BETTER DATE THAN NEVER

UNLUCKY IN LOVE, #2

PIPER SHELDON

QUERQUE PRESS

To J.R., always

And to anybody in it for the story...

1

———

Emma
Several weeks ago

The four gin and tonics weren't what propelled me forward off the couch of the LA club and toward Wesley Cole. Or at least not the *only* thing.

After a tumultuous day of filming the twentieth-anniversary special of *Terraformative*, the four of us, Charlie and Kate, Harrison, and I, unanimously decided to go out on the town and share a small slice of celebrity privilege. Most of the time, being dubbed the Golden Girl of the Intrepid Trio was a sort of pressure that sat heavier on my shoulders with every passing year. Not that I would ever admit that. I was eternally grateful for the empire of Emma Flynn I'd built after our years on TF. Still, this life of always being "on" exhausted me, and nights like this were few and far between.

I wanted to unwind, in somewhat anonymity—or at least what anonymity VIP room status could buy—with my two best friends and Kate, who was quickly becoming a new favorite person.

Kate had subtly pointed out Wesley talking at the bar. As always, my fingertips went tingly at the sight of him, and I had to clamp down long-tampered belly-fizzies. He was still so bloody handsome. My body still thrilled at the sight of him. And how had he reacted to seeing me? He pretended not to. The second our gazes met across the packed room, he looked away as if he hadn't seen me. I pushed down the familiar hurt of rejection and focused instead on the *audacity*.

Oh, the prat!

I stood with a lift of my chin, only slightly unsteady. The calls of the others in my party trying to reel me back in went ignored.

The absolute gall of Wesley Cole. He infamously dismissed me on a press junket. He told Sally, the director, that he wouldn't film any scenes with me. Sally had wanted us to have a segment together to appease the huge portion of the TF fanbase that pushed for our character's—Max and Lucy—coupling, but his agent said he'd only do the special if we never filmed at the same time.

Hot shame burned through me as I recalled Sally's pitiful face. It was like being pummeled back in time to my insecure sixteen-year-old self with a painful crush that everybody knew about. We *had* been friends when we filmed TF together. Sure, he kept it secret and pretended I didn't exist when anybody else was around. That had probably been the first red flag. We had been much more than friends for one intense night before he promptly sent me back to London. Yep. Another red flag.

Then he married someone else—the biggest red flag of all.

What could I say? We were teenagers, and he was my first love, but now I was much older, wiser, and world-weary. All the hurt and shame were packed up tightly and shoved to the back of my brain.

Until the moment I saw him again.

So here in the dark of the bar, the desire for answers *and* the gin and tonics motivated my steps.

I'd been accused of being strong-willed and highly persuasive, that I wouldn't stop until I got what I wanted, and I wanted the truth as to why Wesley ended our friendship without a single look back. It was time to put the past behind me once and for all. Maybe then it wouldn't hurt so badly every time I saw him on the cover of a magazine or online.

As soon as he spotted me crossing the bar through the throng of dancers and toward him, he tried to make a break for it. Despite the thumping music and disorientating flashing lights, I caught the arm of his suit coat and dragged him toward the back of the club to somewhere quieter.

Too late, Buster.

"What are you doing?" he asked in his deep voice, flat with an American accent.

When I first came from England to LA as a child, I always thought he sounded so glamorous. It had deepened to a rich baritone long ago, sending chills as it rumbled down my neck.

"I just want to talk," I said, but my defensiveness sounded sharp and breathy.

He stumbled slightly out of my grasp and straightened. Glancing around, he carded his fingers through his black hair with that flash of white streaked above his brow. His signature look got him roles playing dastardly, morally ambiguous men. He sighed, letting his shoulders down.

"Fine. Outside," he said.

He walked away without another word.

"I'll just follow you then," I said sarcastically, following his hasty retreat. He went out a side exit to the private entrance where a car waited and strode confidently toward the black sedan with every intention of sliding into the back seat. I gasped and ran (carefully in my very high heels, mind you) to put myself between him and the car.

"Are you actually running from me?" I scoffed, arms crossed. He stopped before careening into me.

He froze as his hand grabbed for the door handle. His shoulders tensed almost to his ears. He loomed over me even though I was a few inches shy of six feet.

"Had to give it a shot." His gaze moved up and down the top half of my body, now unavoidable. The silver slip of my satin gown left very little to the imagination.

He closed his eyes and took a steadying breath. Because apparently, being near me was that difficult. When his eyes opened again, they were sharp and glaring down at me, those famous dark eyebrows scrunched. He was *just* close enough to smell the hint of alcohol under the rich notes of his luxury cologne. His suit, as always, was exquisitely cut to his refined figure but slightly disheveled, and his collar was open right in my line of sight.

"Don't I deserve an explanation, at least?" I asked.

His eyes flicked back and forth between mine before his usual unreadable features slid into place. He'd perfected this aloof look since we left the show, and now it was the only thing he wore. I couldn't help but think of it as a mask of indifference —as though twenty years of history didn't stand between us. "An explanation?" he asked.

"You're avoiding me," I pointed out, slightly breathless at his proximity. His scent. His warmth.

I might have rushed into this. Damn those drinks.

His jaw clenched, and I could have sworn he swayed slightly toward me before pushing himself on one arm farther away from the car while still caging me in. "We've agreed in the past that it's not a good idea for us to drink together," he said quietly.

I narrowed my eyes. "You're purposely being obtuse. You

know I don't mean tonight. I'm referring to the past few days. Sally told me that you specifically requested not to film with me."

Wesley leaned over to speak to the driver. His chest brushed against mine, igniting the skin under the sheer material of this barely-there dress.

"Give me a few." His voice vibrated through me as he spoke to the driver.

The window closed, and it was only us two in the quiet back alley. Only the occasional yell and the thumping bass escaped through the building walls.

He straightened but didn't make a move to uncage me. "Sally only wants drama for viewers."

I thought of the recent antics the director concocted for Charlie and Kate. He wasn't wrong, but it was more than that. "You can't pin that on Sally." My hurt was making me reckless. "You really can't even stand to be around me?"

He closed his eyes, and his nostrils flared before schooling them again. "Go back inside. If you still want to talk tomorrow ..." He ran a hand over his face, avoiding me. Lying. "We can try to meet up. But we shouldn't be talking right now."

His eyes had a glassy, unfocused sheen. I wrapped my arms tighter around myself. The LA night wasn't cold, but this dress was thin, and the crystals in my straps kept sending chills down my back.

At least I could blame the crystals.

It had always been like this for me, this allure to his stoic, self-contained persona. Maybe because his mask slipped at times, revealing a glimpse of a man I wanted to know more about, but only for me. It made me feel special and understood, but equally confused every time he took it away. No matter what my brain warned me, there was no denying the physical attraction. My body was a dirty betrayer. It made me question everything. Had he felt something close to this heat that night all those years ago when we gave each other our virginities? Something that seemed so silly now when it had been so huge, so important when we were eighteen. Had he felt anything for me back then? Or was I simply a box to check?

"You can't even look at me," I whispered, the words sounding hollow.

He glared at the ground. "Go back inside."

"No." If he would look at me. Just stare into my eyes and remember who I was, what we were to each other. Not these past few years of resentment and silence. "Tell me why you can't even stand to be near me. We were ... friends." To my utter horror, my voice cracked.

His hands on either side of me balled into fists.

"I'm going through some stuff," he said, deep and fierce. His gaze focused on my neck. My collar. My chin. "The last thing I need is to have the media take *this* and run with it."

"This?" I asked with a hard swallow.

"Us." He looked around as if somebody might pop out from the back alley to snap a picture. Honestly, it wouldn't be that surprising. He added, "You know how they are with Max and Lucy."

Max and Lucy. Definitely not Emsley—our would-be celebrity couple name, given to us by fans ravenous for us to get together.

"Right," I said coldly, blinking.

His eyes hardened as they finally met mine. "Jesus, Ems. Did it occur to you that maybe this isn't about you?" he growled, the mask slipping.

I flinched like he'd shoved the words at me, swaying slightly. I hated his sharp tone, but I hated more how hearing his nickname for me made me want to reach out and pull him against me. How it made me want to turn back the clock to a simpler time. Before all the flags turned red.

He sighed and softened his words as he stepped closer yet. "I'm getting a divorce."

The revelation sent a thrill of elation through me before I was quickly overcome by remorse and compassion for a man in obvious pain. His gaze shuttered, and I could see now, outside of my initial reaction to him, that he wasn't doing well. Those glassy eyes had bruises under them, and his usually meticulous appearance presented minor signs of upset. It wouldn't have meant much on anybody else, but with Wesley, strands of loose hair meant constant fussing, and a shadow of a beard meant neglect. None of these were typical for the son of Hollywood's biggest dynasty.

"I had heard a rumor." I fumbled for words as the shift in topic threw me off.

Not that I ever felt fully in control of my faculties around Wesley.

His gaze moved over my face. "Do you have any idea how humiliating that is? My wife is dating her director. My parents are ... Everything is a mess." He tugged at his hair again, looking away.

"I-I'm sorry. I thought—" A fresh wave of sympathy and regret for pursuing him so doggedly soured my stomach. I couldn't leave well enough alone, could I?

"The last thing I need is a media circus off the rumors of us from a show that's twenty years old. I wish people would leave it alone. Every time I start to move forward—" He cut himself off, sucking in his lips with a glare.

It hadn't been about me. He was going through hell, and I'd projected so much meaning into it.

When he wasn't even thinking of me at all.

I had built up this reunion between us when I'd not even crossed his mind.

That hurt so much more than I wanted to admit.

"Wesley, I didn't know."

"You couldn't know." He let out a breath. "Look. I'm sorry I got upset. I promise this isn't anything you did. I want to get through the next few days, then get back home and deal with my life falling apart. I'm sorry if you thought—"

"No. Stop. I'm sorry." I couldn't meet his gaze now. I couldn't stand to think how he might finish that sentence. I saw myself from his point of view again. The pitiful little girl from his past who couldn't let things go.

I swallowed down the hurt and shame.

"Please stop apologizing. It's all ... complicated," he settled on.

"I'm sure." I chewed my lip in indecision. I felt myself about to do something stupid when I had already determined that pursuing him out here was a mistake. "I *am* sorry about Natasha. She always seemed so lovely."

He shrugged so defeatedly that I couldn't stop the bad idea. I reached forward to wrap my arms around him. Even as I squeezed his stiff shoulders, my rational mind screamed, *will we never learn?*

I had been about to release him—and put him out of this extended misery—when he sighed the tension out from his body. His breath tickled down my neck as his arms looped behind my back, returning the hug with ferocity.

"Ems," he said softly.

God, hearing him say my name like that and feeling it rumble through me with our bodies pressed this close. It was the man who I remembered that nobody else ever seemed to see. It was too much. It was not enough.

Wesley was right. We really shouldn't be together when

drinking. Every cell in my body felt lit up like Nakatomi Tower at the end of *Die Hard*. My stomach tightened with nerves and the hope that we would let ourselves make a stupid mistake. Consequences be damned.

We'd allowed ourselves one night before. When we were both eighteen and about to leave for the real world. We'd been friends forever, even if we weren't open about it, and that night we finally gave in. But everything changed after that.

I leaned back to break the embrace and give my brain thinking space. My brain *really* needed thinking space. As I tried to step back, his warm, calloused hands smoothed down my shoulders to grab my elbows, stopping my retreat.

His gaze dropped to study where we were still pressed together, his thumbs moving over the sensitive skin of my inner elbow. That look in his eyes. I would have given my entire net worth to know what was playing through his mind.

He was still married. I was the Golden Girl. I should go since we both drank too much. It wasn't about me. Rational thoughts tried to make their way to my tongue, but my brain had gone offline. It put an out-of-office sign in the window and stomped off, sighing about not getting paid enough for this.

My body was in control now.

I should have let him be. Why couldn't I quit him even after all these years?

He leaned ever closer. His lips were close enough that his breath mingled with mine.

It would be so easy. I could lean in. Give in. Be someone else. Do something for me for once.

Yet ...

"I should go in," I whispered as hot tears began to burn the back of my eyes.

He stilled in his descent to my mouth. "You should."

We held each other's gaze, waiting for the other to end this moment.

Neither of us moved.

I brought my hand up and placed it on his cheek. The stubble tickled as he closed his eyes and nuzzled into me.

"I hope …" What? What did I hope? "I hope things get better," I said.

He nodded against my palm. I rose onto my tiptoes and pressed a kiss to his other cheek. I lingered a moment too long, letting myself pretend for an instant that we were two people sharing a friendly kiss. Not a married man going through something awful and not the Golden Girl balancing on the edge of a career-ending freak-out.

He was hurt, lonely, and drunk. He didn't want Emma Flynn. He wanted a warm companion. I needed to guard myself against these long-buried feelings. I couldn't let myself fall back into this pattern. I'd moved on and made a difference in the world. I owed it to those who relied on me to remember that I was more than my physical wants.

People counted on me.

With a sigh, I stepped out from the comfortable warmth of his embrace.

His head dropped, jaw tense, glaring at where I had just been. He let me go without another word. We both knew that way led to nothing but regret.

I went back into the club, fighting stupid tears for a life that could never be. Letting go of a future I could never have. I *would* move on from Wesley Cole once and for all.

2

———

Podcast Nosy Nelly Celebrity News

Season 4, Episode 6 *Here's my number. Call me, "Emsley"?* transcript excerpt

Co-hosts: Gabi Ortega and Liz Kane

[excerpt starts]

GABI: Okay, so we all saw the pic by now.

Hosts gasp.

LIZ: The kiss that made a million fans all scream out in excitement.

GABI: Then you really think it's Emma Flynn and Wesley Cole?

LIZ: You don't?

GABI: I dunno. It's pretty dark, and even if that is them, they could just be hugging.

LIZ: Hugging with their faces, maybe. That's a pretty intimate embrace for two people who claim they aren't even friends.

GABI: We all remember the infamous interview at the opening of the *Terraformative* amusement park when Wesley

Cole explicitly said that he and Emma Flynn never spoke, were not friends, and we all needed to just, and I quote, "move on."

LIZ: Oof. Yeah, not a great look for him. Normally, he's so collected. Sexy, cool, calm.

GABI: Well, to be fair, the media has badgered those two since they filmed *Terraformative*. You can tell he snapped. All his years of training went out the window. Being the youngest and *last* born in the Cole Dynasty, how could he be any other way? I'm sure the pressure is on.

LIZ: True. I, like many "Emsley" shippers, want these crazy kids to be together. But let's be real. They've known each other for what, twenty-plus years, and nothing's ever happened before now? I feel like if it was going to happen, it would have happened by now.

GABI: But he was married.

LIZ: And before that?

GABI: They were kids.

LIZ: Eighteen. But they had just wrapped the show.

GABI: Exactly. Babies. What eighteen-year-old knows what they want?

LIZ: I'm thirty-five, and I can't even figure out my deli order without second-guessing myself.

Laughter.

GABI: It's true. I have witnessed the cashier's expectant stare cause her to crumble.

LIZ: Listen. It's a lot of pressure. Cold or toasted? Tuna or turkey? It's too much! *Anyway*. Do you think that the people want Emma and Wesley, or do they actually want Max Malachi and Lucy Lennon together?

BOTH: Yes.

Hosts' laughter.

GABI: We should explain because this is a huge fandom, but it is still a niche one for those outside of it.

LIZ: I forget there are people who exist that don't ship these two.

GABI: Same. For you non-nerds listening, Max Malachi is the bad boy of *Terraformative*—TF for short—the television show based on the ongoing book series of the same name written by G.S. Sedar.

LIZ: We love a bad boy. **Loud sigh.** A love that could never be.

GABI: Right. Max is the bully that made the Intrepid Trio's life miserable. Specifically, Emma's character Lucy, who was bio-mechanical and therefore not "pure" human to Max and his elitist beliefs. Well, his family's beliefs, a terribly bigoted family.

LIZ: Ugh, the reformed bad boy who now sees the errors in his way. I've read so many good fanfics with these two.

GABI: So. Many. It's basically canon in my head now. But it should be noted that it is actually not canon. Technically. Meaning these two never did actually get together on the show or in the books.

LIZ: There were hints, though, don't you think? And there should be more books. I still hold out hope.

GABI: Sure, so long as Sedar is writing them, I will hold out hope. The show may have ended in our youth, but the books continue.

LIZ: That's bananas. Sedar has to be a thousand years old.

GABI: Roughly. But that won't stop him. Those last two books were so good.

LIZ: So good. But back to Emsley.

GABI: There were hints in the books, but maybe we were just looking for them. Regardless, TF is not real. Max and Lucy are not real people. However, Emma and Wesley are real people, not their characters. It borders on getting weird, you don't think?

LIZ: No!

GABI: You're yelling.

LIZ: Sorry. **In a lowered voice.** But no. These two are clearly in love and have been since they were kids.

GABI: You're seeing things based on the super popular fanfiction written about them.

LIZ: No. Listen. This isn't even about the characters, in my opinion. The actors. They have clearly been in love.

GABI: Hmm. Despite repeated and insistent claims otherwise?

LIZ: Remember the picture from the season four premiere? The way he was looking at her when he didn't know the camera was on him?

GABI: Ooh. I do remember that. Like someone caught him off guard. His gaze is practically burning into her.

Both hosts sigh.

LIZ: Exactly. And that's just one example. At the TF series finale, there was a definite *vibe* between them. These two get shipped in and out of fiction for a reason. Their chemistry is palpable! These two both have led incredible lives. Her with all her philanthropy since she retired from acting at nineteen. And he's Hollywood royalty.

GABI: Right. If she's the Golden Girl of the Intrepid Trio, then he's the Prince of Hollywood. Heavy is the head that holds the crown. Four generations of Hollywood elite in his family. Talk about pressure. But no proof that leads us to believe that they have ever been anything other than childhood co-stars.

LIZ: ChicChat, that app that shares anonymous celebrity insider information, says that several people saw them checking into the same hotel room separately only to check out within twenty-four hours the night the show wrapped. Well, before he got married, of course.

GABI: Can we trust ChicChat?

LIZ: I don't know. That app leaked a lot of good stuff that was proven true later.

GABI: They did leak the stuff about Charlie Downing and the fanfiction writer Kate Dubois secretly emailing each other long before they came out.

LIZ: Oh my God, that was so epic and romantic.

GABI: It was. We have a whole other episode on it and will link it in the show notes. But back to the *number one* trending photo on the internet right now. It may be wishful thinking, but the evidence stacks up.

LIZ: Right? And that's only one example of many. Not that I've done extensive research on these two.

GABI: Clearly. But okay. I know I'm a skeptic and jaded, but look, it's Hollywood. This supposedly happened at the premiere of the twenty-year special. That was over *four* months ago. It's weird to me that these are suddenly popping up now? It doesn't look good for Emma or Wesley. Wesley, whose team, incidentally, just announced that he and his wife are divorced.

LIZ: I agree. Totally suss. And can only be related to the fact that Wesley's ex-wife was spotted out and about with the director of her last movie.

GABI: Or did Wesley cheat with Emma first? I mean, these pictures are from months ago. I don't even know if it's true, but I didn't think either one of them was the cheating type. Natasha and Wesley might not have been the couple of our fangirl hearts, but they at least seemed to be good together. They seemed happy.

LIZ: I agree. Is nothing sacred in this industry? God, I hope he didn't cheat. What a cliché that would be.

GABI: Agreed. It would make me hate him, and I don't want to hate him!

LIZ: I can only root for Wesley and Emma if they are together, and this is the real deal forever and ever. So help me God.

GABI: Amen.

Laughter.

GABI: I just hope this doesn't come back to bite them. Not everybody ships Emsley. They're wrong. But they exist. The internet isn't happy about it. So many thought he was really happy with his wife, and now they're calling the Golden Girl of the Intrepid Trio a home-wrecker.

LIZ: That's the patriarchy for you. Emma's been doing charitable work for ten-plus years, and now, with one picture, she's being labeled a home-wrecker? That's bull—

GABI: I agree with you there, but that's a whole other episode ...

[excerpt ends]

3

Emma
Present Day

HARRISON ANSWERED MY CALL RIGHT AWAY.

"Hey, I was about to ring you," he said carefully.

"Lovely. Let me in." I leaned against the large window and banged on the glass. He turned, phone to his ear, and jumped when he saw me.

"Hullo!" I called through the thick glass.

He winced, pulling the phone away from his head.

I'd already let myself in through his security gate and up the drive. I needed out of these heels, a cup of tea, and a good long vent.

"Coming." He shook his head with a laugh, and I heard him through the phone.

I had several calls from my agent and publicist, but I wasn't ready to give them the download from the meeting I had just left. I glanced over to where Harrison's incredible home jutted out from the California rocks over the Pacific Ocean sparkled in the October sun. What if I tossed my phone over the edge? I imagined the soft little gasp I'd make like Rose's elderly character throwing the Heart of the Ocean over the side of the ship. Let it all sink into the murky depths. What if I never called anybody back and slipped away into anonymity? I could find a cozy cottage in the middle of nowhere like Charlie. He had the right idea. But as long as the offers continued, I was morally obligated to keep up the Golden Girl title. I enjoyed using my celebrity powers for good, even if I was a little exhausted. Even if I forgot what it felt like to make a choice without a team. Or how it felt to eat whatever I wanted. Whenever these feelings of ennui crept in, I pushed them down to remember all the good my team and I had done. Emma Flynn was no longer a person but a team of people branded and set upon helping the world.

It was bigger than me and my wants.

He chuckled, and I heard it on the other side of the door. "I wasn't sure if you were coming back before you left. Isn't your flight soon?" The call ended as he opened the door. "Hullo, love," he said, and we embraced.

Harrison was handsome as ever in his jeans and T-shirt. His brown waves and glasses gave him that nerdy appeal that seemed handcrafted for the female gaze. Only it wasn't. That was just Harrison. He'd save a kitten and then make you a bath after a long day. He leaned into his playboy persona, but one day, I hoped he'd find a partner to shower all that affection onto. It was not a subject he liked, so I left it alone. My protective sister side only wanted to see him happy.

I stepped past him and set my tote bag on a side table as I slid out of my heels. "I have a few hours to kill."

"I'm glad you popped over," he said.

"You know the rules. We can't be in the same city and not at least see each other."

"My favorite rule." He kissed the top of my head.

"I've had the oddest morning," I started, and headed back toward the kitchen. I set the kettle as Harrison followed close.

"No doubt."

I turned to face him. He looked concerned, almost hesitant, as he leaned against the kitchen island, hands deep in his pockets.

"Did I tell you I had a meeting with CrunchyCouture today?" I filled the kettle. "I didn't think I had. But maybe I mentioned something in passing."

"Yeah. No. Wait. What meeting?" he asked.

"The one about the ad campaign. They were pushing hard for thirty percent but you know your girl," I said the last part in a strong California accent. "I got them up to forty percent proceeds to charity."

"Oh." He nodded up and down. "Right. Right. Well, good for you, no surprise there."

I reached into the cupboard and got out a teacup. "Cuppa?" I asked him, and he shrugged, so I reached for another one. "The weirdest thing, though. Halfway through the meeting, their director of PR got really weird. He made a comment about the importance of my reputation."

As if my every waking moment wasn't already dedicated to maintaining my impeccable reputation. Be the good girl. Eat right. Floss. Don't stumble out of nightclubs drunk, flashing my knickers as I sag into a taxi. Don't be too thin but don't gain weight. Stand up for what's right, but don't be pushy.

What it might be like to breathe without the world watching

...

Harrison's eyebrows shot up—his mouth opening.

"I know. Utter rubbish. As if I don't know that. The entire persona of Golden Girl Emma Flynn is based on my stellar reputation as if I haven't been honing it to perfection for the past twenty years. The slightest slip and—" He watched me closely with a furrowed brow as I cut myself off with the flip of my wrist. "Well, you know all this. It was weird. I had to pull out the big guns, so to speak, to close the deal. It's been a while since I felt like I needed to prove myself."

"Well, everyone's bound to have an off day," he supplied.

Harrison fiddled with his teacup, avoiding my gaze. His shoulders were tense and his jaw tight, a far cry from my usual gregarious good-natured friend.

He was being weird.

"You're being weird." The kettle whistled, and I poured. "Anyway. Ask me how many times I have not closed a deal?"

"How many—"

"Zero. Zero times. I've closed every deal I've gone into, but the atmosphere felt off today. Like they had been talking about me before I walked in."

Harrison swallowed. My best friend was not a great liar—at least not with me. You couldn't know somebody as intimately as we knew each other and expect there to be any secrets. "Seriously. What's going on? Is somebody over?"

I glanced around, realizing I hadn't checked to ensure he was alone. Just because it was the middle of a Tuesday didn't really mean anything.

"No. No. Just me. But listen." He scratched at his five o'clock shadow. "Have you been online?"

A cold dread seeped into me. Those were trigger words.

"Is something going on? I did miss a few calls. I assumed they wanted to know about the meeting."

"And you didn't immediately answer? Living on the edge, I see."

Normally, I'd banter, but the growing anxiety short-circuited my brain. I set down my tea and went to my tote for my phone. I had several more missed calls and texts.

"Don't get that look," Harrison said. "I'm sure they were

calling to clear everything up. It's the media doing what it does best."

Harrison tried his best to placate me, but it was too late. Fear caused any good feelings about closing the deal to morph into instant worst-case scenarios. Something terrible had happened. My career was over. It would only come crashing down, and I couldn't do anything to help anybody anymore. I'd be nothing more than an answer on the occasional trivia night. People would ask, "Oh yeah, whatever happened to Emma Flynn? What a fall from grace, that one."

I pulled up the most popular social media account and went straight to the trending hashtags. All at once, the dread coiled even tighter around my insides, and the tea burned like acid. "Emsley" and Wesley Cole and Emma Flynn were all trending along with one photo.

"No." A shaking hand covered my mouth.

Harrison stepped up behind me, looking over my shoulder. "Obviously, it's just some fans stirring up controversy as they do. When were you even around Wesley? That doesn't even look like you two."

It was us. Wesley leaned over me, looking at me with his features contorted into *something*. I had been kissing his cheek, but it looked like more. I could almost feel the tension pouring out of the image. All the emotions of that night slammed back into me after months of repressing them. I had wanted to throw it all away. I had wanted to kiss him and have something just for me, but I managed to stop myself.

And all for nothing.

I tried not to see the comments, but I saw enough. While some were thrilled at what they thought was proof of a romantic relationship, many more were throwing around terrible accusations, and my gold was tarnishing fast.

I swallowed, my fingers shaking as I zoomed in on the photo.

A fresh wave of shame and humiliation burned through me. Every time I thought I was over my crush on Wesley, every time I thought I had finally put the past behind us, I went and did something that drudged everything back to the surface.

But he'd been so sad that night ...

Enough. It was *enough*. He'd made it more than clear over the years he wanted nothing more from me. I had to stop this. He had people, and I was not one of them.

I tapped out of the picture, locking my phone. The screen wallpaper of Harrison, Charlie and Kate, and me from that night looked back. We had been having such a great time. Then Wesley happened as always.

"It could be anybody. Look how dark it is." Harrison stepped in front of me. "Emma, you're being awfully quiet. Are you okay?"

I looked up at him, chewing my lip to keep it from wobbling.

"It's not even you two, is it?" he asked, the last of his hope fading away.

I flicked my gaze to the side. "It's us. It was the night we went out on the town with Charlie and Kate while filming the twentieth anniversary special."

His shoulders sagged, and his pity only added to the humiliation and fear coursing through me.

"Emma ..." The sympathy in his voice made it so much worse. "Why do you keep opening yourself up to him?"

I shook my head. It was too much to explain. "It's ... complicated."

"That was months ago. Why did these pictures leak now?"

I shook my head. "I don't know."

"Did he hurt you?" Harrison asked seriously. My heart was desperate to spill all the details of that night, but they weren't mine to share.

I shook my head again.

"No. I was drunk, and … I was just talking to him. It's taken out of context."

"And nothing happened?" Harrison asked with gentle frustration.

"No," I said quickly. "I had hoped. I don't know." I tossed out my hands. "I was all afloat from Charlie and Kate. Being around everyone from the show and talking so much about it got me all up in my feelings, and I had a moment of weakness. I was so angry when I saw him that I wasn't really thinking clearly, and then I realized … well, it wasn't really about me. At all. And he was upset."

Harrison's frown grew. He reminded me so much of my childhood friend, overlaid with this grown man.

"I was comforting him," I went on. "The photographer must have been hiding. We didn't know anybody was out there. That isn't even a real kiss. I'm giving him a friendly peck on his cheek."

We both looked back at the photo. Nothing about the way he leaned over me, face twisted in torture and me looking at him like he could heal world suffering seemed remotely friendly.

"Right. Out of context," he said.

I sniffled, hating the wave of emotion that hit me. I felt idiotic. I didn't even let myself have the moment I wanted with him, and it still wreaked havoc.

"Oh, Emma. I'm so sorry."

I shook my head and squared my shoulders. "It's my own fault. You'd think I'd get the hint. He's been very transparent about his feelings for me. Or lack thereof."

"He shouldn't dick you around. You two should have never slept together unless—"

"Unless what? He committed to marrying me? Come on, Harrison. You know how it goes. We were consenting adults, and it was ages ago. Trust me, he doesn't even think about it." He grimaced, and I rolled my eyes but went on, "It was one night. It was never meant to be any more than that."

Maybe if I said it out loud enough, I would start to feel it as a truth.

"But he knew how you felt. Everybody knew your feelings for him."

"Stop." I pressed my fingertips to my temple and spun away from him. "I'm already embarrassed."

It would never be enough. I would always be that backwater Brit who stumbled into the role of a lifetime ...

I pushed the thoughts down—buried them deep—recalling that I had helped people and made a difference. I wasn't that girl anymore. Harrison pulled me back in for a hug. I rested my chin on his shoulder, knowing it was bony and poked him. Normally, he'd chide me for that, but today, he held me tighter.

"I'm sorry. I just hate this. I hate that he continues to mess with your head."

"It's not his fault. I allow it," I said.

"You deserve a man who will fight for you. Who won't hide your relationship."

"We never had a relationship," I reminded him sadly.

Not as far as anybody else was aware. But we had been something. And that something kept messing with my head when I should have long moved on. I'd spent the past two decades nurturing a one-sided crush. And sure, maybe he was attracted to me on some level, but he had ended things. He had gotten *married* in the end.

We aren't even friends. The words from the infamous interview burned into my brain. As always, it caused a very physical wince. It was more complicated than that, but those were the only facts that mattered.

Enough was enough. I had to stop this ridiculous obsession

with a man I didn't really even know. I certainly wasn't the same person I was at eighteen. And neither was he.

He wasn't a bad guy. He was always clear about where we stood with each other. It was my fault for projecting more on to it. To hope that I'd be someone in his life he couldn't live without.

I'm done. I can't do this anymore. I can't keep having these feelings for him. Every time I see him, I'm sixteen again. I am self-conscious and floundering. I was the Golden Girl of TF. I could make CEOs hand over millions. I brought water to struggling communities. Yet whenever I was near him, I didn't remember how to hold my head or how long to make eye contact. I was the little sister, the awkward co-star.

It had to stop.

I gently pulled myself up and off my best friend. I took a steadying breath. "Okay. Please, let's stop talking about him. I need to figure out what I'm meant to do."

Harrison rubbed at the back of his neck. "The timing isn't great. He's announced his divorce and this picture leaked."

"It's rubbish. That explains the weirdness at the meeting. Even though it shouldn't. You know, the fact that my personal life is even—"

Harrison nodded as I warmed up, feeling an indignant rant about the patriarchal systems in Hollywood and the media, but on cue, my phone vibrated in my hand. It was Sofia, my publicist.

"Better get it over with." I took a steadying breath before I answered. "Hullo," I said, bracing myself. Sofia was one of the people closest to me in my life. She'd come to LA straight out of college with an MBA and a fierce understanding of the business. She was young, beautiful, and motivated; I was lucky to have found her. But she still worked for me, and every relationship based on business balanced on a razor's edge.

"Hey, Emma. I heard that the meeting with CrunchyCouture was a success," she said.

"I thought so."

Harrison sipped his tea and watched our interaction. I made a wincing face as Sofia said, "But obviously, that's not why I've been calling."

"Right."

"Mind if we push your flight back? We'd like to meet up and discuss our plan of attack for this." We were a team of about five people who helped keep Emma Flynn LLC afloat, but Sofia ran the ship. I was the face of the brand and made the toughest negotiations.

"That's fine." I'd been looking forward to a few days off in London, sitting in the quiet of my flat, reading and recharging my social batteries.

"Where are you now?" she asked.

"Harrison's."

"Oh, perfect. Can you be at the address I text you in the next hour?"

I glanced at my watch. LA traffic was a crap shoot, so being anywhere in an hour felt optimistic. "As long as it's within a mile."

"Closer than that."

I braced myself before glancing at the address she had sent over.

The good news was it was just up the road. The bad news was it was a house I vowed to never see.

We finalized a few more details and hung up the call. I stared at the address, wishing more than ever I could go back in time.

"Everything all right, love?" Harrison asked.

Nope. Not at all. I made a stupid offering of kindness in a weak moment, and I'm paying for it.

"It will be." I smiled at him. "Just a quick meeting."

I slid my sore feet back into the binding heels and centered myself with some deep yoga breaths. Thankfully, I'd stayed in the posh suit I'd worn for the meeting; I'd need all my battle gear for this. The Intrepid Trio had weathered more than our fair share of media emergencies over the years. I would grin and bear the renewed interest in Emsley before it all blew over and on to the next scandal.

4

———————

Wesley

THERE WERE NO GREETING CARDS FOR BREAKING UP WITH YOUR toxic family. No helpful pamphlets at the grocery store checkout that explain the best way to divorce yourself from the people who claimed to care for you but wanted to control every aspect of your life to fit an unattainable standard no mortal human could live up to.

But there really should be.

The security system on my phone alerted me that my mother and father had let themselves into my Hollywood Hills home. I asked them to come over to discuss something, but they only responded that they were already on their way.

"That them?" Mac asked.

I nodded at my personal trainer and the closest thing I had to a best friend.

"Okay, well, we're done down here anyway. Want me to go up with you and flex my old bodyguard muscles?" Mac offered.

I huffed a laugh. Mac was the epitome of a teddy bear inside the body of a pro wrestler. He hated conflict more than most, which was why he'd switched to personal coach from celebrity bodyguard.

"I'll be okay," I said, feeling anything but. "I imagine they are here about the divorce announcement."

"They don't approve?" Mac asked as he wiped down the bar.

"They think we'll work it out, but that's hard to do when she's in love with someone else," I said flatly. As far as I was concerned, our marriage was over a long time ago. I didn't harbor any bad feelings toward my ex, Natasha, but there was more chance I would win a Broadway Tony before she and I ever got back together.

Mac frowned. "Sorry, man."

"It's for the best." I stood and clapped my hands. "It's a big day."

I was about to drop the news that the final Cole, the last born of all the generations, was separating from the Cole Dynasty. I wanted nothing more to do with this supposed family. I'd spent months talking with lawyers and making plans to leave Holly-wood once and for all. As far as anybody was concerned, I'd just disappear. Save for the few people who actually gave any fucks about me, I would *poof* vanish into thin air.

I'd be alone, but I'd be free.

"I'm excited for you, man. This is the most relaxed I've seen you in months. You have so much less tension in your form. And you've hardly lifted a pretentious eyebrow at me once."

I raised a pretentious eyebrow at him, and he laughed.

"I guess I didn't realize things were so bad around here." He scratched the back of his neck.

It wasn't his fault. We'd only been working together the past year or so, so he hadn't seen the life of generational trauma being passed down.

"It's the sort of stuff I save for therapy, but trust me, it's been a long time coming. I'm ready." Another wave of nerves hit me. It felt too good to be true. As though even talking about it with Mac could jinx it.

"You sure you don't want me to just come and stand around looking beefy? I'm not scared of them." He crossed his massive arms before scratching at his chin. "Well, your mom is actually terrifying."

"You have no idea." I mentally blew on the hot coals that had been driving me the past few months. The years of emotional abuse and neglect and Natasha. The biggest betrayal of all. I let the flame grow inside me until any remaining doubt singed into dust. "You can let yourself out down here. Go. Be free. Save yourself."

Mac stood and put a hand on my shoulder. "You got this, man. It's going to be hard, but it's worth it."

I swallowed and, after taking a quick shower, made my way up to the living room.

There were no final sentimental glances as I made my way through this ostentatious mansion that was way too big for me. No happy memories would be remembered with longing. Just the absolute freedom of knowing that soon I would never have to be here again.

My father was slumped in the three-thousand-dollar chair that the interior designer insisted completed the room—according to my mother, at least. I was not a part of the design process for this house. I was lucky enough to get to pick the location. My mother perched in an impeccable cream silk two-piece skirt suit on the edge of his chair, arms crossed and waiting for me. She'd gifted me the streak of white that ran through my hair at the temple, but she had bleached her hair for so long that it was hardly noticeable when coiled into her coiffure.

"About time," my father said by way of greeting.

"Hello, Father. Mother."

Normally, I'd kiss her cheek, but today, I went straight to the minibar.

"Really, Wesley. It's not even noon." She came to stand next to me. Quietly, she said, "Play nice today."

I grunted.

She sighed loudly.

Perhaps other thirty-year-old men would fly out in outrage to find their parents waiting for him in his living room. But alas, those men hadn't grown up in the twisted complex "family" that was the Cole Dynasty.

"Care for a drink?" I asked while I poured a whiskey.

They ignored me.

My first gulp burned its way down my throat. Several weeks of portion-controlled meals, hand-delivered by my personal chef and hours a day spent in the gym, meant I was at peak performance. I hadn't had a drink since the night at the bar, and the heat burned my empty gut. I welcomed the strength it would give me.

"Let's get right to it," I deadpanned.

"Yes. Let's. You were supposed to wait to announce your divorce," my father said, voice low and controlled, still not looking up from his phone.

"But we have a plan," my mother spoke up, voice perky with hope. I didn't know how she managed it after all these years with him. "Your father and I have come up with the perfect solution."

They had come up with a solution? They didn't even know the problem. Their unplanned arrival was the first hint. This was the second. Something was up, something outside of the divorce.

"Solution?" I asked, wishing for another drink but knowing damn well I needed my full mental capacity for this battle.

"Don't play dumb. It doesn't suit you," my father said.

I ground my jaw.

A paranoid thought: Had they somehow tapped into my brain and heard my thoughts about leaving this family in the same manner targeted advertising managed to show products based on recent conversations? Because that was the running thought on a loop in my brain every day since Natasha and I split. *How can I leave? How can I get away? How can I make choices for myself?*

But they couldn't know. I had been neck-deep into filming this award-winning role with an award-winning director from the award-winning script whom which they had to pull all the strings to get me. I was doing everything they asked, playing the good son. Behind the scenes, I made my own plans. My escape would be in place before I committed to starting my next role.

For now, there was nothing I could say that wouldn't instigate a fight, so I simply stood, hands clasped behind my back, stomach growling loudly in the silence.

My mother curled her lip as though I'd been obscene. After sixty years of existing on salads and fad diets, hunger was a regrettable state of humanity she found uncouth.

"I don't even understand. When were you two even together?" my mother asked.

My heart tripped.

"Natasha and I?" I asked, genuinely confused.

This wasn't how this conversation was supposed to go. I was supposed to drop a bomb. I should have left without telling a soul ...

Damn me for still feeling like I at least owed her a goodbye. My mother shot an anxious glance to my father.

After clicking around on her phone, my mother held up a picture. My heart sank into my stomach, evaporating any hunger. It was Emma and me.

That night slammed back into the front of my brain.

Thoughts of her reluctant and gentle embrace would play on a constant loop if I let my control slip. She'd been so sweet and gentle and a little pissed off—which, if I was honest, always sort of did something for me. But as soon as I thought of her sexy body or her gentle touches, I pushed them down. The point was to start a new life, not go back down an unbeatable path.

Not the time.

If I hadn't spent my entire life perfecting a no-reaction face, they would have seen everything sweep across my features; fear, sadness, hope, and regret for a life I would never get.

Thankfully, I was a pro at playing dead on the outside.

"So?" I asked. "It's nothing. The teams will sweep it under the rug like they always have over the years. You know how the fans are."

"Unfortunately, not this time, Wesley." My mother took the phone away.

"I don't understand the infatuation with this girl," my father piped in, ever so helpful. I bit my tongue to keep from snapping that she was hardly a girl. But they continued to see me as only a problem child who needed constant supervision, so it would do little to support my point. My father sighed, addressing an invisible audience. He always acted as though he was the star of his own dramatic documentary. "I'm sure he's painted us as the bad guys for forcing them apart. A real tragedy, the like of Romeo and Juliet."

I ground my jaw, knowing my dentist would have plenty to say on the matter at our next visit. That was *exactly* what they had done.

"The picture was taken out of context," I simply said instead. "I don't understand the issue."

"The issue is that you also had to announce your divorce today. Don't you understand how that makes this family look? Do you care at all about the Cole name?" he snapped.

I clenched my jaw so hard I could feel the sharp bite into a nerve. Did I care about the family name? After a lifetime of being their show dog.

I glanced to the side and caught my reflection in a decorative mirror. The Wesley Cole from interviews wore the smooth, emotionless mask I'd perfected in this family. Every strand of hair in place, suit perfect and creaseless. The familiar image stared back, yet it always felt like looking at a stranger. Or a version of myself in an alternate universe.

I often felt that I had stepped into the wrong timeline at some point. That somewhere out there was a version of myself living happily and still friends with the cast of *Terraformative*.

I tried not to think about that lucky son of a bitch.

My mother fidgeted with the flap of my jacket. "What is this? Off the rack? Really, Wesley." She patted the area of my suit jacket she'd just peeled back to examine the label. "We've coordinated with your team. We have a better idea in regard to Emma Flynn."

"You and the *girl* are going to date," my father finished.

Shock and disbelief had me huff a laugh. Their gazes were serious, despite what must be a joke.

"I won't do this. You can't make me," I said with force.

My mother sighed again. The sigh that used to tighten my stomach with fear of disappointing her. Now I was used to these games. I was done with being a pawn for this twisted family. "I had a feeling you'd make a fuss about this," she said. "You know, it's easier to go with whatever your father wants," she said quietly.

"Mother. This is my life. I'm an adult. This is a ridiculous conversation." My temper shook my voice, and I hated even giving her that much satisfaction.

"You know more than most how this industry works. People date for publicity all the time. I could name ten 'couples' right now who are only dating to promote their next release." She used air quotes around the word couples as she spoke.

"This is different. It's too soon. After Natasha." The elephant in the room. The topic we never brought up. Another failure in their eyes.

This wasn't the plan. This wasn't how this was meant to go down. I wouldn't abort now; I had to stay strong.

My mother waved away my comment as though I hadn't even said her name. "We've had to regroup, to move on. This is what's best for you," she said, trying to soften her voice to maternal tones.

My father added, "You wanted this for so long, didn't you? Well, you got what you asked for."

Not like this. Never like this! I wanted to scream. My jaw was locked so tight my temple began to throb.

Instead, I dropped all emotion out of my voice. "Emma will never go for it. She hates me."

Because of what *you* made me do. My insides roiled, replaying her reaction to my hurtful words all those years ago. The interview that officially snapped any remaining thread that may have connected us. I pushed the image away, knowing it would only pop up again in my nightmares. Nightmares when she yelled at me and called me all the horrible names that I deserved.

"She will do it for you," my father said coldly. "Everybody knows she's been in love with you since that pathetic little show."

My father lied. Emma hated me. She *had* to hate me. Any other option was incomprehensible.

And that *pathetic little show* was the only time I ever felt like I belonged. It brought me to Emma.

"I've done everything you've ever asked of me," I said evenly. "I just wrapped a movie where I starved myself and shot eighteen-hour days in the high desert sun." In the hopes of adding another trophy to this family's shelf. I kept the last part to myself.

But that was before I learned about Natasha. Nothing could make me stay now. I was going to leave it all. Leave this family and run away and hide like Charles Downing had. He had the right idea.

"That is your duty to this family," my father snapped. My mother winced, hand going to her clavicle.

"This is what we must do." She smoothed her skirt and lowered her voice to a defeated level. "We have all made sacrifices for the good of this family."

"A Cole under pressure makes diamonds." My father regurgitated the family motto. I swear that had been woven into my baby blanket.

I'd still do the plan. Leave. Run away. Change my name ... I had plenty to live off that they couldn't touch. I scrambled to make it work. Nothing had to change.

"Darling." My mother put a hand on my shoulder. "I know ... I know it's not easy being a part of a dynasty. Always in the public eye. Constantly having to turn the other cheek and endure." She didn't look at my father, but the brief silence that followed was pointed. He'd been careless with his affairs over the years but duty, always duty first and foremost. She gestured to the house around us. "But look at all we have. Look at all that we have to be thankful for. Do you know how many thousands of people come to LA every day just to dream a glimpse of this life?

"Emma is a lovely girl," my mother said.

"At least she's made something of herself," my father added.

Tasteless and classless, they used to call her. A country bumpkin who lucked into the role because she had a specific look.

I snorted. His nostrils flared subtly at the gauche show of emotion. *Now* Emma was lovely. After years and years of them pushing me away from her and toward Natasha. Now that Emma had made an empire of her own, she was acceptable.

"We admit we were hard on her at first. We couldn't predict what a success she'd become. So many young people come to Hollywood only to fail. But we recognize her talents now," my mother said. "She walked off the streets and got the role. She wasn't even classically trained."

"There's no point in arguing. It's already been decided. It only makes sense with award season coming up and the dissolution of your marriage. This is the right plan. I'm done discussing it," he said with finality, standing.

I tasted blood now. No point in pointing out that they were the reason. "Now that she has made a name for herself, you mean," I said. "Now that she carries more power, you want me to attach myself to her?"

My mother looked at me pleadingly. "Why are you fighting this? This is how the real world works, Wesley. And yes. She has proven herself of value. The same way an intern has to work their way up the ranks. There is no shame in admitting that."

"You want to use her," I said.

"You allowed this photo to happen." My father sharpened his tone as he pointed a finger at my chest. "If you had stayed away like you were supposed to and made your marriage work like you were supposed to, we wouldn't even be in this predicament."

I had been so desolate that night—so hurt and alone—and my life was falling apart. I had been drinking, and Emma was there with her large concerned blue eyes, pulling me in to comfort me. After resisting her for thirteen years, I allowed myself one hug. And now we would all pay for my moment of weakness. This. This was why my family learned to shut down their emotions before learning their ABCs.

My mother waited a beat. "I know how cruel the media can be to women," my mother said gently. "We aren't allowed to make any mistakes. We aren't allowed to gain weight or, heaven forbid, age." Despite myself, I softened at her words.

The women of my family undoubtedly were held to entirely different standards than the men. It was why I was always so protective of Emma. I knew as her fame grew, even as children, the world would stop seeing her as a little girl and only as an object to be used and abused. I had never seen my mother or grandmother eat a complex carb. I had seen their bruised faces wrapped up like mummies to defy the natural process of aging. I watched as their husbands strayed, and they kept their bodies tight.

Then the viper attacked, and I realized too late that I had let my guard down.

My father held my gaze as he spoke. "The media can so easily turn. One day, she's the Golden Girl of the Intrepid Trio, and the next, she's a dirty home-wrecker who destroyed your perfect marriage."

The words hit me so hard I stumbled backward. I couldn't take a full breath. All that Emma had done. All the people she helped with various charities and ventures over the years.

"That's not true, and you know it. Natasha and I—"

"The media can easily be swayed. We're in a position to help her. We can spin the tale of two long separated childhood friends finally together. All is forgiven if it's for true love. Otherwise, who knows how they will take this out on her." He glanced at his million-dollar watch. Done with this conversation.

There it was. The threat.

Do this or her career was over. I never had a choice. From

the moment I walked into this room. From the moment I was born ...

I wouldn't be leaving. I was a fool for ever thinking I could.

I felt numb. I felt nothing.

"How long?" I asked.

"What?" My mother blinked at the ice in my tone.

"How long do we put on this charade until you promise to leave her alone?"

"Oh." My mother exchanged a look with my father. "Three months. Until you finish promotion for the movie you just wrapped and get your Oscar nomination."

Three *months*. I could and would survive three months. Three months and my plan would still be on track.

I could do this for Emma. I had to do this for Emma. At least I could make something right for her before I dropped off the map.

It was going to be hard enough to be around Emma. It is my personal form of hell to be near her and not have her. Thankfully, I'm well-practiced. But I wouldn't let myself hurt her. Not again. Public outings. Safe spaces. No drinking around her. I could make it for three months. I would do this to keep her safe from my family.

And from myself.

"Then you will leave her be?" I asked.

"Of course. By then, all this will have blown over, the next thing will be happening, and you will be announced as an Oscar nominee," my father said.

"You can't know that."

He tilted his head, a patronizing smile on his face. "Of course, we can." My dad glanced at his watch again. "We've already contacted her team. We're meeting in less than an hour. Clean yourself up."

I felt numb as my father went out the sliding glass door to the terrace, answering his phone.

My mother put a hand on my shoulder when he was out of earshot.

"Do this for her. Convince her, so that we don't have to," my mother said before following her husband outside.

I would do what they asked one more time, and then I would get away.

I could do this. I could fix this and repent for all the years I've pushed Emma away.

Now how the hell am I supposed to convince the woman I made hate me to pretend to love me?

5

———————

Emma

It was an ambush.

The realization came too late as I was led into the luxury dining room of Wesley Cole's modest Hollywood Hills mansion. If modest and mansion could be used in the same sentence. I lifted my chin, a fake but neutral smile plastered in place, feeling all their eyes on me as I moved across the room. I found Sofia, my only ally, at one end of the sleek table, with several familiar faces at the other. She gave me a comforting nod.

I refused to meet only one gaze as I quickly analyzed the guests sitting around the table.

Wesley Cole.

The very man I vowed never to be in the same room with again. Never make any contact with. Yet here I was, a glutton for punishment, it seemed.

I gripped the back of the only empty chair—left for me next to Wesley, but of course.

His gaze burned the side of my face, but I refused to give him the satisfaction. They may have thought they were running this, but I was Emma Flynn, and I wouldn't be pushed around so easily.

"Let's get started, shall we?" I remained standing behind the chair.

"Thank you for joining us on such short notice, Miss Flynn," Rex Cole said.

I flopped my tote bag onto the table and ignored his lip curl of disgust. I'd been carrying this bag since my time on *Terraformative* despite the ribbing from Harrison and Charlie. The sturdy bag had lots of pockets. It had nothing to do with the fact that Wesley gifted it to me at the shooting finale. He likely didn't even remember.

"We have a situation to handle, thanks to that leaked photo," he said.

I hardly acknowledged Wes's parents, who also felt the need to come to this business meeting. When family was business, I guess that was to be expected.

Another reason I was thankful for my gentle parents and their modest life back in England.

"Emma. Have a seat," Sofia said with a genuine and hopeful smile. "Do you need anything? Sparkling water?" She gestured to where a smorgasbord of untouched sweet and savories were arrayed. Because, of course, a last-minute parley between the Prince of La-La Land and the Golden Girl required caterers.

"No," I said too quickly. The polite Golden Girl facade was shaky with all these eyes on me. It was impossible not to feel the judgment coming off them in waves. "Thank you. I'm fine."

I managed to keep from biting out, *let's get this over with.*

A middle-aged man, bald with a stylized mustache, I think was his agent, pressed a button on the side of the table, and a sleek screen rose from the center. How very James Bond this all was. Another of Wesley's team members typed on the tablet as they spoke. "The Cole family lawyer is joining us remotely."

This was going to take longer than I wanted.

Feeling silly for remaining standing, I took the chair next to Wesley, still refusing to look at him. I ignored the frisson of goose bumps that danced up my arm closest to him and that familiar rich, luxuriant scent. We were sat on one side of the long table, like two children being scolded for nicking holiday treats. I kept my gaze forward, eyes not quite seeing but taking in the room around me.

On Wesley's other side sat his father, then mother, and then two familiar-ish faces that I assumed were people from his team. The man who pulled up the screen and a woman close to our age that had her thick hair twisted in a ponytail on her head with the lower half shaved. Sofia sat to my other side and gently tapped my foot once with hers, as if for encouragement.

His mother was the first to speak. Diana Cole. As elegant and pristine as ever. I thought of the contrast between her against my mother in Wiltshire. Where Diana was long and lean with a perfect twist of white-blond hair, my mother was red-haired and rosy-cheeked, stout and ample, perfect for snuggling into to have a good head pet. I missed my family back home with such an acute longing I felt like a little kid.

Wasn't that the effect that being around Wesley always seemed to have on me? Instant youth-inizing. All my deepest, most tumultuous feelings were brought to the surface. At this moment, I almost preferred actual euthanizing.

His father spoke next, but I couldn't look at him other than a quick nod to register that I was paying attention to his supercilious lecture. He was too close to Wesley. Physically, they were sitting next to each other, but also in appearance. Wesley might have inherited his mother's notorious streak of white hair, but he was a replica of his handsome father in all other ways, albeit younger. But I would never mix them up when one look at Rex

Cole made my skin crawl, and Wesley ... well, Wesley had the opposite effect.

But we weren't worrying about physical reactions when those could be pushed deep, deep down and buried in a tiny little hole of the subconscious.

The summation was that we were two naughty school kids being scolded, so I wasn't far off.

Rex Cole droned on in his nasally Californian accent. The elite of America tried so hard to sound posh.

Wesley's house was and wasn't what I expected. It was lovely, luxurious, masculine. The chairs we were seated in were upholstered in emerald green velvet that must be a nightmare to clean—not that this family ever needed to worry about such pedestrian things. The chandelier above was gold and almost vulgar in its contemporary structure, vaguely reminiscent of a Russian space station. The entire house I'd seen thus far was thoughtfully put together, elite, and not even remotely Wesley Cole.

But then, what did I know of the man? Nothing in actuality.

The person I thought I knew was encased in whoever the man next to me was, like Han Solo cast in carbonite.

"... Reputation such as Miss Flynn's needs to be protected ..." Rex droned on.

I glanced at Sofia. She rolled her eyes subtly, and it eased some of the tension out of my shoulders. Nothing could be that bad if she was willingly here with me. I needed to wait it out.

Wesley shifted next to me. The edge of his suit brushed my elbow, and my arms snapped in closer to my body, hands gripping each other in my lap. Who wore a bloody suit to an unplanned lunch meeting anyway?

He exhaled softly. Annoyed? Unimpressed?

His feelings on the matter were not my concern. He was here, so that said enough. I took slow and silent breaths while keeping my features serene.

"… Suggest the relationship would last until award season."

Ears pricking, I tuned back in.

This was when the man introduced as Burt, Wesley's agent, stood and spoke. His head was polished so shiny the light of the space station reflected in it.

"Miss Flynn and Mr. Cole would make several appearances, at least one ad campaign, one premiere, and several 'plandids,' aka planned candids, together will be leaked in that time. There would need to be several posts on their social media accounts expressing …"

The bald man had been reading from his device, flicking a glance to me as my jaw fell closer and closer to the floor.

"So long as both parties agree to the terms," he finished and sat back down.

The room was silent, but obviously, they were all waiting for me to speak. But how was I meant to when the ringing in my ears was so loud that I couldn't form a thought, let alone a word?

"I'm sorry. Are you suggesting a relationship between Wes— Mr. Cole and I?" My voice was surprisingly calm despite my turmoil. Something else I'd picked up over the years. No longer the reactive teenager. My west country accent was smoothed out to BBC poshness, so long as I kept my cool.

"Temporarily."

"But Wesley and I are not even friends," I said, thankful at how aloof I sounded.

Wesley shifted in his seat.

"It would be a relationship only outwardly. Obviously, nothing but the appearance of dating is necessary," the other publicist said. Her nails tapped on a copy of the document now sitting in front of me.

"And how would this help mitigate anything?" I asked. Was I really the only one who found this tasteless?

Diana spoke up. "Wesley has just wrapped filming what will

surely be a shoo-in for an Oscar. We need him on everybody's radar."

Christ, but I hated how she said his name. As though she owned it.

"To clarify, despite him just getting divorced, you think pushing him into another supposed relationship is good?" I asked.

"There's no bad press," Rex said simply.

Of course, a man of such morals would feel that way.

This was a nightmare of my own making. Any moment, I'd wake up, and this whole day would start over. What if I stood and screamed? What would they do then? I imagined myself in slow motion, throwing all the papers into the air, a snarl twisting my features.

I blinked at Sofia, *how,* I screamed with my eyes, *did she think this was okay*? She knew enough of my feelings toward Wesley, and if nothing else, everybody knew about the bloody interview where he coldly dismissed me.

"We need to take control of the story," Sofia spoke up. "Emma, we've already heard from CrunchyCouture, and they've said they are no longer interested in the campaign." My heart dropped to the floor. She cleared her throat and went on, "Unless ..." Sofia glanced at the Coles.

"Unless?" I asked, voice cracking.

"Unless the younger Mr. Cole joins the campaign for a couple's photo shoot." I impressively held my wince at her confession. But she must have sensed my apprehension, nonetheless. "I wouldn't even be here if I didn't feel like this publicity stunt would mutually benefit both parties," she added.

Et tu, Sofia?

"You can't be serious?" I asked, appalled.

"People love you two together," Sofia said gently.

I didn't mean to guffaw. People loved Lucy Lennon and Max Malachi together.

"We don't understand it either," Rex said with an aloof shake of the head.

"That's enough," Wesley admonished.

He speaks!

"We'd be happy to support the CrunchyCouture company," he added with a lip curl that conveyed anything but happy. "To support this new union, so to speak."

"Ah. So in order to keep the campaign that I fought for that will literally put clothes on the back of needy children, I need Wesley to smile pretty for a camera and pretend to like me? Bloody brilliant." My accent slipped through, but I couldn't care less. I walked into this room two steps behind.

My entire career was on the line to be rescued by a man who detested me.

"I'm happy to clear up this misunderstanding with Crunchy-Couture. You say the word," Rex said smoothly, phone in hand.

"What about the fact that Wes—Mr. Cole has made it quite clear over the years that he and I are no more than long-ago co-stars." And that was putting it genially.

"We have a plan in place. The world will accept it if you make it convincing. All is fair when *true love* is on the line," Rex said, emphasizing true love as though he were explaining stomach trouble.

I noticed a slight tensing in Diana Cole that had dissipated by the time I looked at her.

A distinct sense of panic began to claw its way up inside me. I had spent enough time avoiding my feelings, burying them deep, but now they shook and rattled their confines, waiting for their shot at freedom. My deepest insecurities on full display to suit the games they want to play? He may be a great actor, but I'd never been. He would see everything. My heart already felt raw and exposed, and we hadn't even been in the same room for ten minutes. Forced proximity to this man could ruin everything.

"Pretend to be in love?" I asked, looking around at everyone but Wesley. "He can't even stand to be near me. Nobody is that good of an actor," I said sharply.

This time, he definitely flinched a fraction at my side, but I wouldn't apologize. Not after everything.

This was ridiculous. This was absolutely absurd, yet I seemed to be the only person in the room who had any touch with reality.

I took a deep breath. This was exactly what they wanted. They wanted me to throw a fit and show how beneath them I was. The very fact that I walked into this room as the only unsuspecting party to this plan said everything.

But I hadn't spent the past thirteen years in the industry to be the same naive girl they expected.

I took a collecting breath and sat up straighter. "Prove it," I said to Rex.

He raised an eyebrow. "What exactly?"

"Get my campaign back, and then I will think about it."

Rex smiled. If I hadn't spent my entire adult life negotiating with men like him, I might have been shocked by his callousness. But I'd built some callouses of my own.

I sat in awkward silence, fraught with tension, as Rex typed on his phone. A shockingly short amount of time later, he set the phone down and looked up at me, clasping his hands to mirror my posture.

Sofia's phone pinged, and I looked at her. She nodded, nostrils flared.

"Let me look at the proposed schedule and contract." I reached out a hand to Burt. "I will be in contact. Is that all?" I asked.

The others exchanged glances.

What? I didn't throw the fit you hoped for? "You've made it clear that I have little choice. The personal preferences of Mr. Cole and I hardly seem to matter at this point. But I can control what I can. My team will be in contact."

His mother sniffed with a raised eyebrow. Was that begrudging respect? Or allergies?

Wesley was stock-still at my side. I was tempted to look at him to make sure he wasn't actually in carbonite. But I resisted.

"So glad you saw the light," Rex said as he stood. "Make your changes by the end of the day."

I smiled sweetly at him. "Absolutely."

Diana said, "Let's leave the kids to discuss this, shall we?"

It took an eternity for them all to leave us. As they left the room, Wesley stood to busy his hands with something behind me. I refused to look and give him the satisfaction of my curiosity. With every second that ticked by, I would have to get over this childish reaction.

Not quite yet.

After they left, still looking straight ahead, I said, "They know we're in our thirties, right? At any point, will they ever see us as adults capable of our own choices?"

After a frozen moment, fearful I had already said too much, put too much out on the line, he finally spoke.

"Doubtful," he said from behind me.

He reached around to set down a glass of amber liquid. I felt the heat of him briefly encompass me. He smelled of that same rich cologne and a hint of cinnamon and oak. I didn't dare move and risk brushing up against his chest.

"Poisoned?" I asked.

He stilled briefly as he straightened. "Not yours."

I hid a grin that tried to sneak out as I took a large sip, downing the whole thing. My barking cough ruined the effect.

I didn't have to look at him to see the mocking smile.

I had to get this over with and stop acting like a child. Once my air passage remembered how to function, I turned in the chair and met his gaze. He tilted his head, right imperious eyebrow raised at me. I wondered if he knew it was always the eyebrow with the bits of white that he wielded like a weapon.

"Ah, she can look at me," he said in his deep gravelly *man's* voice.

It still hit me at the most random times that we were both so *old.* At least older than we'd ever been. I forgot that he was such a man. When I replayed the moments of our past, it wasn't this voice that I heard. It was more of a feeling. A feeling that threatened to bubble out of my chest as I took in the sight of this man before me. He was so aloof, so smooth and confident. It had the unwanted effect of making me feel like a bumbling, needy fool. I'd have to keep my eyes and tongue sharp.

"Are you aware your father does that judgmental eyebrow thing too?" I asked sweetly as the words hit their mark. Wouldn't he feel complimented to be compared to the older man?

He turned to the side, eyes narrowing and jaw clenched. He stood, propped against the high bar, long legs crossed at the ankles, one arm supporting him as the other lifted his glass. The picture of indifference. All my nerves came to attention, like hair rising right before a lightning strike.

"I don't see you looking at my father like that," he said coolly.

I barely fought back the blush.

"Oh, get over yourself," I said, standing. I came to his chin and felt decidedly less intimidating.

"Cheers," he said ironically to my empty glass. He toasted the air as I watched his lips fit on the rim and the way his throat moved with the swallow.

Bloody hell, I shouldn't be watching him drink.

I was too close to him to be aware of that. I stepped back and pretended to examine some art on the wall without seeing it.

The whiskey hit my empty stomach hard but gave me the needed courage. "I thought we weren't allowed to drink together," I said. "Wasn't that what got us into this trouble to begin with?"

He swallowed, his strong jaw flexing in an all too appealing way, causing me to regret looking at him at all. Once had been enough for this day. But even as I told myself that, I fought to keep my gaze away.

"We aren't allowed to be drunk together. There's a difference. And it was hardly my doing that got us here."

He did blame me, then. It shouldn't hurt, but I could build a house of all my "shouldn'ts" at this point. I turned slowly back toward him. He swirled his drink, not looking at me. If this was going to be uncomfortable, at least we'd both suffer. There was some schadenfreude in that.

"Right. I couldn't keep my hands to myself," I said. "Just look at what the internet says."

He looked me up and down slowly. "Let's get through this."

6
___

Wesley

It was good that Emma Flynn couldn't muster the will to look at me more than once because her direct attention was too much to bear. My gaze drifted over her figure with her back to me once again. Tall and lithe, she was so much a woman of grace and elegance now. It was impossible not to compare her to the gawky girl with all knees and elbows from our youth. Her body was very, *very* well-proportioned.

When she turned around, I quickly averted my gaze from her ass to my drink.

This meeting had gone differently than expected. I really tried not to get emotional. I tried to remain aloof and cold, but something about our personalities when we were together had me snapping. We both had the instinctual ability to cut the other to the quick. I didn't like to think about why that might be.

My feelings for her were ... complicated. You couldn't give up your freedom for somebody without feeling a little resentful. Rationally, I understood that wasn't her fault. None of this was her fault. Except that she technically *had* followed me out of the bar. She always pushed and pushed back when I tried to keep her away. Why wouldn't she leave me be? I wouldn't always be able to maintain the strength needed to keep her at bay.

"At least you have to think this plan is as absurd as I do," she said almost as a question.

"Ah. There she is," I said, knowing it would only goad her more. I set the drink down with a tink of glass on marble and finally met her gaze.

"What is that supposed to mean?" she asked with ferocity.

"Didn't think you'd roll over so easily."

"Before or after your father blackmailed me into cooperating?"

"I expected some fight."

"You think it would have mattered?" She glared at me with hatred. I should be relieved because that was the plan, after all.

But God, she was gorgeous. I told myself whenever I wasn't around her that the pictures of her online were photoshopped to emphasize her gleaming red hair that flowed like waves and her shocking blue eyes. Most people tend to reveal their flaws in real life. Lighting and filters only did so much to cover when personality was revealed. But Emma was only somehow more breathtaking this close. The cameras did little justice to the burning beauty she carried, this fire that she'd muted over the years as she became the Golden Girl for the public to worship.

I remembered her ferocity. I had already been so jealous of her zeal for the mysteries of the unknown future when I had known my place since I was born.

"Our opinions don't matter," I agreed.

I needed to hurry this along. I was waxing poetic every time she deemed to look at me, and it was getting harder to remember why I thought I could get through this pain-free.

"Clearly." She set her empty glass next to mine, but when the heat of our shared space made itself known, she stepped away again. "Nobody will buy this. This plan they've concocted is sure to fail."

"People en masse are simple creatures. We have to make it seem like it was their idea. Let them be the geniuses who figured it out," I said, invoking my father's haughty tone and hating how easily it came.

Was I destined to become like him? That fear constantly had me acting on behalf of first my mother, then Natasha, and now Emma. Again. This wasn't the first time I'd made sure she would be safe from the Cole sadists.

"God, the arrogance. Do you really take yourself this seriously?" she asked, exacerbated.

It stung that this pretense easily fooled her, but it was better to have her angry; better she felt pressured into this arrangement than to have her do it out of the goodness of her heart. Better to see heat than icy indifference if I was being honest with myself. Heat meant emotion, and any feelings were better than none.

I was hopeless.

"You know I'm right," I explained. "If we come right out with it, then yes, people will think it's fake. We have to make them put the pieces together. You know the superfans will."

"The Emsley shippers."

To think people who had no idea who we were thought they had any claim over what would make us happy. People who thought they knew Emma were fooling themselves. They felt like they had a right to her, and it made me sick. The disgust on my face must have shown but for the wrong reasons.

"That terrible, is it?" she asked. "Yet Mummy and Daddy asked you to do this, and you just rolled over?"

Looked like we both unleashed our sharpest tongues. Now my anger was real, not a tool to push her away.

"Oh, hit a sore spot?" she taunted.

"Don't put this on me when you're the reason we're even here," I said sharply.

She crossed her arms.

"You wanted this, didn't you?" I spat the words back at her that my father had said to me earlier, and there was no taking them back.

She flinched. "Excuse me?"

"You just happened to be there that night? Fake concern for me and a camera was there? That's convenient."

Her color drained.

I couldn't stand myself.

"Christ. You're more jaded by this industry than I ever thought if you could possibly think me capable of that," she said.

Of course, I didn't, but every minute standing here trying to convince her to do this was another minute of torture.

I ground my jaw.

It took forever to get her to even look at me. And now I wish she'd stop. Those crystal-blue eyes always had a trance-like power over me. They pierced me, and I swore she could see my resolve weakening.

I could play this role of villain if it was for a good cause.

"You owe me for this. That picture has really fucked me over in tandem with my divorce," I said.

"Your marriage was over far before that night." Red spread over her neck. "And I was a bloody fool for trying to comfort you."

"I didn't ask you to."

Her eyes were wide in disbelief. Long-buried feelings bubbled over. "I didn't ask you to be there. I never asked you to come around, and time and time again, you show up. Just when—" Just when I'd start to move on, she'd show up and remind me that I'd never feel about anybody else the way I did with her. "You show up and ruin the plan," I finished and felt sick.

Her jaw snapped shut, and her jaw clenched.

She turned away, smoothing her hands down her thighs. "I-I don't know. I don't know why I continue to try to convince myself that someone I know is still in there." She spoke to herself in annoyance, head shaking.

"We were children, and we never knew each other," I said, lying so blatantly now. I wanted to back up and start over.

She pivoted back to me, lifting her chin. "You're right about that."

"You owe me." I took a step toward her.

"You cannot possibly be that arrogant." She mirrored my action.

"I'm a realist."

"You're a prat."

Emma stood toe-to-toe with me, eyes fierce. Our faces were inches away from each other. Both of our chests heaved. Wasn't my goal to go into this in a rational and calm manner, and here I was, a second from grasping her shoulders to push her away ... or something.

Her gaze flicked over my face, and then she registered the lack of space between us. There was a tangible buzz in the air.

She turned and ran her hands through her hair, talking to herself again. "We can't even stand to be in the same room without fighting."

She hates you. Remember that she hates you.

"This only has to be as difficult as you make it," I said.

"As *I* make it?"

"People do this all the time. It's not that big a deal. You're overreacting."

The wheels turned behind those eyes, shifting from the crystal blue of a sparkling ocean to a deadly dark sea. Her emotions shut down. I'd cut too deep. Down to some exposed nerve I wasn't even aware of. I wanted to rile her up, find the sign of life that had to be in there. I never meant to hurt her. Yet again, I hit too hard. I really was my father's son.

We had both changed over the years. We weren't the people we used to be, but some things never changed. Deep down inside, I needed her to know I was aware of this. I needed her to understand that this was one battle in the war. One piece of a game of chess to be moved. She and I had to endure this and not let the arrangement take us down.

I wasn't sure she remembered as much of our time on set together as I did. I always feared that I had a habit of romanticizing the past through the lens of adulthood, but we always played one game. One way we allowed ourselves the freedom to push the boundaries set for us.

"I didn't take you for a chicken," I added and looked up to hold her gaze.

She stilled, watching me intently. The challenge called to her? Or the memory of our shared past?

She leaned forward slowly, purposely brushing me, as she grabbed our empty glasses. "A bit of a top off?"

My dubious reaction must have been written all over my face because she lifted the glasses in emphasis. Wearily, I filled them, the liquor sloshing in the silence.

She lifted her glass. "Cheers."

I mirrored her, waiting for the catch. "Cheers?"

As our glasses clinked together, she said, "Hold there." She produced her phone and held it up. "Scoot a little to the left." I followed the orders yet again, still unsure but too curious to fight her. She nodded succinctly. "Right."

The phone clicked ominously before she slid it away. She threw back the rest of the drink. I still held mine, wondering if I had misplayed this whole scene.

Before I had time to react, she grabbed her bag and the contract off the table. "The team will be in contact."

She didn't look back as she strode toward the exit. Right before she left, she released one last parting shot.

"I'm not the same woman I used to be, Wesley. I won't be made the fool. Not anymore." She sauntered out. I watched her hips sway with confidence as I sat in silent contemplation over what had happened.

If this had been the first battle in the long war, I was pretty sure I'd lost.

A few moments later, my phone began to vibrate with calls and notifications, and my suspicions were confirmed.

7

———

Podcast Nosy Nelly Celebrity News
  Season 4, Episode 12 *Gilded Prince* transcript excerpt
  Co-hosts: Gabi Ortega and Liz Kane

[excerpt starts]

LIZ: I told you!

GABI: Again with the yelling.

LIZ: Sorry. But the truth is out, and I am excitable.

GABI: The truth? Hardly. It's an overzealous fanbase.

LIZ: You're never going to let me have this, are you?

Laughter.

GABI: Maybe I'm dead inside.

LIZ: Maybe?

GABI: Okay. Okay. Regardless of my emotional well-being, you said you had proof that Emsley was officially happening. Hit me.

LIZ: So October twenty-second, the "intimate embrace" photo is leaked, divorce announced.

GABI: Conveniently, taking the attention away from the announcement of his divorce. But we did another episode on that, and I'll link it in the show notes.

LIZ: True. But then that day Emma Flynn posted a picture of her clinking a glass with an unidentified mystery man—with very toned forearms, I must say—and captioned it "Cheers to a new adventure and old friends." Old friends? Felt a little pointed, in my opinion. And it is so clearly Wesley's hand.

GABI: How is that clear? Was he tagged? Did she say specifically?

LIZ: No. But I know that arm.

Scoff.

Liz: *And* she's talking about a project she's excited about, and look at these hashtags: #oldfriendsnewfriends. #Gameof-Chicken #TFreunion #yourmove Emma Flynn has never been an overzealous hashtagger.

GABI: Because that's a word.

LIZ: Language is fluid.

GABI: Okay, but tagging aside, this could mean in business or personal relationship or maybe even a movie? She hasn't acted since *Terraformative* but never explicitly said she was against it. But maybe she's talking about the anniversary special. It could be Harrison Evans or Charlie Downing?

LIZ: Except she always shows their faces when she's with them. They are the "three best friends that anyone could have."

GABI: You're just being hopeful.

LIZ: I'm telling you. Then, the following weekend, Emma posted that she was in New York. Guess who also happened to be in New York? They posted the same landmarks.

GABI: Hmm. I will admit that's strange.

LIZ: Right? And one says she posted a picture of her brunch, and he posted a similar food selfie on the same place setting.

GABI: That is interesting.

LIZ: If it was one thing, but almost every other post could be tied to the other person.

GABI: Okay, okay.

LIZ: Oh. And ChicChat had exclusive information from, and I quote, a source close to the family, who spilled that they're doing an ad campaign together and have been spending a lot of time together.

GABI: Really? So if they're dating, why not just say it?

LIZ: I don't know. Maybe they want privacy.

GABI: Oh, right. Fame and boundaries from the press always go hand in hand with celebrities.

LIZ: In the past two weeks, at least seven different posts between Emma and Wesley can be linked. She posts a picture from the Met; he posts one from Central Park. He posts a picture of a California sunset, and she posts about hiking the Brush Canyon Trail.

Several beats of thoughtful silence.

LIZ: It's occurring to me now that anybody listening who isn't a longtime fan may think we sound totally unhinged.

GABI: Hey, if they're still here at this point, then that's on them.

LIZ: I know, I know. But it's facts, just facts, that I'm pointing out. People can do with it what they will.

GABI: But have we actually seen them together?

LIZ: Technically? No. Not since that last picture.

GABI: Hmm.

LIZ: But it's only a matter of time.

GABI: Ever the optimist.

LIZ: Listen. I need something to believe in these days.

GABI: True that.

LIZ: How much more evidence do you need?

GABI: Not until I see them holding hands at an event will I buy it. Maybe not even then. I might need him to confess his love for her on camera. Live.

LIZ: Damn, you really are a cynic.

GABI: The world has hardened me.

[excerpt ends]

8

———

Emma

It was yet another ambush.

"Hi, Harrison. To what do I owe the honor of this unexpected call?" I squinted at the image of my best friend on the phone, unable to tell where he was.

I had to fly back to New York for the weekend, but Wesley and I had kept up our social media game while I'd been away. For over a month, he'd been doing the same on his end, but we were not talking except for the occasional text to share photos to make it seem like we were together. I wouldn't imagine a life where we actually spent time together and even took the imaginary trips we were meant to have been on. A futile waste of perfect brain processing power.

Instead, I focused on what was to be an intervention from my concerned friend. Charlie, Harrison, and I had vowed to up our monthly calls to weekly since Charlie had expressed concern over our growing distance a few months ago. We'd all made more of an effort to be a regular part of each other's lives. Even still. This unexpected call was clearly motivated.

"Hullo, love. We just wanted to check in," Harrison said.

"We?" I asked right as Charlie's face appeared in another cube of the screen, a little puffy with sleep and hair mussed up.

"And Charlie." I waved at my other best friend.

"Hullo, Emma." He rubbed his eyes as he spoke.

"Hi!" Kate's head popped up next to him in the same room. He smiled sleepily as he scooted over for her, slinging an arm around her. He kissed the side of her head as she leaned over to wave.

Where Charlie had clearly just rolled out of bed, Kate looked flushed and wore a workout tank top. The country life suited her. Or maybe that was the glow of being in love.

I smiled, genuinely happy for them, despite bracing for the inevitable.

"I won't stay long," Kate said. "I just wanted to say hi."

"Stay," I said too quickly. Maybe it would cause the guys to filter some of their thoughts. "You're welcome here as much as any of us. Plus, it's nice not to be overwhelmed by testosterone."

"Manly energy simply radiates off me," Harrison said as he flexed his biceps.

Charlie snorted as he secured Kate more tightly to his side. "*Mi amigos es su amigos.*"

She blushed but settled down next to him. Kate wore her brunette hair in a chic bob that I envied. This long red hair took so much upkeep, but it was part of the brand. Sometimes I dreamed of pulling a "Felicity" and cutting it all off in a fit of rebellion. It would probably be breaking news.

"I have a feeling I'm going to need the cool logic of a woman around these two hotheads," I said.

Harrison mocked being offended. Charlie was distracted, twirling a strand of Kate's hair around his finger.

Maybe it was juvenile to be so upset about a fake relationship when they happened all the time. Truthfully, after my team tweaked a few things into the proposal that would ensure my reputation—and therefore protect the charity—Sofia and I discussed the benefits of this arrangement. It would be good for our reputations and had a relatively short expiration date. I would avoid Wesley as much as possible to get through it, but then I looked at what Kate and Charlie had, and suddenly, wanting something genuine didn't seem so ridiculous. What it might feel like to be looked at like I was the most precious thing in the world? To find a person who made you feel safe and secure? Would Wes look at me when the cameras were on him? Could I stand it if he did?

"Shall we get straight to the point of this call? I'm assuming it's serious if Charlie was able to get out of bed," I said.

"Actually, Charlie's here in Minnesota helping me pack up my place," Kate explained.

I guffawed. "Charlie! That means it's lunchtime there."

"I was up late reading Kate's newest manuscript. Couldn't put it down." He smiled softly again at Kate.

"Still, I don't have a ton of time, so let's get right to it. I imagine this is about some of the press management after the photo leak," I said.

Charlie and Harrison frowned and crossed their arms.

"Press management is the most PC way of putting it. You two seem to be in the news quite a bit lately," Harrison said. "I thought this was all to be swept under the rug like every time the Emsley fans go mad?"

"The rumor mill online is like nothing I've seen before." Kate chewed her lip before she added, "I have to admit some of your posts do seem to be purposely hinting at things between you and Wesley."

"You're fueling the fire," Charlie scoffed.

I sat up straight and proper, taking a deep bracing breath to lay it out there. "That's intentional. Wesley and I are dating." When all three blinked at me in shock, I added, "For publicity only. Obviously." I waved my hand casually in the air. "We'll be doing several appearances as a couple for the next few months until his next movie comes out, and then we'll break it off. The teams felt this was in the best interest of both brands."

My hand twitched restlessly in the following silence.

"But ... why?" Charlie asked.

"It's the smart move. The Emma Flynn brand is bigger than me at this point. It's an entire team, but unfortunately, that reputation still lies squarely on my shoulders. I have to make up for my stupid mistake that night we went out. He needs to get back in good favor after his divorce. It makes sense."

"You weren't stupid," Kate said softly. "That was one of the best nights of my life."

"No. I know. I shouldn't have followed Wesley. You all tried to stop me." I shook my head and sat up confidently. "It doesn't matter. What's done is done. We can only move forward, and it's all temporary."

"This won't end well, Emma," Harrison said bluntly. My eyebrows lifted in surprise.

"No beating around the bush, then," I said, feeling ganged up on again like I had at the meeting with the Coles. At least these people cared about my best interests.

"We promised we would always be honest about things in our career and lives," Harrison said. "He's never been kind to you. We don't want you to be the one hurt in this situation."

"I won't get hurt," I said. "You have to care, and I shut that off."

"You don't think he's using your feelings for him to get what he wants?" Charlie asked.

"I haven't fancied him since we were children. I appreciate you, but this is purely a business decision."

Three sets of concerned eyes looked back at me. If I couldn't even convince them, then I was hopeless.

I sighed. "Look, I know I made an arse of myself once or twice, probably too many times, but I'm telling you that I have everything under control. Have a little faith in me, would you? I'm not the overemotional little twit I was twenty years ago, okay?"

"None of us think you are," Harrison said vehemently. "We don't trust him. He's only concerned about his career and will do whatever he needs to further it. He's made that clear over and over again," Harrison said.

I hated that a part of me wanted to defend the person I used to know. He wasn't always distant from me. He wasn't always aloof and cold. He used to be the person I turned to when I couldn't talk to Charlie and Harrison. It didn't matter who he was now. I knew myself now. I knew what I could and could not handle.

"How does Wesley feel about all this? Are we allowed to ask that?" Kate asked gently.

"I'm sure this was his bloody idea," Charlie said.

"Now that Emma is a sensation, he has the time of day for her," Harrison said, nodding his head in agreement with Charlie's sentiment.

He was abnormally grumpy. Charlie usually held that role, but maybe now that Charlie was distracted and had little butterflies of love flitting around his head, Harrison decided to take up the mantle. Although he'd seemed more and more distracted lately in general. Maybe the pressure of his latest role? I'd have to keep an eye on him.

Back to the current crisis, I took a breath and looked at them each on the screen. "Wesley is just as much a victim of this arrangement as I am, if not more, since technically, it was my ... slipup that night that got us in hot water."

"He's the one who got divorced. He needs you more," Harrison said.

I shook my head. "People divorce all the time. It wouldn't have even made the news if the photo hadn't leaked. Their split is amicable," I said, which was mostly true, as far as I knew.

"He told you that?" Harrison asked.

"Things aren't as black and white as the news wants them to be. As you guys want them to be. It's silly that people even care about this," I said. "I shouldn't have to make business decisions about my personal life." I shook my head. There was no point going down that path, and the guys looked like they were bracing for a tangent. "Anyway. He wants to get through it as much as I do. He looked like he sipped vinegar the whole meeting."

"He should be so lucky to even look at you at this point, let alone pretend to date you," Harrison grumbled.

I decided not to mention the fact that we were not only convincing the world we were dating but also falling in love. Maybe best to take that elephant bite by bite and save that bit for later.

"He's had a lifetime to make up for treating you like shite," Charlie said.

"I always wondered about that interview." Kate's brow furrowed. "It seemed so out of character for him." She flushed. "But then again, I obviously don't know him like you guys do."

"We don't know him at all. He was always separate from us on set," Charlie explained. "He never wanted to hang around the riffraff."

Christ, that was such an oversimplification of our time together on set; I couldn't even begin to explain how hard his family was back then. And that was as a child. I shuddered to think about what had happened when he left the show.

This conversation had the opposite effect my friends

intended. Instead of helping me to see the light about the situation, it made me feel bad for Wesley. Reminding me how he's always been isolated and left with no choices. At least I had choices. I had freedom. Or I did before I became Golden Girl Emma Flynn.

"Can we not talk about the past anymore? This showmance is happening. We're moving forward. And doing it on our own terms as much as possible."

"Fine. Just know we love and support you," Harrison said.

"I know. Thank you. I love you too." A new sense of guilt warred with my frustration. Who was I trying to protect at this point?

A fourth cube popped up on the screen with no warning. It was Agata, Charlie's housekeeper. "He a good man?"

Charlie jumped a foot in the air. Kate snickered and patted him on the hand. Agata had entered Charlie's life a few years ago and into our hearts. Mostly by sheer force of will at first, but now we wouldn't be anywhere without her.

"No." Charlie and Harrison said in sync.

I scoffed with a sigh. "He's not bad. He's under a lot of pressure."

"You make excuses for him?" Agata said. "Does he woo?"

"Ha! Not likely," Charlie said.

Kate smirked.

"He doesn't need to woo. We only need the pretense of woo," I explained.

"Miss Emma can make her own choices," Agata said sharply. "You boys do not own her. She is not livestock."

"Thank you, Agata," I said, crossing my arms.

"And maybe her and hot man can get freaky. So much sexual tension between them," Agata added with a knowing shrug.

"Absolutely not," both men said at the same time.

Kate nodded before she caught herself and flushed.

I rubbed my fingertips to my temples.

"If you're done with the inquisition, I have places to be," I said, feeling a little bad for my brusqueness.

"Check in with us," Harrison demanded.

"Of course I will. You all will see. In time, this whole thing was just a business choice. One day down the road, it'll be like it never happened."

I'd done the work and built an empire to change the world for the better. I wouldn't let a single man threaten any of that.

———

Wesley

"Can a person break their spleen?" I asked Mac through gritted teeth.

"I'm sure you can break anything if you try hard enough," he said.

I told him everything about how the plan to leave was on hold. How my father threatened Emma. He remained surprisingly quiet but offered support in the only way he knew how—by pushing my body to the brink of death.

I made an otherworldly growl I wasn't proud of.

"I thought we were done with these intense trainings for a while. Thirty more seconds," he said.

I grunted as I alternated swinging the heavy ropes as the muscles in my forearms and back screamed for mercy. "Me. Too."

The only good thing about pushing myself this hard was that there was no way for my brain to play my last interaction with Emma. We hadn't spoken. We'd flirted online, if it could be called that. It was a hint of the start of a ruse, and the superfans were eating it up.

Having her back in my life, even in this limited capacity, was like being transported back in time. My feelings for her were a kind of grief. They never went away; in time, waves would crash over me less and less, save for the sudden smell or sight that would cause a memory to accost me at the most random time. But then, seeing her leave again was to lose her all over again.

"They talked about some photo shoot?" Mac took mercy on me and tapped my shoulder. "Okay, two minutes' rest."

I dropped the ends of the rope and had to fight my now weightless arms to stop their inertia from smacking me in the face. He tossed me a water bottle I barely managed to catch. I nodded as I took heavy pulls.

Ah, so the only time I wouldn't think about it was when I was physically not able to. Because as soon as I could breathe, the image of her glaring face popped into my head.

"It's an ad campaign for an eco-friendly, high-end clothing company Emma supports. The research I did about it was actually impressive."

"That's great. It sounds like a win-win. What did she think about you taking it seriously?"

"I didn't tell her that."

"Why?" He gave me a long-suffering look. I should know, I invented that look.

"Because I'm a total goober," I said flatly. And it somehow feels like I'm giving something up. Sharing too much. Showing my soft underbelly just so she can slice at it when this all ends.

He nodded—a little too quickly, if you ask me—in agreement.

"But the fake dating is going good?" he asked.

"Define good. The public seems to be buying it." I frowned at my callused hands. "My parents have backed off a little."

"They're really invested in your personal life." Mac frowned, flicking a look at me.

The weird factor of the Cole Dynasty always surprised those outside of it.

"There is no difference between professional and personal to them. They think they own it all. It's part of the reason I was trying to separate myself."

"Yeah. Damn, I'm sorry, man. No more plans to leave?" he asked.

I glared at the floor. The plan remained the same. Get through these next few months, and then I would get the hell out of this life. But talking about it before had jinxed it. I would keep my dreams to myself for now. "I'm taking things one day at a time."

Mac nodded in sympathy. "Will you see her in real life?"

"Not if I can help it," I said. "When I'm around her ..." I paced in a circle. "I always try to ..." I slumped back onto the bench, head dropping. "I don't know how to be around her."

"Is this how you were when you had a calm, rational conversation about shared goals just as you intended? Because if so, I see the problem."

I looked at him without lifting my head. "I blamed her for everything and insinuated that even pretending to be with her made me physically ill. She called me a pretentious prat."

"Wow. Impressively bad."

I wiped the sweat off my face. "I don't know what it is about her, man. I try so hard to keep my distance. Stay calm. And within seconds, we're in each other's face."

"It's almost like there are decades of unresolved tension," he said, eyebrows lifted innocently.

"Yeah. Yeah." I threw a towel at him. "I'm supposed to see her at this photo shoot in three days. I have no idea how to get through it. This time, I won't bait her." I wouldn't let myself get emotional. It was better to shut myself away. I would do what I had to get through it.

He nodded, shifting on his feet and avoiding my gaze. The ground groaned with his weight.

"What?" I asked.

"Not my place." He held up his hands.

"Out with it."

"Honestly, your ice-man demeanor? That shit you pull on TV? It probably pisses her off."

I looked at him skeptically. Had he been in my head?

"That's the face," he snapped and pointed at me with a chuckle. "It's probably triggering for her. You look like your dad," he said with a shudder.

"Ouch." In the reflection of my home gym, I saw the pretentious raise of my eyebrow and a curl to my lips. "I can't help my face," I said. Or who made me. Was I destined to become him no matter what I did?

"Yeah, you can, man. You aren't like that with me. Well, except now. Or when I make you do burpees."

"You're a cruel man."

"You're nothing like your dad," he said sincerely, holding my gaze.

I blinked away, unable to look at him.

"You and Emma were friends, right?" he asked when it was clear my father was not a topic up for discussion.

"A lifetime ago," I grumbled.

"She probably hates that fake front you put on with everyone else when it's just her. She's known you longer than most people in your life." He gestured to the rack of weights. "Thirty seconds more, then curls."

"I guess." I stood back up and went to the free weights. "When did you become such an expert of all things Emma?"

"It's not her. Don't forget, I was a personal bodyguard before this for ten years. I've seen all kinds in this industry. I get the persona thing, but maybe you don't need to do that with her. Maybe she resents that about you."

"Yeah," I said, processing. I guess that could be true. She didn't like being relegated to the same treatment as strangers. What were my other options? If I was myself around her, if I let her see the truth …

I couldn't voice my real fears. How was I supposed to act around her, then? Before, when I was young and naive, I wanted to touch her. Protect her. I wanted to keep her away from the world that was trying to use her.

"I think the real issue is that I've spent over a decade convincing her that I wanted nothing to do with her," I admitted, shocking myself. I'd never shared the truth with anybody.

Mac stilled. "Why?"

I ran a hand over my face. "Remember when I told you how messed up my family was? When we were younger, she and I were more than friends. We were …" I looked away as a flush burned my neck. That night when we were eighteen had been the greatest moment of my life. It was ripped from my grasp way too soon, but I had tasted pure happiness with her. "We were everything to each other at one point," I finished. "My parents found out and didn't approve. Long story short, it was either lose her or hurt her. I managed to do both."

When I braved a look at Mac, he was glaring. "Damn. That's more fucked up than my family. And that's saying a lot."

"I know. I was a little too good at pushing her away."

"Sounds like you better start making amends."

I swallowed. Nothing I could ever do would make amends.

If I relaxed a little, then I'd lose any control I held on to. Now, I worried about being one of the people who took from her. It wasn't like she needed a protector anymore. She'd made her empire entirely on her own. She wasn't the same woman I used to know.

But he didn't need to know all that. I cleared my throat and changed the subject. My emotions were embarrassingly close to the surface when I thought about Emma's and my complicated past.

"Do you miss it? The bodyguard business?" I asked instead.

Mac was one of those intensely sensitive guys, all muscles and a big heart. Not that I would use these words, but he was a definite teddy bear. Or more like a real bear. They looked cuddly, and then they ripped off your arm for crossing a line. So long as he didn't open his mouth—and there were no cute, widdle babies around—he was very intimidating.

"Not even a little. Spoiled starlets and terrible hours. You couldn't pay me enough to go back there," he said.

"Also. Your whole aversion to violence and any sort of confrontation." I smiled as I picked up the weights he handed me.

He flushed and glanced away. "That too."

I whimpered when he let go, and my arms dropped.

"You can do this. We're almost done. Don't you want to impress Emma at the shoot?" He watched me closely as he asked.

"I just want to get through it without it ending in tears. Mine. Not hers."

He laughed and crossed his tree trunk arms. "Well, we'll leave her speechless at the sight of you shirtless, and then nobody will have to talk at all."

I snorted. As much as I would love to think she'd be impressed by something as trivial as my body, I doubted she'd care. Let alone not find a reason to unleash her aggression on me. God, how I wanted her to release her aggression on me.

And I deserved them all.

9

———

Emma

ARGH.

Of course, Wesley looked bloody fantastic in the Crunchy-Couture clothes. He strode by; his head held high as he nodded to the photographer. He raised his pretentious eyebrow at me just as I started to glare. I huffed and pretended not to notice him.

They had us in the formal wear collection for this first set. He wore custom-tailored charcoal dress trousers and a white button-up under a matching blazer that fit his elite form perfectly. He was almost always in suits. I'd rarely seen him dressed casually, and there was a reason. It was in his blood to look dipped in luxury. I frustratingly understood why the brand wanted him too. Aside from our notable history together, we were a good match for this campaign promoting ethical elegance. I brought the ethics, and he brought the elegance. His trademark hair was perfectly disheveled and long enough on top to be slicked back. Some longer pieces fell over his eyes, including the white strip that gave him an air of mystery and otherworldliness.

He was barefoot as he passed and made his way to the waiting camera and photographer. They spoke in low voices, and he nodded, head lowered to listen. Still no sign of his mood to be seen in his features. He had nailed the aloof look before the rest of us hit puberty. He didn't even flick a glance in my direction once. The woman doing final touches to my hair clicked her tongue in approval.

"At least you'll enjoy the view," she said.

Lovely to look at so long as he doesn't open his mouth.

"He looks very ... fit," I said softly so he wouldn't hear and let it go to his head. The last thing he needed was any more ego. I was here representing the brand of Emma Flynn, so I kept the bitter commentary to myself. Could I get through a photo shoot without direct eye contact or talking with Wesley? We would find out. I brought my focus to my phone. I took a selfie and posted it to my socials, talking again about the project I was excited to work on.

Focus on the goal. Focus on the timeline.

After a final spray of hairspray—I did not even mention the toxic impacts of aerosol on the environment—my hairdresser helped me from the chair. I thanked her before being brought to the rack of gowns I'd be wearing. The first they selected for me was carefully slipped over my head behind a privacy screen. At this point, I was used to having bits of myself on display and didn't worry that my modest breasts were free swinging, so to speak, under the super-fine silk. Not a pastie or bra to be seen.

"Ready for Miss Flynn on set," the coordinator called. After a few final touch-ups, I was brought to the main stage.

I thanked the coordinator on the way. The set looked like a darkly furnished sitting room with a finely upholstered chaise lounge in the center. It was a deep crimson edged with gilded scrollwork. The whole room could have been taken from the bits of Wesley's home I had seen.

The PA brought me to a mark near a small bar where shatterproof cocktail glasses filled with "liquid" didn't move when Wesley picked it up and turned it upside down. I walked to my mark, looking above Wesley's shoulder. We stood near a small bar with matching velvet stools.

"Chat and relax. We're about to start," the assistant said. "Probably nice to see each other after all these years." She winked.

"I'm sure we will have a great time," I said with a quick smile.

He didn't say anything, just set down the pseudo-cocktail and sighed. I thanked her, and she walked away.

I would remain a professional to get through this day quickly. Make some posts and move on.

Only a few hours into hair and makeup, my social meter had started to run low. I'd kept my smiles polite but not at full wattage because I wasn't sure of the tone of the shoot and didn't want to fatigue my smiling muscles. What a silly thing to think outside of this world. I used to be thrilled about photo shoots like this, but now I found them tiresome.

The silence between us was blaring. Onlookers probably wondered why we weren't speaking. If we were supposed to act like a couple, I'd have to extend some olive branch. Be the bigger person.

But I didn't want to. I crossed my arms.

Wesley took his time to acknowledge my presence. His gaze moved over me slowly before his eyebrows angled down into a scowl. I felt like a prized pig as he looked down his nose at me. The halter top of the long black gown they'd selected sliced almost down to my belly button and hardly covered my breasts. The back was so low, the dimples in my lower back showed. My red hair teased and high up, exposed my neck. Smeared charcoal darkened my features, making my bright eyes even more intense. If I had hoped on some pathetic level—I'd never admit to—he'd compliment me, I'd been dead wrong. So much for playing nice. Christ, how he could get under my skin faster than pushy paparazzi.

His jaw clenched as his eyes scorned their way from my bare feet to the heels dangling in my hand. The shoot details were sent earlier, with the day's vision board and color palettes. Dark and broody to play up the Max and Lucy fandom. "Just returned from a night on the town."

I would not be the first to speak. I had to maintain the high ground.

"Careful, or you might exhaust yourself too soon," he said, stepping closer onto the tape *X* on the floor in front of me. I sighed and looked over my shoulder, away from him.

Ha! He lost.

"What are you talking about, Wesley?" I shouldn't rise to his bait. Really, I knew better than that.

I fidgeted with my glass on the sleek bar top, avoiding the bit of his exposed chest where his shirt was unbuttoned. I couldn't ignore the alluring scent of him as easily. Those synapses formed early on and still reacted as though no time had passed.

"All the brownnosing to every person on set. You won't have anything left to pretend with me," he said.

I found his gaze and glared. He'd been perusing my body again and quickly snapped his focus back to my gaze, features neutral.

"You would see basic human decency as sucking up. Heaven forbid you're polite to somebody without an ulterior motive." I leaned in closer to make sure we weren't being heard, keeping my own face friendly and open in case they watched.

"Heaven forbid *you* show any emotion other than the perfect Golden Girl," he mocked.

Now he was trying to goad me. My toxic trait was falling for his traps. Every time. I leaned even closer. "You can be nice. It costs nothing."

"I can be very, very nice." His low words tickled down my spine. "When I want to. They're not your friends."

"It has nothing to do with that. You treat people as though they work for you."

"They do. We're the talent. They literally work for us," he said.

Ugh. The arrogance ... Did he hear himself? He wasn't like this on set growing up. When had he turned into such a prat?

"Do you understand how much work goes into these shoots?" I started. "They've been planning it for weeks. The level of coordination alone. Every person plays a role, and if they all feel valued for their part, then everything operates as it's intended to. A well-oiled machine—"

"Ah, it's been a minute since I've been on the receiving end of an Emma Flynn lecture. Don't pretend you care. You just have to make every person feel special so you don't feel bad about yourself."

My jaw dropped open before I could catch myself. I snapped it shut, teeth grinding.

I *liked* making people feel good. Sure, things did go smoother when they felt appreciated. And more than that, I had to learn very early on to be my best self whenever I was in the public eye, or I'd be the first person complained about on various platforms. Random people gave firsthand accounts of what a stuck-up swot I was if I didn't.

"You don't know anything about me," I said.

"I know this is all an act." He gestured to me. "It isn't you."

How dare he pretend to know me? He might have thought he knew me once, but he had no idea who he trifled with.

"I have a brand to represent," I said.

"You can be polite while still maintaining boundaries."

"Is that what your daddy taught you? Don't interact with the peons when you're elite? Make sure everybody knows that you're a Cole?"

The words hit their mark, and as always, I regretted them. His mouth snapped shut, and his eyes burned into mine. This was quickly going off the rails. I pictured us rolling around on the ground in a cloud of dust and expletives. He opened his mouth to retort, but I cut him off.

"I-I'm only saying that I'm not allowed to act like a total wanker because I'm good-looking and have a penis. There are different standards."

And an inheritance of a Hollywood dynasty that could protect me. But I kept that to myself, trying to make the peace as I was.

The smallest smile threatened the side of his mouth. "You did say I looked 'fit.'"

"Oh, bloody hell, put your eyebrow away. As if you didn't know."

Instead of soaking up the almost compliment, he flicked a glance to the side. "At least if you have to be nice to everyone else, you have me to take out all your frustrations on."

"Exactly," I snapped and then regretted it. Again.

Mere *minutes* in and I'd already lost my cool. We were inches away from each other's faces. I stood on my tiptoes, and he leaned toward me. Nothing about our body language portrayed the professionalism I'd been going for. His lips twisted in a condescending scowl. My shoulders were to my ears as I heaved, breathing heavier than a conversation should elicit.

"Oh good. Yes. Keep that energy up," the photographer, Aybike, said, camera in hand. She clicked, and we both stiffened. "Just test shots. But this is perfect. Originally, we envisioned you came home and were having a nightcap together, but I like this better. Maybe you fought because he had a wandering eye, and she was ignored. Go with this."

I stepped back and collected myself with a quick smile. "Right."

Wesley ground his jaw but kept his mouth shut. He flicked a look at my flushed chest under the deep cut of my dress and then quickly looked away. He grabbed the fake drink and went to take a sip and then grimaced with it halfway to his mouth. I sneered and turned to hide the smile.

I researched Aybike before the shoot to make sure she was shown the respect her reputation garnered. Her name was pronounced Aye-bee-kay, and she was a London transplant originally from Turkey. She came from a large family, and in the past several years, her photographs had made her one of *the* hottest photographers on the scene. See. There was no reason not to do a little research to show respect and humility. I doubted Wesley had even remembered there was a shoot today. He likely flopped out of his golden throne when his personal butler brought the limo around.

The photographer gave more instructions and positioned us in various poses around the bar—leaning on our elbows facing each other, back to back, side by side. The surround sound pumped out bass-heavy sensual hip-hop in a language that might have been Turkish. The rhythm thumped through my chest and overstimulated my already fried nerves. She attempted to capture that tension from a moment ago, but being called out had calmed me to a more professional mode. I really had to keep my head. With every click and flash, I felt the growing frustration of the photographer.

"Relax, you two. You are friends?" she asked.

Wesley snorted without anybody else hearing.

"Get comfortable. Maybe move closer. Mr. Cole, can you sit on the stool? Miss Flynn, come over." Aybike directed me to his hips. She tossed her long and incredibly shiny black hair over her shoulder as she changed positions to crouch on the floor.

I hesitated.

"Come on, friend, don't be a chicken," Wesley said, pulling me between his spread legs.

Chicken.

"Hardly."

I brought my knee up into his lap, exposing my entire leg and a bit of my bottom. Before I left no secrets for the camera, he brought his arm up protectively and smoothly ran his hand down my back to hold the silk dress in place over my backside. It glided farther down yet to the deep slit of the gown, as though learning the area, before heading back to hold the material in place. His hand held in place, but his outstretched pinky brushed the base of my spine, eliciting chills. I let out a shaky breath and studied the side of his face. He protected my modesty while enough of me was still scintillatingly exposed to the camera. All without even looking.

He was *not* thoughtful or professional. He probably wanted to cop a feel.

"Good. Better. Now. Look back and up at her. Emma, look down. Good. Maybe put your hand on his collar to draw attention to his shirt."

As he tilted his head back to lock eyes with me, I pulled from the deepest well of professionalism that I had. We were coworkers. He pointed out that I had been taking out my frustrations on set with him while being kind to everybody else. I didn't want to give him a reason to take the piss out of me. I wanted to get through this. Like the business partners that we were.

I could do this. We were actors, after all. His features softened as he looked at me. His eyebrows contorted effortlessly to convey longing. His dark eyes pierced into me, like he was desperate to hold me.

Christ, he really was a great actor. Not that I would ever admit that to him.

I brought my hand to the sharp line of his jaw and felt down his neck to his exposed chest. His sharp intake of breath was the only warning before he tugged my lower body more firmly to him, still angling himself to reach up to me.

I misjudged how good he was going to be at this. My heart began to beat faster.

I lowered my head closer to his. My thumb moved over the pulse at his neck, thrumming back to touch me. Images flashed through my mind of our night together so many years ago. The feel of this same jaw under my palm as we kissed for hours, so different but also so much the same person. We stared into each other's eyes, and as we did, his features relaxed into something else ... something more wistful? Did he remember that night too? Was he wondering if I was the same person?

"Good. Good," Aybike said distantly. "More passion. Anger. He's yours. Nobody else's."

Thank goodness years of training had gotten my blush under control because the photographer's words flashed instant heat through me.

We were each other's firsts, and he would always have a piece of my heart. Nobody else understood that. But I had a piece of him too, a part of him nobody knew.

Mine.

I grabbed his head and ran my hands through his thick black hair, bringing our glares even closer. Wesley was famous for the streak of white, but I've always found his thick dark waves, in contrast, to be the most tantalizing. He had a way of styling it, always slicked back or to the side, begging to have fingers run through it. Around season seven of TF, he and a lot of the guys went through a long-hair phase. My crush had been bearable before that, but watching him constantly run his hands through his chin-length hair just about wrecked my teenage hormone-addled brain. I spent so many nights fantasizing about playing with the dark locks. Just like now. The thick strands were still soft despite having product in them. I pulled his head farther back to study the way his tendons and Adam's apple moved on a swallow. I wanted to bend my head and lick it, feel his swallow against my tongue. What was it about his bloody neck that almost had me undone?

"Head in the game, Flynn," he rumbled the words quietly. His nostrils were flared, and his dark eyes burned.

How long had I been staring at his neck? I glared back. How dare he tell me what to do when I was the one being professional? I could play these characters as well as he could.

I *was* in character. I was a jealous girlfriend, reminding him of what we had.

And the thing we had was off-the-charts sexual compatibility.

I tugged harder on his hair. He growled, following my lead. His arm shifted so his large palm spread over my hip and a good portion of my bum. Squeezing it tight to show his own form of ownership. Now both of his arms were wrapped tight around me, cocooning me in his heat and masculine scent. Desire flooded me, and I gasped, holding his head possessively. He raised a cocky, challenging eyebrow, and I glared down at him.

"Yes!" Aybike called out, breaking the moment.

There was a camera here and a room full of people, but the yearning in his gaze crushed me in, sucking me closer. Despite the music and the crowd, I swore I could hear his dry swallow before he licked his lips.

"Okay. I think we got some great shots. Let's do the next set," the photographer called.

The second she spoke, Wesley's indifference slid back into place. He shifted to lower my leg, instantly grabbing his phone from where it was hidden behind the bar. He leaned forward on his elbows, totally ignoring me. I blinked back to myself and took two steps away. The set was quiet because the whole room was watching us. As I scanned the crowd, they broke their stares to busy themselves.

I cleared my throat and went to change. Okay, I had a bit of a moment. My body reacted to the history between us, but it all went toward the greater good. I got through it. He made a convincing display.

We were really good actors, after all.

10

Wesley

I GLARED AT THE PHONE IN MY HAND, THUMBS CLICKING OVER THE screen but seeing nothing. I bit the inside of my mouth, trying to cause enough pain to get this reaction to her under control. If I stood now, this fucking erection would call me out.

I heard her scoff and stomp away, but I didn't dare look up.

Why did she have to be so damn beautiful? Why did she have to get under my skin like nobody else? Why did she have to look at me like I was hers? Her hand on my face and tugging through my hair instantly sent me back in time.

I couldn't keep control over myself with her beautiful body pressed against me. With her hands running through my hair and her lips beckoning and her eyes looking at me like that ... like she wanted *me*. I'd done several intimate scenes before with different actresses, but nothing had pushed me to the brink like her running her thumb against my jaw had.

It was too much.

I shuddered and forced myself to think of the grossest thing possible. My go-to erection killer was that time on set, early on, before the explosive success and major funding of the later seasons of TF, when half the crew got food poisoning. The colorful explosions cut short the whole day of shooting. It was a nightmare.

I shuddered again, this time in disgust. *That'll do it.*

I'd riled her up to purposely shake her out of her Golden Girl perfectionist head, and it backfired on me. I had promised myself to keep it light, but then she treated me so differently than everybody else. I deserved it, but it didn't help the sting of her derision for me. It was more than that. She was exhausting herself with people who didn't deserve her. Sure, she had matured into a confident and elegant woman, there was no questioning that, but it made me miss the woman I used to know. The boisterous, curious, somewhat gangly redhead of my youth. She'd spoken her mind and stood her ground. She didn't exhaust herself on an unmaintainable persona.

I took a breath and stood to stretch. I found her glaring in my direction from behind the privacy curtains. It blocked most of her body except her head and her arms above her head as they lifted the "dress" off her and put on the next outfit. If it could have been called a dress. It felt more like a second skin as I rubbed my hand up her long leg to her perfect ass.

Nope. Projectile vomit. That is the focus.

When she noticed I was watching her, she looked away, and her glare melted into a smile for the person helping her.

Okay, well, the worst must be over. The photographer seemed like she got some good shots. Aybike was now across the room talking to her assistants, pointing at the chaise lounge and nodding. The three of them looked back at me and then toward Emma. I didn't trust their looks, like they were one step away from rubbing their hands together and laughing maniacally.

A little while later, Emma was brought back to set; we'd both been touched up and changed. She looked just as beautiful in a slightly different gown. This time, I was prepared. Last time, she walked in with that black silk piece of fabric, and it was like getting sucker punched. I didn't understand how she continued to get more beautiful every time I saw her. It made me lash out in frustration. Well, we couldn't all be perfect.

But this time, I was ready. I hardly looked over her dress at all. It might have been a rusty metallic satin, but I wouldn't know. It may have complemented the shade of her skin and red hair now flowing in waves over her shoulders, but it's hard to say because I barely noticed.

As Emma walked up to me, I was determined to get through this last part with a level of professionalism. Maybe even compliment her taste.

I plucked at the suit coat and cleared my throat. "This clothing is actually pretty nice for granola gear," I said. There. A compliment to the company she helped finance.

Based on the way her eyes narrowed, the intent had not been received. "I'll have you know this is higher quality than so many of those designers you insist on wearing." She poked my chest. I tilted my head. "And if you took any time to prepare for this shoot, you would know the material is ethically sourced, and the people who sew them are paid fair wages. The stat—"

I pressed a finger to her lips. "Save your sales pitch, Golden Girl. I was just saying it wasn't that bad."

She flared her nostrils before her shoulders moved up and down in a slow breath.

I dropped my hands into my pockets and looked away. Well, so much for that. I tried. She was determined to take everything I said as an insult. Why had I expected anything else?

Thankfully, the photographer walked up. "You can take off your jacket now, Mr. Cole. Let's undo the buttons."

Aybike was a first-generation British citizen who grew up in London. We chatted a bit before Emma got to set. Despite what

Emma thought, I actually did make an effort. I just didn't spread it all on so thick that people couldn't swallow. I liked Aybike and did as told without hesitation.

Emma stiffened at my side.

"Fantastic," I said. "My trainer will appreciate that his efforts haven't gone unnoticed."

Emma snorted ever so elegantly and crossed her arms.

"Plus, Emma's dying to see me in my pants."

Her jaw dropped. "That'll be a cold day in—"

Snickers sounded around the set, and she stopped herself and flashed a fake smile. A memory popped up unbidden of the time on set for TF when I'd talked about my pants, and Emma blushed from the tips of her ears to her toes until somebody explained that was what Americans called trousers. Was she thinking of my briefs now? I missed those blushes of hers. Did she remember that day? Did she remember all the things I did?

I purposely took my time undoing the buttons and flexing my abs as I tossed the sides of the shirt out. Mac had pummeled me into this physique, so I might as well make the most of it. That was my burden.

When I looked up and found her biting her lip as her eyes raked over me, the burden felt so much lighter.

She quickly looked away.

We were directed to the chaise lounge, and it became apparent Aybike had an evil genius side.

Emma was directed onto her back, her head thrown back. I sat on my knees at her feet on the other end.

"Don't be shy," Aybike said.

I really, *really* did not care for this. I made my way over Emma. Crawling swiftly until I hovered over her, balancing on my arms. This was actual torture.

They tested the lighting around our heads, and I did every-thing in my power not to have too much of my body touching hers as I knelt on either side of her legs, but my chest was inches from hers.

"This is ridiculous," she grumbled.

"Careful, somebody may hear that you're slightly unhappy," I said, keeping my thoughts on food poisoning and not the soft shape of her nipples peaking under the dress. Nipples that I once had the chance to ...

Nope.

She shifted her hips and brushed my groin. Her stiff body made it obvious how much she hated this. Was she uncomfortable because I was too close or because I wasn't close enough? She understandably didn't care for me, but our bodies seemed to have forgotten all that. Or maybe that was wishful thinking. This version of Emma was impossible to read. Affable and polite but astoundingly insincere, yet I was the only one who seemed to notice.

I ground my jaw and gripped the edge of the chair. "Could you stop moving?"

"I'm sorry," she said with absolutely no remorse in her tone. "This is uncomfortable. How does this ... *angle* sell the clothes?"

"You think it's about the clothes still. That's cute." I balanced precariously to touch the tip of her nose with my finger.

"Did you just boop my nose?"

"Sweet, summer child. They're selling us. The fantasy of all the Max and Lucy shippers." I couldn't say Emsley shippers because that felt a little too real at the moment. I tried to shrug, but the last-minute workout this morning exhausted my arms, and I started shaking while holding myself off her.

"Ugh. You're such an arsehat."

"Now that's an image. Would it be like a tiny fedora? Or more like a baseball cap?"

"Bend over and I could show you." This time, her smile was genuine.

"Promise?" I said lower to her ear.

"Ugh." Her frustrated growl vibrated through her and straight to my cock.

God, I loved how easy it was to work her up. Golden Girl was nowhere to be seen now. This was what I fed off of.

"Good. That's good. Bring that anger and heat," Aybike said.

By the time Aybike started clicking away, the position wasn't working, and Emma grew more frustrated with every minute that ticked by. We all did. My stomach growled loudly from the ever-present sugary cinnamon scent of Emma. If I licked her, would she taste as sweet as she smelled?

"Stop being so tense," I growled. My arms shook, and she was so damn stiff. If she didn't relax, we'd be stuck in this erotic position for hours.

"You make it sound so easy."

"Give them what they want. Remember, I'm the bully asshole, and you're the long-suffering innocent."

"Well, at least that's easy," she said.

I blinked at her. That was what I wanted, right? To have her hate me. It was easier this way. Wasn't it?

"Emma, let's have your hair flowing down now over the edge. He's over you like a vampire. Like you want to suck on her," Aybike said to me.

I looked down at the long column of her exposed neck. I suddenly couldn't swallow. I would suck and lick every inch of her.

Fuck.

It took every ounce of control to keep my body from reacting to her. A massive erection would not go unnoticed. Her chest heaved in shallow pants. She wouldn't look at me, couldn't in this position, but the heat emanating off her felt so good. I wanted to sink into her, relax my body, and give in. Even the worst Mac workout would be easier than this.

"Gorgeous, Emma. But we need more of the dress," Aybike said. "Can you lift your hips to angle the dress more. I know it feels awkward, but I promise it'll be stunning."

Emma started to shift but wasn't understanding what Aybike wanted. Instead, her thigh flexed and relaxed under my *family dynasty,* causing a different set of problems. She was seconds from inadvertently rubbing against my now half-hard cock. That would be great for the tension between us.

"Not like that," I grunted.

"It's not an easy angle," she hissed.

"Lift your hips. My arms are tired. Hurry."

She tried again with a grunt of frustration.

"No. Just." I groaned. "Like this."

I slipped a hand under her hips and heaved her up effortlessly. God, it felt so good to lift her toward me. To have her give under my direction. Soft hip, hot skin.

A sound came out of her like a squawk. I couldn't tell if I had hurt her or ...

"Are you okay? You made a weird sound," I asked, throat tight.

"No, I didn't."

"Yes. Like you're in pain."

"Shh. Fine," she whispered tightly.

"Stop talking," the photographer said. The camera snapped.

She was breathtaking. Her red hair spread out under her long, graceful limbs above her head. I did feel like a vampire lurking over her. It was like an alternate universe Lucy and Max, in which I hunted her to this point. I could envision how lovely it was going to be finally having her under me. Her waist in my arms, my body straining over hers. Moving and positioning her long, flexible limbs in any which way I wanted ...

The strain to control was too much. I couldn't hold her and myself up. Her ass muscles were flexed under my grip, and my grasp slipped. I heaved her up to release the tension in my arm and switch positions, but everything happened so fast in the next second.

The sudden rough jostling caused her core to brush against my now full erection briefly. There was no hiding it. Her eyes closed, and a gasp combined with a soft whine escaped her. Nobody else could have heard, but it shot straight to my cock. Sounds I remembered from our night together. A sound of longing.

I watched her in awe before the loud click of the flash reminded me where the hell we were.

"Yes!" Aybike shouted. "That's it, that's the one!"

Emma's eyes shot open, gleaming and bright. Color high on her cheeks. My arms finally gave out, and I collapsed on top of her. Thankfully, I was no longer poking her, but I couldn't lift my head quite yet from the crook of her neck.

"Get off. Get off!" She whacked my shoulders.

"Give me a moment." I inhaled her deeply. *Ah well, when in Rome.*

"Wesley!"

I groaned and sat back on my knees. No hiding it now. Her eyes went wide as they moved from my jutting erection to my face.

"Can't be helped." I shrugged.

She stood and put her back to me. "You're ridiculous," she spat.

So she had an entirely different experience than I just had.

"You've got to see this. Come look," Aybike called us over, not seeing anything but the screen on her camera.

I winced as I adjusted to tuck myself discreetly into the waistline of my *trousers*. Not much to be done at this point. The vomit-fest memory wasn't ever going to replace the sound of her moan and the way her hard nipples looked pressing up against the fabric of the dress.

I made my way over to Emma and Aybike, who huddled over the camera. Emma had her head tilted, brow furrowed.

"Absolutely stunning. You two. Just stunning," Aybike said, holding the image up higher.

I came to stand behind Emma to get a look. She stiffened, but I was careful not to accidentally brush her again. Point taken.

The photo took my breath away. Emma was in a state of blissful nirvana. I didn't think anything but an actual orgasm could have given her that look. Meanwhile ... I gave everything away. I looked at her with such blatant desire that it had to make all my feelings clear. She had to see everything I had been shoving deep down inside me since I met her.

I ran a hand down my face.

"Excuse me." Emma turned and pushed past me. I was afraid to let her go without knowing what she was thinking. Had she suspected?

I flicked a look at Aybike, who smiled slightly confused. She said, "Let's pack up, everybody."

"Be right back," I said, and quickly followed after Emma. I had no idea when I would see her again but wasn't ready to let her go yet.

11

———————

Emma

LET ME MAKE IT TO THE BATHROOM. LET ME GET AWAY. PLEASE LET ME get a minute to breathe.

I had gotten so good at suppressing my turbulent feelings over the years, but they were so close to the surface right now. I was nothing but exposed nerves, and the slightest irritant would cause me to cry out.

"Emma, wait," Wesley called out after me.

Speaking of irritants.

"Christ," I mumbled, tears burning at the back of my eyes as I glared up at the ceiling, pulling it all back down.

I'd almost made it to the bathroom. Almost.

"Emma." Wesley grabbed my shoulder.

And I flinched away so hard I stumbled.

"Shit. Sorry. What's wrong?" he said, glancing around to make sure we were alone in the hallway.

I shook my head, pressing a hand to my chest. My heart still raced under my palm. My skin was on fire. I was so ridiculous. All these years and he still did this to me.

"I need a moment," I said.

Heat burned my cheeks again to find him looking at me with concern. Like he didn't know exactly what he did. The sounds that came out of me when he grabbed my waist. The way my body melted under his touch.

"Hey. Hey, talk to me." He swallowed and tucked his hands in his pockets. He glanced around again before pulling me even farther from set. He turned to me, shoulders still hunched.

I backed away from him. "Is this because of, uh—" He gestured to his now under control trousers. "I didn't mean to make you uncomfortable."

"Oh, please." I rolled my eyes.

He glared.

He knew exactly what he was doing. I was nothing but a game to him.

"I couldn't help it. That dress is ..." He carded his hands through his messy hair. He almost looked remorseful.

I crossed my arms. My emotions were too close to the surface, so I had to be angry. If I wasn't angry, I would cry. Honestly, I might still cry, but I had to wait until he was gone. I would not let him see. I had already given him too much satisfaction.

I closed my eyes against the flash of heat as I recalled the photo I'd just seen. I was in ecstasy when Aybike snapped that picture. When he'd grabbed my waist so coolly and confidently, it threw me over the edge I had been carefully clinging to. My desire had been so close to the surface, and with the simple movement of him yanking my hips up, my barely controlled desire crested like a wave. He moved my body expertly. He lifted me with smooth ease. He knew my body better than I knew it myself. He understood what would make the camera salivate, how to make us look genuine for the lens, yet I ... I hadn't even remembered the other people in the room. Having him so close to me again threw off all my pretenses of not being attracted to him anymore.

My body wanted him and yearned for him in a way that hadn't been muted even after all these years. No, it'd been slowly simmering, and the moment his erection brushed my hot core, it went full explosive boil. I was hit with a wave of desire so strong I almost passed out. I had never experienced anything like that. So intense. So vulnerable. He *had* to sense it.

It was humiliating.

"Talk to me," he asked softly. He was so sincere and timid that I could almost believe his regret. He was such a convincing actor. Wasn't that what all this was? Just acting for him and life-altering for me.

"Why? We aren't friends," I snapped.

A flash of hurt hardened his features.

"Trust me. You've made that perfectly clear," he said, teeth gritted.

"Don't act like you have feelings that can be hurt. This is nothing but a game to you," I said.

"A game? What the hell are you talking about? You're the one who can't even be nice to me for a second."

"You know exactly what you're doing. You love to humiliate me. Make a fool out of me. Show how beneath you I am," I said, nose stinging as I fought back the angry tears. Every past pain I'd pushed down rose to the top. He didn't deserve an explanation.

I was fourteen again, hoping to be kissed. Waiting for his lips to brush mine, only to feel the cold air as he turned his back to me and walked away.

I couldn't be the laughingstock to him again. I would have smacked him and walked straight off the set if it wouldn't have caused a scene that would inevitably end up online.

"A fool?" he asked, aghast. "I'm pretty sure I was the one who should be embarrassed." He ground his teeth, jaw flexing. "I couldn't even control myself for a fucking photo in front of a room full of people."

I pressed my icy fingertips to my overheated cheeks.

"It's so easy for you, isn't it? All this ... *pretending*?"

"Easy?" He scoffed with a shake of his head. "Yeah, I'm having a great time." He glared and looked to the side. "I don't understand what you're upset about. That picture looked amazing. It's going to be huge. Isn't that the point of all of this?"

He had to know how this brought me back. How everybody in that room could see how my body reacted to him, whether I wanted to or not. It was written all over my face. Poor little Emma, in love with the boy who wouldn't give her the time of day.

I was humiliated, and the more I reacted, the more immature and embarrassed I became. I hated being this person. Why did he always revert me to my most base self? How could he stand there looking cool and confident?

I collapsed back against the wall, ready for this day to be over. Ready to go home, take off all this makeup and clothing, curl up, and be alone.

"Right." I took a deep breath before I did anything else I regretted. I was better than this. "We got the shot. That's all that matters. Now we don't have to see each other again. Until the next scheduled event." My flat, professional tone said it all.

He lifted his chin and looked away before locking gazes with me again. His eyes instantly hardened, and his familiar mask was perfectly in place. "Fantastic. I'll be seeing you."

With that, he turned on his heel and stepped away briskly. I let out a sigh of relief, thankful to have made it out alive with my pride mostly intact. I had an ever-present fear that once I started crying in front of Wesley, I might never be able to stop.

I dropped my head back against the wall with eyes clenched

tight as I steadied my heart rate with deep yoga breath cycling. Wesley's retreating steps stopped suddenly. I glanced up to find he'd turned back to me, his eyebrows pinched and his shoulders hunched as though struggling with some internal debate. Decision made, he stomped back to me.

He stepped close, face leaning down toward mine, his figure looming over me menacingly. Or at least menacingly to me. "Is this really how you want it to be?" he asked.

"What do you mean?" I shifted off the wall, expecting an attack, taken aback by the question and the softness of his voice.

"You want us to spend the next however many weeks angry with each other? Constantly at each other's throats?" His question was earnest, like it was on *me* to decide. Like I was the one who could shift the dynamic.

Blinking, I shook my head because I couldn't answer that. I couldn't imagine a scenario where we could be *friends*.

I opened my mouth, unsure if it was a trap. It shouldn't feel like a trap. It shouldn't feel like it cost so much to admit that I didn't want to fight with him constantly, but then ... how could we go on?

He frowned and took a deep breath, closing the space between us. "Because I don't want that," he offered, the words catching in his throat.

My heart lurched in hope, like it was demanding to take the lead on stage. Could it be that simple? After all this time, could we leave the past behind and move forward?

"What do you want?" I asked, despite knowing that the answer, deep down, could never give me what I wanted.

He looked almost pained as he considered his response. "What I want is ..." He leaned over me, not touching, but somehow, I felt him over every inch of me. I had no room to back up, so I was forced to tilt my head back to meet his eyes. "I want you to—"

"Wesley." A cold man's voice popped our bubble.

I'd forgotten we were still in public. Still on set. I stood off the wall.

Wesley stepped back instantly. His eyes promptly shadowed. It was like he tucked whatever version of him I'd just glimpsed back behind a wall.

He clasped his hands behind his back, his voice emotionless. "Father. What are you doing here?"

"I came to check on the photos." Rex Cole looked down his nose at me in a quick glance. In a fraction of a second, I was relegated to nothing more than a piece of furniture on set.

Wesley stood stiffly, several steps away from me, refusing to acknowledge me. Wow, if this wasn't a blast from the past. A glimpse at a softer Wesley in private, only to be brutally ignored when someone else showed up.

"Excuse me." I brushed past Wesley and made a run for it.

Neither of them acknowledged me. If I had hoped that he would stop me, grab my wrist, and tell me to wait so we could finish the conversation, his cold mask grossly disillusioned me.

What had he been about to say? What was it that I hoped for? Because before that mask slipped on, I saw a person I remembered.

I *knew* that man. If only for a second. I recognized him. And for the first time, I felt the stirring of hope that the person I knew existed somewhere deep inside him.

But then a wave of crashing despair. Because if he was still there, if this aching in my chest was just from a glimmer of hope, then I was in even more trouble than I thought.

I went around the corner and slumped back against the wall, chest heaving.

I thought being around him would be so easy. I thought I would always have the upper hand. I was Emma Flynn. I was somebody now, not a child.

"The photos look acceptable," Rex said.

I didn't want to hear this but couldn't move. I closed my eyes, blocking out whatever his futile opinion was.

Wesley said something, but his deep voice made it too hard to decipher.

"I see she's still mad for you," he said.

Silence.

I closed my eyes against the humiliation.

"Thankfully, you're a great actor. Otherwise, I'd think that you—"

"What is it that you want, Father? Don't you think it's a little weird you showing up like this?"

"A progress check."

"This is my career, and I'm a grown man."

"Don't you dare take that tone with me. If it weren't for me, none of this would be happening. Don't forget, this is all temporary. In a few weeks, you won't ever see that girl again."

That was enough. I couldn't take another word. I busted out of my hiding space and went to change without even sparing them a backward glance.

I knew this was all a game to him. Trying to soften me up with promises of friendship.

I wasn't angry. I wasn't hurt.

I was determined. I wouldn't be made the fool again. I wasn't the little girl they thought they could mess with.

12

———————

Wesley

THE ONLY THING WORSE THAN A HANGOVER WAS A HANGOVER IN MY parents' company. Thankfully, I might have been a little drunk still, and that would help me survive whatever this parental intervention entailed.

I groaned to myself as the hostess pointed at the table across the patio. Clammy with sweat, I made my way through the Sunday crowd as the trendy LA brunch spot tilted to the side. Last night, I left the photo shoot and promptly met Mac for drinks. I had no reason to be alcohol-free anymore as I wasn't shooting anytime soon, but the lack of food in my system, combined with the fact I hadn't had more than that one whiskey in months, made for me getting pretty wasted, pretty quickly. He commiserated in my regret of my reflexive asshole tendencies and pushed drinks at me until we closed down the bar.

Mac got me home close to two o'clock.

My mother called me five hours later at seven o'clock to tell me we were meeting for brunch.

And this was why drinking to excess after thirty was no

longer fun. My stomach roiled as I passed a plate of croque madame being set down and toward the table awaiting my doom. My mother and father, who I *had* expected, were waiting, slightly annoyed at my three-minute late arrival. The third person at the table was not expected. She tilted her head up, a large white hat blocking her from view. I'm not saying it was intentional, but I suspected the look of surprise wasn't well hidden on my end. But not entirely unwelcome. Seeing her could never be bad. Despite how things were left after the shoot.

The fresh, fully made-up face of Emma smiled patiently at me. There was a tug in my chest so acute at the sight of her that I almost stumbled. I blamed the hangover.

My father had warned me that getting closer to Emma would only make it harder when the arrangement eventually ended. Now, seeing her sitting here with my parents in the dappled light under the vines covering the trellis, she took my breath away as always. She wore a pale-green thin-strapped dress with little white daisies all over it. The soft material gathered at her breasts, and her long neck and smooth shoulders were exposed as her long red locks flowed over one shoulder. The oversized straw hat blocked the California sun from freckling her pale British skin. On any other person, I would think they looked ridiculous dressed to the nines in that hat, but Emma reminded me of an old Hollywood starlet, her chin pointed at just the right angle to make her full red lips perfectly alluring.

But not enough to distract me from the fact that I had walked into some sort of trap.

I hadn't spoken to her since my father interrupted my attempt at a white flag. I assumed we were back to not talking and not acknowledging each other except for when we absolutely had to.

I went to my father first and shook his hand. He nodded and

pumped it once before going back to his phone, a half-drunk Bloody Mary in front of him.

"Mother." I bent and kissed her cheek. She smiled hesitantly at me.

I hated this charade so much, but it was habit at this point.

"Darling." I stood to go to the chair awaiting me when my mother held my arm, stilling me. "Don't forget to kiss your lovely girlfriend hello," she said through a forced smile. "You never know who's watching."

"Of course." I straightened.

Emma's smile faltered as I made my way to her. We'd not discussed public displays of affection yet, as we had not had any public displays in general. And affection was no more than a faded memory of our past.

She blinked slowly up at me, waiting for me to make a move.

"Emma," I said flatly. I had been about to brush a polite passing of lips against her cheek, hovering right above her skin, no reason to go all in for an unexpected brunch date with my parents, when she turned her head at the last minute. She had been going for my cheek, but we both miscalculated, and our lips met. Her eyes widened in surprise before fluttering closed briefly. Her full, soft lips pressed against mine and shocked down my lower back and into my balls. It was just that she was so damn soft and smelled so good, even with the world tilting slightly.

It was over in a flash, but I hesitated above her as we looked at each other, shock on my end, and ... *something* on her side.

"Hello, Wesley," she said softly.

She quickly reached for her tiny cup of espresso as I made my way to my chair and sat down, slightly dazed. My body remembered the way her lips felt all too acutely.

"No tie, really? It's Sunday," my father said without looking up.

I was in dress slacks and a button-up shirt. A regular heathen. I was still dressed up for the last-minute plans and the hangover currently jackhammering my skull.

"Take off those sunglasses," he added.

"We're outside," I said, knowing it was futile.

He gave me a look that brooked no arguments.

Emma, who seemed to have picked up on the state of me— that or she caught a whiff of the booze from last night wafting off me despite a shower—raised an eyebrow. "How was your evening, Wesley?"

I blinked at her behind my shades before sliding them off, folding them, and gently setting them on the table. "Great."

I sighed as the light from the patio added to the hammering. It was partly shaded, but the California sun found a way.

"Oh my," Emma said.

I ignored her reaction and reached for the glass of water sitting in front of me.

"Tie one off, son?" my father asked, looking up from his phone at my mother's gasp.

I chose to chug my water rather than respond. When I left the house, my eyes were bloodshot and puffy. Their reaction said they hadn't gotten much better.

"Wesley. You're too old to be drinking like that," my mother chastised.

"That we can agree on," I croaked in my rusty morning voice.

Emma pretended to study a menu, but her sucked-in lips told me she was trying not to laugh at me.

"Did your trainer say it was okay?" my father asked. "You're older now. Your metabolism won't bounce back so fast. You've always gained weight so easily. You get that from your mother's side."

"Mac had opinions for sure," I said. I didn't mention that he was the one pushing the shots toward me while berating me for being a clueless asshole.

Emma gave me another barely concealed amused look. After we made our orders, a greasy meat-filled option that had the women curling their noses and my father looking longingly—take that, metabolism—my mother cleared her throat.

"I appreciate you two meeting us," my mother said.

Emma nodded but remained politely aloof.

I sipped my black coffee and felt it corrode my empty insides like battery acid. "What's this about?" I asked.

"Sit up, you're slouching," my mother said.

"Christ, Diana, he's a grown man," my father snapped.

Her face went red, and she dabbed at her lips with a napkin.

I straightened and looked at Emma, waiting to see if she knew what this was about. She seemed to be back to pointedly ignoring me.

"Your father and I agree that this current setup is simply not working," my mother said.

My stomach lurched up my throat. I wasn't ready for this to end. We were supposed to have weeks.

The unexpected thoughts were pushed aside.

Emma stilled, her gaze flicking back and forth between my parents. Was she having similar thoughts, or was she flooded with relief?

"It's not?" I asked in a level voice, despite a racing heart. "Last I checked, we were trending within the top twenty hashtags online."

My mother spoke with a determined set to her shoulders. "You need to be seen together more."

My father nodded, only briefly looking up from his phone.

Emma's mouth opened and closed.

I swallowed as an anxious, nauseous, sour taste filled my

mouth. At this point, I had no idea if it was the hangover or my reaction to the news.

Emma and I barely made it through that photo shoot. I had tried; I really had. I was close to throwing away all pretense and admitting that I hated the constant anger rolling off her. I thought it was what I wanted, no needed, to get through these weeks, but when I felt her wrath firsthand, it only made me miss the way it used to be with her as kids. Before my parents ruined everything. The way I rarely let myself reminisce.

"Seen together more?" I repeated.

My mother nodded.

My father grunted at something on his phone. "You two had your fun with the little hints on the social platforms and what-not. And I appreciate your generation's attempt at subtlety. But let's be honest, the people of the world are idiots and need things spelled out."

I avoided Emma's gaze. My father's words mirrored what I had said to Emma at the start of this setup. It was so easy to slip into the role of who I was expected to be: a perfect replica of Rex Cole.

My father continued. "We need hard and fast proof, starting with today. Cameras are waiting for some plandids when we leave."

I nodded.

"And then next week at the hospital's charity gala, you will be going as an official couple," he said, watching my reaction closely.

I clenched my jaw and rubbed my eyes. "Okay."

Honestly, I was shocked at my relief. These plans for our fake relationship had already been discussed. I thought Emma had met with my parents without me and was ready to end this, and my visceral reaction scared me. Even though it was pretend, being in her orbit was better than another galaxy.

"Okay?" Emma asked skeptically, her eyebrows bouncing up subtly.

"I agree that it makes sense to be seen together more," I said, even though I knew it would only be a form of torture. But my hands were tied here. I now understood how Emma must have felt at that first meeting.

"The gala is crucial. Your mother has been organizing it since last year. Don't mess this up," my father said.

My mother sat up and preened at his words. "I'm sure it will all be lovely."

We politely discussed what we would wear for the charity gala until the food came, and I waited for the other shoe to drop. That had been too easy.

At least they waited until after I'd mostly finished my plate before they spoke next.

"One more thought," my father said.

I sat back with a sigh, wiping my face with a cloth napkin and setting it on my plate. A server appeared a moment later to take it away.

"Thank you," I said and smiled up at the server out of reflex, forgetting too late that I was with my parents.

My mother cleared her throat pointedly, and my father huffed out. "Don't encourage the help or they expect a tip." He said it while they were still in earshot, and I cringed internally. Thankfully, my face was well-trained after a lifetime of comments like that.

Emma was not as accustomed. Her mouth opened—likely about to go off on a tangent about tipping and deplorable living wages—but at the last minute, she managed to hold her tongue. Her mouth snapped shut, and she reached for her water instead. A twisted part of me would love to watch her go off on them. Let them see the passion that writhed under this pristine facade.

"He's always been a bleeding heart." My mother dabbed at

her mouth with her napkin even though she'd hardly eaten anything but a few bites of her grapefruit. "He gets *that* from your side."

My father looked up from his phone, sucking his tooth behind a mouth pulled tight. He'd been about to retort something but instead went back to typing out something on his phone. My mother blinked rapidly and turned back to Emma and me.

Emma looked between the awkward display, a little furrow forming between her brow.

My mother cleared her throat. "Your father and I have decided that Emma should move into the LA house. It makes the most sense."

I didn't move or breathe. Was this their plan of attack? Putting us together *more*? Had Emma known about this? Was she secretly hoping we'd end up in some knock-down, drag-out fight to end things faster?

Emma was motionless. Only the racing pulse at her collar gave anything away. "Move in with Wesley?" she asked calmly.

I was impressed that she was even able to ask that. But she must have known this meeting was another move by my parents in this chess game of our lives. I half expected Emma to have black smears under her eyes, ready for battle. This Emma had built the empire. I preferred this version to the Golden Girl.

My father finally glanced up to share a look with my mother. Maybe they had similar questions.

"I do agree that, logistically, it makes sense," Emma finished.

Maybe she was hiding her disgust. Perhaps I should be afraid of the calculations running behind her eyes.

Yet a huge part of me was thrilled about this idea. I wanted to scream out hell yes. To have her close all the time ...

"Think you'll be able to keep it in your pants, son?" my father asked in that sarcastic "joking" way men of his generation used to get away with saying truly deplorable shit, only to laugh it off as a joke.

"His house is plenty large enough for us both," Emma said curtly before I could reply. "Wesley and his pants aren't any of my concern."

It always came back to my pants.

I let out a silent breath that had been locked inside me.

I shot a look at Emma. Her hand reflexively went to her old tote bag before going back to her lap.

"I'm perfectly aware this is only temporary. I'm counting on it," Emma said before innocently taking a sip of her espresso. "You just have to make sure your son doesn't fall in love with me."

I coughed. My mother was struck speechless.

"He's smarter than that. We all know that this is a business arrangement. Coles know what's best for them," my father said and looked down his nose at Emma, but she acted impervious to it.

"No Cole would be foolish enough to ruin the family name by thinking with their hearts," my mother said quietly. "Not again." I couldn't be sure, but was that a little sarcasm from dear ole Mother?

My father turned his steel-melting gaze to my mother now. "His uncle was foolish enough to go against the family's wishes, and Wesley understands the cost."

"This is hardly the same. Your brother made his choice too," my mother said, ice in her tone.

"Is now really the right time to talk about this, Diana?" he asked in a low and menacing tone.

I looked out at the road, hardly visible through the tall shrubs surrounding the patio. My parents' bickering faded away. A family of four strolled by hand in hand, smiling and pointing around excitedly. I had few memories of Uncle Ace because he was out of the family before I was six. I remember laughter and joy from riding on his shoulders in picturesque golden light like something out of a prescription drug commercial. Side effects might include crippling sadness when separated ...

It was enough to push the thoughts away over the years. This dirty family secret was a dark spot on our family name and only brought out to prove a point.

Look. See. This was what happened when you forgot about your duties to the Cole family.

Not all Coles turned to diamonds under pressure. Some got pulverized to dust and wiped out of existence.

I eventually tuned back into the conversation as the bill was dropped off. Emma watched me closely, but the polite smile she'd been sporting all morning was no longer there. Instead, a small furrow had formed between her brows.

Ah, it was one thing to hear about the Coles, but watching the live show was another thing entirely. At least I didn't have to worry about her wanting to be in this family because nobody would choose this. Soon, it wouldn't be my issue, either.

She glanced away and reached for the bill. My father grabbed it first and gave her a look that had her blinking back in shock. Rex Cole paid the bills. It wasn't kindness; it was ego.

She and I exchanged a look when he signed with a flourish. The tip line blank.

The four of us made our way to the exit.

"Oh, excuse me, I forgot my phone," Emma said and headed back inside.

I didn't blame her for avoiding the awkward goodbye.

I gave my own goodbyes to my mother and father with the usual platitudes to check in with them soon.

"Keep an eye on yourself. Remember the goal, and don't do anything stupid," my father said, cuffing me on the shoulder one last time before they left.

Once they were out of sight, I went back to the table to drop some bills on the tab.

Emma was there already, doing the same thing. As I dropped the cash on top of hers, Emma gave me a look daring me to say something.

"I just couldn't stand the thought—" she said.

"I get it. They've never had to work to survive, so they don't understand," I said.

I wasn't excusing them. Maybe it sounded like I was. It was just easier to do it this way. I met her awaiting gaze and the ensuing lash-out.

"Neither did you, yet here you are," she said.

I didn't like how she looked at me. Like I was somehow changing in her estimation. But I was like them. I was a literal product of the two people she saw today. I was a Cole, and she needed to remember I had a darkness in me. I shrugged.

"See you at *home*, Golden Girl."

Turning, I left. I needed to mentally prepare for my new houseguest.

The last thing I heard was her sigh, but I would bet money she rolled her eyes.

13

Emma

After Sofia gave me the information to get into Wesley's house, I brought over my suitcases from Harrison's. It didn't take me long since they were essentially neighbors, but Wesley was nowhere to be found, even though he must have beat me back to the house. The island in the kitchen contained a note in his lilting script handwriting, not easily deciphered, that told me I could pick whatever room I wanted.

Just not mine, please.

I huffed quietly. I briefly debated deliberately disobeying his single request and strewing my clothing all over his room. Instead, I chose a large bedroom on the other side of the house from the room I presumed was his.

On my way to drop my bags, I stopped by his almost barren room, like the designer had lost steam by the time they got there. It had a king-size bed, a soft-to-the-touch dark-green duvet, and a few pieces of modern furniture. The only signs of life were the unmade bed and the en suite bathroom filled with his cologne. It was as though he'd hurriedly showered, his trousers and shirt from the night before thrown on a chair in the corner.

I unpacked quickly before making my way out to a lounge chair beside Wesley's pool to replay the events of brunch this morning. The air up here in the Hills had a chill, so I sat wrapped in a large jumper.

This new plan his parents concocted was jarring and confusing. In theory, I understood their reasoning, but a part of me thought they just liked to prove their point. When Wesley showed up at breakfast hungover and on edge, I'd enjoyed poking the beast, but after one meal in his parents' company, I felt slimy. I didn't want to be another person at that table taking a jab at his expense. The hurt from the photo shoot was washed away.

His father was even more dreadful than I'd imagined. Throughout brunch, Wesley had worn that familiar, cold mask, slipping further away into his thoughts with every moment. When they brought up the uncle I'd never heard of, he completely checked out of the conversation. His eyes had taken on a soft haze as though looking out to the horizon. The way they spoke to Wesley was unimaginable. My parents had only ever encouraged and supported me. The closest thing to a critique my mother had was to thrust sweets at me when I came home.

"So that's the smell that clings to you."

"Bloody hell." I jumped and, too late, tried to hide the e-cigarette in my hand.

"I thought you had a weird habit of tucking your pockets full of Cinnamon Toast Crunch," Wesley said from behind me.

I placed a hand over my racing heart. "Hello, Wesley. I didn't hear you slither up behind me."

"Clearly. Caught with an e-cig. I would have never guessed, not in a million years."

I lifted my chin and ignored him.

"Calm yourself, Golden Girl."

"I hate when you call me that," I snapped.

Why did he have to be like everybody else and size me up with a single nickname? Or did he purposely push my buttons because he knew I was anything but perfect? It never felt like a compliment when the media dubbed me that.

"Do you?" he asked and plopped himself into the chair beside mine. "Too bad. I so enjoy that face you make."

"Are you done?"

"That's the one. And no. I need to drag out your suffering as long as possible. I still can't believe you smoke."

"You're acting like I eat live spiders."

"That's a terrible example for you to pull from your hat so quickly," he said.

"What sort of hat? A fedora? Or a baseball hat?" I mocked him by quoting his words from the photo shoot.

He nudged my foot with his and quirked an eyebrow at the vaporizer.

I sighed. "It's only CBD. It helps with anxiety," I explained. There was just so much pressure. So much expectation all the time.

A little crease formed between his brows before he smoothed it away. He gestured for me to hand it over. I hesitated. "No cooties, I swear."

"I beg to differ," I said but passed it.

He took a deep pull and widened his eyes comically before coughing. "I felt that in my toes."

"And a little tobacco-free nicotine," I added, reaching to take it back.

He tilted his head to look at me more closely. "So, there is a chink in the armor?"

"Piss off."

"I'm teasing. It's encouraging to know that you aren't totally perfect."

"Nobody's perfect."

"Well, you're as close as they come," he said.

I gave him a skeptical glance, but he studied the little black device, refusing to give it back yet. That felt too close to a compliment for comfort. "It helps me relax," I explained, dropping my waiting arm.

"So why hide?" he asked, taking another less enthusiastic pull this time.

His mouth pursed over the mouthpiece, where mine had been only a moment ago. It made me think of our accidental kiss this morning at brunch. That kiss had caused a flurry of emotions in my chest. Lesson learned. No more kisses unless a camera was present or given express permission.

Not that I would ask.

Not that *he* would ... I needed these thoughts back on track.

"Do I really need to say why?" I said in answer to his question about secrecy.

"I suppose not."

"With how little is known about the health risks and how bad the disposable pods are for the environment, it makes me a complete hypocrite. Plus, the thought of little kids seeing me do it and think it's something to look up to." I suddenly felt sick with guilt again.

"Ah, well, now I feel like a bastard. Don't make that face." He nudged me again, but this time kept his foot (and most of the leg attached) on my lounger instead of bringing it back to his own. "It's really not as bad as eating spiders." He pinched his thumb and pointer together. "Like a step below."

I groaned.

"I'm messing with you. So you indulge a little. Better than many other vices," he pointed out.

"The worst part," I started. A small, secret smile spread over my lips. I couldn't help it.

"It gets worse? I'm learning so much about you G—Emma."

"The worst part," I said, ignoring him, "is that I absolutely run Harrison over the coals for smoking his." I tucked my face in my hands.

"That's the best part," he said with a laugh.

"You like Harrison," I said, sure of myself. Though I couldn't think of many times they'd been together.

"I'm not the one with the issues. Harrison is civil to me, but he's never been warm to me."

I mulled it over. "He's protective. He's always been."

Wesley made a sound that told me he had differing opinions on the matter but wasn't going to explain.

"Anyway, my nagging is justified. He smokes his all day, every day. This is just a little bit. When I'm exceedingly stressed."

He pretended to brush something off my cheek. The subtle and quick gesture was still enough to make the world go wonky for a moment. "You're tarnishing that golden facade," he teased.

Facade indeed. I wanted to tell him how exhausted I was. How I hated my reputation. The problem with being seen as perfect was not only that there was no room for errors, but I could never be perfect enough. There was no standard I could ever meet when I'd feel like I could relax.

The problem with being seen as perfect meant you could only ever disappoint.

I pushed those thoughts back down.

"You're deranged. You're genuinely happy about this discovery," I said instead.

He shrugged. "I'm happy to see that you do something for yourself. I wished it wasn't that health-wise, but knowing that you allow yourself a bit of naughtiness in the world makes me happy. I was starting to suspect you'd truly transformed into some infallible super being."

"Hardly." I snorted. Then flushed.

"Oh man, I remember that sound."

I tucked my face back in my hands. Along with the blushing, I had thought I had my awkward laughter under control. Seemed Wesley brought it all back out.

I tucked the device back into the pocket of my jumper.

"Why are you exceedingly stressed?" he asked.

I gave him a questioning look. "Hmm?"

"You said you only need it when you're stressed."

Did he really not understand how hard this was? Was the thought of moving in with me and pretending to date me that easy for him? After brunch today, I was starting to understand that I could hardly read this man next to me at all.

"You know the brunch was an attack. A way of getting the upper hand," I said.

"Very on brand for them." He shrugged. I snapped my head toward him.

"You did?"

He nodded. "Did you plan it?" he asked me.

"No," I said instantly. I was upset after the photo shoot. I had wanted to gain control, but I wouldn't ever have thought being together *more* was the answer. "Why would you think that?" I asked, slightly hurt.

"You didn't build your charitable empire by being polite to everyone you work with," he said. "Something in you pushes harder than the rest and gets you what you want. I heard about the deal with Harlow. He's notoriously a penny-pincher. My own parents couldn't convince him to back any project, yet you swept him off his feet."

I had to make sure my jaw wasn't on the ground. Had he

really been following my career all these years? That deal hadn't even been publicly announced.

"That's different. That's business. This is …"

"Personal?" he finished.

"Maybe it shouldn't be." I sighed and pinched the bridge of my nose. "I heard your father at the shoot yesterday," I admitted, putting some of the cards out there. I was so tired. "I planned to make you squirm when they said they wanted to meet."

"Ah, yes. But then?" he asked. I felt him studying my profile as I looked out over the rolling hills behind his house. The clouds moved so fast that the light changed every minute.

"Turns out, I'm not the vengeful sort. Plus, you looked miserable enough," I said.

"The bleeding heart."

"Harrison and Charlie would absolutely agree with that," I said. "I tend to lean a little too much toward making excuses for people. Imagine their hardships."

"At the sacrifice of your own happiness," he finished.

I cleared my throat. That was precisely what the guys worried I was doing with Wesley. I projected an entire life onto him to soften the way he'd treated me in the past. But they also didn't see Wesley the way I had.

"Then I had lunch with your parents and realized I wasn't even needed to make you squirm."

He tossed his head back with a genuine laugh. "Who needs torture when you have family?" He looked out at the water of the pool, his sunglasses back on his face. He sounded happy enough, but there was a tightness in his jaw.

"I mean, I knew your family had expectations but bloody hell. You must always have to be on guard around them," I said.

He shrugged. "We all have an image to maintain. You know a bit about that," he said softer.

I let out a sigh. "Right, but it's your *family*. I have an uncle who's always blitzed out of his gourd every holiday and spews horrid Torie talk, but we still keep inviting him back. The way they treat you like an employee ... it's sad."

He looked away. "All families are different."

"And your poor mother," I said without thinking.

This surprised him. His head turned to me, brows raised behind his Ray-Bans. "My mother?"

"She's so lovely," I started, and that same brow furrowed. "She tries so hard to get your father's attention, and he won't ever look up from that blasted device of his," I explained.

"I don't think much about their relationship. It's always sort of been there but never felt like ... Well, it's not like in the movies. At least the happy ones."

"To be married all those years and feel like strangers," I said.

"She will always choose him," he said with flared nostrils. A darkness that spoke to a history I wasn't privy to passed over him. He cleared his throat, looking increasingly uncomfortable. "Now *that* is just business for them. It works for them."

"Does it? It's just that ..." I thought about my words, shocked by how much we were conversing but not wanting it to stop. "I always thought your family was the way they were because you were your own little unit. You were proud and rich, but I thought it was because you protected each other. Loved each other. But now I'm wondering."

He pulled his leg back to his lounger. I had gone too far. It wasn't my place to talk about his family like this. His cool demeanor wasn't ever an act. That was how he was taught to behave. It was how he protected himself.

"Anyway, I'm sorry I brought it up," I said.

"My mother brought it up when she mentioned Ace Cole."

"Who?"

"Exactly." He turned to me.

I rolled my eyes.

"Careful or your face will freeze like that."

I crossed my eyes and stuck out my tongue, if only to make him smile after prodding too deep. I was happy he wasn't storming off. This conversation was a white flag waving between us. It was like the old days, the secret visits between scenes. I knew *this* man.

"Much better," he said.

I laughed, and he went on after a long breath out. "Uncle Ace was my dad's brother, as I'm sure you gathered. He was always different, always going against the grain, and he never wanted to be an actor or even be in Hollywood. When he fell in love with a woman who didn't fit the bill of who they wanted him to marry, they told him he had to choose. I never got the full story because Uncle Ace is a skeleton we pretend doesn't exist. That's what Coles do." He shook his head and went on. "He wanted to run away with this woman. When he chose the life he wanted, he was completely cut out of the family. He was completely blackballed in the industry. Nobody would work with him, even if he wanted to come back."

"That's terrible."

"It's the cautionary tale."

"At least he's happy right?"

"No," Wesley said, his throat tight. "It ended with the mystery woman, as far as I can tell. It's impossible to get information about him. He had no money to fall back on. No one in the family is allowed to talk to him. I've thought about it, but I wouldn't even know how to find him. He was forced to change his last name after being hassled by family lawyers. Last I heard, he lived in some city in the Midwest."

"Oh God," I said, aghast.

"This is why you never go against the Coles," he said solemnly. "Generations of Hollywood life have left this family so completely detached from reality we wouldn't even know how to operate in the real world." He frowned at the horizon again, his mind drifting to some far-off thought. "All because he was an idiot who fell in love." He swallowed, jaw tight.

A cloud moved over the sun, and I shivered.

"And that's why you're going along with all this? Really?" I asked. "Not just to recover from the business of divorce but because you don't have a choice?"

His face darkened. "Something like that. I'll tell you about it one day."

"Hmm," I said. One day. What did that mean? Our days were limited.

I took out my phone and snagged a selfie with a hint of the corner of his shoulder at the edge of the shot. I posted it with a caption about old friends and California air.

"What are you up to?" He smirked. "I normally charge to be in photos."

"Bill me. But only for your shoulder. I was thinking about what you said when we were leaving the photo shoot. About trying to be more copacetic."

The side of his head rested against the back of the chair, slightly hunched, he looked oddly young despite his suit, and I remembered he was nursing a hell of a hangover.

"Oh yeah?" He blinked softly at me. I could see because the light shone through the side of his sunglasses. I wondered if he knew his emotions were on display.

"Well. I've been thinking about things anyway. I would like it if we w-were friends. At the gala next weekend, our first official outing. I promise. I will come in peace." I held up my empty hands.

"I think I'd really like that." He pushed up his glasses and blinked against the muted light, then reached out his hand. The tension around his eyes melted away as I reached out and shook him.

We held still, looking at each other.

His large, calloused hand sheltered mine. There was a time when this sort of contact would have fueled my adolescent brain for days. I would have played it over and over, remembering how it made my heart race and made me feel safe and protected. This peace offering of friendship was the best I could hope for now.

I wanted to tell him that he was different from his family. That he wasn't like them. But then, I remembered Harrison and Charlie's warning. Was he different, or did my heart want him to be different? He was doing this fake-dating scheme. He was going along with it even if he wasn't thrilled. Yes, his family was powerful, but he chose his family on some level every time. It wasn't a judgment. It was facts. I couldn't imagine having to choose between freedom or family, toxic or otherwise.

I was rehashing a decades-old crush only to get hurt again. It didn't matter. This was a temporary arrangement. I didn't have to be so defensive, but I would remain on guard.

I released his hand and faced forward.

14

───────

Wesley

After almost two weeks of living together, I'd heard from Emma even less than before she'd "moved in." She must have taken my previous words to heart about her always showing up, because after moving in, she made herself scarce.

I missed her. Initially, the promise of friendship had left me on edge. At any moment, an unguarded look from me might give everything away. But as the days ticked by, it became clear she was avoiding me.

I couldn't blame her. It was most likely for the best.

In the downstairs gym, I took out some frustration on the rowing machine. I wasn't training as hard as I had when I was filming, but that didn't mean I could relax either. Also, I had sexual energy to burn. Even though Emma was the quietest roommate ever, she may as well have been stomping through the halls with a megaphone for as often as I thought of her. Little signs of life in the form of her soft voice echoing down the hall or the waft of perfume in a hallway she'd recently passed through. Knowing she was only a few rooms away at night was torture and oddly comforting.

It allowed me the fantasy of pretending this could be life—that she was always just outside the bedroom, about to come in. I'd open my arm, she'd burrow into the sheets, and I'd pretend to be mad when she put her ice-cold feet on me.

"Jesus. Get it together, Cole," I swore to myself.

As I wiped my sweat-drenched brow, it occurred to me that if I wanted to see Emma, I had a little tool at my disposal. The whole point of this living arrangement was to tease the fans and be seen together more. So that was what I needed to do.

Time for a little game of chicken.

I showered and changed into a comfortable pair of gray sweatpants and a black T-shirt. Word on the street was that it made women go crazy, so I would test that theory with Emma. I wasn't sure that she'd seen me in anything but suits since we'd known each other.

After ensuring my hair was appropriately styled to appear dashingly disheveled enough, I grabbed my phone and logged onto the social media account with the most followers. My hair was a point of pride, so sue me. It used to be the thing that caused teasing, but now it was my signature look, and I'd fully embraced it. Also, it helped that it was the defining feature that separated me from my father.

It only occurred to me at that moment that I would have to dye my hair when I left. I was too easily recognized with it. The idea troubled me ... and that bothered me even more.

I shook the thoughts away and focused on the here and now.

I went in search of Emma. She was curled up on the couch next to the window, book in hand. The afternoon sun ignited her red hair, which flowed over her shoulder. Her bright-blue eyes were downcast onto the page, and her dewy pale skin all but glowed backlit as she was. I wasn't a total asshole. I would make sure that she was camera ready before I bombarded her. Luckily, or unluckily depending on how she saw it, she was always camera ready. While I arguably benefited from this, I didn't envy the time she had to spend just to feel like she could leave the house. But if it made her feel more comfortable, I couldn't blame her. See above: my own hair.

Truth be told, she was beautiful all the time, so it was difficult to know when she found herself in an unacceptable state.

I thumbed into the app and ensured the camera pointed at me. Making sure she couldn't spot me yet, I grinned and waved at the camera, then held a finger to my lips. At first, I wasn't sure if the live video worked because there was no interaction, but soon, the comments started rolling up. Hearts and thumbs-ups dotted the screen so fast I couldn't keep up.

"Hello, all. Just wanted to say hi."

I had almost a thousand viewers already.

"Did you say something?" Emma called from around the corner.

I held a finger to my mouth, miming, "Be quiet," to the viewers as if they were making any sound.

The comments exploded.

I'm sorry, but that voice sounded familiar!

Was that who I think it was!?

OMG OMG OMG

And so on and so forth.

I came around the corner with the phone held high, obvious that the camera was on, but still pointed at my face.

"Wesley!" She covered her head with a pillow. "Are you taking a picture of me?"

I couldn't take my eyes off her but felt the comments practically explode my phone.

"I would never do that," I said.

She lowered the pillow and looked at me.

Just as she looked skeptically hesitant, I added. "It's a live video. Say hi!"

She shrieked and brought the pillow back up. "You better be lying," she squealed. "I'm not dressed or made up."

"Really?" I tilted my head. I guess now that I looked closer, her lashes were paler than normal. It was hard to tell from this far. I stepped closer but kept the camera on my face. "You look beautiful. But don't worry, I won't put you on camera without permission," I said. "Unlike some people I know."

She slowly lowered the pillow and narrowed her eyes. "That was your shoulder. Hardly the same," she muttered.

I glanced at the comments. They came so fast I could hardly keep up.

He called her beautiful. Dead. I'm dead. I'm writing this from beyond the grave.

OMG, LET US SEE HER.

That is definitely Emma! I'd know that accent anywhere.

FLIP THE CAMERA!!

And chorus after chorus demanded more information. We were already up to twenty thousand viewers.

Emma grabbed her phone and clicked around. A few seconds later, I heard my voice delayed back.

"You really are doing a live. You're absolutely mental," she said to herself with a shake of her head.

"I wanted to show the world my lovely guest."

Her eyes moved rapidly over the screen, hand over her mouth. She looked up at me and widened her eyes. She mouthed, "I'm going to murder you." Then her eyes seemed to snag on the gray sweatpants, glancing away before returning once more. I would take that as a win.

"What are you reading, *friend*?" I asked.

She gave her best attempt to ignore me, putting her phone down.

"I'm sorry, ladies and gentlemen. My friend is being shy and doesn't want to be on camera." I somberly tilted my head, giving my most pitiful puppy dog face in her direction.

She rolled her eyes so epically I thought her head might fall off her shoulders.

There was another burst of support for me in the comments when I glanced down.

A hundred thousand viewers.

"Oh no," I said, heavily sarcastic. "Somebody has called you a chicken on here. Not me. I would never. *I* know you're not a chicken. But somebody here is calling you out."

She smacked her mouth in exasperation before—very dramatically, in my opinion—placing a scrap of paper in the pages and closing her book.

"Oh. She's making her way over," I said, my voice dropping with sudden nerves. "She doesn't seem happy with me." There was a fifty-fifty chance she'd go along with this risky game. Otherwise, there was a strong possibility I was about to be kneed in the balls.

Nah, she would never do that.

Her eyes narrowed as she got closer, her arched eyebrow saying it all.

I flinched. She might do that.

The viewers were now climbing so fast, I couldn't keep track. Hundreds of thousands, with the number clicking higher every second.

Emma came and stood next to me and, without warning, slid her arms around my waist and tilted her head onto my shoulder and into the frame.

"Hello." She waved sweetly. "Wesley is being dramatic, as always. I'm happy to pop on and say hello."

She was the right amount of demure and pseudo (hopefully) put out. Her shampoo smelled so good, I had to fight leaning in to inhale her. My free hand pulled her closer. If we were going to do this *act* or whatever it was, I was going all in.

The comments exploded.

"What are you up to, Wesley?" she asked.

"I thought while we're both here hanging out, maybe we could answer some questions for the loyal fans," I said. "Maybe about *Terraformative*? The reunion special was a hit."

"Hmm, I should have made more tea."

"There will be no tea spilling. Just answering questions."

She chuckled. "Very funny."

Unfortunately, she untangled herself from my side and tugged me over to the couch. She roughly pushed me down, and I'll be damned if I didn't like that.

"I'll answer some questions so long as I get the option to pass," she said as she curled her knees up to her chest and snuggled close to me.

It would be like this if we were a real couple. We could freely cuddle and touch and never worry about doing it for pretense or what other people thought.

"Okay, fair," I said. "Let's start with some easy ones."

I lifted my arm so she could come closer yet, and she scrolled through the comments.

Are you a couple?

Or some variation was by far the most asked question, and I fully intended to ignore it.

"Oh, that's a good one," Emma said.

I squeezed her side, instinctually understanding we were on the same page and that page was ignoring the most obvious questions. To drive them wild in anticipation.

"'How long have you known each other?' this person asks." I looked down at her, squinting in thought, making sure the camera still focused on both our faces in the frame.

She glanced up at me with warm eyes, and my heart tripped.

"Well, let's see. We met when I was eleven. So over twenty years," Emma said.

"Feels like forever," I said.

Her sweet lips puckered in thought. "I can't tell if you mean that in a good way or a bad way."

I couldn't fight the genuine, spreading smile. It was like the warm feelings that her nearness caused in me. As though she raised my internal temperature by several degrees. She blinked at me and then swallowed as she brought her attention back to the phone.

"Hmm," she said. She scrolled until she found one that wasn't about us dating. "How about this one. 'What are you working on now?'"

"These are great questions," I said. "We really thought you all only cared about one thing, but we're glad to see you're invested in our careers," I teased. "I'm between projects, just finished wrapping a movie that I'm very excited about."

"Oh, I've heard good things about that one. Words like 'Oscar-worthy performance' are being thrown around," Emma said so smoothly you'd think we'd rehearsed this repartee.

"Well, I don't know about that, but it was a great project with a phenomenal cast and crew," I said modestly.

She squeezed my thigh in support.

"And you're about to start the library campaign, right?" I prompted her.

She gave a spiel about her newest project, invested in getting funding for a major city in the Midwest down to one public library. She was so perfectly elegant, so graceful and well-spoken, and passionate. How could anybody listen to her and not be totally enthralled? This was how she built an empire—with the perfect combination of intelligence, compassion, and enthusiasm.

"What?" she asked, looking at me, and I realized I'd been staring openly. God, I loved *pretending* with her.

"What do you mean?" I asked.

"Have I got something on me?" She looked at our faces on the phone more closely.

"I was listening. It's fascinating."

Her eyes narrowed. "I can't tell if you're pulling my leg."

I laughed and kissed her temple without thinking. "I'm not. I'm just listening."

Look at how he looks at her.

They have to be doing it.

That forehead kiss tho.

Good lord, the sexual tension could be cut with a knife.

"Anyway." She flushed. "I think I've gone off the rails a bit. Let's see. Oh, and we just finished a campaign with Crunchy-Couture. We're both very excited about that."

"The pictures are incredible. Can't wait for you to see."

Fire fire fire.

My Emsley loving heart is literally exploding right now.

Are you a couple?

They are so dating.

We answered a few questions about filming TF and kept things light. We both seemed to register another question at the same time. Emma was ready to ignore it, but I had to address one of the bigger elephants in the room. This room was getting claustrophobic.

"This user asked about the infamous twenty-twelve interview," I said, sobering my tone.

"Hmm." Emma didn't give much away.

"I think we all know that I was a massive asshole in that interview. If I haven't apologized to Emma by now, I will."

She looked up at me.

"I'm sorry," I said, holding her expectant but guarded gaze. I poured all my sincerity into it because no words could possibly justify how awful I felt after I went off like that. "I don't have an excuse. I was young and temperamental and an all-around ass."

Her brow furrowed, but then she seemed to remember herself. "I know." She patted my cheek lovingly but hard enough to sting.

"Not that I can defend my actions, but I had started dating someone very special to me at the time." I swallowed. *Or so I had thought.* "And it turns out, women don't love for their partners to be asked about other women."

Emma blinked up at me. "I didn't know that."

"I'm still sorry."

"Thank you," she said before letting out a low and slow breath.

"So long as I'm alive, Emma Flynn will have a superfan. Sometimes it just takes time to realize what's in front of you," I said.

I noticed the briefest furrow of her brow as though she had more she wanted to ask, but then she remembered the giant mass of people watching us. She smoothed her features.

There was so much that we still needed to discuss. So much that I needed to apologize for, without almost a million viewers watching. So much I needed to explain. Once I was free of the Cole name, I could put everything out there. For now, there was too much risk to her.

Suddenly, I didn't want to be doing this live anymore. I didn't want to push her away or cause her pain. I wanted to live in a reality where this was our life. A life that could only ever exist in my fantasy, where my only job was to make her happy.

"I think that's all we have time for today," I said.

"There really doesn't seem to be any other questions," Emma said dryly.

"True. I think that's answered all of it."

She laughed up at me, and I leaned forward without thinking. I had been about to kiss her. Again. It was the reflex of the other version of me in the alternate timeline. I stopped in the nick of time and reached next to her to grab her book and hand it to her.

If I thought antagonizing her was fun because it got a reaction out of her, nothing could compare to what I felt when I made her laugh. I used to love this. I'd locked it down for so long, not even allowing myself to remember, but my God, her laugh gave me life.

"We better let her get back to reading. The woman works hard and deserves her rest."

Exclamations of *TEASE* and *Noooooo!*

Emma discreetly pointed at the screen where the viewer count was now almost a million views. We shared a look. This was huge for publicity. Our gazes held as though daring the other.

Kiss. Kiss. Kiss!

Y'all need a life. They're just friends.

Click on my profile to see xxx women.

"You know the people want us to kiss. The naughty little pervs," I said.

I looked at Emma. We hadn't discussed this.

"Don't look at me. I'm not kissing you without permission anymore," she said. "That hasn't ever worked out in my favor."

The comments exploded. Between the leaked picture early on, the brunch, and the photo shoot. The media was getting more than its fair share of us almost lip locked.

"Well, then I'll just have to kiss you," I said, determined. Ready.

I cleared my throat, softened my mouth, and leaned closer to her. With every bit of air disappearing between us, her eyes widened.

15

———

Emma

WESLEY WAS GOING TO KISS ME. HE WAS GOING TO KISS ME ON camera with over a million people watching. His gaze went all soft as it flicked back and forth between my eyes. I licked my lips and realized how that would look.

"No, I wouldn't do that to Emma. If I recall, you told me boys had cooties," he said and shifted away.

"Well, to be fair, I was barely eleven when I said that," I clarified, shaky and fake sounding.

He smiled. "Words cut, Ems."

I flushed hearing him call me that.

"I guess he's afraid of *my* cooties," I said to the camera.

I couldn't see the comments anymore because they were coming so fast. My heart was racing at our almost kiss. I couldn't focus on them even if I wanted to. I was too aware of how close he sat and how tightly our bodies were pressed so we could both be seen on screen. Or at least that was how I rationalized his proximity.

I made the mistake of putting myself out there one too many

times. If he wanted to kiss me, he could be the one to initiate it. But this was all an act. The tease was working brilliantly.

He lowered his head and kissed my cheek. This time, I didn't accidentally steal one on the mouth. I let it be innocent and vague to drive the viewers more insane.

It was chaste and sweet, and I was desperate for more. I made a show of smiling for the camera.

"All right well, better get back to work. Thanks for hanging out with us," he said.

"Bye. Nice chatting with all of you."

He ended the video, and we sat in awkward silence.

"Well. That should keep my parents happy for a bit."

"Just waiting to hear from the team about it," I said, voice shockingly calm.

"But it went well, didn't it?"

"Yeah. I think so." I fiddled with my fingers. Neither of us had moved.

I played back before the Kiss That Never Was to his apology. He had seemed so sincere. I needed to hear that sorry for so long, and I appreciated it. But how much stake could I put in it if it was on camera? Was it only for the viewers? It had felt sincere, but everything felt so real when we pretended. He was so bloody good at all this.

On the other hand, hearing it from his point of view reminded me that I *had* made everything about me back then. I was so young and self-centered, and truthfully, I was obsessed with him. I might not have enjoyed the media attention, but I relished that they felt the tension between us, as I had. I hadn't known he was trying to start a relationship with Natasha then. The whole thing felt so small and far away now.

I held on to the anger for so long. I wished ...

"It was true," he said as though my thoughts spilled out of my head. "About dating Natasha at the time." He nudged me until I looked at him. "I shouldn't have apologized like that on the video, but it didn't make it any less sincere."

"Okay," I said. A lot of the hurt was still there, simmering under the surface. It was the well of hurt I pulled from when any other pesky feelings about him got too intense. He was the one who insisted we weren't even friends. He was the one who never had feelings. The embarrassment and pain of it all kept me protected from falling for him time and time again.

"I think about that interview all the time." He frowned at where I sat curled up next to him, gaze distant. "I never should have said those things about us. I never should have let that interviewer get to me. It was exactly what they wanted, and I fed right into it and snapped. And you were the one who suffered."

"I understand how those things go. I know what the world sees isn't always the truth," I said.

"You're too gracious. You have every right to be mad."

"Oh, I cursed you many times. There are several fake troll accounts out there just to hate on you," I said.

"Really?" His eyebrows shot up.

"No. Not really. But thank you for apologizing. I needed to hear it. I never understood what happened after *Terraformative*. Why you changed so much," I admitted softly.

His features contorted in obvious pain. "It's complicated. But just know that ..." He carded his fingers through his hair. "This sounds ridiculous, but those years on set with you were the happiest years of my life. Pathetic." He flicked a glance at me and swallowed as though he'd admitted something awful.

"It's not pathetic. I'm surprised, is all. You seemed very remote back then," I said. *Except with me.*

"I was as happy as I could be," he said vaguely.

"But I get it, missing that time," I said. "Seeing the past through rose-tinted glasses. Charlie, Harrison, and I talk about it sometimes. But honestly, I can't think about it too much. It hurts to recognize how far away it is. That unbridled joy of having everything ahead still and nothing to look back on with regret. The way of being young and carefree, you know?"

His eyes darkened, jaw flexing. "You were always so hopeful about the future." And it was one of the few times he referred to our history.

"Like I said, I can't think about it too much, or I get ennui. Although I did want to quit at one point," I admitted without meaning to. I never even confessed that to Charlie or Harrison.

"Wait, really? You did?" He sat back, shocked, but didn't take his arm off me, and I was thankful for the warmth and safety of it.

"Yes, around the fourth season. It was when things really started to explode globally. I was becoming aware of what lay in store for me. There would never be going back to any semblance of a normal life if I stayed," I explained.

"The media was terrible to you," he said sadly. "More than Harrison or Charlie. I hated it for you."

I smiled at him. I thought of the obsession with my weight, who I was dating ... and much worse. I was barely fifteen, and they were making Halloween costumes that sexualized my character's flight suit.

"The world of TF without Emma Flynn. I can't even imagine," he said. "What made you decide to stay?"

I swallowed hard. It wasn't him. It wasn't *just* him. I picked at a piece of lint on my knees. "I love the stories. I love the world Sedar created. I love the fans, the ones who love it as much as we do. The impact we had on so many people was incomprehensible. It was amazing to be a part of something that meant so much to so many people. The energy with the cast and crew was so palpable. We were family and knew we belonged to something that would change the world. Even as young and maybe self-centered and scared as I was, I knew I would regret it if I left.

I knew that if I stayed, it would mean pressure and expectations like I never imagined. But I couldn't walk away. I loved it too much."

I cleared my throat, wondering if I'd said too much.

"I'm so thankful you stayed on," he said, his voice tight. "Some of my favorite memories were the ones of us talking between scenes."

"Mine too." I wanted to scream, So what happened? Why were you so different to me in front of the rest of the crew? Why were you so awful to me later?

But I couldn't ask. I couldn't ruin this moment. Not when we'd laid down the weapons. Not when my turbulent emotions bubbled just below the thin skin of this conversation.

"Sometimes, I worry I'll never be that happy again," he said seriously.

I held his gaze. "You don't really think that?"

He chuckled but waved me away. "No. Not really."

But I knew that fake laugh by now. What was Wesley like when he fully let his guard down? When he stopped holding on so tight? I wouldn't ever be the person in his life who got to see. Time was passing, and we only had a few weeks together. That was the point. The end was a way for me to feel safe.

But now I wanted time to slow down a bit.

I was so close to him, I was practically sitting in his lap. Neither of us rushed to move.

"You know. Maybe we should be comfortable with more, uh, public displays of affection," I hedged.

He watched me closely. "True. With the gala this weekend."

"Our first official outing. It would behoove us to be comfortable with physical intimacy. Know each other's boundaries. Not that we—"

"No, I know. I agree."

"Right." I nodded.

"Yes. So then. Maybe some agreements on what's okay?" he asked.

I nodded again. My speech escaped me temporarily.

"Hand holding?" He reached for my hand where it sat on my lap. He watched me closely as he wrapped his fingers through mine. Like at the pool, my body melted into the comfort of his touch.

My head bobbed on like the arm of those Japanese cat figurines. His hand was warm and dry around my icy fingers.

"Your hands are freezing." He grabbed my other hand, rubbing them both like trying to start a fire.

"I run cold."

"I knew it," he mumbled, mostly to himself.

When they were decidedly warmer—my whole body was quite hot, in fact—his eyes never left mine as the soft skin of his lips traced my knuckles. His breath tickled me before he gently lowered them back to my lap.

"An arm around your shoulders?" When I consented, he brought me in even closer.

I was tucked under him, more than half of me pressed into him, closer than on the call. My heart beat so hard I felt my shoulder shaking slightly against him. His heartbeat called back a tempo on my shoulder.

"A kiss?" His voice was so deep and low that I clenched to grab it.

"We've done that." I swallowed.

"That wasn't a real kiss." The rumble in his voice tightened my insides.

I made a sound I wasn't proud of. Similar to the one when he hoisted my hips up into him at the photo shoot. God, but the way this man drove me up a wall. I'd never felt so heavy with desire around any other person as I did with him.

"I meant ..." *The night we never talked about.*

"Ah. That doesn't count. I was eighteen." He cleared his throat and shifted slightly. "Let the record show that many upgrades have been made since that night."

"Duly noted," I whispered. "Not too many. I quite liked that night."

I turned in his arms so we were face-to-face and risked a glance up.

His gaze was so molten it melted me.

"Did you like it?" I asked. We never talked about it. It was outside of time and reality to even be bringing it up now.

His fingers threaded into my hair, tilting up my chin. "God, Emma. So much. You have no idea how often—" He cleared his throat again. "I'm glad it was you."

I stilled. "Even after all this time?" Was it pathetic to want to know if he regretted losing his virginity to me? Another thing that felt so small now, so insignificant, yet the feelings surrounding that night were big enough to fill up twenty years.

"It couldn't have been anyone else." He took a steady breath in as my insides folded in on themselves with relief I didn't know I needed. "Still. Permission to show that I've learned some things since?"

I was back to nodding in waving kitty mode.

He dipped his head slowly toward me, giving me plenty of time to stop him. I didn't. I couldn't. I'd never wanted anything more, even if it was just practice.

His mouth finally reached mine. We both sighed as our lips greeted each other after so long apart. Like our lungs had finally cleared enough to inhale properly.

He still tasted the same, and his lips still felt like him. But he wasn't kidding about learning some things. His hand moved from my hair to cup the base of my throat, his thumb brushing my ear as his tongue dipped into my mouth. I moaned and opened wider to him. We kissed deeply and eternally. Time was insignificant. There were no deadlines or places to be. I couldn't have him close enough or kiss him deep enough. I scurried into his lap and straddled him. He shifted up to make room for me, and his length prodded my thigh.

I broke the kiss to gasp but immediately dropped back into the kiss before we could stop ourselves. He chuckled against my mouth. "God, Emma."

His hands were everywhere, groping and squeezing my backside, trailing up my back and shoulders, tracing my neck. I clawed at his hair and ground against him. Soon, the heat was pricking sweat on his brow and my back, and our heavy breaths filled the air.

His hands tentatively traced along the waist of my yoga leggings, cascading goose bumps up my body. His thumb went higher, covering my rib cage with his whole hand. Rough skin gently slid until he grazed the bottom of my breast.

He groaned as I sucked in a breath, and his hips tilted up, brushing against my hot and wet core. His sweatpants did nothing to hide his girth. I wanted to rub against it until we both came like that, grinding and taking what we needed, greedy and giving no figs about any expectations upon us.

I broke away to tell him more. Anything. Whatever he'd give me.

My shirt was lifted partially, gripped in his hands as though at war with himself. He was panting, and his hair was a mess, and seeing him this level of undone almost pushed me over the edge.

"You know, this may be a little much just for the cameras," I teased.

"Well, you never know." He leaned forward to nip at my bottom lip, his knuckles brushed across my rib cage, still gripping my shirt. "Have to make it look authentic."

"We could practice all day and night," I said coyly, biting my lip.

"I'm very committed to my craft," he growled.

I giggled as he tugged me back down. I'd been about to lift the shirt over my head when there was a loud banging at the door.

"Knock, knock!" Harrison shouted.

Wesley cursed. His alarm system chirped as his phone buzzed on the coffee table.

"You have too many friends," Wesley groaned, throwing his head back on the couch.

"I'm about to have one less," I grumbled and stood off him.

———

Wesley

I collected myself on the couch while Emma answered the door. Praying for enough self-control to not end up in the news for assault. That would really mess with all the fans who shipped Max Malachi with Harrison's TF character, Adam Abbott.

Kissing Emma like that was too perfect. She was too good. I wouldn't have stopped myself. I wanted to lay her back and slowly strip her clothes off to see if my memories still lined up with the reality of her. Maybe I should thank the nosy bastard, actually.

"What are you doing, Harrison?" Emma asked.

"Can't a neighbor and friend pop in and say hello?" he asked with too much cheer.

Funnily enough, all these years of living up the road from each other, and he's never once "popped in."

"I saw your live video and thought we could do a mini TF

reunion. Since we're all friends," Harrison said, exaggerating the last word.

"Really, Harrison," Emma said, exasperated.

"Christ, Emma, you look like you've been properly snogged." He pushed past her and into the living room, where I sat with my elbows on my knees. "Heya, mate!" he said to me.

"Harrison!" she called, following him.

"Please. Make yourself at home." I waved around the room.

"Well, if you don't mind the company," he said, hardly looking at me.

"Not at all. Excuse me. I need the restroom." I walked away stiffly, hoping my flagging erection was tucked out of sight and regretting the sweatpants.

As I retreated, I heard them argue.

"What are you doing here?" Emma growled.

"Nothing more than I said," he said in an easy tone.

"Hmm."

I tucked myself into the nearest guest bath, ears straining to listen.

"After all, I wouldn't have to be worried about you. Not when you said this was all business, and your feelings were well protected," Harrison said.

"Right."

Feelings? The only recent feelings Emma expressed were those of loathing.

Emma might have *reacted* to my touch, but bodies and minds weren't always on the same page. How could she feel anything else when I've pushed her away and been appalling to her? Harrison was being overprotective. Emma would never ...

"Because I saw that live, Emma. And that man is really good at what he does. The viewers' comments were mental." He made his voice pitchy and switched to an American accent. "'The way he looks at her. Oh. Em. Gee. There's no way that's pretend.'"

"I get it," Emma snapped.

Why wasn't she defending herself? Where was that fiery denial of even liking me?

"Good. Because I don't have to remind you that this is all for his career. He doesn't care for you, and he will abandon you as soon as his family says."

I glared but didn't speak because he was right. I felt sick. It didn't matter that our chemistry was explosive. In the end, I was leaving, so Emma would be free from the cancer of the Cole name.

It was more effective than an icy shower. After I collected myself, I flushed the toilet and made a show of washing my hands before loudly announcing my arrival back in the room.

"I've been trying to see him more, but it's so hard with my schedule," Harrison explained as I walked back into the room.

Emma had her arms tight around herself. "Is everything okay? You seem—"

"So it'll be the weekend before Christmas. Can you make it?" Harrison cut her off when he spotted me walking in. "It would mean a lot to Sedar."

"Of course." Emma nodded her head. "Yes. Of course."

"Brilliant. Charlie and Kate are flying out too. It'll be just like old times." Harrison smiled, but there was tension around his eyes. I stayed tucked back against the doorway, feeling like I was intruding. It felt like when we were filming together, watching their friendship from the outside. An unexpected wave of jealousy overtook me, and I looked away.

"Wesley. You should come too," she said, stepping closer to me, her bright eyes hopeful. "Sedar is hosting an early Christmas at his house a few hours north."

I pushed off the wall and stepped closer, still feeling like an intruder. "You don't have to invite me."

"It's a great time. Very casual. No cameras," she said.

"So it wouldn't be for publicity?" Harrison asked, but I wasn't sure for whose benefit or what he'd meant by that.

"No. Just a bunch of old friends hanging out. Literally, these days," she said. "Gosh. It's been so long since we've all been back there."

Harrison nodded, his face tight.

"You never went as a kid," she said to me. "We used to go every summer for weeks. It was almost like a camp. Do you remember?" Emma asked.

"Yeah. I just ..." I hesitated.

Of course, I remembered. I was desperate to go, but my parents yelled at me the first time I asked. It was one of the many ways they isolated me from the rest of the cast. When we'd start shooting again in the fall, they'd all have freckled cheeks and tanned skin with inside jokes that were never quite as funny upon retelling them to me.

"He never wanted to then. Don't force him to hang out with us now. Just because you two are ... dating for the public." Harrison grimaced as he spoke.

Emma elbowed Harrison, and he winced. "Christ. You're bony."

"Wesley, you should come. It'll be brilliant." Her brow furrowed. "Unless you really don't want to." She looked so hopeful, her wide blue eyes blinking up at me.

I glanced at Harrison. He was glaring at me, not even pretending to hide it. Emma stepped in front to block him. "There's no pressure, but I think it would be fun." Hope twinkled in her eyes, and it was over for me. I wasn't sure what she thought a weekend trip could accomplish, but she was so excited about it. How could I say no? I couldn't.

"I could get us all up there on the family jet? If you're sure," I offered.

"Oh, you don't have to do that," Emma said.

"I'm sure my father wouldn't mind," I said, smiling at Harrison. Rex would be absolutely bothered by it, and I couldn't wait.

"Well, if you insist," she said. He fixed his features before Emma turned back to look at her best friend. "Yay!" She clapped. "This will be lovely."

"The more the merrier. Sedar did say to invite all 'the kids,' so I'm assuming that means us," Harrison said. A shadow passed over his features. "It occurs to me that we're about the age our parents were when we first started filming. But we are the adult generation now."

The three of us flinched. To think our own families had been formed by this age and had children old enough to be palling around.

Emma nodded slowly, looking a little ill.

"Thought I'd have a bunch of littles by now myself." Harrison laughed but with no humor. There was a sadness behind the sentiment that I couldn't place. It made me feel a bit of a bastard for pushing to come. He shook his head and smiled easily at Emma, seeming to return to himself. "Right. Well. I'll email him back and let him know we're all coming." Harrison smacked me roughly on the shoulder. "It'll be good to spend some time, man-to-man. Mano a mano."

It was not even a thinly veiled threat at this point.

"Welp. I better let you two get back to it," Harrison said. "And by it, I mean only things that friends would do."

Emma rolled her eyes as she walked him to the door. "Are you sure you're okay?"

Harrison did seem to be carrying more tension than usual. I didn't know the man, but he always seemed jovial to everyone. Else.

"Yeah. Just quitting smoking. Your nagging finally got to me," he said.

Emma and I shared a look, and I turned away before she could catch my smile.

"Oh. Brilliant. Good job, Harrison," she said, overly bright.

Harrison softened and bent to kiss the top of her head. "Sorry, I'm being a right bastard." He looked up at me, and I busied myself straightening some books on the shelf.

"This trip will be great. You'll see. We can all be together again," he said with childlike hopefulness. I never took Harrison for the sentimental type. I always thought he enjoyed his bachelor movie star lifestyle. It seemed we both had things to learn about each other.

"I'll call you later," he said.

Once he was gone, Emma turned to me. If I was worried she'd want to continue what we'd been doing, I was very wrong. Her mind had shifted gears.

"Something's going on with him," she said.

"Maybe it's work stress."

"Yeah. Maybe." She came back to herself. "He's right, though. This little getaway will be a good reset."

I sure hoped so.

At least it wouldn't just be the two of us. Every day we lived together, it was getting harder to stay away.

16

Emma

"Are we ready for this?" I asked, wiping my palms on a tissue in the back of the Town Car.

"I don't know that we can go back now," Wesley said. If he had any trepidation about this evening's performance, he wasn't letting it show. He was as collected as ever. I took a deep breath in and out. I wanted to pull out my e-cig and take a calming hit before we were unleashed on all the cameras, but my nerves were too close to the surface. If he made even one comment, I'd likely bite his head off.

I was trying to be better about that sort of thing. And not just because of the snogging.

"You look incredible tonight," he said.

"Thanks. You too," I added. Because I had manners. I glanced up at him with a perfunctory smile.

"I do. Thank you," he said with cheek as if to get a rise out of me.

"Modest as always."

The city lights flashed by in a blur out the dark window. Wesley grabbed my hand and lowered where I'd been about to bite at my thumb. My nerves were making me twitchy, but that wasn't his fault. It was more that my mind played a hundred different versions of what could go wrong, and I was made a fool in every one.

"At least you left that ugly old tote at home tonight," he said.

"It's not ugly," I said out of reflex before processing his words. I flicked him a look and found him grinning.

"I didn't think you'd still have it."

So he had noticed that I carried the bag he gave me the night we were together.

"Charlie calls it my Emotional Support Bag." I shrugged. "It holds all my stuff."

"Sure." I didn't care for how closely he was watching me. Had I given too much away? "We're pulling up," he added, ducking his head to look out.

Right on cue, the car began to slow, and the flashes of cameras and the sound of the crowds burst in.

"And you're prepared with what to say? We'll be hammered with questions," I asked.

He pointed at his head. "Got it."

My leg was jumping. I shouldn't be this nervous. I'd done a thousand charity events before—of course, I wasn't usually pretending to date a man who secretly made me hot and heavy and had kissed me to the brink of orgasm a few days earlier.

But those were *not* the thoughts to be having right now. He rested his hand on my leg and squeezed in an effort to comfort me. That did not have the effect that he thought it did.

"You're all jumpy, Ems. Nothing to worry about. If you want to leave all the talking to me, you can," he offered.

"Not bloody likely."

"I'm offended," he said with a grin.

Just what I needed; him telling the press that I'd been crushing on him for twenty years, and he finally gave in to my demands. This whole thing wasn't even making sense. Nobody would buy any of this rubbish.

Hand still resting on my exposed thigh, he said, "It's going to be fine." He cocked a charming smile at me, and I shuddered. His smile did things to me. When he was real about it, it unlocked the memories I'd wrapped up in chains.

Defenses up. Stand on guard. Ignore the thrumming pulse that demanded I lean in and kiss him.

We hadn't talked about the practice kissing cut painfully short by Harrison, but it was probably better that way.

"Ju-Just stick to the lines we discussed. Timing and friends and all that rubbish," I said.

"Wow, you really are such a romantic," he said dryly.

"Hmm." I chewed my lip as the car came to a full stop.

"Honestly." He grabbed my hands from where I'd been twisting them in my lap. "Nothing to worry about," he said. "We both look insanely hot and are literally professional actors. Slip into the role."

"Right," I said, gaze flicking to the cameras already going off like fireworks outside the window, like piranhas to fresh blood.

He squeezed my hands. "It's just me. We've known each other since we were kids," he said as if that was supposed to help. As if I had any idea who this man was now. He and I were strangers, and with every passing day, I felt like I understood less about him, and my feelings for him grew more complicated.

"You are Emma fucking Flynn. You run an empire saving the world one Scrooge McDuck billionaire at a time. You can handle some cheesy press questions."

This time, I took a deep breath in and out.

"You're right. This is just another night of schmoozing for donations. This is my wheelhouse."

He winked, looking handsome as ever.

The explosion of lights was harrowing as the door opened. Wesley was out first, extending a hand to help me out of the car.

The questions were already being lobbed, but we were to wait until we reached the first mark for our first scheduled interview. After that, we would stop and talk to a handful of interviewers. The rest we smiled and stood for, posing enigmatically as they clicked away. Wesley made a show of letting me step forward, twirling me in my gown, and grabbing me back to him. He was a bloody natural. I tossed my head back and laughed as he bowed to me.

Everyone wanted us together, throwing out questions about this as an official announcement of our relationship.

It was all a blur as we made our way down the red carpet toward the old hotel, hand in hand.

I checked back in when he took the lead on the questions, as I was unusually tongue-tied. He gripped our clasped hands and brought them to his lips, brushing my knuckles with another kiss.

"Emma and I have never had the timing down. But everything feels right now," he explained.

He looked down at me with such unbridled admiration that my knees nearly gave out.

Somebody, get this man his damn Oscar.

The interviewer gushed, but the blood pounded between my ears. He smiled at me and squeezed my hand in comfort. I smiled up at him, and the cameras clicked wildly all around.

"I'm lucky to have her," he said. "I ask myself every day how I ever lived without her." He looked at me while he spoke, and his sincerity was so genuine I began to question everything.

This was the plan. He was an actor. Yet my hammering heart obviously believed every word he spoke.

Back inside, I was able to let out a breath. The tough part

was over, and it all went off without a hitch. The charity gala was to benefit a hospital that the Coles supported in downtown LA. It specialized in programs to help those with addictions, as well as free healthcare for those unhoused citizens of the city. Honestly, I was shocked to learn about the Coles' association with this charity. They didn't exactly strike me as the type, but I supposed not everybody was totally evil.

The room was extravagant, as these events always were. Massive bouquets, endless amount of hardly touched food, live music, etc.

Once we were seated, Wesley leaned over and whispered into my ear. "Just so you know, Natasha is expected to be here. She was a big part of the committee that organized this with my mother."

I blinked at him, then smiled and said through my teeth, "Thank you for telling me this now."

He reared back at the ice in my tone. "Honestly, there's nothing to worry about. She and I—"

"I'm not worried about that," I snapped. "I'm worried about what the press here will say."

His mask slid in place. "Of course." He leaned back in his chair and looked around. "There isn't much to say. We're exes, and it's a big small town in this circle. Chances are, we will run into each other from time to time."

I let out a breath. "You're right. I'm sorry. We just have to act the part and get through this."

His jaw clenched with a hard swallow. "Yep. Another night to pretend."

We were sat at one of a dozen gorgeous tables overflowing with dazzling glass vases and rare flowers spiraling up to the ceiling. Occasionally, a passing guest would stop to say hello. The crowd was a mix of celebrities, billionaires, and other ne'er-do-wells looking to dress up and show off the fact that they're not completely driven by greed.

Christ, when had I gotten so jaded? I'd been to so many of these over the years and experienced the same disappointment over and over. There were so many who needed so little and so many who could change all these lives and not even notice the hit on their finances. The balance of fortune made me ill, and every day, I felt more drawn into this club. It was so easy to ignore the pain of millions when flying above it all in a private jet.

"Hey," Wesley said as he nudged my foot with his own. "What's going on in that little brain of yours?"

"Little?" I asked, offended.

He huffed. "You're more combative than normal. Aren't you supposed to pretend you like me?"

I turned in the chair to face him and grabbed his hand. "You're right." I tried to smile.

"Pathetic attempt." He lifted a thumb to brush against my cheek, eliciting a breath I hadn't known I'd been holding in.

"I'm being morose. I'll be better."

"Just be you."

I leaned forward and kissed his cheek. "Charmer."

His eyebrows shot up in surprise. "How can I get more of those?"

I laughed, and some of the tension eased from his shoulders. "I really didn't think Natasha would be an issue. I'm sorry I didn't—"

I shook my head. "No. It's really not that. It's all this. This whole thing ..."

These were his people. This was his life. He never knew any other way, so I shouldn't offend him by feeling so disgruntled.

"I know. It's such a sham. Most of these people will write a check and ease their conscience for another few months but never worry about the conditions that drive this gala to begin with."

My eyebrows shot up this time. "Yes. Exactly."

"It's a dog and pony show. I hate it. Sometimes I daydream about standing up and yelling about the hypocrisy of it all."

My jaw dropped. I had no idea he even ...

"But then wouldn't that be hypocritical when I am a literal product of it and the biggest benefactor of a broken system? I'm not exactly living off the grid in protest."

"I—"

"I can see you're beating yourself up. You know you can't solve all the world's problems, right? You do more than most. This isn't all on you, Ems. You are not at fault here."

I frowned at the gilded plate in front of me, the seventh course left untouched. The excess. The unnecessary extravagance.

"I just want to help." That's why I did all this. That's why I wore the title of Golden Girl, even though I hated it more every day. "I genuinely want to help people."

"I know. And that's one of the many things to love about you. That big, beautiful heart of yours. You've had it as long as I've known you."

I blinked up at him, mouth dry. His gaze moved over my face.

"Come on. Let's go dance," he said.

He stood and extended a hand, one arm tucked behind his back, looking rather dapper.

"You can dance?" I asked.

He scoffed, the extended hand coming to his chest in mock offense. "I'm a Cole. I'd better know how to dance."

Despite myself, I grinned. I took his hand and smiled. "Show me, Fred Astaire."

He pulled me into his arms, and I felt several gazes stray our way. My hand fell to his lapel.

"Is this CrunchyCouture?"

"It is," he said, smiling. "You like?"

"It's stunning."

"I have to keep up with you," he said.

I rolled my eyes. "I didn't know you were contracted to wear it."

"I'm not. But I like it." He shrugged so casually, but I couldn't help my smile.

It said something about me that his choosing to wear the clothing meant more than the compliments. It was almost as though he understood what mattered most to me.

As we headed to the dance floor, his mother and father found us.

I smiled and greeted them as one might their actual in-laws. *Smile for the camera, don't bare your teeth.*

"The flowers are lovely, Mrs. Cole. Did you help with the table displays?" I offered an olive branch.

She blinked rapidly. "I did, yes. Thank you."

Rex Cole stepped in front of his wife. "I trust you two are behaving."

"You know, I had thought about proffering me cap for coins. But now that you mention it, best not, Gov'na," I said in my most ludicrous cockney accent.

"Charming." He sniffed. "Some things never change."

Wesley moved to block me from his father and grab my hand. "Excuse me, but I owe my love a dance." He pulled me toward the floor, but not before I saw the grimace his father tried to hide. It was an almost brush-off from Wesley. I bit back my smile.

My love.

Christ, it would be too easy to live like this.

"I can't say I didn't enjoy that a little," he whispered in my ear while his hands settled around my waist as though we did this all the time.

"It just slipped out." I shrugged coyly.

"Please, just ... be careful with him," he said before lowering his head to brush his nose along my exposed neck. I glanced around for a camera, wondering about the action.

I shivered. "I can handle Rex Cole."

"I don't doubt that, but—" He broke off with a frown. "Just be careful." His genuine concern unnerved me.

"I will." I pressed my finger to his arched eyebrow. "You can take a break tonight," I spoke to his tensed brow. His features relaxed under my touch.

A live quartet played instrumental covers of pop songs, and it made for perfect waltzing and other partner-style dances. True to his word, Wesley swung me around the dance floor in a dazzling display of smooth grace and talent. My skills were negligible, but he swept me up and pushed me around so that onlookers wouldn't know the difference. One hand clasped my hand as the other rested on the exposed skin of my lower back. Had I chosen this low-back dress hoping for this exact scenario? I honestly couldn't say.

When the music slowed, instead of leaving the floor, he gripped my body up tight against his own, not bothered by the fact we were both damp with sweat. His cologne, confidence, and whatever other magic radiated out of him tricked my body into releasing all the previously held tension. He slowly spun me out with grace. I laughed, head back, enjoying the freedom of dancing with him. I wasn't pretending this time as I had for the cameras out front.

Nearby couples watched us with interest, but my attention was only on him. When he brought me back, he placed my wrists behind his head, and both hands moved to my waist. The hard planes of his body flexed and moved against me as we slowly rocked to the lilting romantic music. It sent flickers of desire shooting across my body, tightening my insides, making me fully aware of every place our bodies pressed against each other.

"Okay. Fine. You can dance," I admitted.

"I know," he said.

"Your modesty is unmatched."

"Modesty is pointless."

"Says the cis white man."

He guffawed but covered it quickly. "I've trained for years. I wouldn't expect you to be modest about your talents. I'd expect you to shout them from the rooftops."

"Women aren't really allowed to do that."

"Now who's letting the patriarchy win? If you won't, then I will." He brought me closer yet so that my head naturally rested against his shoulder. This was just so ... nice. My naive brain imagined this exact scene so many times over the years. His strong arms made me feel safe and protected. Was it all for the cameras?

The pressures of our roles in the outside world didn't exist in his embrace. All we had to be was Emma and Wesley. It was a potent daydream.

"You're doing it again," he said, nudging me slightly with his shoulder.

"Hmm?"

"Getting morose."

I narrowed my eyes. "I'm starting to worry that you can read minds."

"I can read you."

I lowered my head back to his shoulder with a sigh. "I wish you wouldn't."

"What's wrong, Emma?" he asked gently.

"Nothing. Hormones or something. Ennui." I laughed

without humor and squeezed him tighter. I would wrap my arms under his suit and burrow against him if I could. "I like this."

He stumbled slightly. "I have a confession," he said in an uneven voice.

"Tell me."

"I'm remembering the seventh season. The dance?"

I groaned and kept my face hidden.

I felt him chuckle. "What?"

"I *hated* that night."

"Why?" he asked, genuinely surprised.

"The director was awful. He was trying so hard to get Charlie and me to dance for that scene, but it was just terrible. We had no chemistry whatsoever. Awkward and forced." I shuddered, and he laughed.

"Wow. I remember that night so differently," he said.

I tilted my head back to look at him. He had a blurry-eyed smile as he recalled our past life. He cleared his throat. I was starting to recognize this as his stall tactic—almost a nervous tic. Maybe I didn't want to know.

He swallowed and looked directly into my eyes. "I remember thinking that you looked gorgeous."

I couldn't hide my shock. "What?"

"I was terrified," he said softly.

"Terrified? Of what?"

"You were always so stunning. But that night, the rest of the world finally seemed to notice. I knew that whatever peace you had was going to be taken. The world would wring you out like a washcloth."

I couldn't hide the hurt that washed over me. I had hoped he meant that he wanted to kiss me that night because I remember seeing him in his tuxedo and thinking the same thing. He was beautiful. He was refined and handsome, and I wanted him to be the one dancing with me and not Charlie, who couldn't tell my toes from the floor.

"A washcloth?" I repeated, lip curling.

"I knew that this industry would be as captivated as I was. They would use you up and wring you out until nothing was left." He tucked my hair back as I swallowed. "I wanted to protect you from this world. It can be so ugly."

"I don't know what to say." He was right. For my teenage years and on, the media was oppressive and incessant until I learned how to make Emma Flynn the Golden Girl and provide some distance. Knowing that he worried about me back then and saw coming what others couldn't gave me a flash of hope. This was the Wesley I knew.

Captivated.

"Thankfully, I didn't need to worry, did I?" His thumb brushed over my cheek as he looked down at me with reverence I didn't know I deserved. "You managed all on your own. Better than anybody could have ever imagined. You're an absolute wonder, Emma Flynn. The whole world sees what a wonder you are."

I swallowed with difficulty. Nobody had ever been so genuinely kind.

But then the doubt crept in. If he thought that, *thinks* that, then why had he been so cruel for so long? Why had he acted as though he couldn't get enough of me when it was just us two and then pushed me away the second somebody was looking? It made me so unsure and insecure for so long. Everyone around me used me as my fame grew. Charlie and Harrison were the only people I could fully trust outside my family.

"I'm sorry I never told you that before." He paused to lift my chin and look deep into my eyes. "I should have told you a thousand times. I didn't want to be another person in your life objectifying you. The whole world was coming at you, and I felt so ... I didn't think there was a place for me."

I couldn't process this. I wasn't sure what this meant or how it fit with the picture I had painted in my head. We stood in the middle of the dance floor, long gowns swirling past us as we stayed stock-still.

"I always thought—"

I wanted to tell him that there was always a place for him. There would always be a place for him, and *that* was a problem. No matter how many times I tried to evict him from my heart, he was always there. He'd made a home so deep in the cracks and crevices of my young and forming heart that as I grew older and hardened, he was like tree roots through concrete. He had formed with the muscles, so to cut him out would be to take away the flesh of my own body.

A few passing couples looked us up and down. We must have painted the perfect picture. Once again, he knew how to look at me to make me feel like I was flying. I was sure that my face betrayed everything I felt.

"Don't say anything. I just needed to tell you," he said. "There were so many memories I wish I could rewrite."

I needed to tell him. I couldn't go on pretending I was fine. I would never be fine again.

"I—"

"Wesley?" a sweet high voice said at his side.

I blinked back into consciousness, seeing Natasha, his gorgeous and elegant ex-wife. She wore an emerald-blue empire waist gown that made her long blond hair look smooth and silky. She smiled tentatively at me.

"Natasha," Wesley said. His softened features hardened into his neutral mask.

"I'm so sorry to interrupt. I have to leave soon, but I was hoping we could talk for a minute? Hello, Emma. Nice to see you again." She seemed genuine, but I couldn't understand what was happening. The reality of where we were slammed down, cracking the shell around us.

I stepped back in shock, unable to think of what else I could do.

There was nothing I *could* do.

I smiled and turned away. Let them discuss whatever they needed. They had been married. I was ... a publicity stunt.

17

Wesley

"Are you okay, Wes?" Natasha asked, chewing her bottom lip.

I swallowed, nodding numbly.

"I know it's all fast." Her voice shook. She was terrified to tell her news, and suddenly, I remembered that this information wasn't about me at all. I still cared for this woman in front of me, glowing and beautiful.

"It's wonderful." I shook my selfish thoughts away and reached for her hands. "Truly, Nat. This is wonderful." I stepped back, still holding her hands, and looked her up and down. "Are you happy?"

Her face broke, and the tears she'd been holding back came all in a rush. She nodded and sniffled, reaching between her ample cleavage to pull out a tissue. "I'm so happy. It's almost scary. I didn't think it was possible." She dabbed carefully at her pristine makeup so her mascara wouldn't run.

A tightening in my chest must have shifted my features.

"I'm sorry. I didn't mean—"

"I understand. I know what it was like for us," I said.

She nodded with a watery smile. "I'm still so thankful for our time together."

"If nothing other than to know what real love feels like," I said ruefully.

She tsked. "No. That's not true. We were some of the lucky ones. We loved each other. In our own way."

"In our own way," I agreed.

"Wesley. You look at me," she said sternly.

"Uh-oh, you've already got the mom tone nailed."

She sniffled. "That's right. You listen carefully. You are a wonderful man. You have come out of a terrible situation with more ethics and kindness than most people I know. You *are* a good person. Do not let that family take that away from you."

I couldn't stand the compliments. I couldn't believe the words. I was my father's son. I had hurt Emma so much already. When I extended the smallest bit of kindness, the shock and disbelief on her face told me everything about her expectations of me. And I had only shared the tip of the iceberg of my feelings for her.

"I'm so glad you and Emma are finally giving it a go," she added.

I flicked a gaze over her face. I hadn't expected her to buy my new relationship with Emma, not after our marriage.

"I know," she said. "Don't look so surprised. It's okay. You have loved her for so long. I'm glad you're letting yourself have this bit of happiness."

My gaze snapped to hers. "No. Nat. I never."

"I know. You really are a good man. I know the rumors of you two were never true. But I also know you better than most. The way you look at her. The scene I walked up to." She fanned at her rosy cheeks. "There's no doubt in my mind now. I always wondered. You can't fake some of those looks." When I couldn't speak, she added, "It's truly okay. We both get it now. We know the real thing."

"Real thing?"

"Real love. I see the same glow coming from you that I feel. Promise me you'll hold on to that? Promise me you won't let this cold industry harden you."

"Okay, Nat. I promise," I said and wished it could be true.

After I gave Natasha a final hug, I made my way around the banquet hall, half numb.

Had I been so obvious all those years? I thought I was so good at pushing down all those wants and desires. If Natasha knew, then who else could see it?

I found Emma on a small terrace, hidden by large potted plants that I had missed the first two times I'd circled the hall. She leaned on an intricate concrete balustrade, balancing on her elbows, looking out at the lights of LA. We were farther up the mountains, and from up here, the city was a hazy blur. The back of her shimmering emerald-green dress was cut low, showing her slender curves and lean strength. Also, her ass looked incredible.

The rush of emotion and desire that hit me upon finding her, especially so soon after talking to my ex-wife, confirmed any lingering denials. There would never be anybody else for me. I spent my entire adult life trying to tell myself everything I felt was the love of a young boy, but there was no doubt now.

I loved Emma as a fully formed adult, and I always would.

"You're hiding," I said, closing the French doors behind me, hoping for a few minutes of privacy.

She stood and turned toward me, tucking away her CBD pen in her clutch. Her features were unreadable but not guarded exactly. More wary, hesitant.

"Not hiding. Exactly." She tucked her hair behind her ear and looked up at me. "Just breathing."

"Gotcha." I came to join her, leaning against the short concrete wall, side by side, sliding my arm around her waist. She tensed slightly before melting into me.

"Is someone watching?" she whispered.

"Sure," I lied.

I'd install hidden cameras everywhere if it meant she'd let me touch her like this every moment we were together. Her eyes narrowed, and she looked up at me.

"Everything okay?" she asked.

"Of course," I said casually. "How are you?"

She pulled her hair over her shoulder before pushing it right back into the position it was in before. I didn't release her from the prison of my arms. "Good."

We were silent, and I bit back a smile.

Every second I didn't share about my talk with Natasha, the more her curiosity grew.

"And Natasha? Is she okay?" she asked.

"Ah. You managed one whole minute."

She huffed and turned away, but I held on to her tighter. "Never mind. I was just being polite." She tried to put space between us, but I kept her locked in. I ran my lips up and down the column of her elegant neck and inhaled deeply.

She gasped softly but stopped struggling.

"You make it too easy, Ems," I said.

She kept her mouth shut, but I tucked her under my chin and held her close, slowly rubbing her arms up and down. No plan in mind, just touching. Something changed in me. I wouldn't be wasting any of the time we had together. Natasha may think higher of me, but that didn't change the reality of the expiration date in this scenario. Unless I could somehow ... no. I wouldn't let myself dream too big.

I would luxuriate in every moment I could, for the here and now.

"Natasha is having a baby," I said bluntly.

She reared back to look up at me, almost smacking her head into my nose. I flinched back just in time. "Oh my God." She shifted and struggled. "Would you let me look at you?" I loosened my hold so she could turn in my arms. Her gaze moved over my features. I knew I had a soft smile on my face, happy to be here. Happy for my ex. Buzzing on the high of Emma's scent and the heat of her body.

"Are you messing with me?" she asked, taking my smile the wrong way.

"No." I laughed.

Her hands covered her mouth, and the color drained from her cheeks. I tugged her hands back down and held them in my hands. She frowned down at us entangled. "How far?"

"Five months." I rubbed my lips over her knuckles. I didn't know why I loved doing that so much. I bet her shoulder would be smoother. I tested the theory.

"W-Would you stop that?" She smacked futilely at me.

"I can't. Someone may be watching." I kissed up her neck.

"Wesley. This isn't funny." She wrapped her arms around her middle. "W-What are you going to do about Natasha?" she asked.

"Be happy for her, I guess. She was always on the fence before about having kids. Said there was no rush. I guess there was some rush." I tried to pull her back into my arms, but she put her hands on my chest to stop me.

I pouted.

"This is serious. This is ... What about—you don't want to be a part of the baby's life?" Her hand went to her chest, her eyes wide. "Does she want to get back together?"

I stilled.

I suddenly understood this line of questioning from a

different angle. "What? God, no. No. It's not *my* baby. Is that what you thought?"

She sagged back, arms dropping away. "Of course, that's what I thought!" She lowered her voice when she realized how it echoed on the marble around us. "She was your wife."

I ran a hand over my face. "Fuck no, the baby isn't mine. Literally. There was no fu—relations between us for some time. Over a year or more and before that ..." I shook my head, cutting myself off.

She smacked my arm. "Ow."

"You did that on purpose," she said.

"I did not. It wouldn't even occur to me that you would think that. Or that you would care so much."

She crossed her arms again with a frown. "Obviously, I care. It's a *baby*."

"I know. It's hard to wrap my mind around." But honestly, I wasn't thinking about it much. I was thinking about how I could get her to practice kissing me again.

"Are you okay? Really?" she asked.

"I think so. I don't feel as much as you might think. Maybe I should? I feel happy for her. Why are you all the way over there?"

"You're in a mood." She shook her head and came closer. "I'm sure your feelings are complicated."

"She was letting me know because she won't be able to hide it much longer."

I saw the moment she did the math in her head. "And that means this all happened while you were still married."

My jaw clenched. "Exactly. That part doesn't feel great, but I can't say I'm surprised. I knew they were together. We were waiting to announce the divorce until everything was finalized."

She blew out a breath. "I'm sure you need time to process."

She tried to get away, but I growled and lifted her leg up on my hip to get easier access to her ass.

"She's happy and loves him," I said, pressing my mouth against the pulse at her collarbone.

"That's good." Her head tilted to the side. "I-I suppose."

I didn't say anything. Was it good? I only cared about why Emma wasn't kissing me. I had an idea. "My pride has taken a ding. I admit."

"Has it?" Emma frowned, looking at me closely. "You seem fine."

"I may need to make her jealous. Or you know, for the cameras or whatever."

She threw her head back. "You're ridiculous. I don't know what's gotten into you."

"I'm heartbroken. Heal me. Fix me." I grasped her ass and rubbed against her.

"Oh. Wow. We'll have to be extra convincing tonight." Her hand went to the back of my head to run through my hair. I closed my eyes and shuddered.

I wanted more. *Give me more.*

"We're in public." She laughed again but pulled my head more firmly against her neck.

"Didn't know I said that out loud," I mumbled against her skin.

"Gosh, you seem very happy."

"I'm very happy." I kissed up her arms.

"It's worrying."

I laughed harder. "Sorry to terrify you with my good vibes."

"I don't know if I can keep up."

"I bet you can. Chicken."

She tugged harder, and our mouths crashed. We kissed deeply.

She broke away suddenly.

"But wait." She pulled back to look at me. "You were so upset the night at the club. I thought maybe you still had feelings for Natasha," she said hesitantly.

I let out a breath, putting some space between us. But not too much. Probably best not to totally ravage her on a balcony anyway.

"Ah, that. I was a mess that night, but mostly because I found out that my entire marriage had been a sham."

"What do you mean?" she asked.

"Just that. I found out that my parents had arranged our marriage from the beginning. Before we were born actually." I hadn't admitted this to anybody else. This was the thing that pushed me over the edge. It convinced me I needed out of the Cole family. Natasha and I were essentially blackmailed into marrying each other. "Our families were business associates. Friends would be a strong word. They knew our marriage would be great for publicity. They were right, but they didn't account for one of us falling in love with someone else."

I held her gaze as I spoke, wondering if I had given too much away.

"I knew they were controlling, but I never would have thought they'd go that far," she said, shaking her head. "I don't understand. You met on set, I thought?"

"Yes. It was all arranged. We were pushed toward each other. Everything we thought had been organic was in fact part of their plan. It was essentially an arranged marriage. I think we both hoped that what was there was enough. And it was for a while. It was working. But then she fell in love and realized that the real thing pales in comparison. That night, I realized I never had any control. I never would get control."

"I can't understand your family."

"There's not much to understand. Ask yourself why enough

times, and it always goes back to money and power. That's all they care about."

"But that's not all you care about," she said softly.

I held her face, so close to telling her everything. So close. "No. That's not at all what I care about."

Her eyes fluttered close, and I brought my mouth to hers. Slower this time, deeper, pulling strength and pouring back all my love into her.

I felt a fever grip me. I needed more, crowds be damned. I kissed her with intent. My hands roamed chaotically over every inch of her.

"Wesley," she moaned my name as I squeezed her breast over the silk of her dress.

I pulled at her nipple, loving how it responded to me.

"God, I want you," I said, slightly delirious with all the emotions of the evening.

"We've made our appearance. Nothing is keeping us here." Her hand was creeping under my shirt, tugging it from the hem of my pants.

"Let's go."

"Ahem." My father's voice broke through the air.

I closed my eyes and dropped my forehead as Emma straightened and pulled away.

"Save it for the cameras, kids."

Emma gave him her back as she situated her dress.

"They're about to do speeches." He turned on his heel and left.

"The man has timing, I'll give him that," she said.

"I'm going to buy an island full of locked doors and no other people," I mumbled. "I've never lost an erection so fast," I said, and she snickered.

"Maybe we should be embarrassed?"

"Nah. Let's put on a hell of a show instead," I said, tucking my shirt back in.

"He's probably not happy about that."

"He wouldn't know what it was to be happy." I proffered my arm. "Come on, let's give them a hell of a show."

"I think we already did," she said, double-checking her dress. "Was my boob out?"

"Not as much as I would have liked."

She laughed, and we entered the ballroom arm in arm. I wished it could be like this forever. I couldn't help but find my father's interruption an ominous warning of what was to come.

I looked at the beautiful woman in my arms and decided my worries could wait a little longer.

18

PODCAST NOSY NELLY CELEBRITY NEWS

Season 4, Episode 22 *Fool me Once, Shame on Emsley* transcript excerpt

Co-hosts: Gabi Ortega and Liz Kane

[excerpt starts]

GABI: It would appear that Emsley is official.

Pause.

GABI: Okay, okay, I can feel the sanctimony wafting off you.

GABI: Just say it.

Gabi sighs.

GABI: You were right.

LIZ: I WAS RIGHT!

GABI: You will never let me live this down, will you?

LIZ: Never. Is it too soon to make wedding predictions?

GABI: Yes. I'm still not convinced this isn't an elaborate ruse.

LIZ: Boo. Always the contrarian.

GABI: I prefer unsentimental. Practical. Scientific.

LIZ: LAME.

GABI: Somebody has to be. Practical, that is. Call me a party pooper, but until they are walking down the aisle and maybe even then. Look at him and Natasha? They seemed so secure.

LIZ: Speaking of! Am I crazy, or was that lady rocking a baby bump?

GABI: It was the cut of the dress—

LIZ: That women specifically wear to hide a baby bump.

GABI: Well, if she is showing, then she's pretty far along.

LIZ: Poor Wesley.

GABI: Poor Wesley? You don't think he's a proud papa-to-be?

LIZ: Nah. He and Natasha haven't been spotted together in months. She's been with her director beau more than him this last year.

GABI: I see your point. Plus, in the gala pictures, Wesley and Natasha seemed to be glowing with their prospective partners.

LIZ: So you agree? Wesley was looking at Emma Flynn like she hung the moon!

GABI: He definitely wasn't looking at his ex-wife that way.

Long pause.

GABI: Liz? What is that face for?

LIZ: No face.

GABI: You have a "I know something you don't know face."

LIZ: Well. Since you asked. This morning on ChicChat, an anonymous source—

GABI: Let me guess, "Close to the couple?"

LIZ: Yes. But don't ruin this for me. This source said that Wesley and Emma were caught in flagrante at the charity ball.

GABI: This anonymous source sure happens to be at all the right places at all the right times for being too chicken to give their name. Only so many people can be that "close to the couple."

LIZ: My point is, if they are faking it, then why were they

gettin' jiggy with it secretly? You'd think they'd make a show of it.

GABI: You did *not* just say gettin' jiggy. Is it 1997? You're aging us.

LIZ: I'm ignoring you. All of this right after the live video they did, where they were basically eye-banging each other the whole time. This cannot be faked!

GABI: Yeah, actors are notoriously terrible fakers.

LIZ: La la la. I'm not listening to you. I am manifesting their love story. Did you see the way he looked at her on the red carpet too? Did you hear how he talked about her? I was swooning!

GABI: I fully admit, they looked smitten and very into each other. That being said, if this turns out to be a hoax, I don't think I'll forgive either one of them.

LIZ: I agree with you there, and you are not alone. If they continue to play with our hearts like this only to find out it was all pretend? The world would never forgive them.

[excerpt ends]

19

———————

Emma

"OH LOOK, FREE COOKIES!" KATE MADE GRABBY FINGERS AT A plate of biscuits a handsome flight attendant offered as he made his way down the short cabin of the private jet.

I sighed. "Sure. Cookies make up for the fact that private jets are one of the worst things for the environment."

"Yay, Captain Buzzkill is here," Charlie said and tossed a cookie at my head.

Wesley snagged it out of the air before it made contact and popped it into his mouth.

"I'm surprised you got Emma to go along with it," Harrison said to Wesley, referring to the use of his family's private plane.

"Well, it was just sitting there," he said after swallowing.

He shrugged and put his arm around me. I flicked a look at him and then back at the others. Harrison blinked very pointedly, and Charlie seemed not to notice. I gave Harrison a look that expressed, "Let me have this," and I relaxed against Wesley. A girl could get used to all this casual flirtation.

"I'm not a ridiculous person, you know. I just know that if

everybody in the public eye were to be aware of their global footprint, it could really make a difference. And the fact of the matter is—"

"Ugh," came a collective chorus from everyone except Kate, who was my only real friend. Wesley pulled me closer to him and kissed me on the mouth. Just like that. In front of God and everyone. I was thrilled on the inside, even though a tiny voice warned me not to get used to it.

I chose to ignore that voice.

"I think it's great how much you care." He ran his thumb over my cheek. "But I like to spoil you too."

"To be fair, it's no different from when you took me out on the town. You just want to share some of the perks of your lifestyle," said Kate, formerly known as my only friend.

I crossed my arms but stopped my speech. It was the holidays, after all, and teasing aside, I was quite pleased to be spending the next few days with my best friends at the home of George Sedar. If that meant I had to put my ethics on the shelf, so be it. The shelf was overcrowded these days.

At least the flight was short up to Northern California, where Sedar's house sat perched on top of the Mayacamas in a small mountain town tucked away from the realities of Hollywood. As children, it was the perfect getaway, and our parents loved the free stay in wine country.

The five of us would stay with George for the next few days, and then we would be off to England, sans Wesley, for the holiday to be with our families. I briefly wondered what Wesley's holiday would look like. Had he ever experienced a proper British Christmas?

"I can't believe I'm really going to meet G.S. Sedar," Kate said. "He's been my idol for so long."

"You can call him George. He's never been one for pretense, even though technically he's *Sir* George Sedar," Harrison said.

"He was born and lived most of his life in London before moving out here when the show started filming. After that, he never left."

"He'll think you're brilliant," Charlie said as he kissed Kate's temple.

I smiled to myself at Kate's look of awe. She and Charlie were so happy together, it was hard to look at them directly. It felt too personal, or maybe I was a little jealous.

"I know people think the show is the best part of *Terraformative*, and it was amazing, of course," she added quickly, and I grinned at her. "But those books. They have literally always been a part of my life. I remember waiting in costume for the midnight release at bookstores with a hundred other fans ..." She trailed off, and a blush burned her cheeks. "I've said too much."

"Don't forget we were fans before we were actors too," I said to make her feel better. "I literally dreamed about being Lucy Lennon, and then there was a casting call. Honestly, sometimes it still doesn't even feel real. I was a regular kid one day and then the next ..." It was my turn to trail off. "Anyway. I'm glad he continued writing them."

"There are over thirty of them now, aren't there?" Charlie asked.

Kate nodded eagerly. "And the last two. Gah!" She rolled her eyes dramatically to the back of her head. "He really seems to be leaning into the romance side more, and I have no complaints there."

"It's impressive that he has managed to keep it fresh this long," Harrison agreed.

"Right? I can't imagine. But as the Intrepid Trio grew up, the stories only got better and richer in character growth." She shook her head and pressed her fingers to her cheeks. "Okay. I'm stopping now. My fangirl is showing a little too much."

"I like it," Charlie beamed at her. Then he turned back to Harrison. "Oh yeah, Harrison, how was your visit out here last month?" Charlie asked.

I turned to Harrison, mouth agape. He hadn't told me about that.

Harrison looked out the window. "It was fine."

"You were just checking up on him, yeah?"

Harrison nodded, his leg bouncing in the chair.

"Was everything okay?" I asked.

Harrison scratched at his hair. "You know what we should do while we're here?" he said brightly, pretending not to hear the question. "Play flashlight tag! Remember how many nights we'd be up playing that? Or sardines!"

"Sardines? I haven't played that since I was a kid. Might be a little harder to get us all tucked away," Kate said to Harrison.

I shared a quick look with Charlie as Harrison and Kate chatted. We mentally agreed that that was a weird misdirection and change in subject. Whatever was going on with George, it was clear Harrison wasn't ready to talk about it. I would have to investigate more in private. That might explain why he'd been acting so weird lately. More tense than normal.

"Those summers sound magical," Kate said.

"They really were," I said.

"We would swim all day. Eat rubbish until our bellies ached. Watch movies in his home theater." Harrison sighed. "Remember the time Charlie ate so many of those sour gummy worm things he made sick in the pool?"

"Oh, God," I covered my mouth as a wave of queasiness passed over me. "I'd quite repressed that, thank you very much."

"Cheers, mate. Thanks for bringing that up." Charlie turned to Kate. "Don't listen to these buffoons. I've always been the epitome of class and culture."

Kate snorted. "I'm sure." Turning back to us, she said, "Tell me more. I want every embarrassing moment." Her brown eyes widened in excitement.

"You wound me," Charlie said.

Charlie, Harrison, and I went back and forth, sharing more of our summertime memories as Kate listened on, laughing and asking for more details.

Wesley kept mostly quiet with the occasional soft chuckle. I wondered if he felt overwhelmed by our strong personalities. When the Intrepid Trio reunited, we could be a bit much.

"Are you okay?" I whispered in his ear.

"Yeah. Just listening. I like hearing about the memories." He moved his gaze out the window. "Makes me wish I'd been there."

"How come you never came?" Charlie asked.

"It was a bit beneath him, no?" Harrison said, sounding casual, but the cutting bite of his words stung nonetheless. "A posh sort like him wouldn't slum it with the country bumpkins from across the pond."

"Sounds like you've been talking to my parents," he said softly.

"Harrison," I chided.

"Timing never worked out, I guess," Wesley said, almost detached as he continued to look out the window.

"Not in eight summers?" Kate asked gently.

Tension gathered in his shoulders and around his eyes.

"My parents always booked me to shoot movies as much as possible during the summer weeks. That was before the golden age of television, and truth be told, they looked down on TF. They wanted me to be a staple in Hollywood by the time the show ended. They never expected it to go on so long."

"You never got a break? You worked year-round even when you were in school?" I asked.

"As much as was legally allowed. Yeah. And even that was a little blurry. Education was never the emphasis when your future was already planned out." He shifted uncomfortably in the chair with everybody's eyes on him.

"That's a bit much for a kid," Charlie said, and I couldn't help but agree. I assumed he was off holidaying somewhere exotic.

"Yeah, well ... the Coles have big expectations." He cleared his throat. "I did ask. The first few times you invited me." He looked among the three of us. "Don't get me wrong, I really wanted to go. I was pretty jealous after summer break when you all had your stories and inside jokes."

Guilt ate at me. I had always assumed the same as Harrison, that he thought the trip was beneath him.

"But, uh, truth be told, my parents weren't big on me mingling with the rest of the cast." He looked around the small private jet as though waiting for someone to save him.

"Why?" I asked softly.

"They never really saw TF for the phenomenon that it is. Even now." He shook his head as though not understanding. "I still have fans coming up to me for Max Malachi, more than any other role, I've ever played. It's the thing I'll always be most known for."

"Does it bother you?" Charlie asked seriously.

"Not at all." He smirked. "I kind of like that I'll always be known for the role my parents hated the most. Feels like I'm sticking it to them in a way."

"Why didn't they want you spending time with us, though? We weren't *that* bad," Harrison asked.

"They didn't want me to form attachments. I was never allowed to spend time with anybody from the cast." He flicked a glance at me, still keeping all our rendezvous secret. "They said they worried it would be harder for me to leave when the show ended. But then it kept going and going, and they grew angry about it. They pulled me away as soon as they could."

But really, it was a tactic to maintain control over him. That was left unsaid but understood. The plane was silent outside the constant roar of the engines.

Harrison frowned at the floor. Kate and Charlie snuggled closer. I grabbed his hands and held them.

"That's terrible," Kate said sadly.

"Those were some of my best memories. The cast and crew and the bonding between shooting," Charlie said.

Wesley cleared his throat. "Yeah. I still ..." He hesitated. "I'm still so thankful for the show. I'm still most proud of that show and its impact on the world. More so than anything else I've ever done." He smiled tightly. "Probably sounds insincere, but it's true."

Harrison had a serious deep furrow between his brows. His usual gregarious nature had melted away. "Not at all, mate. We all get it."

Charlie nodded somberly. Kate smiled a watery smile.

"Shit. I brought down the mood," Wesley tried to laugh it off. "How very Max Malachi of me."

"Nah. You didn't ruin anything. We're just reminiscing. Sentimentality goes hand in hand with age," Harrison offered.

"Cheers to the show that brought us all together. It never ceases to amaze me how much *Terraformative* has bonded so many people," Kate said, lifting her glass of sparkling cider.

"Here, here. Best thing that ever happened to me. And it brought me Kate," Charlie said with gleaming eyes.

"It brought us all together," I said, sneaking a look at Wesley.

"And cheers to the Coles, who let us borrow their private jet," Harrison said with a wink in my direction.

Perhaps my best friend was softening to Wesley after all.

"Unbeknownst to them. Which makes it all the sweeter," Wesley said.

We all laughed and clinked glasses.

Wesley

THE REST OF THE FLIGHT WAS OVER IN A BLINK. I SILENTLY ruminated on my oversharing. Emma kept sending me soft, pitiful smiles, and I hated it. I wasn't sure if their pity was any better than them all thinking I was a huge snob.

It felt better to get it off my chest, at least. I still needed to tell Emma the rest of it. The truth of just how controlling they were and everything I did. I needed to come clean before our time together was up. I wouldn't waste any more time.

"It's exactly how I remember it." Emma looked around, head twisting everywhere and eyes wide as we stepped into the house. Harrison had let us in with his copy of the key.

The outside looked like a typical Spanish-style California mansion, but from the large foyer, the grand house managed to feel like a cozy cottage with the vastness of an English estate. Off to the left was an overstuffed sitting room with shelves of books stacked high and a cozy brick fireplace decorated with garland and stockings. The couches looked well-worn and comfortable, with mismatched patterns and deflated cushions, multicolored knitted throws, and quilted blankets decorating each one. Large taper candles dotted most surfaces, circled with rings of ivy. The air smelled of cooking and cinnamon. And at least two squat, fat, real trees sat with strings of berries and popcorn. There wasn't a single cleared space or empty corner. If I were to imagine what a home felt like, it was something like this and not the sterile "luxury" I'd grown up with.

"It's not changed a bit," Emma said in awe.

"Bloody hell! He's even still got that same old chair." Charlie pointed at a recliner in the corner nearest to the fire, heavily indented, next to a side table stacked with several books and as many pairs of glasses and teacups. "I broke that once, messing about on it. The back popped right off," Charlie explained to Kate.

Emma and Harrison laughed. "We were terrified he was never going to invite us over again," Emma said.

"I think it's being held together by tape and hope." Harrison craned his neck to look.

"What do you think?" Emma whispered to me. I tucked her against my side and smiled down at her.

"It's fantastic. I don't think I could have imagined it better," I said honestly.

She grinned widely at me. "I'm so glad you're here."

The way she looked up at me when she said it caused any remaining doubt to vanish. There was no hesitation. I would tell her everything this weekend. It was time to put our history to rest. I would never let her question herself again when it came to my past actions.

"Me too," I said tightly, suddenly wishing we'd be shown to our rooms so I could talk to her. We had discussed separate rooms, but hopefully, we'd be close.

"Hello? George?" Harrison called out as we placed our weekend bags down.

Just then, a little princess came bolting down the stairs and slid to a stop in front of us.

"Welcome to my castle. I am princess fairy queen Colette." She bowed deeply in her bright pink tulle dress before us all. "I am six years old, and I have two wiggly teeth." She pulled her lip down. "Wanna thee?" she asked, tongue already prodding the loose tooth.

"Here, let me take it out for you," Harrison said, reaching for her.

She squealed and swatted him away. "I remember you!" the little girl said to Harrison. "You're the man who came last month. I beat you at Go Fish."

"You absolutely slaughtered me," he said, kneeling to return the hug she launched at his knees.

"You are very bad at maths," she said.

"I'm an actor. I just have to look pretty." Harrison winked.

Colette giggled, and then her whole face turned into a pout. "You didn't stay very long."

"Work called me away. I'll be here up until Christmas this time. Then off I pop to England."

All her dramatic features squished in thought. "I suppose that will have to do."

A moment later, an elderly man hobbled in on a cane. "I see you've met my granddaughter, Frankie."

She giggled. "*Great*-granddaughter, Papa George! Silly man. And you know my name is Colette!" Her sweet little voice was mostly American, but certain words were certainly inspired by George's strong English accent.

He frowned, leaning on his cane, and shook his head back into a smile. "Well, whoever you are, you're quite adorable."

I'd seen Sedar on the set once or twice back in the day, but he didn't come often. He was happy with the writers of the show and acted mostly in a consultant capacity. He'd looked old to me as a child, and the man before me looked even more aged and had to be in his nineties now. His fully white hair floated in wisps around his head like an aura, and the laugh lines tugged his features more acutely. Years of writing at a desk had taken their toll as his shoulders hunched severely over a cane. But his cloudy eyes were as lit as his open smile.

Harrison's passing comments flickered through my mind. Emma flicked a glance to Harrison after she took in the state of the man. She fixed her features before anybody could see the wobble of her chin.

"Adam, my boy. Handsome as ever." Harrison and George

exchanged a hearty hug and pats on the back. "It's been too long. You need to come more often."

Emma shot a look at Harrison, who kept his smile in place but shook his head once discreetly at her. Emma frowned, biting her lip.

"Papa George! That's Harrison, you know that." Colette lost it to another fit of giggles.

"Of course I do. I was just testing you all. Now, where's my granddaughter?" He looked up through his bifocals at all of us, hesitating on Kate for a moment.

"Mom is gone, remember? But she won't be back until next year. I told you that this morning," Colette explained with an exaggerated eye roll. "How many sleeps is that?" Before anybody could answer, she'd already switched subjects. "But Frankie said she'd be back before Christmas."

George frowned. "Quite right," the old man said.

He stopped before Kate and looked her up and down. "Pretty young lass. I don't remember you."

"This is my better half, George," Charlie said.

"George? Now I'm sure that that's my name," he said.

"Hi. I'm Kate," she said, her cheeks pulled wide with a smile.

Everybody laughed. But Emma was watching Harrison closely, her brow furrowed. Harrison had a smile locked in place but tension around his eyes.

"I'm a huge fan. Thank you so much for having me," Kate said, hugging him with eyes gleaming.

"I don't know how Charlie managed it, but you're always welcome." George straightened.

Emma stepped forward, taking the old man's hands in hers. "I've missed you," she said.

They gave cheek kisses, and she gestured to me. "This is my —this is Wesley Cole," she settled on. I couldn't blame her for not wanting to lie to the man who was like family, but a part of me winced at the pain it caused. If only to hear her say that I'm her *something* and mean it.

George turned toward me, and I extended my hand as Emma came back to my side.

"*You're* Wesley, eh?" He shook my hand with a large, genuine grin. "I would recognize Max Malachi anywhere. That hair and glare give you away."

"Glare? This is just my face." Instead of smiling, I made my fiercest glower, hoping and succeeding in another fit of giggles from Colette.

"You do have a bit of Resting Smolder Face," Emma said.

"I think he's very handsome," Colette said, the first time displaying a hint of shyness.

I bowed slightly at her. "Thank you, your highness."

She tucked herself behind George with a blush.

"He's all right." Harrison sniffed. Emma rolled her eyes and reached out to goose his side. He yelped, and that caused another peal of laughter from Colette.

"Well, glad to have you here, boy. It's about damn time," George said to me.

"Thank you, sir. I've been meaning to come out for the past twenty years or so. Give or take," I said sheepishly.

Emma chuckled at my side, and I slung a hand around her waist. After all, we were still in public, and I didn't have the strength of will not to touch her at all times now.

"Well, yes. Quite right. You know I called this. Many years ago." He took a hand off the cane just long enough to gesture back and forth between the two of us. "Took you bloody long enough."

Emma and I exchanged a look, neither sure what the protocol was.

"I was a bit of an idiot these past twenty years or so. Give or take," I repeated. There. Another truth.

Emma sighed, and I wasn't sure what that meant.

"You know, I pushed Max and Lucy. I wanted Max to have a more fulfilled arc," George said. His wispy brows furrowed in concentration as he looked over our shoulders and into the past. "I wanted you two to have a relationship the final year. So that Max wasn't such a one-dimensional bad guy. Yes. Yes. If I recall, the writers were strong-handed. I guess one of the show runners was quite adamant against it."

I stilled, jaw clenching. I'd bet my kidney that would be the Cole Foundation, one of the original producing investors. Despite never having approved of the show, they still had to have their control where they could.

"That sounds right," I said.

Emma looked up at me with that same look of pity she'd had when she met my family.

"Oh my gosh, the fandom would lose their minds to hear that," Kate said in awe.

"It's a shame." George's gaze came back in focus as he took Emma and me in. "You two have always had palpable chemistry."

"Emma is extraordinarily talented," I said.

"Alas, this old writer only had so much pull over the show's direction." He sighed and suddenly looked much older as he looked at all of us. "Ah, well. We are all here now."

"Cheers to that," Harrison said.

"I'm talented too. Can I sing them a song?" Colette asked.

"Oh, please do," Harrison said.

The little girl began to sing a song clearly made up on the spot, with several mentions of ducks over and over. To be fair, she actually did have a nice singing voice. This little one had child-star potential written all over her. God help her.

Before long, George cut her off. "Okay, love. You don't want to make the others too jealous."

"True. Frankie says less is more sometimes," Colette nodded regally.

"I've never found that to be true," Harrison said, and she grinned triumphantly.

"All right, all right. Enough chitchat in the entry. Let's get this party started. I have a roast beast waiting in the oven."

"Papa George," Colette said with all the exasperation a six-year-old could muster. "It's a turkey."

"Let the wild rumpus begin!" shouted George, and we all followed them farther into the house.

I smiled over at Emma, my heart fuller than ever. It was then the anxiety began to seep around the edges. If all good things came to an end, what did it mean for things that felt like a dream come true?

20

───────

Wesley

THE REST OF THAT FIRST DAY PASSED IN A BLUR. IT WAS GOING TOO fast. It was already the holidays, which meant award season was right around the corner. My time with Emma was coming to an end. I debated how to get her alone and tell her everything.

After dinner, I was so anxious I could hardly focus on the book in my hand. We sat in the living room area next to the fireplace. Emma read, her head on my lap as Kate, Charlie, and Colette played a vigorous game of Chutes and Ladders. George walked into the room wearing an excited grin and a sparkle in his eyes.

"You'll never believe what I've dug up," George exclaimed.

Harrison came up behind a moment later and dropped a heavy box on the table in front of the TV. "Who dug it up?" He wiped at his brow. "The man has an entire *Terraformative* museum up there. You really should organize all that."

George waved him away with a harrumph. "It's on the list."

"What list?" Harrison asked, standing akimbo.

"Never you mind. Now look what I have here!" George

pulled out a few cases of nondescript DVDs, black with handwritten notes on the covers. He set to work trying to figure out the DVD player for all of ten seconds before Harrison came up to manage the tech.

Emma sat up and set her book to the side. Charlie and Kate scooted in next to Emma.

"Scoot on, mate, and we can fit," Harrison said as he squeezed between Emma and me.

Emma flicked his ear, and I reached behind him to rest my hand on her shoulder.

He looked pointedly at the arm that rested around him.

"Cozy," I said.

He glared as the TV came to life.

Sedar made his way to his chair, and Colette jumped into his lap. "Oomph. Stop growing so fast."

She laughed. "I can't!"

On screen, dated footage flickered to life. It was eleven-year-old Emma Flynn, shifting in front of a camera with a plain white backdrop behind her. Her hair was frizzy and red, her teeth were a little too big for her mouth, and her already long limbs looked knobby under the jeans and T-shirt. The sight squeezed my chest. I remembered the day I met her so clearly, looking just like that.

"Anytime you're ready," a woman off-screen said.

A tiny Emma lifted her chin, and her whole face changed into Lucy Lennon. She took her job very seriously as she recited early lines from the pilot episode.

"Oh my God!" Emma moaned on the other side of Harrison.

The room filled with laughter.

"Is that you?" Colette asked, looking back and forth between the screen and Emma. "You're so old now."

Charlie and Harrison cackled even louder.

"Yes," Emma moaned. "Look at my hair."

"You are absolutely adorable," I said.

Harrison scoffed. "No points for lying, mate. That hair lives on in my nightmares."

"I hadn't learned the importance of conditioner yet. Let's wait and see how you two look," Emma said.

Sure enough, up next was Charlie Downing, reading his lines with deep, dimpled humor. He was loud and goofy, just as I remembered him as kids. His cheeks were rounded out with Freddy Finks's chubby childish looks.

"This is the greatest moment of my life," Kate said in awe, her eyes wide and sparkling as she stared at the screen.

Charlie sighed and brought Kate closer.

Harrison came on next, and I had to admit, even as a tween, the kid had charisma. No doubt for a second that he was made to play Adam Abbotts for *Terraformative*.

"There's our boy!" George clapped. "As soon as I saw his casting photo, I knew he was the one."

Harrison smiled at his idol with open admiration.

"I remember this so vividly," Harrison said. "It feels like yesterday. How was it over twenty years ago?"

Emma squeezed his hand, and Charlie grabbed hers. These three were so close for so long, I felt like an intruder for the first time this weekend. I had been so envious of their friendship as a child, and even now, I envied what I could only ever dream about. This place. These friends. It felt so far removed from my reality, I couldn't think about what waited for me back home without an ache threatening to drag down my good mood. I forced the thoughts away for Future Wesley to deal with.

The screen went wavy as George fast-forwarded to my audition.

I scowled on the screen, curling my lip as Max Malachi. I sneered my lines about what being a human meant, all too convincingly. This was how people saw me. How Emma saw me for years.

"Okay, that's good," the woman off-screen said.

Instantly, my face transformed into a wide grin.

My childhood version flicked a look to the side, where both my parents stood off-camera watching me. The smile on my face faded at whatever their reaction had been. I schooled my features as I listened to the casting director's feedback but remembered her words had fallen on deaf ears. I was reeling at my father's reaction, knowing I'd been about to get a lecture as soon as we were alone.

Emma reached across Harrison to squeeze my hand. So she'd seen it too. I cleared my throat. Even now, all these years later, the pain at their disappointment still managed to cut like a knife. Shouldn't I know better by now?

Harrison looked at me, jaw clenched, but didn't speak.

"This is incredible. I can't believe these have never been seen before," Kate said.

"I offered them for the reunion, but there wasn't enough time. I think they're saving them for something else. Squeezing every penny out of the fans," George said.

"I'd pay for it," Kate said.

"Adam, put in the next one. That one there," George said, pointing at another box on the table.

Harrison and Emma exchanged a quick look.

George frowned. "Did I say Adam? Ah, it's all these memories. Mixing things up in this old man's head." He chuckled and so did Emma and Harrison, worriedly but happy to laugh it off.

Harrison did as directed, and soon, the screen came to life with behind-the-scenes footage of us actors. It was a classroom set early on in filming, maybe the pilot episode.

"We are babies," Emma said. "Omg slaps! Christ, I hated that game."

I slapped at Emma's downturned hands on-screen as she tried to pull away in time.

"You're just saying that because you could never beat me," I teased.

Harrison and Charlie snorted and tried to cover it when the women at their sides smacked them.

"I'll take you any time, Cole," Emma said, leaning around Harrison to glare at me.

"Bring it on, Flynn," I said coolly.

"Ugh, could you two contain it to the bedroom? Oof." Harrison rubbed his ribs where Emma elbowed him.

Back on the TV, George's various set clips played on and on. Colette grew bored and went to play in her room. On-screen, the three best friends laughed between scenes, wrapped in robes far too big for their little frames.

"The sets were always so cold," Emma said.

"Until we were filming under the lights and then I couldn't ever cool off," Charlie said. He turned to Kate. "My cheeks would get so red."

"Remember the pit stains on your flight suit?" Harrison asked. "They always had an extra one on hand."

"Thanks, mate," Charlie said. "Don't believe anything he says."

"She wanted the insider info," Harrison said with a shrug.

"You're precious. This is amazing to see," Kate said before kissing Charlie's cheek.

"There're those red cheeks," Harrison said, and we all laughed when Charlie shoved Harrison's head.

On-screen, the camera zoomed in on Emma and me in the Communication Cube. The tiny cube was mostly a green screen for Emma's character, who was in charge of the tech stuff while Charlie and Harrison, or rather Freddy and Adam, went to visit the surface of planets. In the show, with after-effects added, it looked like a small room filled with flashing lights and buttons with sparkling space floating by outside wraparound windows. In real life, it was a green cube, hardly big enough for Emma and me both to fit in it.

"Oh Lord, the Cube of Solitude," Emma said. "All the hours spent in that sweatbox."

Emma and I played handheld gaming units on-screen, laying on our backs laughing as we elbowed each other, trying to mess the other person up.

Emotion tightened my throat as I watched us so young. I was so obviously happy just to be spending time with her.

"I've never seen this before," Emma said softly.

I was suddenly very annoyed that Harrison sat between us.

"We spent a lot of hours in there." I cleared my throat. "I'm really glad you got this," I said to George. "I would love to get a copy made."

George nodded. "It's on the list. Make all this digital."

"Seriously, what list?" Harrison asked.

George ignored him.

Emma chewed her lip, nodding, her eyes shining as she stared at the two of us on-screen. I wondered what thoughts swirled in her head and if they matched my own warring sentiment.

"I didn't realize you two hung out so much," Charlie said.

"Yeah, well, Adam and Freddy had a lot of trips to the surface that were 'too dangerous' for Lucy," Emma said sarcastically.

"I hated that they separated you three like that." George frowned as he spoke. "The Intrepid Trio were always meant to explore together."

"I grew to hate the Cube of Solitude," Emma said with a frown. "Wesley would visit me all the time to keep me company between scenes." Emma smiled at me.

Harrison cleared his throat. "I guess I didn't think about all the times you had to film in there." Harrison flicked a look at me. "Thanks for taking care of her when we were gone."

I clenched my jaw but nodded. "She didn't need taken care of. She just needed a friend." I shrugged.

"She was lucky to have you," Harrison said.

I flicked a look at Emma, whose mouth lifted with a smile.

"Remember the time Wesley lost his mind on the director?" Charlie said to Harrison.

Harrison frowned. "I don't think so?"

Emma sat forward and looked at me. I kept my gaze locked on the screen. God, I hated that day. That was one of our worst fights.

"What happened?" Harrison asked.

Emma sighed. "Wesley yelled at the director because of what I was wearing."

I snapped my head to her. "What? No. That's not at all what happened."

She looked at me, eyes narrowed. "That's exactly what happened."

"No, Emma," Charlie spoke up. "Wesley went mental because that bloody director was being a total wanker."

Her jaw dropped.

"He made you do that scene a thousand times, remember? You were on the verge of tears, and he made you do it over and over. Wearing that skimpy outfit." Charlie's face twisted as he spoke. "Christ, looking back, he was a total perv, wasn't he?"

"Yes," I said instantly.

Emma blinked. She looked at me. "I thought you got mad because of what I was wearing."

I ran a hand down my face. "No, Emma. I never got mad at you." How could she think that? I remembered getting so frustrated that she wasn't standing up for herself. That she was being objectified by this creepy old prick, and nobody was doing shit to stop it. I held her gaze. "I got mad at the director. And we were fifteen, and I went off on whoever was nearest. I'm-I'm sorry if you thought it was because of what you did. It was never you," I repeated.

Harrison watched this whole exchange with his mouth open. "Where the crap was I for all this?" he asked. Emma and Charlie shrugged.

I looked back to Emma, and she smiled softly. "Thank you for putting him in his place. That day really was awful."

"Yeah," I said. "My dad was not pleased." I wished I'd not said anything the instant the words were out.

"He said something to you?" Emma asked softly.

"He was friends with the director of that episode."

"Thank Christ, that prick never came back after that episode," Charlie said.

I nodded. I'd made sure of it. Even though my parents were livid with me. I refused to do the movie with him over the summer until they agreed he wasn't the right fit for the show.

"I was a Cole. Not some 'hot-headed brat.'" I cleared my throat. "Anyway. It's all in the past now. Let's keep watching." I turned back to the screen but felt the eyes of the Intrepid Trio on me.

Eventually, though, we all got back into watching George's behind-the-scenes footage.

The clips went on, and as they did, the children on-screen transformed into gangly pre-teens, then awkward regular teens, then rather good-looking young adults. Us in the room grew quiet as time went on. We all went from laughing at our younger selves to a heavy silence that sat on my chest, making it hard to take a full breath. The whole room felt filled with a tangible sort of sweet sadness.

I wasn't alone. Charlie had his face buried in a crying Kate's hair, and Harrison was leaning forward, elbows on his knees and his hand covering his mouth. His brows were pulled together, and I could tell he was trying just as hard as I was not to get too emotional. Watching our entire childhoods pass in a few minutes was harrowing.

Emma had given up and was curled, knees to her chest, sniffling silently as she dabbed her eyes with a tissue.

"It shouldn't feel this sad," she said eventually, letting out a slow breath. "Why do I feel like my heart is breaking?" she asked, and her voice cracked.

Harrison leaned back and put an arm around her shoulders. "It's watching our entire childhood pass by. It's bloody sad. Think of everything we didn't know. Think of what dreams we had."

I wished I was holding Emma now. Harrison flicked a look at me and stood. Maybe I wasn't hiding my thoughts at all. I instantly went to Emma and scooped her up. Harrison noticed but didn't say anything as he moved to sit on another chair.

"Well, I didn't mean to bring the whole mood down," George said. He, too, had grown quiet, and the sagging skin around his eyes had moisture pooled in them.

"That's usually my job," I said.

The others tried to laugh at my attempt to lighten the mood, but the sentimentality sat too heavy on all of us.

Harrison stood and shut off the TV when the clips stopped playing.

George cleared his throat, demanding all our attention. He leaned forward, hands clasped on the handle of his cane.

"Take it from an old man who's lived a long and wonderful life. Time moves much faster than you can ever imagine. Make the most of it. There's a reason old mugs like me are such a sentimental lot. I've been blessed beyond imagination, and I don't regret a thing. I'm so thankful for you in this room." He paused to gather himself. "That show had magic. You kids were magic. We hit on something that changed the world, and I'm so thankful. But it all moves so fast," he repeated, almost to himself. "Don't waste time doing things that don't fill your soul with purpose. Don't waste your life on people who don't care about you. Save your cares for those who matter. Find those people and hold on tight. The things that feel so big won't even matter one day, and you'll regret having wasted even a moment."

I clenched my jaw to keep my emotion at bay. I pressed my mouth into Emma's temple and held her tighter. She trembled in my arms with a sniffle but gripped me back with her own hands.

21

———

Emma

After a few seconds of heavy silence, Kate said, "I better go get ready for bed." Her nose was red from crying too. Charlie stood and looked at Harrison and me, then George, a fierce scowl on his face.

"I bloody love you all," he said almost angrily before following after Kate.

I scoffed a wet laugh. "Love you too, Charlie."

"Love you, mate," Harrison said.

George nodded, and Wesley remained silent at my side. Probably unsure if he was included in that sudden declaration. Charlie followed after Kate as the turbulent emotions bubbled up in me.

It was too much.

I couldn't sit still anymore.

Seeing those memories and the way I looked at Wesley, I was so clearly in love with him the whole time. Everybody had to know. Twenty years later and we were right back in the same position. I needed to get away from him and his hand squeezes and casual touches. What did it mean that he protected me from that creepy director? Was he really the man I hoped he was, or was I setting myself up for disappointment yet again?

"Excuse me," I said. I jumped up from the sofa, hiding my face from Wesley, knowing that it betrayed every thought flying through my head. These last words from George were too much after shuffling through my entire childhood. Cloying emotions made the room feel claustrophobic. I fled without looking back.

I made a beeline to the mudroom, quickly pulling on some wellies and an old mac. If I hurried, maybe the memories wouldn't catch up to me. I had always loved Wesley, and everybody in that room could see it. Twenty years or one day, it didn't matter. I was always back here to square one.

I needed space from him. He made me want and feel too much.

Wesley chased after me, but I couldn't stop my retreat. I had to protect myself.

"Ems, wait!" he called after me.

I raced out the back door and toward my old hiding place. Even in the near-dark, I remembered how to get to the secret cove under a pine so massive I could sit comfortably out of sight from any nearby properties.

"Shit," he yelled as he stumbled.

I marched through the wildflowers of George's backyard, past the boundary line of a fence to the fields that blanketed his property, before stumbling up over loose rocks and knee-high grass of the hillside. I slowed only enough so he wouldn't impale himself on a fence. He followed close until I made it to my spot.

I pulled the mac tighter around me. The tree grew on a peak of a hill tucked away on Sedar's property that allowed a view of the vineyards below but protected from the city's lights. The moon and stars sparkled through the spiny foliage, casting the scene in a surreal light, like a distant planet we would have traveled to in TF.

He caught up a second later, a bundle under his arms.

"What are you doing here, Wesley?" I spun and asked him, stopping him dead in his tracks.

He gestured to a massive coat and blanket he brought. "It's cold. I didn't ... I wasn't sure if you wanted to be alone."

"That's not what I mean. Why are you *here*?" I asked, emotion wobbling my voice. Everything was so close to the surface.

"I-I thought you wanted me to come," he asked, wounded. "What's changed?"

I shook my head, looking toward the stars so my tears wouldn't overflow. "What's changed is that I just had twenty years of unresolved pain thrown back in my face."

He took a hesitant step forward. "I've been wanting to explain."

"I feel like such a fool." I paced in the small area, needles crunching under my boots. "Time and time again, I open myself to you, only to get hurt because I'm right back here, like that little girl in those videos. I'm back in that same spot, heart on my sleeve, and what's going to happen? This ruse will come to an end. You'll get your Oscar, and you'll never talk to me again.

"I can't do it again. It's too painful. I thought I would be okay. I'm not okay." I stopped, the wind out of my sails. "I will never be good enough for you."

"Good enough for *me*? What're you talking about?" He held up his arms, dropped the blankets, and stepped toward me. Even in the low light, the color had drained from his face, and he looked horrified. "Where are you back to? I'm trying to understand."

I stepped back, holding my arm to stop him from coming

any closer. His touches made rational thought impossible. I needed to get this out once and for all.

"I'm fifteen years old and falling for someone who wants nothing to do with me. I'm twenty-three hoping to just talk to you and hearing you say you're not even my friend. Years of getting my hopes up just to be near you and being rejected."

He blinked at me. "Falling? Wait." He shook his head.

"I'm eighteen. Twisted in sheets where we just made love and watching you walk away from me never to return. Totally in love with you."

His hands covered his mouth. "It's not like—"

I scoffed. "Do not tell me how I feel."

"No," he said calmly. "That's not what I'm saying. What feelings? You hate me. You always have. I thought maybe we were close when we were young, but you've hated me for so long. And I never knew on set you had feelings for me."

I almost believed his earnestness. "There's no possible way you didn't know I was in love with you for most of filming. Were you watching those tapes?"

"I was. And I saw a dumbass kid who was terrified of losing the only thing that mattered," he said with growing frustration.

I shook my head, his words not sinking through the barrier of protection I'd built around myself. "Everybody knew. I was a laughingstock. I'd think that maybe you felt something for me too, and then when it wasn't just us, it was like a switch was flipped. I was nobody to you."

His hand ran down his face. "Fuck!" He swore suddenly, turning away to kick rocks. I jumped as a shudder wracked me. "I can't believe this. I never knew you had feelings. Never. That night when we made love, I—" He shook his head, stopping himself. "You don't understand the lengths my family went through to shelter me from you."

It had felt like the whole world had known, but he seemed

so knocked off balance by this declaration. Was it really possible he hadn't known? "And the media always painting me as the needy little girl?"

"As if we could ever trust the media?" His head was shaking. "No, Ems. I never knew. Even if anybody were to make a comment about your feelings for me, I couldn't let myself even hope for that. Because it was too much. It was a reflex to remind myself that you hated me. You had to hate me or ..." His hands gripped his stomach. "It was all pointless."

"What was?" I threw my arms out.

"I have so much I need to tell you. That I've been wanting to tell you."

"Then start talking because I'm not interested in being the fool anymore."

"Okay. Okay. Let's get one thing clear. I never knew you had a crush on set. I never meant to hurt you. I wanted to protect you. Everything was to ... I know that I did ... if you knew how fucking awful ... Let me explain." He was as incoherent as I felt.

Suddenly, my stomach was tight with nerves. He looked so wrecked.

But I was wrecked too.

"Okay," I said cautiously.

"I've said how my parents purposely isolated me from the rest of the cast and crew. Didn't want me to form bonds." He rubbed at his eyes. "I'm pretty sure they're the reason Max and Lucy never had the scenes that Sedar pushed for."

"I'd wondered." I huffed.

"Yeah. It goes much deeper than that." He took a steadying breath. "I know there have been so many times when you've questioned why I changed so much after the show. Why I pushed you away when we were on set. Why I kept our friendship a secret and never let anybody know." His throat worked a tight swallow, and he reached for my hand. I let him take it. Because I was emotionally and physically taxed to the brink of exhaustion, and Wesley's touch felt like a lifeline and a chance to finally move on from our past.

"Rex and Diana found out we were getting close," he continued. "They had people on set watching me at all times. They knew how much you were growing to mean to me and used that information to control me. Every time I went against them, they threatened you."

I gasped sharply, unable to fathom a world where the people who were supposed to be your biggest supporters could be so cruel. It made me want to fly to Wiltshire to my parents and hug them tight.

He let out a long, slow breath.

"I'm not excusing the way I treated you. Just like with that interview—"

"You've already apologized—"

"I know, but I'm just saying I don't expect that to be an excuse for being a shit kid. I was, at first, so desperate for their approval. They were my family, you know. My parents. I wanted them to be proud of me. I wanted to live up to the Cole name. So when they told me that I couldn't be around you, I listened. I pushed you away."

I chewed my bottom lip. The fury and emotion had stolen all my words. I let him speak the speech he'd clearly practiced a thousand times.

"But you … You kept coming around. No. Not true." He shook his head once. "I sought you out too. I won't pin this on you. I couldn't stay away. Even as kids. I wanted to be with you as much as possible while we were filming. So I got greedy. I wanted to have my cake and eat it too. I visited you secretly. We grew closer. You were the most important person in the world to me."

The tortured look in his eyes almost broke my resolve; his features twisted in pain.

"I am so sorry I hid our friendship. It kills me to know the pain I've caused you. To think that you may have thought that you weren't good enough somehow. That you thought I looked down on *you*. It breaks my fucking heart. You are the best person I know. Truly. Then and now." He slumped forward onto his knees, head in his hands. "It's me that's never felt worthy of being near *you*," he said through his hands. "Look at where I come from."

"Wesley." I never thought I could feel someone else's pain so viscerally, but watching him fall to pieces hurt as if I were being cut open. I quickly opened the blanket, needing to do something to help him through this. I tugged him over onto it. He followed my direction while still not looking at me. "Thank you. For apologizing. I always wondered what I did wrong."

"Never you, Ems." He lifted to hold my gaze, his Adam's apple bobbing. "I wish I could go back and do it all differently. I wish I was strong enough to stand up to them."

"You were a child. They were all you knew."

"Yeah, but then on set, being around you and the other kids, seeing their parents visit, the pieces started to add up that my family was massively fucked." He laughed, but it came out like a muted sob.

I grabbed him and pulled him to me. He wrapped his arms tightly around my body as I held on to him. All the anger and humiliation I'd felt only a moment ago had drained away. He trembled in my arms, head on my chest, and I absorbed as much of his pain as I could.

"You did your best. There's no going back. If I hadn't been the emotional, self-centered teen that I was, I could have easily seen how bloody awful things were for you." I grabbed his hands and kissed his knuckles like he'd done to me so many times.

"Please. No. Don't do that, Ems. Don't make excuses. I can't take it. You never did anything wrong. We couldn't help that we were drawn together," he said, returning to wrap himself around me.

"We really were. So many happy times." I smiled, recalling the goofy grins on our young faces.

"Seeing those memories. It felt so raw still. I loved every single second I stole on set with you. All my favorite memories are tied to you," he said.

I lifted his chin and lowered a quick kiss to his lips. He looked at me like I'd given him the most precious gift before his features twisted in pain once again.

"There's one more thing." He leaned back to hold my hands as he spoke, and I genuinely wasn't sure that I could take any more. How had he endured all this alone? At least I had my family and the guys. Wesley was so alone. "The night that we made love. It meant everything to me. If I wasn't such a dumb kid, I would've told you then that I wanted to stay with you. I was prepared to come with you, wherever you went."

I remained stock-still. I almost couldn't hear the truth. I couldn't fathom any of the cruelty of all this time spent misunderstanding each other.

"They found out. My father cornered me the next morning. Warned about what would happen if I got you pregnant. Told me I was an idiot. Berated me and emotionally beat me down." He looked over into the trees as he spoke. "He said that if I went with you, if I didn't go into acting, that not only would my own life be over but he would ruin your life too."

"No," I gasped.

"He knew people at Oxford. He said he would make sure that you were kicked out and that you would have no future at any other prestigious university. He said we were dumb kids and that by following you, I would ruin any chance you had at a future. And he was sort of right. Look at all you've accomplished. I would have only ever held you back."

"That's not true." My voice sounded far away to my own ears.

Rage like I'd never felt boiled me from the inside out. How could anybody be so controlling and awful? I couldn't think about the implications that he *wanted* to go after me when we were eighteen. I spent all these years convinced it was a fling to satisfy our curiosity, but I *knew* it'd felt like more. I knew that night wasn't typical when it became the measuring stick to which I compared all other relationships.

"I shouldn't have let them control me, but it seemed like the best way to protect you. To let you be away from me and the evil that is my family. I had to push you away. Time and time again. Whenever I saw you after TF, it was a fresh wave of pain. That night of the interview, I wanted you so badly. You looked so beautiful, and I understood then that I would never stop wanting you, and it made me furious. I was supposed to be dating Natasha and having those feelings for her. Every time I saw you, it made me colder in my anger because I only saw what I would never have."

"Wesley," I said.

"I am so sorry that it made me awful toward you. I'm not justifying it, only trying to explain how fucked this family has made me. They found the one thing that brought me joy and took it away."

My heart broke for the boy and the childhood he never had. It broke for how I interpreted it, and I felt like I was lacking because of my own deep insecurities. It broke because there was no going back and fixing any of the pain that was caused.

"I was so easily manipulated. My only consolation is that the pain I caused you might only be matched by the pain I've caused myself," he said.

"Stop," I snapped. "That isn't a consolation. That is right and truly fucked up. Wesley, they are your family. We're designed to love our parents and it makes not trusting them very difficult."

"So fucking sorry." He hesitantly leaned forward to kiss my cheek. I met him halfway, his cold nose and lips sending chills down my back in the quick brush. "It killed me. After everything we had." He kissed my forehead. "How you treated me, how you always welcomed me back like no time had passed. I'm so fucking sorry." I closed my eyes and let his kisses cover me. Let the apology wash over me.

"I'm so sorry," he said.

"It's in the past," I said.

He kissed my neck. "I want to stop being the person who makes you hurt." He ran his lips up the column of my neck. He pushed the mac and jumper off my shoulder to get more access to my skin. "I want to only bring you pleasure. From here on out."

I grabbed his face and kissed his cheek. "I forgive you." I kissed his forehead. "I forgive you." I kissed his lips. "I forgive you."

We dropped our foreheads together, shaking slightly, breathing each other in. "From here on out, we let past hurts go. Let's move on together."

He squeezed his eyes shut tight. "I don't know that I can do that. The guilt. It eats at me."

"You have to. I demand it. Let it go and so will I. We can move forward. Now that we understand. It's time you forgave yourself."

He sighed long and low, his breath tickling down my cleavage.

"Emma, I—"

I stilled, unable to breathe. My heart raced at the words unsaid and maybe too soon. I let myself just feel.

"I want to make you feel good." He was kissing my skin again. "No more interruptions. No more people popping up." He pulled me closer into his embrace. "It's not a private island, but it will do," he mumbled.

I gasped as his mouth moved over mine. We kissed deeply, pouring all the words that remained unsaid. We kissed to make up for years of hurt and pain and misunderstanding.

He put his arm around me and smoothly moved me onto my back, our mouths never breaking their kiss. Just as he had at the photo shoot, he moved me expertly as though he'd known my body forever. And in some ways, he has. I've always been his, even if I forgot for a bit. The way he touched me showed he never forgot that I was his.

He climbed over me, warming me up until I had to shrug out of the jumper. He kissed me as his hand rubbed up and down my body, adding more heat, exploring every curve and exposed bit of skin. He went in search of new skin, brushing up my shirt to lavish my rib cage and hips. I arched up into him, thinking of our first time, thinking of all the ways I wanted him the past few weeks. At the photo shoot, on the couch. Anytime he looked at me with his dark, guarded expression. Knowing now all the truths behind that cold mask.

He whispered my name as he kissed down my body.

"Let me make you feel good. It's all I ever want," he said.

"Yes." All tension melted out of me.

He tugged my leggings and my knickers away in one movement. I was too lost in the moment to care about being outside. The rest of the world didn't exist on our blanket in the secluded corner of the estate. The cool evening air brushed my wet core, notching up my desire even higher. He tugged up my shirt and pulled down my bra to lick and suck on my breasts as I sucked in a breath.

Finally, finally.

He nuzzled my belly and placed open-mouthed kisses on my inner thigh. He told me how much he adored me. He told me how beautiful I was and how good I smelled and tasted. He pampered me with kisses. When his tongue finally licked at the center of me, I was almost already undone.

I gripped his thick hair and moved against him, letting our bodies move in syncopation.

He coaxed me closer to the brink. He whispered words of encouragement between breaths for air.

"You're so beautiful." *Kiss.* "You taste so good." *Lick.* "God, I love this." *Kiss.*

I couldn't speak for once. He explored me with hooked fingers as he sucked me into his mouth. I was too lost to sensation as I climbed higher and higher. My body coiling. Loving that this was finally happening again. I was here with Wesley, and he was bringing me pleasure.

"The nights I dreamed of this."

Had that been his words or mine? I groaned, and he hefted me closer, hand gripping my bottom as he devoured me.

"Yes, Emma. Please. Let me feel you come."

This was how it always should have been, how it could have been. I left my body as the orgasm ricocheted through me. My eyes shot open as wave after wave lifted me higher and away from myself. Above me, the night glittered.

Wesley took me to the stars.

22

Wesley

Emma lay panting as I kissed my way up her body, covering her back up as I went in the cool night. She was so perfect and so beautiful. I felt light as air with the weight of the truth off my shoulders. She might have forgiven me, but she didn't know yet that I intended to continue showing her pleasure as long as I could. I wouldn't be absolved of my sins against her until I'd spent the rest of our time together bringing her joy. There would never be enough time.

I wouldn't think about life outside this house. I couldn't let myself.

"Wesley, that was ..."

"Good."

"I think I might have died for a minute there."

"A little death, as they say."

She made a sound. "I get it now."

She was boneless in my arms as I scooped her up, wrapped in the blanket, and started the journey back to the house.

"But you—"

"Shh." I kissed her forehead and brought us silently to my guest room. The house was silent as it was close to midnight, just the occasional crack of the fire and creak of shifting floors.

She watched with heavy eyes as I stripped her down to her panties and tank top and tucked her into bed. Her eyes stayed on me, widening silently as I stripped out of the slacks and dress shirt I'd been wearing. They snagged briefly on the erection that hadn't even begun to wane. It probably never would, so long as I could still taste her on me.

She opened the blankets to me, and I slid in next to her, feeling a level of contentment that I never thought possible. She burrowed in under my arm before pressing icy feet against my calves.

"Witch," I said with a hiss.

She smiled against my bare chest and kissed my pec. She kissed up my neck and to my mouth. We spent some time kissing deeply, until the heat began to gather again, her hips ground against me, and my control weakened.

"We should sleep," I said weakly.

"Hmm," she said, but her nails scratched lightly down my abdomen, my core flexing as she went. She pulled back the blanket so I could see her delicate fingers wrap around me. I almost came then.

I groaned, doing my best to hold back. "Emma."

"Shh." She smiled as she continued to kiss me, her hand working me with perfect pressure and speed.

Her touch was confident and soft. I arched up into her. Our quiet breaths. The sounds of our mouths. The shuffling of her arm as she worked me in the small, hot room. The scent of her, the taste of her. It was all too much. I was already so close when I'd made her come. It didn't take long now.

I barely had time to warn her before I quietly groaned. With my head thrown back, I spilled over her hand and onto my chest.

"Thank you." I kissed her as she grinned sleepily.

"Hmm," she said.

After a quick cleanup, we were both back in bed, silent and watching the stars through the window. There was so much to say still, so much I wanted from her. But the silence was a balm, and all I wanted could wait until the morning. Her breaths smoothed out, and soon, I followed her into sleep.

The next morning, I woke to her rubbing her backside against my morning wood. I wasn't fully awake as my hands cupped her breasts under her sleep shirt. Her nipples pebbled as I toyed with them. I rubbed my nose along the column of her neck, and my hips pressed into her. My greedy hands felt everywhere they could.

"We have to get downstairs soon and I need to shower," she said as she pressed her ass more firmly against me.

"You started it."

"I was sleeping innocently."

"Shh, I'm sleeping," I whispered.

I nodded against her as my hand trailed down her stomach to her wet center. I teased her, and she arched back, her ass cradling my cock.

"Wesley," she groaned.

"Definitely a dream. I know this dream. I've had it a thousand times." I used her moisture to explore her more and felt as she grew wetter and swollen. My fingers teased along her vulva, into her, and back out to brush her clit.

"Weird. I've had this same dream." She sighed.

Her hand reached between us to tug down my briefs and found me rock hard. I rocked into her hand as she ground against mine. My cock slipped between her thighs. She was so slick it was almost as good as being inside her.

"Fuck," I swore.

She gripped her thumb and pointer, making a tight ring at the base of my cock, and I continued to rock between her slippery thighs.

"You're so hard," she said. "I feel like I can't get enough of you."

The angle had to be awkward. We were sheened in sweat and rutting against each other's hands like we'd just discovered our bodies. It was quick and dirty grinding, desperate, making up for time but still not enough. She groaned into the pillow, her body clamping along my fingers, thighs squeezing around my cock. I followed her a second later.

We lay panting, sweaty, and sticky. It was fucking perfection. I kissed her hot shoulder and gently brought my hand away.

"I *really* need to go shower now," she said.

"We both do."

"That was ..." She flopped onto her back, a hand pushing her hair out of her flushed and sweaty face. "I can't believe how fast I came. Part of me feels like I should be embarrassed, but mostly I'm just impressed. I don't even think I was fully awake."

I smiled against her shoulder and toyed with her breast. I would never tire of this body, of this woman. I was still half hard and felt the blood begin to rush back in.

"You better get out of here before it's too late."

She chewed on her lip and seemed to contemplate. I nudged her hip as I got harder.

"Emma," I warned.

"I'm just saying, we've already slept away the morning."

"You really want to give Harrison any more reason to hate me?" I asked.

"He doesn't hate you. He's protective. But you're right. Off I pop!" After kissing my temple, she jumped out of bed and into the bathroom. I watched her perfect ass as she went.

"Ugh," I groaned and fell back onto the bed. I would truly never get enough of her. My heart hammered with the knowledge. I let her go, though I desperately wanted to follow her. I wouldn't have the self-control to resist her naked and lathered-up body, and every second I lay in bed was another second I couldn't remember why that was so bad. Now that I'd tasted her and made her come, I couldn't get enough. Best to put space between us so we could get downstairs eventually. Otherwise, I'd be tempted to tie her to the bed.

Oh, I'd have to save that for another time …

Back downstairs, after both of us showered—separately—we made our way to the living room hand in hand, a sheepish smile on her face and what I was sure could only be described as a "cat who got the cream" smile on my face. Everybody was around the fire as we joined them. Sedar dozed quietly in his chair.

"About time! We're playing games before pretend Christmas dinner." Colette sighed dramatically. "You guys must have been very sleepy."

Harrison's nostrils flared at the blush that spread over Emma's face. I lifted my chin and swung my arm over her shoulder, a big ole smile for Harrison. Charlie and Kate exchanged a glance and reached for each other's hands on the couch.

Sedar snorted in his sleep.

Conversation chattered on as I sipped coffee, absently toying with the strands of Emma's hair, bright red in the afternoon sun.

She glanced up at me, and another flush followed whatever she read on my face.

God, I adored this woman.

I never thought I'd be so thankful to see a blush on her cheeks again. She was so relaxed here. Funny and charming, quick-witted and teasing. It was as though she was able to return to herself without having to be the image of whatever she perceived as perfect. This was how she should be all the time.

Her hair piled into a messy knot on her head, and she wore comfy-looking leggings, an oversized sweater, and fuzzy slipper socks. I didn't think she'd even touched any makeup since we got here.

She'd never looked more beautiful, which was really an accomplishment for her.

I wasn't even pretending to hide my feelings anymore. Everything I had ever felt for her was out there. I was so comfortable in this safe space.

"What?" she asked quietly when she caught me staring at her again.

"Just like looking at you." I shrugged.

Harrison huffed.

"Are you okay?" she asked.

"I'm happy. Relaxed."

"Oh, that's why I don't recognize it," she said dryly.

Though she was joking, she wasn't wrong. I pulled her hands into mine and whispered, "Being here. It's more than I ever thought it could be." She frowned, but I continued. "I'm not looking for pity. I really don't want it. I have a life so many would be envious of. But being here has shown me how sterile and lonely that life has been."

"Oh Wesley," she said. "I—"

"I'm happy, Emma. You make me so happy."

She grinned up at me. "I'm happy too."

I let out a long sigh, and she settled into me. I would be happy here and now for as long as we had.

Because as happy as I was now, there was no doubt this sort of joy could last.

23

Emma

Sedar had been right yesterday. Life was fleeting and never was that clearer to me than now. Wesley was a good man in horrible circumstances who still managed to be a more decent person than most. His confession last night had cemented in me two things that I always knew to be true. He was a good man, and my feelings for him would never go away.

I'd been digging into things before this trip, and though I had more research, there had to be ways to help him. His family threatened to take everything away from him time and time again. You didn't get to be that huge, that powerful without some skeletons of your own in the closet. There had to be something we could leverage to protect him, but for now, one thing was absolutely clear; he needed to leave that horrid family.

"Earth to Emma?" A parsnip hit my plate, and I jumped back to the present moment.

Charlie was waving innocently from across from me.

We'd all spent the day relaxing or walking around the estate. Now, we all sat around George's massive dining room table adjacent to the kitchen and warmed by another fireplace. For being California, it had all the feel of a cozy cottage back home. Paper crowns sat askew on our heads, and Colette had already gone off to play with the cheap toys from our crackers. I was starting to wonder about her parents, but as nobody else brought it up, I wasn't about to. I'd have to ask Harrison later. In fact, I had several questions for Harrison, but the time hadn't felt right.

George had gone to digest in his chair by the fire and snored softly, leaving the five of us to chat and pick at our plates.

"Sorry, just woolgathering," I said.

"She's scheming. I know that face," Charlie said around a huge mouthful, a tiny fleck of pie crust flying as he spoke.

"Classy as ever, Charlie," I said dryly.

"Hey. It's a casual event. Save that one." He pointed at Wesley, who looked up innocently.

The rest of us wore ugly holiday jumpers for our faux Christmas dinner, except Wesley, who was dressed to the nines, dapper as always, making the rest of us look like absolute country bumpkins. I didn't mind as long as I got to look at him.

"I dressed for the occasion," he said, delicately slicing bits of his turkey with all the grace of a duke.

"Well, you're making the rest of us look bad." Charlie looked at Harrison for support.

Harrison gestured at Charlie with his knife. "You've got gravy on your jumper," Harrison said.

"Lot of help you are," Charlie grumbled as Kate dabbed at him with a wet towel.

"I'm not scheming. I'm content," I said honestly. My overly full belly was sore from laughing so much throughout dinner. My cheeks were rosy with wine and tender from smiling. I was so happy being here with my best friends and my ... Wesley.

Wesley grinned at me, and the warmth in my chest blossomed so great I thought it might start overflowing into golden light all around the table.

"So now that you've had a taste of a truly Brit Christmas, Wesley, is it all that you imagined?" Harrison asked.

"It's great." *My* Wesley sat back with a contented sigh. "I think this is the best Christmas I've ever had."

"The bar is that low, then?" Charlie asked.

"Charlie," I said, throwing the parsnip back at him. "Could you just stop quizzing him?"

"It's fine." Wesley put his hand on my thigh and squeezed. "We aren't a big Christmas family. My parents have a massive New Year's Eve party and all their attention tends to go in preparation for that. It's been that way my whole life."

"Bloody depressing," Charlie said.

Wesley shrugged but didn't disagree. Instead, he changed the subject. "I haven't had so many different versions of carbs in so long I can't remember."

"Those filming diets can be rough, mate," Harrison said. "You just wrapped a film with Martin too, didn't you? How was that, then? I almost chose a role with him, but the rumors around his work ethics were not brilliant."

"Safe space?" Wesley asked, and Harrison shrugged as though it was a given. "He was awful. Martin would make us reshoot over and over. He screamed at us. All of it was just ... brutal."

I frowned. I hadn't known that. Why wouldn't he have quit? Said something? But I knew the answer because it was always the same. He was controlled by his family. I was determined as ever.

"All worth it for the Oscar, then?" Charlie asked around a yawn.

"The Coles certainly think so. Another statue for the shelf," Wesley answered evasively.

"We'll find out soon enough," Harrison said. "Aren't they announcing the nominees in a few weeks?"

Wesley nodded and stole a glance at me. That had been our deadline. He got the nomination, and I got freedom. It had been what I wanted for so long, but now it only felt like a looming end to something wonderful I'd only begun exploring. It didn't feel fair.

Only one thing mattered to me now, and I needed to talk to Wesley about it sooner rather than later.

24

Emma

After cleaning up and saying our good nights, Wesley and I made our way up to the room we shared at the top of the stairs before the attic. I hadn't even pretended to stay in the one designated for me. I hadn't noticed the stained glass window before or at least didn't appreciate the beauty of it when I was younger. It was a mermaid or maybe a siren staring at a ship in the distance.

We had an early flight in the morning, but neither of us felt in a hurry to go to sleep.

I moved to sit next to him on the bed.

"It was a lovely dinner," I said.

Wesley hummed his agreement and pulled me closer until he could rest his head in my lap. I chuckled and ran my fingers through the thick waves of his hair. This hardly seemed like the same man from only a few weeks ago, now so open with his affection. I didn't pretend it was for the cameras anymore. We both knew better.

"Has everyone else already gone to bed?" I asked after we sat in silence for a few moments. I'd gone to change and help clean up the kitchen before the housekeeper waved me away. George was the first to head out after dinner, but the rest of us stayed up chatting, listening to Colette explain the ways of the world to us with all her infinite six-year-old knowledge.

"Kate and Charlie were 'quite knackered' and went to bed," Wesley said, rumbling against my leg.

"Likely story," I said.

He chuckled and rubbed his face along my thigh, sending a wave of heat through me. "I wouldn't go knocking, that's for sure."

"Harrison?" I asked.

"I think Papa George's spiced punch packed more of a *punch* than he'd expected. I heard him reading a bedtime story to Colette on my way to the restroom, and by the time I walked back, they were both snoring."

I smiled at the image of the two of them passed out, mouths open wide, zzzs floating above the *Charlotte's Web* spread across his chest. "Those two really seemed to have bonded, haven't they?" I thought out loud. Harrison had always put his career first, but more comments about wanting a family had slipped in. I worried he was projecting a dream life onto a child who already had a family. I worried more and more for him.

"It's sweet. She's a precocious little one. If she wanted to, she could be the next Shirley Temple." Wesley lifted his arm to brush his thumb along my cheek until I looked down at him. "What's the worried face for?" Apparently, even now, he could read me.

"I don't know. Something's going on with Harrison. He's being cagey with me. He didn't tell me he came out here last month, and now I'm worried he's getting too attached to being here."

"Is that so bad?"

"I don't know. There's something he's not saying. And I think he's lonely. He's mentioned a few times about how he thought he'd have a big family by now, and I just worry about him. I should visit more."

"Let him come to you when he's ready. Maybe he's worried about George." The unspoken passed between us in a concerned glance, neither of us ready to talk about the lapses in George's memory. I couldn't even think about it without my throat growing tight.

"Hmm," I said.

"Though, I wouldn't complain if you came to LA more," he said softly.

It was the first time we spoke about a life after this arrangement, and I was desperate to know his thoughts. I wasn't even sure of my own thoughts, though I was pretty sure they were contingent on knowing his first. I knew what I wanted *his* to be.

"I would like that," I settled on.

Wesley shifted off me to sit up. "Is that all that's on your mind?" he asked softly, brushing my cheek.

I shook my head, stomach suddenly anxious.

"I've made a decision," I said.

He watched me while loosening the tie he wore at dinner and chuckled. "Should I be worried?"

"I don't know," I said honestly.

"Ah. So Charlie was right. You were scheming at dinner." He cocked a grin at me, though a strain of worry gathered around the corners of his eyes.

"I've been thinking. Yes." I cleared my throat, not to be distracted by his charm. "You have to leave them," I said.

He pulled off his tie and tossed it onto the chair. "Who?"

I took a steadying breath, speech prepared. "Your family."

His eyebrows shot up.

"I know it won't be easy. In fact, I'm sure it will be quite messy. But I'll help you. I've been looking into some things—"

"Shouldn't do that," he said seriously.

I held up my hand. "Now, just hear me out. I know that family can be tricky. I know that you likely feel a lot of confusion and guilt. They're your family. How could you ever leave them? It feels like going against nature." I grabbed his hands. "But family doesn't act the way the Coles do. Family shouldn't want to control you. They should love you and support you unconditionally. That's their only job, as far as I'm concerned."

He swallowed, brow furrowing. "I agree."

"You do? Because I have more to say." I stood and watched his gaze move over my legs, shown off in the short nightie I'd changed into.

"Well, I don't want to cut your speech short. Out with it." He brought my knuckles to his mouth to brush his lips against them.

"You-you aren't alone. You have people who care about you." I lifted my chin, holding his gaze intently. "I care about you. I will help you through this. We'll get lawyers and make sure you're protected."

A soft smile played on his lips as he squeezed our clasped hands. "*We* will?"

"Yes." I nodded primly. "You have all of us. I know the guys are warming to you. They will only ever want me happy. And you make me happy. You aren't alone," I repeated, and my voice cracked.

I thought of the little boy who fought for me, the little boy who never had a support system. The man whose parents controlled and pushed him around. I mourned for a life he never got to lead.

"Ems," he said, and his eyes melted.

"That's how your family should treat you. They should only

care about that. So long as nobody is getting hurt and all that. And your family hurts you. They are family in name and nothing else."

He nodded seriously, a hard swallow.

"You are an incredible man," I went on. "You are outrageously talented and compassionate and somehow all that *despite* the rubbish that was your upbringing. You are a lovely human, and it's high time you got what you want. George was right. All this will seem small one day, down the road. We will look back and think about how it felt so important, but nothing is as important as you having freewill and happiness before it's too late."

I let out a breath. I had said it and waited on edge for his reaction. He was still so hard to read, guarded. But there was a somewhat aloof and patient glint to his eyes. "There is so much there I want to linger on and unpack." He grabbed me closer, hand sliding up my bottom. Silk against skin. "But I'm still stuck on the 'you care about me' bit."

"Of course I do, you thick man," I said, chin wobbling. "Isn't that painfully obvious at this point?"

"Not as obvious as you might think." He stepped closer, hands sliding up my arms. "And one day *we* will look back on this?"

I sucked in my lips and nodded. My heart was hammering in my ears. I wanted to tell him the truth about my feelings for him, the unending depth of them.

Just tell him!

But one thing at a time. I wasn't sure how he'd handle my demands to divorce his family. Wouldn't want to throw too much on the fire at once.

"Well. The good news is, I'm leaving them," he said.

I blinked up at him. "What?"

"That had always been my plan. There's so much more than

you could possibly imagine. More than I want to go into and spoil this amazing weekend. I'm sure over time I will tell you. But when I found out their hand in my marriage, I couldn't stay any longer. I had lawyers. I was going to change my name. Probably dye my hair." He shrugged.

A breath whooshed out of me. "Thank God," I said. I stepped on my tiptoes and kissed him. "But let's not rush into the hair thing." I smiled against his mouth, and I wrapped my arms around his neck.

"Noted," he said and leaned down to kiss me deeply.

I held on tight, mouths connected, as he walked me back until my calves hit the bed. The nerves I'd been feeling washed away by his confident hands and luxurious kiss. Could it be that simple? Could I imagine a future where we were together and had peace?

Then his words all sank in. *Had.* He'd been speaking in the past tense. When he found out about Natasha and their sham marriage, he'd planned to end things ... and then what?

I stilled, leaning back to break the kiss. He looked between my eyes, questioning.

"Why didn't you leave them?" I asked.

His nostrils flared.

"You said, you had plans. When? When were you going to tell them?"

His shoulders sagged. "The day the photo was leaked," he said. "The day we met to discuss our fake relationship. I was on my way to tell them, and they were waiting for me."

The dread moved through my body like a physical thing. A growing panic seized my chest as I watched him study me closely. He knew I was putting things together.

I gasped. "It's my fault. That picture from the night at the bar. You were about to leave them when all this happened. That bloody picture."

His clenched jaw was all the response I needed.

"What did they do?" I asked, my voice shaking with rage.

"He ... it doesn't matter," he said. "They don't matter. We are forgetting the past, remember? Moving on."

I shook my head. "Tell. Me."

He sighed. "They threatened you. Your foundation. Everything. They said they'd ruin you."

"They're monsters," I said. A shiver shook through my body, a sort of foreboding of something I couldn't fully understand. I was livid, guilty, sad, and so many things I couldn't accurately voice. Mostly, there was an incredible sadness for a man who spent a life of manipulation and emotional abuse and a sense that I was missing something crucial.

"Yes. But I wouldn't let them hurt. I will *never* let them hurt you." He brushed a thumb along my cheek before dropping his head to my neck to inhale me.

"Oh God." I shook my head, fingers pressed to my temples. "But why? I—you didn't even like me then. You hated me."

"I never hated you." He slumped onto the bed and shook his head at his feet. "Remember, they know you're my biggest weakness. They'll still use you against me."

"Biggest weakness?" I could only repeat words and phrases. Not able to form sentences of my own as my brain quickly tried to rewrite everything from the past few months from an entirely new point of view. He never hated me. He never cared about the Oscar. He did this to protect me and keep my work safe. Just as he had when we were kids. "But *why*?"

"You know why," he said, a patient smile spreading on his lips, tinged with sadness.

My head kept shaking. "No. I don't understand."

"You really haven't figured it out, Ems?" He looked up at me, adoration written all over his features. He huffed a laugh. "You are the smartest, most tenacious woman I know. You started a multimillion-dollar foundation. You can argue your way for just about anything. You really can't think why?" he asked.

My mouth opened and closed. A million thoughts swirled in my brain.

"It's always been you," he said.

My legs gave out, and I slumped into the chair.

"I've never been faking any of this. I have been in love with you since we were eleven years old. Before my pea-sized brain could even understand what love was. I've always loved you," he said simply. Like it was the way things played out. *Oh yeah, been in love with you forever.*

Tears welled in my eyes. "I thought you were just a really good actor."

"Maybe when I had to push you away." He huffed. "The media goes on and on all the time about how I look at you. I was never pretending. Every single look was me letting my guard down. Was me finally getting to take a breath and let myself be free with my feelings after bottling it up for almost my entire life." He ran his hand down my hair as he spoke. It was like he was in confession, freeing himself of a burden.

Tears streaked down my face. I was overwhelmed with shock and joy. My mind reeled to understand that my dreams were catching up with reality. I was the most grounded I'd ever felt but also like my mind was drifting away. Was he really saying what I thought he was? He sat calmly, explaining a truth that caused my entire life to turn upside down.

He shrugged. "I would stay with my family the rest of my life if it meant being with you even for a little bit. Even if it was pretend," he said.

"Wesley. What are you saying?"

"But it was never pretend on my end, Emma. You need to understand that. I love you. I always have. I always will."

His shoulders relaxed away from his body, and it was like he was feeling the sun after a long winter. Like he was living without any pretense. There was no more cold mask. No more pushing down his feelings. Every look he ever gave me. Every time he tried to push me away. It was all to protect me.

Wesley loved me.

I had misunderstood everything. I grabbed his hands.

"Wesley, I—"

"Don't say it," he said, and I reared back.

His eyes were red-rimmed. "Please, don't say it," he repeated with a sad shake of his head.

"Why?" I asked, trying not to feel hurt. "You aren't alone in this. You aren't alone anymore," I said.

"That's enough. To know and feel that. That's enough." He closed his eyes, rubbing his head along my hands. He spoke so softly I almost couldn't hear him. "Because somehow they'll hear it. They'll take it away. I just want this moment here with you now."

He might not be ready to hear it and wouldn't believe my feelings even if I confessed them, but I could show him. I could not waste any more time with wrought feelings of hurt or embarrassment and show him.

Let him feel what love was like for once.

25

Wesley

I WANTED TO HEAR THE WORDS AND BELIEVE THEY WERE TRUE. BUT I still couldn't be sure. I still couldn't believe she could love me when I came from such an awful place. And after all the pain and insecurity I caused in her. I didn't deserve her love. If I heard her say she loved me only to ultimately lose her, my heart would never recover.

Something passed over Emma's features as I watched. Worry to sadness to something else entirely. Something I only saw in moments when she didn't think I watched her. The look in her eyes was the look I saw when I closed my eyes and dreamed of a future we would never be able to have. Her hand lifted to my face with a softness in her eyes that made my heart beat faster in my chest.

I loved this woman so much. No matter what she feared, I would always put her first, and I would always protect her. Even if that meant keeping her far away from the Cole family.

We only had right now. Like George said. We could only

have these brief moments of happiness and couldn't let them go to waste.

I leaned into her soft hand and let myself go. I would take whatever she gave me. She dropped her head, mouth parting, and I lifted my mouth to meet hers. She kissed me tenderly, passionately. I kissed her so that everything I'd confessed could be felt. Tongues colliding, lips moving. My hands went to her backside, smoothing the warm silk around as I rubbed her ass, moving down her legs and back up, lifting it as I came back to her hips.

She broke the kiss and stepped back, holding my gaze, as she pushed one thin strap off her shoulder and then the other, and the gown began to slide down her body. It caught on her hard nipples, and she bit her lip as she wiggled slightly to send it the rest of its journey. It dropped to the floor silently as she revealed her naked form to me.

"Absolutely beautiful," I said.

She flushed and stepped forward between my spread legs. I smoothed my hands over her long, lithe legs, over her ass and hips, rounding over her stomach up to her breasts and shoulders. I couldn't touch enough of her. I loved how her skin broke out in tiny bumps as my fingertips grazed her.

She shivered, and I brought her closer to nuzzle her breasts. She gasped when I captured one nipple in my mouth and then the other.

"Stand up," she said.

I did as commanded, and she began to reverently strip me of my remaining clothes. First my suit jacket, then my shirts and pants—both trousers and briefs. Soon, we were both naked in front of each other, staring at every inch exposed to the other. Her blue eyes had gone dark as she looked me up and down, snagging on my hard cock. Her tongue poked out to lick her bottom lip.

She opened her mouth to speak but stopped herself with another flush of her cheeks.

"What were you about to say?" I asked. I drew a finger slowly up and down the side of her body. She was so soft, so perfect. I was desperate to sink into her and stay there forever.

"Nothing," she said, closing her eyes and letting her head fall back.

I brought my body flat against hers to lick up her neck. My hot skin pressed all along her, and my cock prodded eagerly at her hip.

"You feel so good," she groaned, eyes still closed. "I need more."

"Tell me what you need. Tell me what you were going to say." I kept my touch featherlight, teasing her to get the answers I wanted.

"I-I was just thinking about the photo shoot." Her eyes squeezed tighter still. "Christ, this is so embarrassing."

"Tell me," I growled. "I promise you I have thought about that shoot more than you could possibly know."

A small squeak escaped her, and she swallowed. "You did?" She peeked at me.

I jutted against her, a drop of precum leaking onto her skin. "I've made myself come so many times thinking about that day."

She closed her eyes again with a shiver. "The way you moved me. When you were over me like that."

"Open your eyes, Ems," I demanded. "I want you to see how badly I want you."

She blinked her eyes open and looked into mine. She was shy and tentative—two things I would never typically use to describe the gorgeous redhead.

"Tell me what you want, and I will give you everything," I said, nostrils flaring. I was seconds from losing control, tossing her on the bed and licking her until she screamed. But teasing was a form of delicious torture for us both, and I wanted to make this last.

"I liked how you moved me. I liked that you took control. I'd never felt anything like that," she admitted.

I closed my eyes with a groan. I'd been so worried that I'd pushed her too far that day and made her feel uncomfortable. "God, I wanted you so bad. Do you remember how I was shaking?"

She nodded with a soft inhale.

"I wanted to fuck you then, Emma. I forgot about all the people in the room." I brought her close and began to brush soft strokes over her hot core. "I wanted to slide up that dress and slam into you."

"Yes," she groaned, and her knees shook, giving out. I snaked an arm out around her waist and hefted her to me, sliding my thigh between her legs. We both gasped at how hot and wet she was against my skin. I flexed my thigh, and she rubbed herself wantonly against me, my cock weeping against her stomach.

"God, you are so wet. You are so good," I whispered in her ear as she ground against me. "Take whatever you want."

"I need ... more." She demanded even as she rode my thigh.

I hefted her boneless body even higher, flipped her, and laid her out on her back on the bed. Her cheeks were flushed, her red hair spilled out around her, pert breasts pointing up.

My finger traced down her sternum, past her belly button, down, over her mound, and into her.

She mumbled in pleasure, pushing against me so that my finger sunk deeper into her.

"So hot." I added another finger, my pointer and middle thrusting in and out of her, thumb brushing her clit.

"More," she said as she writhed on the bed.

"You've never been very patient." I withdrew my fingers, and she whimpered.

I pushed her knees apart and lowered my face to blow cool air on her wet center.

She groaned, trying to close her legs. I pressed on her knees, forcing them down against the mattress. "No. I want to see all of you."

Her hips flexed and lifted, trying for something just out of reach. Sprawled and writhing on the bed, she was every dream and desire I'd ever had.

"You're so fucking beautiful," I said again. I would never stop telling her.

I released her knees, and she stayed open for me. "Good," I said.

I slowly made my way onto the bed, one knee on either side of her hips. Her eyes shot open to watch as I climbed over her body. I purposely didn't let myself get close enough to brush her, but the heat between us was tangible. I climbed up her until my arms bracketed her, shaking as they had at the photo shoot.

She watched me, waiting for me to make the next move. I would make this perfect for her. She would take everything I couldn't give in the past.

"If I recall, you were farther back, almost off the chaise lounge," I said.

She nodded, eyelids heavy with desire.

I hooked my arm under her waist and hefted her up to my body, just as I had with the camera on us. "Like this?" I asked.

She moaned, her body almost limp as she let me position her however I wanted.

"Not quite," I said.

I pushed her back, perpendicular to the mattress so that her head was over the edge, hair waterfalling over the side. "Getting closer."

My whole body shook as I held her lifted to me. I couldn't stop the way I ground against her. My cock found the warmth between her thighs and slid between them without my meaning to. She groaned at my teasing. I still wasn't in her, but I had to take a moment even in this imitation of being inside her.

I took a steadying breath. "Fuck. Hang on." But even as I said it, my hips flexed, and I rubbed my cock back and forth along the wetness of her core. Sweat began to prickle my back, and my arm muscle was cramping. I licked her breast, and I leaned over her.

"This is what I wanted to do that day," I said, then switched to the other breast.

"Yes," she groaned. "More."

I grabbed a pillow and shoved it under her hips, propping them so she was still angled up but freeing my other hand to touch. I hovered over her as I continued to drive her wild with gentle brushes along every inch of her smooth body.

"More?" I grabbed myself rock hard, harder than I'd ever been in my life as I rolled on a condom. I closed my eyes and squeezed the base of my cock to take a moment before lining myself up at her entrance.

"More."

I teased the tip of my cock up and down, pressing against her clit before dragging it back down. She was writhing and wild, trying to get more. I pressed down as she pressed up.

We both gasped out as I glided all the way into her, settling in deeper and deeper until I could go no farther. She was so fucking wet and swollen. I couldn't move or breathe.

She clenched around me and groaned, trying to rock, but the position didn't allow her much freedom to do so.

"Shh. I need you to be still," I ground out. "Just for a second."

She was too lost to pleasure to hear me. One of her hands went to her breast and the other to where our bodies met. I felt her taunting me, pulling me deeper in with her internal muscles.

"Emma," I warned.

I was holding on by a thread, looking at her sprawled out, taking everything she needed from my cock.

I took a steadying breath and moved over her, pushing as deep as I could. I pressed my weight where our hips met, grinding down, up and back, rocking against her slowly. I moved in slow, torturous waves, hips sliding and never leaving.

"Oh my God," she groaned.

I couldn't speak, I could only focus on not coming too fast. She felt so good. I didn't slam into her, I didn't take, I only gave in long slow strokes. Using my hard cock to press against her clit and hopefully hit the spot inside her. She cried out. Her feet hooked behind my back as she pressed harder yet against me.

"Oh God, yes. There." She pushed and clenched, ratcheting herself up higher and higher against me. I was covered in sweat, biting my cheek, focusing on her. "I'm so close."

I made a sound like a grunt and sucked at a spot on her neck. She was holding tightly on to me, nails clawing into me. Her scent was all around me, her hair tangling in my hands as I held on just as tightly. Everywhere our bodies touched was slick with sweat. It was dirty, sweaty grinding, and it was fucking amazing.

"Wesley," she called out, convulsing under me, squeeze after squeeze as she came around my cock.

My entire body tensed, my balls so tight and tingling. I held out as long as I could. I came a second later.

I ground my jaw to keep from screaming out as I convulsed. I came so hard that I literally saw white spots as my vision returned.

"Holy fuck." I panted after several heavy breaths.

I remained seated in her and gently rocked a few more times, getting my final moments inside her. Her arms were sprawled out to the side, her chest heaving, her head shaking with hair plastered to her forehead. She was totally undone. Eventually, reluctantly, I slowly pulled out.

I should have made it last longer. I wasn't ready to leave her.

I carefully lifted her back up and turned her so she was on a pillow and not hanging over the edge. She flopped about like a wet noodle, still panting. I kissed her gently and tucked her in before quickly disposing of the condom and coming back into the blankets. I wrapped her into my arms and kissed her again.

I smiled against her temple.

It would always be like this for us.

My time with her would never be enough.

Emma

I FOUGHT SLEEP, WANTING TO TAKE EVERY MOMENT I COULD WITH Wesley before I flew to the other side of the planet, or at least the other side of the Atlantic, if I was being less dramatic. But the orgasm he gave me left me with little ability to fight the pull of sleep. I barely managed to go to the loo before the siren call of the warm bed got to me.

"Emma," he whispered. "Are you asleep?"

I must have drifted off without meaning to.

I sat up, panicked. "What time is it? Did I miss the flight? I'm not packed."

"Shh," he said. He gently tucked me back down and to his side. "It's only been a few minutes. You have plenty of time to pack and make your flight."

I let out a long breath. He was kissing my shoulder and neck as my mental faculties returned.

"I didn't mean to fall asleep," I mumbled. I'd been so determined to show him how much I felt for him, so sure that I would make him feel good. But once again, he put me first and wrung me out like a rag.

"It's okay. You can sleep more. I can't stop touching you. I'm sorry. You sleep. I'll just carry on."

I laughed and stretched, arching my back, muscles already a little tight from the intense orgasms he'd given me over the past few days. Long dormant muscles waking up with satisfied yawns.

He took the opportunity to move his attention to my breasts which had broken out of my blanket.

"I don't want to sleep. I'll sleep on the plane." I grabbed his face to get his focus back. His eyes were dark with desire, and he had to really focus to hold my gaze. "I don't want to waste any more time."

I climbed on top of him, straddling his waist and letting my tangled hair fall all around us. "I'd meant to make you feel good. Instead, you gave me that orgasm of a lifetime."

"Trust me. It wasn't a chore."

"Hmm." I tilted my head and looked him over.

His hands were behind his head, biceps on display, and a half-cocked smile played over his lips. I sighed dramatically. "You are ridiculously good-looking," I said, feigning annoyance.

He freed his arms to grab my hips. "I was thinking the same thing."

I kissed him slowly and lovingly. "I want more," I said with no shame. "I want to use you up until you are a husk of a man."

"Is that so?" He brushed my cheek, and I nuzzled into his hand. "I'm sure I should insist that you sleep," he said.

"Oh. I see. You're chicken." I reached between us, where he was already hard again.

"Yes. I'm terrified of you," he said it lightly, but his voice held tension, a raw honesty I didn't like.

I leaned back, pressing against his chest to look him in the eyes. "Really?"

"Nothing has scared me more than you." He held my gaze, and his chest rose and fell rapidly. It was another confession, a charged moment that said so much. "Sometimes the weight of my feelings for you seems like the only thing holding me to the earth."

"Wesley," I said breathlessly, eyes filling. If that was the case, what did he think would happen when this ended? I couldn't fathom that right now. I had only this moment to take his worries away. I would make him see just how not alone he was.

I kissed him, running my mouth along his chest and lower as my hair trailed down his body.

The next time he moved in me, I let him take me however he wanted.

We took advantage of every hour. We made up for years apart. We held each other like there was no tomorrow.

"Wesley," I said as the sky turned pink out the window.

"Yes?" His deep voice was rough from lack of sleep. I loved this early morning voice.

"I was thinking about this whole arrangement. The fake dating," I said.

"Ah. I remember saying it wasn't fake for me."

I kissed his cheek. "I don't want it to be fake for me either. I mean. Here's the thing. Even if and or when you get your Oscar nomination, you know it's really going to be important to go for the next goal. The thing when you have an Oscar and Tony and Emmy?"

"The triple crown of acting," he said.

"Yes, that. Well, we should probably stay together until then. You have any plans for Broadway?" I asked.

"Nope."

I smiled widely and leaned into him. "Yeah, we should probably stay together until then."

He sat up and pulled me close.

"In all seriousness, Ems. No more pretending. No more acting. Just you and me. For as long as you'll have me."

"I would like that."

I didn't care for his word choice. *As long as I would have him.* He said it with such disguised sadness as though he was waiting for the other shoe to drop. I couldn't promise him forever. I wouldn't even know what the next few weeks brought, but it wouldn't be because of me that this ended.

"I hate that now that I actually want to be around you, I have to leave for England." I poked his shoulder.

"I'll miss you too." He brushed his lips against my knuckles. It was his favorite gesture. Even when he wasn't around, I would feel the phantom kiss of his lips against me.

"Come to London," I said. Worried simmered inside me. It felt important we stay together.

"I can't." He frowned. "I have that silly New Year's party, and then I start filming the next movie. It'll only be a couple of weeks."

"That feels like forever now. Promise me you'll wait until I return to tell your parents we are really together. Promise me you'll wait until I'm back before you do anything drastic."

"I promise. I'll just be getting through the holidays. It doesn't even matter to me. Far as I'm concerned, I had the best Christmas. Now I will be counting down the days until you come back," he said.

"Me too."

As I showered and packed, Wesley went downstairs for breakfast before leaving for the private airport. He insisted on letting us use his jet to fly home, and the others were too excited for me to convince him otherwise.

When I came down, Harrison and Wesley were talking, heads lowered. They stepped apart as I entered the room but not before passing a sneaky look.

Colette came forward to where all of us stood. "Before you leave, we have a special presentation we would like to, uh, present." She broke off with a giggle. "You know what I mean. Come over here."

She dragged Kate and Charlie toward the piano in the corner, and I followed, reaching for Wesley. To my surprise, he winked and made his way to the bench, and sat down.

"You can play piano?" I asked.

"I'm a Cole." He sniffed, lifting his chin. "I had to be classically trained in at least three types of dance and an instrument before I could even think about attending kindergarten."

He cleared his throat and made a show of cracking his neck and fingers, getting into position. George came over on his cane, led by Harrison.

Harrison lifted Colette and set her on top of the closed piano lid.

Wesley began to play with a flourish, tickling the keys dramatically. I recognized the old-timey song even though it wasn't one of the more popular holiday songs. In a slow, jazzy tempo, he played "What are you doing for New Year's Eve?" Harrison began to sing first, looking over at Colette. His lovely voice was rich, like a classic crooner. I forgot he was multitalented. But the real delight was when Colette started singing the next verse in her sweet, deep voice. She sounded like a classic movie star, fawning a transatlantic accent as she sang. Her little shoulders rocked side to side as she and Harrison sang. They alternated verses, deciding to make plans for New Year's Eve.

The music built as the song did; Wesley smiled as he played flawlessly, his strong, long fingers moving with perfect dexterity along the ivory. He glanced up and winked at me before returning to the sheet music in front of him. Joy and love swelled to a breaking point inside me.

He gentled his playing as Harrison and Colette harmonized for the song's climax. They made quite the little duet. This was a memory I would treasure forever.

George clapped and whooped.

Kate and Charlie danced arm in arm.

In my periphery, the front door opened, and a woman walked in. She was about my age and very pretty. Her arms were laden with bags filled with gifts and groceries. This must have been the mysterious Frankie. She quietly set her stuff down and stepped closer, smiling widely when she saw Colette.

Harrison belted out the final notes, and Wesley stopped playing so that Harrison's rich voice rang out clearly in the silence. We all clapped and cheered. As soon as the little girl spotted the woman, her eyes widened, and she waved with her whole body. She jumped off the piano, assisted by Harrison, who grabbed her, slightly falling as he caught her. She ran to the newcomer.

Harrison turned around to see what the distraction was. He watched as the woman and Colette hugged tightly. When she stood, and he could see her clearly, the smile faded from his face. His jaw fell open, and his eyes widened in shock before he quickly tried to smooth his features. But I'd seen enough. He looked at me and pretended to smile.

It was too late. I'd seen something, and more questions formed.

The woman then looked up, and her face fell in a similar reaction to what Harrison's had been. Shock and confusion. Her gaze was locked on my best friend as she asked sharply, "What are you—"

She cut herself off as her gaze moved to the rest of the people in the room. "George? Who are all your guests?"

"They are sadly on their way out the door. I was hoping you'd get here in time to meet them," he said.

"Hi." She waved cautiously at all of us. "I'm Frankie. George's ..."

She hesitated, and George finished, "Granddaughter. She helps out around here."

She waved to us all, smiling and purposely avoiding Harrison. Harrison glared at the ground, and my worry for him grew. Who was this woman, and why had his mood shifted so rapidly?

"These are the kids of *Terraformative*," George explained. "Kids, this is Frankie."

I reached forward and shook her hand. "We've heard so much about you from Colette and George. Nice to meet you finally."

"Sorry I'm so late," she said. "You're from *Terraformative*? The show?"

Kate shook her hand next. "You've not watched?" Kate asked in obvious disbelief. "I wasn't on it. Just them." Kate thumbed to the rest of the group.

"No. I never watched," Frankie said stiffly as though ready to be on the defense.

"Frankie doesn't believe in TV. Or movies. Or tablets," Colette said with a dramatic eye roll.

"You're all actors?" Frankie's gaze flickered over Harrison and snagged.

He frowned at his feet, suddenly quiet.

"Mostly just Harrison and me, now. These two have retired from the business. But please don't hold it against us. I'm Wesley," he said as he shook her hand too. The rest made their introductions.

Her handshake with Harrison was comically brief, neither of

them making eye contact. Who was this woman who had elicited such a reaction in my friend? I was left with more questions than ever, and it hurt that he hadn't shared something with me. I glanced at Charlie, and he too finally seemed to pick up on the tension between this new woman and our best friend. He furrowed his brow at me, and we shared a worried look.

Harrison, noticing our interaction, smiled brightly and said, "We better be off."

"I won't interrupt." Frankie tucked her hair behind her ear and reached for the little girl. "Colette, come help me put the groceries away so the old friends can all say goodbye."

"Okay." She ran to Harrison. "I will miss you most of all, Scarecrow," she said, squeezing his legs. "Papa George and Harrison let me watch *Wizard of Oz*," Colette said.

"That's nice," the woman said through a forced smile.

After Colette and Frankie left, the rest of us made our goodbyes, distracting me from my worries. It was harder than I thought to leave. I tried not to cry again as I hugged George. He felt so thin and fragile in my arms.

We waited in the car as Harrison and George spoke lowly on the doorstep. They hugged, and Harrison was distracted the entire drive. When I tried to talk to him, he put in his earbuds and said he had to read lines.

I held Wesley's hand on the way to the airport and couldn't shake the feeling that leaving right now was a bad idea.

As Charlie, Kate, and Harrison got on the jet, I held tight to Wesley.

"We should be together for the holidays," I said.

"We were." He brushed his thumb along my cheek.

"This doesn't feel right," I said.

He kissed me deeply before dropping his forehead to mine. I didn't care if the others saw. At this point, I had nothing to hide.

"It'll go fast. And we'll be together again before we know it."
His eyes were closed, and he said it like a prayer.

"Promise?" I asked him.

"Promise," he said, but he didn't open his eyes.

26

Emma

THE HOLIDAYS WITH MY FAMILY BACK HOME WERE LOVELY DESPITE the nagging feeling that something was off with Wesley. His confession of his feelings was so honest and raw and vulnerable. Our time together at Sedar's house felt like this bubble of perfection, and now we were outside of it. It was like I waited for the needle that would pop it.

I spent Christmas and Boxing Day with my loud and large family in Wiltshire, battling cousins for the comfy spots on the sofa and being humbled in the way only family could. Not that I even needed to worry about my fame causing ego when I had Harrison and Charlie in my life.

Now it was New Year's Day, and we were back at Charlie's cottage, The Vicarage, in Devon. He and Kate had made so many updates while still maintaining a homey, cozy feeling. I, for one, thought the installation of a second bathroom down-stairs was worth its weight in gold.

Wesley and I talked all day, every day, through text and video chat. I got to see him with his guard down, and I was shocked by how often he made me laugh. I shouldn't be though, I'd always found his dry, caustic humor enticing. But it was more than that. I never felt like I had to overexplain or make myself understood. He just got things and listened. And I listened as he kept me posted on the happenings of his holidays, which were brief. Comments like "At least it's over" and "Party was same as always." When we video chatted, there was a strain in his expression, and it took several minutes of cajoling to warm him up back to the unmasked version of himself.

Something still nagged at me, and I couldn't quite figure out what to make of it. I had a deep-seated insecurity that he would cut me off once again. That even knowing how he felt for me and believing it to be true, he'd still find himself falling on the sword of his family name in the hopes of somehow saving me.

I was so afraid of losing him now that I knew how good it could be.

These and other fun thoughts were on repeat in my head as I stepped outside for a walk on Charlie's sprawling country estate.

"Wait up," Harrison called after me, tugging on a mac as he caught up.

I stood at the wooden post in my wellies and hood up, waiting for him. There had been a cold misting rain pretty much the whole time we'd been here, but I needed the fresh air to clear my head and stretch my legs. And I was a Brit through and through despite half a life in the States, so a bit of rain never stopped me.

He was breathless by the time he caught up with me at the end of the drive. I had barely enough time to tuck my CBD e-cigarette away.

"Charlie's joining us too. Is that okay? Or were you wanting more alone time to be in your head and overthink everything?" He cocked a smile at me.

"That obvious?" I asked. "No. It'll be good for us to get

moving and chatting. I have some questions for you actually," I said.

He looked back at the door. "Oh good, there's Charlie now."

"Hmm." So he was still not talking about his issues. I would give him time.

"Hullo," Charlie said. "Kate's working, but I wanted to walk too."

I tucked my arms in theirs, one on either side, briefly resting my head on each of their shoulders before we started off.

"All right. Have we cracked Emma yet?" Charlie asked.

"Nope. Just got out here," Harrison said.

"I don't need cracking, thank you very much. I'm fine."

"You've been distracted since we left George's," Harrison pointed out.

"You're one to talk. Are you going to tell us what's going on with Frankie?" I asked.

"Who's Frankie?"

"Really, Charlie? You're terrible at names. It was George's granddaughter. Or maybe Colette's guardian? I'm not sure."

"Yeah, that was odd, mate, what was that about? What's the story there?" he asked.

"No story." Harrison shrugged indifferently. "We aren't talking about me. What's going on with Wesley?"

"Nothing. He's fine. Surviving the holidays with his horrid family," I said.

"I do feel bad for the ole chap," Charlie said as we climbed the road through the countryside. It wasn't raining, but it felt like walking through clouds. "I hadn't realized his family was so tough on him."

"They were worse than you could even know. He opened up about some things that I had totally misinterpreted from when we were on TF," I said.

"He really did take care of you while Charlie and I were off running about?" Harrison asked.

"Yes. I never really told you guys. A little bit because you never trusted him, and I knew that it looked bad how he was always dismissive of me in public. Gosh, even now it sounds so pathetic the way I fancied him and followed him around."

"You were just a kid," Charlie said.

"We had no idea," Harrison added.

"That's because I didn't want to tell you and make you feel bad. For a few years, things were so hard for me on TF. The media would hound me in ways that you guys never experienced. They were obsessed with my body and love life and other things that a child shouldn't even have to worry about."

"Emma," Harrison said with a frown.

"It wasn't your fault, though. You were teenage boys and having the times of your lives. I just wanted to get through it. And yes, Wesley was there for me. So much. But it was always so secretive. I thought something was wrong with me because he was ashamed of me."

"He's a tosser if that's true," Harrison said.

"Bloody idiot," Charlie added.

"No. His family was even more controlling than you can imagine. It's not really my place to talk about it too much, but the long and short of it was that everything he ever did in regard to me was to protect me."

"And why is that?" Harrison asked.

I let out a long breath, thinking of the best way to explain. "He fancies he's in love with me." I hadn't said it out loud before. It still didn't feel true. I still felt like he might pop out of nowhere to deny it.

"Well, obviously," Harrison said.

"Come on, then," Charlie said.

"I'm sorry, what?" I stopped and untucked my arms to glare

at them. "You were the little chattering monkeys who told me he was using me!"

"Sure, but that was before this weekend. He's clearly mental for you. Always has been." Harrison shrugged, reaching for his pocket and then dropping his hand with a frown.

"Obviously," Charlie added.

"I really want to smack you both." They smiled tentatively at me.

"Right. Wesley is in love with you, and you're having a bit of a panic about it? Is that it?" Harrison asked.

"Am not." I crossed my arms.

"Am too. You've gone all pale and twitchy."

"You've been lost in thought all week," Charlie confirmed, oh so helpfully.

"It's just. A lot. To know all these years, I thought the worst about him and he's been secretly in love with me. It's everything I dreamed for, but it doesn't feel real. He's been all alone in this. He's given up everything for me. The hold his family has over him ... they're monsters, and he's ... He's never had a choice. Not from the beginning. It's awful. And then he finally had a chance to be free and it's all so sad and so much time has been wasted doing what we thought was right for other people but never ourselves."

Harrison looked absolutely gutted.

"And you are feeling?" Charlie asked.

"I-I don't know how to say this without coming off as ..." I flipped out a hand.

"Out with it," Harrison said.

"You're going to think I'm just fishing or something."

"We won't."

I stuck my hands deep in my pocket and thumbed the e-cig. Instead, I started walking again, avoiding their gazes as I spoke. "It's intense. It's a lot. I don't understand why. I know he said he loves me, but ... how could he give up so much for me? How could he love me so much and still push me away? I keep thinking that in the light of day, outside the bubble of Sedar's, he's going to end things. Or publicly renounce me. I'm as insecure as a thirteen-year-old all over again."

To my surprise, they both remained quiet for several steps. Even more, to my surprise, it was Charlie that spoke first. "I sometimes think that the Intrepid Trio, formerly known as the Loveless Trio, has a bit of a hang-up about our early success."

"You think?" Harrison said.

"Sarcasm doesn't suit you, Harrison. Go on, Charlie."

"It's as though by hitting the jackpot at such a young age, we've spent the rest of our lives somehow repenting for it. Because surely, we couldn't possibly deserve it. I've talked about this a lot with my counselor and sponsor. It was the same for me with Kate. I didn't feel I could possibly be worthy of such an intense and powerful love."

"And how did you combat that?" I asked, my throat tight.

"Well, that's the thing with love, innit? Nobody deserves or doesn't deserve love. It's just there. Like our fame. It happens, and we do our best to hold on and make the best of it."

"I can't tell if that makes me feel better or worse," I said.

"I'm talking about radical acceptance. Of our pasts. Of Wesley's feelings. Of yourself. Just pretend that you *do* deserve it. If it changes nothing either way, may as well go for the choice that makes you feel better." Charlie sounded incredibly wise, and I had never been happier that my friend found the help he needed and a partner to support him.

"You won't suddenly be worthy of Wesley's love by making as many sacrifices as he has. Just as he doesn't need to push you away to show his love," Charlie finished.

"I've not done anything," I said. "He's been so alone in this. I feel like I'm showing up to a movie right as the twist has been revealed but have no idea what the movie is even about."

"But you do that. With us. With Wesley. The media. You strive to be the most exemplarily version of yourself since you were cast as Lucy Lennon. Like you somehow didn't deserve it and were waiting for someone to find a single fault with you to call you out and take it all away."

"I don't know what you mean."

"All of this stuff for your foundation. Are you even happy?" Harrison asked. "I sometimes feel like you hold on so tight to the image you think you are meant to be that you don't even know what you like."

I frowned.

"Do you even like being the Golden Girl?"

"Of course not. But I like helping people. I really like using my influence to stick it to people who have too much. Sometimes I feel a little like Robin Hood. Except the rich have so much they hardly notice and instead of stealing it, they get to claim it as a tax write-off."

"And the rest of it?" Harrison prodded.

"I am tired of being in the spotlight all the time. I sometimes daydream of leaving the house without having to worry about cameras catching me without makeup or slacking off for a few days to laze about and read. I don't know who I am or how to act after I've been trying to be perfect for so long."

"You've put too much pressure on yourself. Just breathe," Charlie said.

"I don't know how," I admitted. "It's like if I loosen a little bit on anything, everything will come crashing down."

"I can tell. You wouldn't even tell us about Wesley or being unhappy as a kid," Harrison said. "I thought we didn't keep secrets."

I raised my eyebrows at him. "Is that so?" He looked away,

flushing at his ears. "Plus, I was happy when I was with you guys. I'm so happy with our friendship now. But being the girl when we were kids would always make me an automatic outsider. But it wasn't you. I was so insecure."

"You won't even admit to the e-cig in your pocket," Harrison said with a cheeky little smile.

I gasped and then groaned. "How did you know?"

"I've seen you sneak out only to come back smelling like cinnamon sugar a few times. We spot our own."

"I'm so awful, and after all the grief I give you." I hid my face.

Harrison shrugged. "It's okay. I needed to quit anyway." He stopped himself before he gave too much away. "The point is, you shouldn't have to hide things about yourself or be perfect all the time."

"Wait. Emma is smoking?" Charlie asked, eyes wide.

I rolled my eyes. "Just CBD. You're very sneaky. You know that, Harrison? You act so clueless, but I'm starting to suspect you see a lot more than you let on."

He shrugged. "I don't know what you mean. I'm the good-time guy, right? No more depth than that." He looked out to the horizon as the sky began to pinken. "Are you happy, Emma?" Harrison asked.

"I mean. Most days. Sometimes I dream of getting hit by a car just so I can go into a coma and not have to exist for a little while, but who doesn't?"

The guys stopped and exchanged a worried look. "Emma."

"No. Nothing like that. I don't want to shuffle off this mortal coil or anything. I just want a break, you know? But without the guilt of people thinking I was ungrateful."

"I think that you can do that without potential fatalities involved," Charlie said with a worried glance at Harrison.

How would I even start? Where would I even begin?

"Sofia seems very capable," Harrison offered.

"She is. Incredibly tenacious. And for being barely out of college, she's a spitfire. She could easily run the whole ..." I trailed off, feeling a slight tremor of excitement. "She basically does run the ship ... But I'm the face. How could I walk away?"

Harrison smiled. "One step at a time."

For so long, all I wanted was to hold on tight. Prove that I was worthy of this life and what I had. But what if I could release the reins a little? Maybe allow Sofia to step into the limelight so I could nap in the shade. Could it be so easy? Radical acceptance of a new path?

"And what if Wesley doesn't stick it out? What if he decides for both of us that he should leave?" I asked, and tears spilled over.

Harrison and Charlie swung their arms back around me.

"If he is not a total wanker, he will stay and fight for you. He has to figure out what he's afraid of too," Charlie said. "But you don't have to be perfect to earn that love. Wesley clearly loves you as you are."

"We all do," Harrison said.

I sniffled and nodded. I knew my face would be a puffy mess, and the little bit of makeup I put on last night was streaking down my face. But I actually didn't care. I was here with my two best friends. Wesley loved me, and I was ready to accept that love. I would talk to Sofia and see how she felt about stepping into a more public-facing role. I felt excited about the future for the first time in a long time.

"You've given me much to think on," I said, pulling out the e-cig to puff as we turned the corner to come back to The Vicarage.

"Look at you, little rebel," Harrison said.

Charlie stopped suddenly, head tilting. "Do you hear that? What is that?" he asked.

I had heard a rustle but assumed his ever-growing family of

chickens were up to something. Then I spotted the vans and cars parked just outside Charlie's property down the long drive. It was too late by then. A dozen or more people came running up as soon as they spotted the three of us.

I froze as questions were lobbed at me, while microphones and cameras were shoved into my face. The questions came so fast that there was no telling who said what.

"How do you feel about the breakup?"

"Are you happy Wesley got his Oscar nomination?"

"Who was that woman Wesley was spotted with on New Year's?"

"What about the rumors that you were never really dating and this was all for his new movie?"

"What about rumors that he's having a baby with his ex-wife?"

"Was this all for publicity's sake?"

"What are you smoking? Is that marijuana?"

I was too shocked to move or speak.

The top question spinning in my brain was the breakup.

No. No. No.

"No." The words came out. "Wesley and I are dating," I said.

"But his team just announced your breakup. Said it was not 'working out.'"

"An inside source said it was all pretend anyway."

"Okay, that's enough." Charlie stepped in front of me, his large frame protecting me as my body grew numb.

Wesley wouldn't do that. I told him to wait. This wasn't happening.

Charlie and Harrison barricaded me as they shuffled me the rest of the way to the door. Harrison was polite and calmly reiterated that they would soon be entering private property and to give us space. I was hardly aware of any of it as the thoughts bombarded me. My deepest insecurities back at play.

When we got to the drive, there was an explosion of noise.

Agata came barreling toward the group of paparazzi, a broom raised above her head and Nugget, the rooster at her side, running full speed at the camera people.

"I sue you all! You cannot be here!" She whacked at one man as the group backed up to exclamations of rules and rights. Nugget pecked wildly, plumage on ends as he attacked with her.

One day, I would look back at this and laugh. If I ever laughed again.

But all I could think was that he was doing it again. He was doing it again. I had imagined all the love and feelings and promises. This couldn't be true. I talked to him every day. I trusted him.

Back in the house, I was surrounded by the four of them talking.

"Are you okay?" Kate asked distantly.

"I will sue them. They aren't allowed to be here," Charlie swore.

"Don't worry about this. It's not true. You know how the media is," Harrison said.

Numbly, I opened my phone to see what was real and what was fake.

An official announcement from his team that our relationship was over.

A picture of a beautiful woman on Wesley's arm as he is dressed in a tuxedo, bent to her ear.

Viral audio of me saying nobody would ever believe we are dating. Wesley saying people are dumb from that first night at his place. Our private conversation was leaked ...

A numbness spread over me, making my hands icy, and my mind shut down. It was all too much to process at once.

"It's the worst news possible. It's everything I feared," I

mumbled the words. My brain hadn't really seemed to catch up to the implications.

"It's not real. It is not real," Kate said. "I don't believe any of it. You have to talk to Wesley."

I have to get back to LA.

"You sure you want to go back there?" Harrison said. I didn't realize I had even said it out loud.

"Just talk to Wesley first," Charlie said, I think.

Even if the rest were lies, my reputation was ruined. Everything I feared, all the people I helped, who would ever work with me again? Whether I was ready to be done being the Golden Girl, that option was taken from me. I had no say in how any of this news broke, and everything I ever worked for was ruined.

27

Wesley

"Well, well, well. It's about damn time." Mac stood and hugged me, clapping me heartily on my back. The Academy officially announced me as an Oscar nominee for Best Actor. "Congrats."

I felt numb, and my fingertips tingled. *Emma should be here* repeated over and over in my head.

We were down in my theater. My parents insisted on watching the announcements together, but I needed space from them after the holidays. I'm sure I'd pay for the sleight somehow. I'd been avoiding them as much as possible, knowing I would be too tempted to tell them to fuck off and run away with Emma. But she'd asked me to wait until she came back. And what was another few weeks after almost an entire life of faking it with the family while dreaming of Emma?

I barely made it through the past two weeks without her by my side. I thought of her every waking moment. Texted her a fraction of the time that I wanted to. Daydreamed of her. The holidays felt even more unbearable than normal knowing how good it could be.

"Thanks, man. Doesn't feel real. I probably won't win," I said, thoughts swirling.

"But it's nice to be nominated," he teased.

"Some clichés exist for a reason." I tried to smile.

I felt conflicted. Had I really earned it, or had my parents pulled strings?

"Are you okay?" Mac asked, hands in his pockets and a worried look on his face.

"I don't feel like I deserve it."

"I think they call that impostor syndrome."

I shook my head. "That or my father somehow bought my nomination."

Mac cleared his throat and looked at his feet. We both knew it was a possibility.

"The weirdest thing is, I just want to call Emma and tell her about it," I said.

"That's not weird. Emma is your person."

My smile was genuine this time. "She is."

"I'm glad you talked to her and put everything on the table. Do you feel better?" he asked.

I nodded once, but truthfully, I was as conflicted as ever. When we were together, everything felt perfect and right. Too good. It was a lifetime of having the rug pulled out from me that had me prepared for the worst. They wouldn't let this happen. They would somehow sense my joy and use it against me.

"Yeah. She knows it was never fake for me," I said.

"Yet, you don't seem thrilled," Mac observed.

"I keep waiting for my father to ruin this somehow."

Mac glared. "Your father has a lot of power, but he can't ruin what is genuine between you," he said with more ferocity than I'd ever seen in him. "I thought maybe at first you two were acting, but I've never seen you as happy as when you're around her."

"I don't know. It's hard to explain. I can't believe she would want me. Or stay with me. I feel like I've spent my whole life never feeling good enough for her, and now that we are together, I'm afraid she'll figure it out."

"Ah. That's the feeling of vulnerability. That's the shitty part about loving somebody. You have to trust that what they say and do is true. That you are worthy of being loved and loving." He cleared his throat again and shrugged. "Or so I hear."

"I knew you were a big softy."

But how did I tell him the deepest fear, that it wasn't my father who would ruin this? That I would slowly turn into him as the years went on. That I would become cold and jaded and slowly suck the life out of her until she was a shell of the woman she used to be.

Mac smiled. "You call Emma. Tell her the news. I gotta head out anyway. I'm really happy for you two. Just don't fuck it up by thinking you know what's best for both of you. You're a team now."

"Thanks. She's pretty incredible." I barely held back my sigh. Like a cartoon character in love.

Mac pulled out his phone and was headed to leave when he froze.

He turned back, and worry creased his features. "Hey. Um. There's a rumor going ... no, not a rumor. Wait. Did you and Emma announce a breakup?" He was frowning at his phone.

I went cold with fear, already opening my phone. Article after article bombarded me with rumors and lies and gossip. Each image or clickbait title was worse than the last. My heart beat so loud, the blood rushing in my ears so thunderous that as Mac spoke, the words were drowned out.

Me with that random woman at the party who would not leave me alone.

Pictures taken out of context. A breakup announcement.

Emma's shocked face as the paparazzi bombarded her. She looked so devastated. Again, I'd caused that pain—not directly, but this was all happening because of me. It couldn't happen like this. I'd done everything to protect her from exactly this.

"No. No. Fuck. This isn't happening," I said, my voice breaking.

I would talk to her. She would know this wasn't real. I'd been talking to her every day, she trusted me and knew me. The whole world was crumbling around me.

Except for that, every time I made promises to her before, I was forced to break them. I pictured her then, believing all the lies because, of course, she would. Because this is the family who ruins people. This was what I was trying to protect her from. They didn't just hurt me this time; they hurt her too.

I took the stairs three at a time, rage barreling me forward. Before I was even aware that I had dialed the number, I was yelling out all my anger and frustration into my phone.

"What have you done!" I shouted at my father before he even greeted me.

I was peripherally aware of Mac hesitating to leave before he awkwardly waved goodbye.

"Calm down. You're acting like a child." My father's unruffled tone only added to my fury.

"You had no right." I seethed. My heart raced, and I felt sick. I wanted to break everything in this ugly house.

"I always thought your mother babied you, but you really are still a child in so many ways," he said.

My hand shook as I squeezed the phone. "I'm done with this. Do you not see how insane this is?" I had felt love and family. I wouldn't do this anymore.

"That old song again?" he asked.

I stilled.

"You think we didn't know you were trying to leave?" A thousand thoughts battled my brain at the same time. He wasn't talking about the announcement. "You were never supposed to stay with her. This whole setup was a lesson for your antics."

"My antics?"

"You thought you could pull one over on me? I'm Rex Cole, and I run this family. You cannot leave."

I stumbled back. "You leaked the picture of Emma and me. You started all of this."

"Who do you think took it?" he asked, and I could hear his sneer through the phone. "You're so predictable. Upset over the divorce, you caused by the way, out drinking. We had to keep an eye on you. And we were right too. You behaved exactly as we knew you would the second we learned Emma Flynn was also there."

I shook my head. It wasn't Emma's or my fault. They had been watching me. Set me up. Revenge for trying to live my own life.

"You aren't strong enough to go against the Coles. Generations of work won't be undone by one selfish boy. You don't have the power. You never did. It's time you understand your role in this family and stop messing around."

"Why do you hate me so much?" I was whispering it. I couldn't fathom it. I knew he was awful. "You just wanted me to have a glimpse of happiness so you could rip it away again?"

"You needed to learn that desire is fleeting. This family is forever."

"This is not a family. This is ..." I threw out my hand. "I don't know what this is, but it's not a family."

"I'm protecting you in the long run, son. Love is never enough. You think she'll stay with you now? After you've hurt her yet again? She's too smart to ruin both of your lives and everything you built. You think it's just about money? Or acting? Where will you go? What could you possibly do besides act? You've never worked a job. You have nobody else. If she cares about you, she will understand that this will never work and leave you alone once and for all."

I could only swallow down the bile that worked its way up my throat.

"If she loves you so much, she won't let you give up everything for her. If she's so noble. And if you love her, you will finally do what I say and stop trying to control things you have no idea about."

"You're a goddamn monster," I spat. "You're not even human anymore."

"I do what needs to be done. Somebody has to." He hesitated. "Congrats on the nomination." He ended the call.

I stared at the phone. I loved her. Maybe she even loved me too. I wouldn't let her tell me. God, why hadn't I let myself have that final piece of joy when I had the chance?

Now I would never know.

Even if we loved each other, it would never be enough.

28

———

Emma

My phone was a constant explosion of calls from Sofia and every person I knew except the one person I needed to talk to. Every call that wasn't him, my fears ratcheted. I knew Wesley. I trusted him. I had been lying to myself, pretending I didn't know him. Of course, I knew him, a piece of my heart always had, like knowing how the sun would feel on my face before stepping outside. I understood his soul on the most instinctual level.

I silently comforted the hurt child in me that feared the worst. This was the time to prove that my love was not weak.

When I finally saw his name pop up, I answered with trembling fingers. He was pale, and his eyes were bloodshot. His shoulders were slumped, and the life was out of his eyes.

He was defeated.

"Wesley," I said.

"I didn't leak about the breakup or the audio of us talking about our plans to date for publicity." He held a hand over his mouth and spoke flatly.

He was far away, his eyes detached. I needed him in my

arms. I needed to tell him it would all be okay, but he spoke so garbled and rambled without giving me a chance to speak. "I don't know how they got that audio. I would have never recorded you without your permission. You have to know. Of course. I think maybe they planted something during the meeting. I don't know. I wouldn't have ever—"

"Wesley." I interrupted, and he stopped speaking. "Look at me. Look at me!" He finally brought his gaze up. "I never believed it. I told you that I don't believe anything I see. I trust you."

He looked at me, eyes still shining. "You didn't doubt me? Not even for a second?" he asked.

My hesitation was a fraction too long.

"Look, I'm not perfect," I explained. "I have some issues of insecurity that I'm working on in that regard. I know you, though. And I know you wouldn't do that. The thing I fear is that you're going to push me away again."

"It's never going to be enough. No matter what I do," he said to the side of the screen.

He didn't seem fully present in his body.

"I don't care about any of it," I said calmly. "I believe in you. In us."

"I'm glad you believed me. But the media does care. The media are completely against you now."

"It can be fixed. All publicity is good publicity, isn't that the whole thing?" I tried to keep my voice light and hopeful.

His frown deepened. "Ems, it was never going to last. We both knew that. I'm not allowed to have good things."

I shook my head. No. *No.* He wasn't going to do this again. He wasn't going to let his family win. With every second, I saw how he pulled further into himself. It wasn't even just about us. It was about this constant cycle of abuse he endured. It had to stop. It had to end.

"Wesley. Look at me." He shook his head. "Wesley, *please*." My voice cracked.

Finally, he looked back at the camera, shoulders slumped, mask in place. God, I hated that face. I hated that suit of armor he had to wear to survive. I understood why he needed it but not with me. Never with me.

"I won't let you do this. We are stronger than anything they can throw at us. I won't let you die inside for this family that treats you like garbage. You are better than them. You need to get away from them. You want to get away. That's what you told me. That you were leaving. So let's go. Come to London."

I needed to be there. This could end at any moment. I shook all over, frozen in my packing when he answered my call but now too afraid to move.

He shook his head. "He won't let me leave. He's the one who leaked the picture of us that night at the club. He found out that I was trying to leave the family. This whole thing was a setup to prove he was in control. That love wasn't real." He spoke low and even, sharing the details, but he was detached and checked out, rambling again.

The news came like a shock. "They did this to prove a point?"

He nodded. "Do you see? This is what life is like with me. It's not worth it."

"Stop it," I demanded. "This can't be how it is. I refuse to accept this." I poured all the stubborn haughtiness I possessed into my voice.

Now he looked directly at me, and the words flowed out of him.

"For so long, I thought that this life was my only choice. There was no way I could ever be anything outside the expectations set on me since I was born. I know it sounds so easy to leave. They make you unhappy, so leave. But it was all I'd ever known. It was my family. Then I would tell myself that this was the price I paid for the life so many people wanted."

A lifetime of a thousand tiny cuts had left him one giant open wound, bleeding out in front of me. I watched as the man I loved gave up after holding on for so long.

"You came back into my life, and I felt hope again. I thought about a future where we could have happiness. That was the cruelest thing they could have done. It was better to never know."

A sob broke out of me. I tried to find words to pull him back even as he slipped further and further away. How could I combat an entire life of abuse?

"He let me feel light and love so he could show that it could be taken away without warning. I've been so lonely. But then you came back into my life. And I remembered how easy it was to be happy. No, not happy, how easy it felt to just exist. I wasn't wearing masks. I wasn't trying to convince myself every minute of every day that this was what I wanted, what I should want. I felt alive. So they did what they needed to do. They proved their point."

He shook his head. "This hurts so much worse now."

I had to collect myself. My crying made it impossible to speak clearly. He needed me to be strong for us both.

"Wesley, please. I know it feels hopeless right now, but it's not. We can survive this."

He shook his head, and I wasn't sure if my words were even getting through. "The worst part is, I feel myself turning into him. Into the ugly man that he is."

"No," I gasped. "You are nothing like him."

"I am. Every time I pushed you away and told you I was doing it for you was me being afraid. It was me trying to have control. That's no better than him." His damp cheeks and heartbroken face almost killed me.

"Then be better than him. Choose me. Choose us," I said low and controlled. He looked up at me, some of the fog clearing from his gaze. "You said you'd never let them hurt me. If you give up now, he won. Fight with me."

He opened his mouth and closed it. "How do I stop the Cole curse from hurting you?"

"There is no curse, just loads and loads of generational trauma. It feels like there is no way out, but that's simply not true. You're not alone. I won't let you turn into him. You're not your father. He didn't have anybody who loved him enough to stop him from becoming what he is, but you have me."

A long breath escaped him as his gaze moved over my face. "I don't feel like I could ever be enough to deserve you," he said.

"Lucky for both of us, love doesn't work that way," I said softly, smiling. I took a steadying breath as he started to come back to me. He wiped his face and sat up straighter.

"I wanted to keep you safe," he said.

"You did. And now I will protect you like somebody should have been from the beginning. You love me, and I love you. I love you, Wesley. Do you understand that?" A smile spread over his watery features. I didn't want to tell him while he was emotionally fraught like this. I didn't want him to think I was only saying it out of fear or trying to be another person who controlled him. Christ, but I should have told him that night at George's. I should have told him from the moment I realized it. But I wasn't sure when the moment was. I've been denying myself the feelings for so long that I couldn't even tell how long I've been lying to myself. Since we were children.

"You do?"

"Of course, I bloody do, you nincompoop. I wanted to tell you at George's. Before that, if I'm being honest. You said once that it's always been me. Well, guess what? That goes both ways."

His gaze moved over my face in the camera, tension released from his shoulders.

"I'm Emma fucking Flynn, and I protect what's mine."

He chuckled, and relief rushed into me. "You're a little scary when you get like this," he said.

"Damn right, I am. We'll decide what to do next. I'll come with you to the Oscars, or I will tell the press we are apart. I will smother you and fly to you right away, or I will give you space. But *we* will decide what is best for us and nobody else. I will wait as long as it takes. You promised no more pain. No more letting them control you. You *promised* that you would only make me feel good. Remember at Sedar's? You promised me. If you love me, trust me."

"I love you, and I trust you." He sat up straighter, shaking his head out as though preparing to make a plan. "Ems. He's so powerful. He'll come at us from every angle."

"Let him bloody try."

29

Podcast Nosy Nelly Celebrity News

Season 4, Episode 42 *Fool me Twice, Shame on Me* transcript excerpt

Co-hosts: Gabi Ortega and Liz Kane

[excerpt starts]

LIZ: Just say it.

Pause.

LIZ: I know you want to.

GABI: You know, I really don't.

LIZ: Well, I will because I'm pissed. It was all fake. We were all duped.

GABI: Seems that way.

LIZ: My stupid romantic heart is broken. For those living under a rock, an epic breakup between Hollywood's, nay, this is intercontinental, so the film industry's biggest couple. Duped again by La-La Land.

GABI: Something went down. It's been weeks. They haven't

been spotted together. Their PR teams have been incredibly tight-lipped.

LIZ: Yeah, because it's not a good look for either of them. She was smoking an e-cig! In that audio, she admitted it was all fake. I feel like I don't even know her!

GABI: We don't know her. We don't know either of them.

LIZ: I'm crushed. Aren't you? You don't seem that mad. You seem weird.

GABI: I don't know. Something feels off.

LIZ: Oh, of course, you say that now. You were the biggest critic to begin with. You were the one who said if it was faked, you would never trust them again!

GABI: Yeah. I know.

LIZ: Her reputation is shot. No more Golden Girl. She took an active role in lying to her fandom. A fandom, mind you, who has only loved and supported her. How did she think that would go?

GABI: I've never seen you so upset.

LIZ: I'm livid. I feel betrayed.

GABI: I get it. But does a breakup warrant undoing a lifetime of charity work?

LIZ: I guess not. But I'm still mad.

GABI: Fair. It does feel like finding out Santa isn't real.

LIZ: And where's he? Nowhere to be seen. Apparently, he never showed up for the next film he was supposed to start shooting.

GABI: Hear that from an inside source?

LIZ: Close to the family.

Sad chuckle.

LIZ: This is all just so depressing.

GABI: Okay. Listen. I know I don't say this often, but maybe I was wrong.

LIZ: What?

GABI: I know. I know. Something feels weird. Like something is going on behind the scenes that we don't know about.

LIZ: Yeah, but the breakup is everywhere. His team made an announcement. They literally dropped off the face of the earth. It's been weeks without a single spotting. The audio about it all being a setup has gone so viral it's been meme'd.

GABI: I don't think that's a word.

LIZ: It is now. So much so that the memes have memes.

GABI: I just ... I really thought. I thought this was a real one.

Gasp.

GABI: I wanted to be wrong about these two. Unless they're the world's best actors, and in that case, they both deserve Oscars because that relationship felt real. The gala, the photo shoot, the way her face looked when they broke the news of her breakup. It was like she was just finding out. She looked absolutely broken.

LIZ: She was a mess, I agree.

GABI: My gut is telling me that these two fools are in love, and I can't shake it.

LIZ: But if they love each other, why aren't they with each other? It doesn't make any sense. What could possibly be more important than being together when you love someone?

GABI: Maybe sometimes love isn't enough.

LIZ: God, that's a depressing thought.

GABI: Indeed.

[excerpt ends]

30

Wesley

THE ONLY GOOD THING ABOUT THIS YEAR SO FAR WAS THE FACT that the Oscars were held the first week in March. That meant I only had to get through eight weeks without seeing Emma.

Eight of the longest weeks of my life, miserably pretending for a little longer that I was doing as I was told and staying in my place.

But tonight, I would finally get to see her. She would show up on the red carpet in a gorgeous gown. We'd see each other across the crowd, run into each other's arms, and tell every reporter the truth about what happened. The whole damn truth.

We wouldn't let Rex Cole take away the most important thing in our lives. Maybe it would be safer not to be together, but who cared about being safe when love was on the line. We'd agreed that the publicity needed to die down first. That when we showed our faces again, as a united front, we would have a plan.

Only Emma wasn't here.

I walked the red carpet alone, waiting for her to show up,

and she never showed. I ignored the questions and walked right into the theater.

She'd promised, I repeated to myself. We had a plan. I trusted her.

But every minute that ticked by, the same self-doubt crept in. Had I hurt her too many times? Had my father gotten into her head? Did she decide I wasn't worth the drama and baggage?

Now I sat alone through hours of the award ceremony, an empty seat next to me and pitying glances from the celebrities around me. The hosts on stage announced the penultimate award of the night. The award I'd been nominated for. They listed the names of my peers, my name among them. Years of training allowed my features to be stoic as the camera was held on my face.

Please don't let it be me. Please don't let it be me.

I might have been the only nominee in the show's history who didn't want their name called. But Emma should have been here. Emma should have been at my side. This was an absolute joke as it was. Why was I even here? Who knew what my parents did to pull these strings?

"Wesley Cole." The air warbled around my head like waves crashing against the surf. "This is Wesley Cole's first nomination and his first win." Someone shook my shoulder in congratulatory excitement. The applause all around me was deafening, but I was outside of myself. Autopilot propelled me forward.

I made my way toward the stage. My feet somehow moved. Things were being said. A young woman handed me a gold statue. A microphone rose from the floor, raised to my height.

I blinked at it as though it was an antenna from an alien. Then I glared down at the surprisingly heavy statue in my hand.

This wasn't fair to the people who dreamed their whole lives of this moment. This wasn't fair that Emma wasn't here celebrating with me. All I ever wanted was to protect her by keeping her away from me. How ridiculous I'd been. We should be a team figuring this out together. That was what she said.

Why wasn't she here? She was supposed to be here.

The entire room was silent. Countless wide eyes smiled up at me, waiting for me to speak. With every second that ticked by like a gong ringing next to my head, their smiles started to fade. They shared awkward glances.

I cleared my throat and leaned forward.

Find those people and hold on tight.

A flash of Emma's head in my lap as she read. Her riding me, red hair flowing over her shoulders. Her bright blue eyes as she snorted with laughter. Her angry, impassioned speeches with waving hands and strong sense of justice. She was here with me. Just as she always was, firmly settled in my bones, my lungs, my heart. She was woven into the fiber that made me who I was. The good parts. She was the reason I hadn't turned into my father.

It was always Emma.

"I don't deserve this," I said, still looking down at the little figurine. "I don't mean that in the falsely modest way. I genuinely am not sure I deserve this. I'm sure you know my father. But you may not know that he would do just about anything to have one of these on our family's shelf. I guess this is for you, Dad. If you are watching. Sorry I'm not the son you ever wanted. Sorry that I continue to be a disappointment." I laughed freely and loudly, head thrown back and grinning like a maniac. "I don't even want this. Fuck. I sound so ungrateful. Shit, sorry. You'll probably have to bleep that out. The other one too."

Row after row of celebrities stared slack-jawed or pulled out their phone to record me. I spotted Harrison, features neutral except for a slight furrow of his brow as I continued to go off the rails.

"This is so messed up. This award means so much to so

many people. And I don't deserve it at all. There are people who want this and work for it their whole lives." I gestured to an actor who was a fellow nominee. "Who deserve it so much more. I'm standing up here completely blank because all I can think about is Emma Flynn."

There was a soft shuffling as audience members grew more uncomfortable. "I keep thinking how I should be with her wherever she is. How that's really the only thing that matters." I ran my hand over my face, and my laughter melted. "I have wasted so much time. So much time," I repeated to myself. "That was what George meant. He didn't mean that all good things end. I mean, that's true, they do." I spoke my thoughts out loud, processing them in real-time.

"He meant that we needed to fight for what was real. The things that seem so big won't even matter because the important things will end before we're ready. I don't know what I'm saying. God, I just want to have time with her. Whatever I'll get. Whatever she'll give me. I love that woman so much." I was laughing again, but tears filled my eyes. "It's this physical thing. It hurts so bad." I rubbed at my chest. "It feels like it's eating me alive sometimes. I've never known any person as wonderful as she is. Brave and smart and beautiful but she's a human being. She's treated like this false idol. She's not allowed to be fallible or have flaws or even exist without constant scrutiny. I've been guilty of that because I thought she was too perfect to have my love. That I would only ever taint her with my ugliness, and I've spent so much time pushing her away because that's what I thought was best for her. But this *love* that consumes me, it's not a dangerous thing. Nothing this pure could be bad. Loving somebody this hard could never be bad. Wanting to see them happy and thriving could only ever be good for them. To see them be their best selves, truly alive as who they are. That's the thing." I nodded in agreement with myself. "I'm the only person who could love her this hard. I know this. I know this in every cell. But I didn't think that would be enough. I was made to feel that love was fleeting and cheap and wrong. But love is really all there is, isn't there?" I looked out at the audience. A few teary faces nodded encouragement. "That's really the only thing we will take at the end. Even if everything else fails, it's this feeling, these people in our lives, that matter. It's a damn cliché for a reason."

I scoffed, head back, and stared at the high ceiling. When I looked back out at the gobsmacked room, a few people smiled, and Harrison nodded in a "duh" sort of way.

"I've wasted so much time already. Your time. Her time. The Academy's time. Listen, there's the awkward music telling me I've babbled far too long. I have to go. I have to find her and stop wasting this stupid short life. Thank you. I'm sorry I'm such a massive asshole. I'm sure when I'm not so totally fucked in the head, I will really appreciate this award and probably have to issue more apologies." I smacked my forehead. "And sorry for the swearing. Man, it's really hard to be coherent up here. Bye."

I ran off stage as applause and laughter broke out behind me.

That should occupy the media for a solid evening.

The only thing I cared about was finding Emma.

31

———

Wesley

I called Emma's phone as soon as I was off stage. Just as before, it went straight to voicemail, and my texts went unread. I sprinted through the winding backstage hallways and offshoots, shouting questions at whoever passed for directions to the back exit. I would run to her. I would find her.

"Wesley!" my mother called out.

I froze, shoulders hunching, and took a deep breath to soothe my frustrations and anger. I was on fire with adrenaline, and stopping my progress felt like torture.

What was she doing here? I hadn't spoken to either of them since he told me the truth on the phone that day. I'd avoided them, afraid my anger would ruin the plan. They'd only managed to not make anything worse because the media hadn't found out Emma and I were still in contact. We hadn't told anybody. We kept things secret until we were ready.

My mother stepped toward me in the back hall near some offices with nobody else around.

"I heard your speech," she said tentatively.

My instinct was to apologize for the incredible mess I'd been and placate her, but I clamped it down. "I don't have time for this," I said.

"Wait. Please, just give me five minutes."

"I have to find Emma."

"I know," she said. "It was a … a lovely speech. I didn't know you felt so strongly about her. You never said." She twisted her hands in front of her.

I felt my face twist into a scowl. "I didn't need to tell you. You both saw enough of my feelings to use her to manipulate me. I know about everything."

"I was worried you'd choose her. I tried to warn you. It's easier to just go with it. You think that I'm out of touch, but he's always two steps ahead."

"Why are you here?" My fists were balled so tight they began to ache.

"You are too important to this family to let you go."

"I'm nothing more than those pointless metal statues on your shelves."

"That's not true. I'm your mother. Don't you even care about me? This family? You can't leave me alone here with your father."

I shook my head. "I love her. I won't leave her."

"If you love her, then you will tell her that you can't be together. You went too far this time. He's not happy."

"Why? Why do you two care so much? This makes no sense." I was shouting, over the top, and emotional, and I let her see it all. There was no holding back because I didn't care about their opinion of me anymore.

"It's complicated. Your father doesn't like to be wrong."

"I don't give a fuck," I snapped, and she reared back. "We're leaving. All of this."

"And what about her brand? What about all the people who

rely on her?"

"We'll figure it out."

"You don't understand. Your father has reach. He'll ruin her. Nobody will ever help her again. You are really ready to destroy both of your lives and everything she has built?"

"None of that matters. We'll figure out new ways to help."

"Why won't you do as he says? It's easier!" she yelled and stomped her foot. Her neck was splotched with red, but her face was a pale, cool mask with all the makeup. I'd never seen her like this, so totally out of control. She was the one who taught me to hide my emotions so well.

I blinked in disgust. "Is it easier?"

She twisted her hands. I held her gaze until she broke away first. I stepped forward, steadying my voice to speak.

"I'm not talking about financially easier. Because sure, maybe. But seeing your life, how miserable you seem, doesn't make me think it's easy. You have no freedom. But maybe that is easier for you?"

She looked up at me, lips trembling. "I made hard choices, and you don't get to judge me."

I shook my head. "Well, if that's *easy*, then I don't want that. I want whatever comes with being in love. I want the passion. I want the fear. I want the good times and the hard times. I want to figure out making a family with her. I want to watch her change and grow. Help her find her passions and what makes her happy. I want to struggle and then be happy. I want whatever is the opposite of what you and Dad have. Because if that's the easy life, then I want nothing to do with it."

"Wesley," she said, tears welled in her eyes. It was the most emotion I had ever seen in her.

"I want every heartbreak with her by my side. I want to *feel* things. Anything, so long as I'm feeling. I'm tired of pretending and pushing things down. The more I pretend things don't affect me, the more I feel myself die inside. The more I turn into that man."

Her lips trembled. "Your father?"

I nodded, nostrils flared. "I don't want to be anything like that monster."

She huffed a laugh. "You're nothing like him. The more he pushed you to follow in his footsteps, the more you were your own man. He's a sad, lonely person who came from a sad, lonely set of people who were also driven by greed and fame. I'm not excusing him. He is the product of his environment. He tried so hard to make you his little shadow, to somehow prove that it was all worth it. But trust me when I say you are nothing like him other than the DNA you share."

I glared at the ground.

She lifted my chin with her perfectly manicured nail and gave me a watery smile. "And I've never been more proud."

Despite myself, despite everything, my fucking heart ached at those words.

"Why did you stay? Why do you put up with it?" I asked.

"Fear. You were the only thing I ever loved, and he would take you too."

"Too?"

She fidgeted with her purse strap. "There is more to the story of your uncle Ace." She looked away and then back at me. "We were in love. Ace and me. Before I met your father. We were going to run away together. We were going to start a new life, but I was the match your grandmother wanted for your father because of my family. Your father followed orders. They didn't want me with Ace because he was leaving, or rather being forced out of the family. I didn't have a choice. I stayed for his freedom."

"Mom." I shook my head, not understanding. "Why not stay with him? Why tell me this now?"

"What choice did I have? Ace wanted freedom. I wanted

Ace's happiness. I wouldn't chain him to this life. Your father offered everything else, security, a life of luxury. A family. I'm just saying I understand, and I'm trying to protect you. You think you understand how powerful he is, but you have no idea."

"I know he leaked the picture and set all this up."

"He found out you were trying to leave us. Your lawyers, they knew, and they told us. He has his fingers in everything. This was all a long game. I understand how much you love her, but it will only ever hurt her. I've been trying to protect you."

"I can't look at you. I can't stand this." I moved to brush past her.

A horrible suspicion crept over me, and I stopped and turned around. "Is Ace my father?"

Her eyes widened. "No. No." She reached for me, but I stepped back, and she pressed a hand to her chest. "You know when you were born, you were my fourth IVF attempt. Your father and I never ... He said I disgusted him and wouldn't touch me after I was with his brother. Our whole marriage was a lie."

"Mom. Please. Please don't emotionally manipulate me with this."

"I'm not. I'm not. Listen, please. The moment I held you, I knew you were my miracle baby. I knew I would do anything to protect you from this family. You had that streak of white in your hair like me, and even though you grew up to look more and more like him, I was secretly so happy about that streak. He wanted to dye it when you were young, and I never let him. The one thing I refused to let him have. And then it became a part of your signature look, so he couldn't take it away. But it made me so happy to see that proof of defiance. I thought about taking you away, but this life means something. Sometimes that means playing the long game."

"I don't want to play any game. I want to live my life. I'm exhausted."

"Go to her. Explain that he will take everything. She will make the same sacrifice for you if she really loves you. But it doesn't have to be the end. Maybe you can still have an affair in secret."

I felt sick. I was surer than ever that I couldn't lose Emma. That every second away from her was a second wasted. "You can't be serious. Watch each other marry someone else? I can't even." My stomach roiled.

"If she loves you as much as she does, she will let you go. Just like I did. It will be hard, but you will be okay."

"But you're not okay. You're not. You were in love with a man, and you ... wait, but I have memories of Uncle Ace."

She smiled softly. "I didn't think you would remember."

"How is that possible if he left before I was born?"

"He used to come visit when your father was out of town. He and I tried ... to be friendly, but it was too painful. He had to stop coming." She looked over my shoulder. "He was such a good man. Just like you. Despite his upbringing."

"You made the wrong choice," I said.

"No." She shook her head, eyes gleaming. "I got you. Everything was worth it."

I wanted to believe her. I wanted this mother who loved and fought for me, but I'd been played and manipulated before. Actions spoke louder than words in this family. Words meant nothing.

"I won't make the same choice you made. I choose Emma."

She looked down sadly. "It may be too late. He won't ever be wrong."

My blood ran cold. "Where is she?"

"Your father has her."

32

———————

Emma

I knocked on Wesley's door, jumping with nerves. We were supposed to meet at the Oscars, but I took an earlier flight to surprise him.

We'd waited long enough.

I shifted from foot to foot as a dark shape moved to answer the door.

A shape that was far too big for Wesley.

I clutched my tote closer as the door swung open, and a huge man looked expectantly at me.

"Mr. Cole has asked to meet with you to chat." He had his hands clasped loosely in front of him. Dark sunglasses hid his eyes, but his square jaw was clenched.

"No, thank you." I stepped back with my phone gripped in my hand.

He snatched it from my grasp easily. "I'm sorry, Miss Flynn. It's easier to go along with it." He turned it off and slid it into his suit jacket pocket.

"The Coles have hired thugs now?" I asked, shrinking back.

He ground his jaw, grabbing my upper arm. "Nothing is going to happen to you. He just wants to talk."

I fought him off, and he let go with a sigh. "This is unbelievably ridiculous. Wesley is waiting for me. I do not accept this." Except where was Wesley?

"Wesley is already gone. He went early, hoping to see you sooner." He flushed as he spoke. How did he know that?

"Great." I sighed.

The large man shrugged and easily moved to block any chance of escape. "I don't like it either."

I didn't think I was in physical danger; the man was obviously miserable to be here. Another pawn of Rex Cole. Also, Harrison knew I was going to Wesley's early, but he was already at the theater, and his agent had his phone. I didn't want to be totally at this thug's mercy. I checked my bag for anything I could use. Nothing. Unless he was highly allergic to vegan protein bars or SPF lip-plumping moisturizer.

I was led to the dining room table from my first meeting here. Even then, Rex knew Wesley's plan to leave. Rex was always aware. He knew I had landed early. I wasn't sure how his father knew everything, but I wasn't surprised. I tossed my tote into the center of the table, knowing there was no point in fighting until Rex had his say.

And I had mine.

He could throw whatever he wanted at me, but I was Emma Flynn, and I had nothing to lose. Nothing but the man I loved who already gave up so much for me.

Bring it on.

Hours ticked by. Every time I breathed too hard, the thug would watch me carefully. Poor Wesley was alone, likely assuming the worst. The awards had to be nearly winding down. Rex was waiting for something. Maybe to ensure that I wouldn't be there when Wesley's category was called. He wanted his son to feel more isolated and alone. What an absolute wanker Rex Cole was.

Every moment that passed, my rage grew.

I'd lost track of how long I'd been kept in the room. I sighed with arms crossed at the table, foot tapping. The big man hadn't moved from his station near the door, seemingly relaxed until I made the slightest shift. Then he tensed slightly as though he'd need to spring to action.

I looked around the room and to the dining room table. I thought of everything Rex Cole had controlled from the very beginning. How he really always seemed to be two steps ahead of the game. But men like that always had a weakness, an ego that would ultimately do them in. An idea was beginning to form. My pulse raced, and I needed a minute alone.

"He shouldn't be too much longer," the man said, startling me.

"I'm thirsty," I said.

He blinked at me.

"I can go get it," I offered.

He tilted his head subtly, an eyebrow raised, conveying what he thought about that.

"Please? I feel like I'm being held captive." I gave him my best blue-eyed, pleading look.

His nostrils flared, and he flicked a glance to the attached kitchen. Maybe the man had a conscience.

I slid my tote to the center of the table more. "Look. I'll put that there and I'll ..." I looked around. I unhooked the ethically sourced gemstone necklace from around my neck. I wrapped it around my wrists to secure them to each other. "I won't go anywhere. It's too late at this point. I've not eaten or drunk anything all day to look good in a dress I didn't even get to wear. It's all moot anyway at this point. I really need some water."

I gave my most convincing Emma Flynn pleading look and made my blue eyes large and desperate.

He frowned at where I secured myself to the table. "You aren't being held captive," he grumbled.

"Then I'll just head out," I said with an innocent smile.

He sighed and glanced again to the kitchen. "Don't move," he said.

I nodded.

"I don't get paid enough for this," he grumbled as he walked away.

I worked quickly and had just managed to be back in my chair by the time he returned less than two minutes later. I hadn't quite finished what I needed to do.

I sat in the same spot, heart racing but features pristine. He set the glass of water in front of me.

I made a face. "No fizzy water?" I asked.

He clenched his jaw but snatched the water and turned back.

"And a slice of lemon. If not too much trouble," I called after him.

"Celebrities," he grumbled some more.

This time, I had finished when he returned again and set the new glass down.

"Thank you so much," I said, wrists still seemingly locked together. I took a big drink and smacked my lips loudly with a contented sigh.

My hands shook as I set the glass back down, but he didn't notice as he returned to stand sentinel at the door.

Rex Cole walked in a heartbeat later. I sat up straighter, as did the man on guard. Rex's eyes took in the glass of water and my necklace before he shot a look at the man in sunglasses.

"You can go, McCormick," Rex said.

Ah, so he had a name. The man in question glanced at me again, hesitating.

"Goodbye, Mac," Rex said. "Thank you for your assistance. I'll keep my end of the bargain."

Mac. *Mac.* I swore to myself. I knew that name.

Mac, Wesley's supposed only friend, nodded before he turned on a heel and left. The front door opened and closed.

"I think it's apparent at this point, Miss Flynn, that you have very little control in this situation. Let me say what I need to and you can leave," Rex said. "No need for all the theatrics." He flicked a look to where I untwisted the pseudo-handcuffs from my wrist.

He was dressed as always in a suit, except, for once, he didn't have a phone in his hand. He really wanted my uninterrupted focus.

I kept silent, slowly breathing in and out.

"What's that about?" He raised an eyebrow at the necklace.

"The reason I'm chained here? Your hired henchman told me I had no option to leave, and I was thirsty. It was a compromise," I said loudly and evenly.

"You could have left anytime," he said with a shrug. Infuriatingly.

"It really didn't feel that way when you barricaded me in your son's house."

"Let's get to the point."

I rubbed at my wrist but didn't move from my spot.

"You know why you're here and what I want," he said in his low, I'm sure to many, intimidating tone.

"What?" I said, leaning forward slightly. Just to fuck with him. "I'm sorry I couldn't hear you over the absolute gall."

He huffed once, dryly. "You have a lot of arrogance for a woman who's lost everything," he said louder.

"Actually, I haven't lost anything."

"Not yet." His nostrils flared, and he stepped forward. "These antics with my son need to end. We've tried to be patient, but we've had enough."

"I don't control your son. Unlike you. Wesley is free to do whatever he wants." I grinned ear to ear. "And that's me."

Rex's cool features tensed for a moment. "Classy as always, little girl. I knew you were trash the second you showed up on set."

I shrugged a shoulder. "I really could not care less what a man like you thinks of me."

"This arrangement was never going to last. This was all for show. But now it's time to end it," he said.

"I don't think so."

"Wesley won't do it on his own," he continued, ignoring my snark. "That foolish boy has got it in his head that he loves you and is ready to give up everything to be with you."

I blinked at him. "How awful for you," I said.

"But I know you're smarter than he is. I have seen you take control of your brand over the years. I see you understand this world more rationally than he does."

"Flattery is it now?" I asked.

"No. Just facts. My son won't leave you. But you will leave him. If you care about him like you think you do. You understand that his life will be over if he leaves. Wesley has no skills to fall back on. Nobody in this business will ever work with him again. I have control of his financial assets. He will be absolutely destitute. He needs this family."

"Like his uncle Ace?" I asked. "Isn't that what you did to your own brother?"

"Don't speak of what you don't understand."

"And you're wrong. Even if you pull your strings and black-ball your own *son*," I exaggerated the word. "Wesley won't be alone. He will have me," I said simply.

He sighed as he pinched the area between his eyes. "Everybody has their price. No matter how in *love* they think they are," he said that last bit with clear disgust. "You have worked very hard and helped so many people. I'd hate to see them all left high and dry now."

"Let me get this straight. You're telling me if I don't break up with your son, even though he's happy, and I love him and we want to be together, that you'll ruin my charity that helps people and take away all the money he's made? Do you not hear how mental that sounds?"

"I do what it takes to protect this family."

"That's what you expect me to do, isn't it? Like you've been using your son's love for me all these years to control him, you expect me to do the same. To push him away if I love him."

"He would do it for you. If you really claim to know what love is."

I leaned back, blowing out a long breath through puffed lips. "I'm really starting to understand that you actually have no clue about anything. Love is not a form of control, it's freedom."

"Love is fleeting. I want what's best for him."

"What's that? Money? Power?"

He's silent. "Are you done with this sentimental drivel?"

I laughed. "Not even close."

He stepped closer. I held up a hand. "I'll tell you when I'm done, so you can go ahead and shut up for now."

His lip curled into a snarl. "You have no idea who you're talking to. You've no idea the power I hold."

"Let's circle back to that in a minute, but for now, I want to make it clear what I think of you, for once. I pity *you*. I feel sad for *you*. You've looked down on me my whole life, yet you are the one who hasn't got a clue. Because no matter what you do, how many ways you come at us, Wesley and I have each other. We are family. We know what family and love feel like, and you never will. You think you can put out the flame by dumping gasoline on it because you have no idea how it works. That's your biggest weakness and flaw. You will always assume money and power drives people. And that's why I feel sad for you because, at the end of the day, you may be rich and powerful, but you will be totally alone, and not a single person will remember your name." As I spoke, his face grew redder and redder, my old accent slipped in, and I was yelling.

Let him see emotion. Let it ooze over him like slime he can never wash off.

"You people are all sentimental fools!" His color rose to match his voice. "I've kept this family afloat. I'm always the bad guy, but I've done everything to maintain our status and protect the Cole family."

"This isn't a family anymore. It's a crime syndicate."

"We're done here. You've made your choice. Just because you're too weak to do what it takes to love my son like you say."

"Too weak?"

"You. My son. My brother. All of you are weak. Coles protect this family at all costs."

I stared at him. "Now, I really do think you believe that. I wouldn't be surprised to hear, I dunno, that you were willing to do anything to protect yourself. Including maybe embezzling funds from the hospital that you supposedly donate to."

This stopped him in his tracks.

"Somebody would really have to spend a lot of time researching and digging into your records and have contacts of their own to help them find that out, wouldn't they?" I stood and leaned forward to glare at him.

"You have no proof," he spat. He stomped toward me, but I put the chair between us.

"I'm going to stop you right there before you really do something you can't take back."

"You're a trashy little country whore that's been trying to seduce my son for too long. I should have taken care of you when I first had the chance. Fuck that fucking show."

"Are you telling me you wanted to hurt the Golden Girl? Remove her from the Intrepid Trio of the beloved show *Terraformative*. Because several million people might have a problem with that."

He shook his head. "That show was a pile of shit, and anybody who liked it was a sentimental fool like the rest of you. I should have never let Wesley do that show."

"The fans are not going to like that."

"You think I give a shit about those idiots?"

"The TF fans are the best thing to happen, and you have no idea the power they hold. Now, it's time for *you* to be scared," I said, low and controlled again.

Rex stalked toward me, body towering, and his face contorted in a grimace. It was the first time his outside matched his inhumanity within. His mask had slipped to reveal the true deformed creature of hatred underneath. I had a fleeting and futile thought, *this man will kill me before he lets his son have any happiness.*

I stood my ground even as he stepped right up to me. I glared in defiance. I fought hard and would continue to. I wouldn't give up until I had done everything in my power to stop him.

Footsteps pounded outside as the door slammed open.

"Father!" Wesley barreled into the room, finding me immediately. He took in his father looming over me, and my fists balled at my side. His voice was ice cold. I'd be lying if I said I wasn't relieved to see him. "Get away from her. Don't lay a fucking finger on her." He ran to my side.

His father stepped back, hands up, features cool again. "We were just talking."

"Emma! Don't listen to anything he says," Wesley said. "Whatever he threatened you with, don't listen. Nothing matters but you and me, okay?" I wrapped my arms around his shoulders as he kissed my cheek, holding me tight. "You and me, we'll figure it out. Just don't let him get to you."

I leaned back and placed my hands on his cheeks. "Don't worry."

"Calm yourself, Wesley," Rex said.

"Yeah, we were chatting. Your dad and me ..." I slid my tote bag to the side to lean forward and look at the screen of the small tablet in the middle of the table. "And two million of our closest friends."

Rex's face went pale as his eyes moved to the screen.

I couldn't revel in his astonishment for too long because, at that exact moment, Harrison, the big dude Mac, and Diana Cole entered the room, breathless and haggard.

Mac looked wrecked. Diana looked like she was seconds from wilting. Harrison looked entertained.

Shortly after, Sofia came in, phone in hand, and a handsome older man who nobody else seemed to notice yet. The new man stood, arms crossed, with a familiar scowl.

Well, this was all going splendidly. It wasn't how we'd planned it, but there was no stopping us now.

33

Wesley

I inspected every inch of Emma for any signs of injury. Her wrists were a little red, and I kissed them. As my hands roamed over her, I rambled incoherently about keeping her safe. I was terrified that I'd be too late. That somehow, the final thread that tied my father to humanity would snap, and he would do something he couldn't take back.

"He kept me from you. I tried to be there," she said.

"It's okay. I know. I'm here now," I murmured, kissing her forehead.

"You missed a damn good speech, though," Harrison cut in from behind.

Wesley seemed surprised to suddenly hear from him. Then his gaze moved to the others in the room. "Mom? Harrison? What's everyone doing here?"

"Mac got ahold of me and told me where Emma was. He had been waiting for me," Harrison said.

The big guy looked at his feet. "Not soon enough," he mumbled.

"I followed you," Harrison cut in. "I was worried. I knew Emma wouldn't miss being there for you without a very good reason."

Emma nodded.

I was so proud of my brave, beautiful woman. I turned my attention to my father.

"Did you really try to kidnap my girlfriend? Have you really lost it?" I yelled.

"Please. I just wanted to talk. Ask your friend," he gestured to Mac.

Mac still wouldn't meet my gaze. He glared down but seemed to decide something before a shake of his head. "He told me not to let her leave under any circumstances. I'm sorry, Wes. I thought ... I don't have an excuse, but I knew if I was watching her, nobody else could hurt her."

I was numb to his betrayal but wasn't surprised. Somebody had to be working for my father, and it only made sense that Mac would fall victim to him. I was too distracted by Emma to fully process that my only friend had been another fake aspect of my life.

"There goes my end of the bargain," Rex said.

Mac shook his head and handed Emma her phone back. "I'm sorry, Miss Flynn."

Emma grabbed her phone and shrugged. "I'm sorry I started recording when you went to get me fizzy water. I don't even like fizzy water."

He winked. "I know."

I blinked at Mac, hardly processing everything that was happening.

"And you've been recording this whole conversation?" I asked Emma.

She shook her head. "Not recording. Live streaming."

"None of this will hold up in court. You'll be hearing from my lawyers," my father said.

"Not if you hear from mine first," Emma said with a smile. There was the fierceness of the negotiator that I knew. "And actually, here's one now."

Another man I didn't immediately notice stepped forward. Slow realization spread over me at the same time as my father, based on how the color drained from his face.

My uncle Ace stepped forward, his features serene as he looked between Emma and my father. He briefly looked at me with a nod. "Nice to see you, Wesley."

"Here's the great part," Emma said. "I know how you love to record people without their knowledge, so I really think you'll like this. You remember your brother, Ace? He's a big-time attorney now. I'm sure you know that as you've been doing everything in your power to find him and keep tabs on him."

Rex stared, his mask in place, but the wheels behind his eyes turned.

"I specialize in family law now to make sure what happened to me won't happen to anybody else again." He glared at Rex. His gaze staggered on Diana momentarily. Her mouth opened and closed, but she could only look away. When he spotted Diana, his hard features cracked for a split second. So he had the family Cole mask still.

Rex came forward and stepped up to Ace. To his credit, Ace did not shirk back. He matched his brother's stance, unimpressed. Unthreatened. Watching Rex and Ace square off was like watching the results of a timeline that split in two. Two different lives based on the choices they made. One life that left more laugh lines and freckles that spoke of a life lived and joy. And one pristine mask. Smooth but emotionless and pitiful, like a lake of ice.

"I've been working with Emma to look into your finances

with several other lawyers, specifically experts in white-collar crime. There's a lot of missing money that needs to be accounted for." Ace didn't even acknowledge his brother or their past of pain. "You won't be able to outplay this one, big brother. The whole world was watching. You have some major explaining to do, and I can't imagine anybody would want to support such an awful and pretentious asshole."

"I bet you are so excited to be the hero." Rex sneered.

"I only care about what's right." The older man took a breath and added, "And for the record, Coles under pressure don't make diamonds. They make for second-rate fire starters."

"Yeah, coal doesn't make diamonds, that's an old wives' tale," Harrison said quietly.

"The whole diamond industry is exploitive and problematic in so many ways—" Emma started in response to Harrison. I hugged her tighter, and she quietly added, "I can finish that speech later."

"Someone, turn off that bloody video!" Rex yelled, the final traces of cool being lost forever.

Sofia stepped forward and grabbed the device. "I think we got enough anyway." Sofia tucked the tablet under her arm and smiled at Rex. "Hi. I'm Sofia. You might remember me from the last time we were all here. I'm Emma's manager. I wanted to say that working with you has been an absolute shit show, and I've hated every second of it." She said it so sweetly that my father almost extended his hand, despite everything going on, until the words sank in, and he scowled.

Mac watched her with wide eyes. "I like her," he said softly.

I clapped Mac on the back a little roughly. "Good, you'll be getting to know her well," I whispered in his ear.

He raised a questioning eyebrow, and I looked away. We had plans for Sofia and the future of Emma's company. Mac would be playing a crucial role in making up for what he did.

Emma stepped to my father. "You'll also see a lot more of her as she takes on the business side of things. I'm looking to pull back a little. Your attempt to slander my entire existence has pushed me to understand that I need some time off anyway. So thank you. This has all really worked out nicely," Emma said.

Uncle Ace covered his mouth as he tried to hide his smile. My mother had yet to take her eyes off him. It caused me to go back to Emma's side and put her under my arm protectively. To think that we were so close to going down that same lonely path as my mom and Ace. I brought her hand to my mouth to brush my lips along her knuckles, reassurance that she was here and mine.

My father had grown redder than I'd ever seen him. There was not a single masked emotion in the room.

"Ha!" Harrison laughed loudly out of nowhere. We all looked at him, wondering what could possibly be that funny with the tension so high in this room right now. "Er, sorry. I was just thinking that Emma had an ace up her sleeve. A literal Ace."

Emma laughed with a headshake.

"Enough," Rex snapped and grabbed his pale wife's wrist. "Let's go."

She tugged her arm free and stood her ground. She shook her head and came to stand on the other side of me.

"I only ever put up with it for Wesley. I won't lose him," she said, eyes filling.

"The saddest thing is that you had a chance to really have it all," Emma said, holding Rex's gaze. "You had a wife and a son, and you tortured them into doing your bidding. You might have had it all, and when you have absolutely nothing, you can think about that."

"This is hardly the end, little girl."

"You can't hurt us. You can take everything, but you won't

take us. We are stronger together, and you will never understand that. Even now, you still can't see it."

I looked at Emma, then at my mother. To others in this room who were here for Emma and me. For George and the others at Christmas. I had found my family. I was not alone.

"It's over, Rex," I said. "I'm not afraid anymore. I'm not afraid of becoming you. Not when I know myself and what I want. I will never be motivated by the things that motivate you."

"You're just like me," he said. "You think I'm a monster, but wouldn't you do anything to protect her?" He gestured to Emma. "Doing the unthinkable happens slowly over time, not all at once. You think I thought I'd end up here when I was a kid? You protect your family. That's your job," he said.

I hesitated. I would do anything to protect Emma. Would this ultimately lead to my downfall? Love had been used as an excuse to do deplorable things all throughout human history.

Emma stood and put herself between us. My mother came to stand on my other side. I felt the others stand behind me, forming a wall of defense against my father's slander.

"No," I said. "I won't turn into you. And I'm not worried about that anymore. Despite your best attempts, I've managed to accept the love offered to me. I don't fear it. I look forward to it, and I plan to make the most of it."

He looked appalled.

"Your loss," he spat and left.

Alone.

As soon as he was gone, Emma jumped into my arms. She rapid-fire attacked my face with kisses.

"I'm so proud of you," I said.

"Of me?" She leaned back to look at me in question.

"You did in one evening what I couldn't do my whole life," I said.

"Well, I am the Golden Girl for a reason." She smiled.

"Nah. You're Emma Flynn. And you're incredible."

"I love you, Wesley Cole."

"I love you, Emma Flynn."

I lowered my head and met hers for a kiss.

Next to us, a sniffle broke us from our reunion. I turned to find Mac discreetly wiping at his nose. He cleared his throat and dropped his shoulders in a shrug. "It's a beautiful moment."

"Who's this marshmallow?" Sofia asked, handing him a tissue with an amused smile.

"This is your future bodyguard, Mac. Mac, this is Sofia. She's taking over the foundation so Emma and I can take some time off on white sandy beaches."

"I do not need—" Sofia said at the same time Mac said, "Nah, man. You know I don't—"

He stopped when he saw the look on my face.

"—see how I could say no. When I clearly owe you," he finished.

"Good man."

He swallowed, going slightly pale as he looked back at Sofia. She had her arms crossed and a scowl on her face. "This isn't going to happen," she whispered.

"We'll see," he said back, taking his bodyguard stance next to her, blank face and arms crossed in front of him.

Sofia shuffled a step away. "Let's give the lovebirds some space. I have a feeling the show is just beginning."

She gave Emma a hug. "I'm glad you decided to fake date Wesley Cole. It all worked out." She smiled as though it had been her plan all along.

Emma hugged her back with a confused smile.

Uncle Ace stepped forward and shook my hand. "I'm looking forward to getting to know the man you are now," he said. "I like what I see so far." He smiled freely, grinning ear to ear. It was as unfamiliar yet familiar as looking at an old photo.

His hair was grayer than I remembered and looked remarkably like his brother, but where my father had a constant cool mask, Ace had little crinkles around his eyes and mouth.

"I'm looking forward to it," I said, throat tight.

"Good lady you've got there. She's fierce," he said. "I made myself untraceable, yet she found me and, well, here I am. She's something else. Never thought I'd be back here. No offense."

"That sounds like my Emma."

"Well, hold on tight to her." He clapped me on the shoulder before shaking his head and pulling me in for a hug. I hugged him back in surprise but enjoyed the sudden affection. A lot.

Ace glanced at my mom one last time and hesitated before turning and leaving.

My mother's shoulders slumped as she watched him go. "I will leave you two to chat," she said back to me. "Wesley." She started. "There's so much I need to say and so much to make up for, but thank you for not kicking me out with him. I will try—I will be better from now on."

"It's never too late," I said. "To mend any relationship." I glanced at where Ace had just left.

She swallowed. "I hope so." She remained focused on me. She raised a hand to my cheek and hovered for a moment before placing it on me. She sighed. "You really should shave. I don't know that the stubble—"

"Mother."

"Sorry." She held her hands up and shook her head. "You're right. I'm leaving." I gave her a hug, and she squeezed me a moment longer than she ever had in the past. When she finally let go, she sniffled and fixed my collar like she had done a thousand times before. I always considered it a critique of my appearance, but now I wondered if it was the only way she knew how to express affection.

"My next therapy session is going to be a doozy," I said as I stepped toward Emma.

She laughed and hugged my chest. It was so right and good to have her in my arms.

"Alone at last," I rumbled in her ear.

"Ahem." A voice cleared behind us.

I sighed and dropped my forehead to Emma's. "Harrison. You're still here."

"Well, at first, I felt weird interrupting the family reunion, and then it seemed you both forgot about me. It happens. Everybody forgets poor lonely me these days," he said with drama.

Emma sighed and broke herself out of my strong grasp.

"Harrison, you poor soul. Let me walk you out," she said as she linked her arm through his. He winked at me over her shoulder with a shit-eating grin.

I felt nothing but good-natured love for the man, despite his teasing. "Goodbye, Harrison," I called.

"Goodbye, lovah-boy." He smiled, and this time, it felt like a sincere gesture.

I was exhausted to my bones. The last hour had left me with a post-adrenaline tension headache. The whole situation was messy and complicated, but as I watched Emma kiss him goodbye, I felt more joy than I could remember feeling in so long. Maybe ever. I had friends and family. I had hope.

I had Emma.

Finally.

———

Emma

"WELL, NOW THAT IS A LOT TO UNPACK." I STEPPED TOWARD

Wesley, who'd remained quiet after everybody left. "Are you okay?" I asked, reaching for him.

He brought my arms behind his neck and bent to inhale me. I let out a breath and the tension melted from me.

"I'm perfect," he said.

"After talking with Ace and the team, there's likely a long battle ahead of us," I said.

He nodded, rubbing his nose up my neck. "That's true." He leaned back to hold my eyes in his. "Thankfully, we have nothing but time."

"And you're really okay?" I asked. "I know he was still your father. None of that could have been easy."

"The more time that passes, the more I pity him. He's truly the cautionary tale of what could have happened. It makes me all the more thankful for you. I don't know how I got to have you love me as much as I love you, but I won't be so stupid to ever lose it."

"You're a wonderful man."

"I love you." When he said he loved me, this time, it felt like the future. It felt like hope and promise and not anything like a goodbye.

"I love you," I said. "What's that face for?"

He raised his white and black eyebrow in question.

"That gooey-eyed look," I explained.

"I have to tell you something."

A sudden, knee-jerk reaction of fear filled me, but I quickly pushed it back down. I had no reason to be afraid. Whatever he was about to tell me, I would be okay. *We* would be okay.

I sat on the couch and gave him my undivided attention as he sat next to me, carefully taking my hands.

"Tell me. The buildup is honestly killing me. After the past few months, I really don't think my heart can take any more surprises, family secrets, or ambushes," I said.

He nodded seriously, but there was still that glint in his eyes. That soft smile that he knew something that I didn't. It was the look he'd always held since we were fourteen and playing games in the Cube of Solitude, or when we were twenty-three passing each other at an event, and he didn't know I was watching him.

"My face. This is how my face looks," he said, then turned slightly in profile so I could see it more clearly with a cheeky grin.

"Oh, bloody hell, Wesley, you gave me a scare."

He started to laugh and scooped me closer. "No, listen. I'm being serious. This face, what did you call it? The 'gooey-eyed' look? That's really what I look like when I'm looking at you, being near you. Or even thinking about you. Which is any time I'm awake. *That* is my actual state of being. And it hardly comes close to representing all the ginormous feelings inside."

"Ginormous, huh?"

"Yes. Stop interrupting. Because for all these years, every time you've seen me, I'd been hiding behind my Cole mask. Keeping myself at a distance because I knew at any second, I might slip and give it all away. Couldn't have you knowing how I felt about you. I have loved you as long as I've known what love is and probably a little before that."

"Oh."

"All that to say, get used to it. It's my mug, and you'll be seeing it for the next … oh, sixty to eighty years? Give or take?"

"Is that so?" I kissed the side of his mouth.

"God, I hope so."

"Hmm," I said. "That feels like a challenge."

"It is. It definitely is the ultimate game of chicken," he said seriously. "And I won't lose. I will absolutely love you with my entire being for the rest of my time on this plane of existence."

I narrowed my eyes. "I could probably beat that. I'm really, really good at getting what I want, as we know."

"If anybody could negotiate us into the next realm, it would be you," he said.

I flipped my hair over my shoulder. "True."

"Thank you for everything," he said, suddenly serious. "For standing up to my father. For tracking down my uncle." He shook his head, breaking off. "I still can't believe it."

"I'm so sorry I missed your award. I heard you gave a pretty good speech."

"I was a wreck. Unprepared and rambling."

"I can't wait to see it. I like Wesley Cole a little messy."

"Is that so?" He flipped me back onto the couch and crouched over me, the easy grin melting into something much darker and more titillating. We'd been patient enough. Waited long enough.

He grabbed my hands in his and pressed the backs of them against the cushions as he ground his already hard cock against my hip. His mouth moved over my neck, shoulder, everywhere, gently seeking it all out.

"God, I've missed you," I said as I tugged my fingers through his hair, guiding him to where I needed to be devoured the most. Everywhere. Forever.

He was worked up, as he tended to get in these moments. No filters or masks. No pretending or preplanning words. Thoughts tumbled out of him without stopping. He mumbled against my lips and breasts.

Oh, when had he taken those out?

"I will never tire of this." He groaned. He hefted me to wrap my legs around him and ground deeper against me. I was already heavy with arousal, and the press of him against my dress was a tease. "I will never tire of spending time with you. I want to learn every square inch of you. I want to know what you like and what makes you laugh."

"I feel like you know more about that than I do already." I panted.

I thought of how easily he brought me to orgasm with his mouth, his fingers, and the slow, steady pressure of his cock as he held it in me and pressed it deep.

I needed that *now*.

"I will be the world's only expert on Emma Flynn's body," he said, lowering to lavish my breasts. "Media's Golden Girl: A case study on orgasms. How to find them and make her scream." His fingers trailed up my thighs to toy at my core. I cried out as his thumb pressed against my clit. "Just like that," he said, self-satisfied. But I was benefiting far too much from his arrogance to knock him down a peg. "I will write the book of your body and sell exactly zero copies because I will be the only person who ever gets to make you writhe like this." His fingers had found their way into me, swirling to make me do just that.

"Nobody else even has the default instruction manual."

"Good," he growled.

"Also, we're retiring Golden Girl," I said, losing focus as his hands moved everywhere.

"About damn time."

Somehow, I was totally undressed. He was not. I groaned against him. I loved how my exposed skin felt against the fabrics of his suit, but not as much as I loved him naked with me.

"Nobody has ever made me feel like you do. Not even close," I confessed. "I don't think I ever even realized you were the measuring stick I measured all other men against until I found them all coming up short."

"Men are overall, painfully underwhelming."

"Exactly." I arched up with a whine. "Now get naked."

After we'd cleaned up and cooled down, I lay on his chest, listening to the beat of his heart, overall feeling rather sappy with orgasm.

"You know," he started.

When he spoke, I was startled, lost in my own thoughts as I'd been. He chuckled, and the vibrations traveled through me. He kissed my hair before he went on. "All these years, I've been wondering how this will hurt you. How I would hurt you."

I sat up with a shake of my head. I opened my mouth to speak, but he pressed a finger to my lips.

"My turn. I would feel this overwhelming pull of love and like a reflex, I'd immediately imagine how it would be used to cause you pain. How my love had *already* caused you pain."

I chewed my trembling lip to keep from speaking.

"It's so clear to me now. So ridiculously obvious. All those thoughts were wrong. I was asking the wrong questions. What will this love bring? What could my love give you? What joys and wonders and peace? Tiny moments of contentment and big moments of pleasure and quiet moments of awe. These are the questions I should have been asking."

"Wesley." I gasped, tears balanced on my lid. He tucked my hair behind my ear to brush his thumb against my cheek.

"And now it's like a whole new world has been opened to me. There are endless ways to make you happy. Endless joy yet to be discovered."

"Yes," I said. "Endless."

"Remember when we were talking about how after leaving TF there was this sense that we'd never be the same again, never feel as hopeful and happy?"

I nodded.

"I was wrong. I feel that with you. Every time I'm around you, I feel excited about anything and everything as long as I get to experience it with you. See it through your eyes. I haven't felt as hopeful for the future as I do now."

My heart beat a frantic tempo in my chest, and my body literally felt like it could explode with love. "I feel that way too. I thought I had to suffer to earn what I'd built. I thought the only way to make up for the dumb luck of getting that role of Lucy Lennon was to be perfect all the time and do as much good as possible. You've shown me so much, Wesley. Your ability to love, despite everything you've experienced, gives me so much hope. It's not all on my shoulders. It's not anything I did wrong or right. I am allowed to just exist and be loved."

"Your capacity to love knows no bounds, and it is awe-inspiring," he said. "You dug up all the best parts of me. I thought I'd lost them forever but I've found them in you."

"You are my home," I said.

"You are mine."

34

———

Podcast Nosy Nelly Celebrity News

Season 5, Episode 01 *'Bout Damn Time* transcript excerpt

Co-hosts: Gabi Ortega and Liz Kane

[excerpt starts]

LIZ: Well, the truth is out!

GABI: And how!

LIZ: What an epic reveal of the ultimate douchebag that's ever douched.

GABI: Ew.

LIZ: Yeah, sorry, that felt like too much the moment it left my lips.

GABI: I knew we could trust Emma.

LIZ: She would never betray her fans.

GABI: I never doubted her for a second. She loves the TF fandom.

LIZ: And the fandom loves her back!

GABI: She is such a badass.

LIZ: And more importantly, they are so in love. Did you

watch the live?"

GABI: Of course. Who didn't?

LIZ: Nobody, it seems like. It held the title for most watched live for weeks. Well, until the live Diana Cole did exposing Rex's lifetime of fraud. She tore Rex Cole a new one. I hope the multiple lawsuits work out.

GABI: Me too. But there's no doubt that Rex has been completely blackballed in Hollywood. Nobody will work with him now. All his so-called friends and associates have jumped ship to save face.

LIZ: Good. To extort a hospital that was supposed to help people. What an absolute monster.

GABI: Not to mention the emotional manipulation of the people he was supposed to care about.

LIZ: Mostly that. Yes.

GABI: I heard a rumor that Wesley might change his last name to Flynn when they get married.

LIZ: Emma and Wesley Flynn. I like it! Are they engaged?

GABI: Not yet, but I have a feeling about these two.

LIZ: Oh, for sure. They're the real deal. Never doubted it for a minute.

GABI: It has also been announced that Emma has stepped back from her charity work for a while.

LIZ: About damn time. That girl needs a break. They both do. After everything they did and fought for. I'm getting emotional just thinking about it.

GABI: It was a lot.

LIZ: A lifetime, basically, of loving each other.

Sighs in unison.

LIZ: They earned their happy ending.

GABI: And then some.

LIZ: An inside source, close to the family, told ChicChat that her former assistant will now be running the charity. There is something going on there too. She always has a bodyguard with her.

GABI: Oh, interesting. I wonder what that's about.

LIZ: Me too. God, I love the drama.

GABI: Speaking of. The Cole saga continues. The former Diana Cole has been spotted with her ex-husband's *brother*, Ace Cole.

LIZ: Oh, this is very juicy. What do you think the story is there?

GABI: I would love to know. I'm just happy to see she got her fair share and squared up the money owed to the hospital Rex was embezzling from.

LIZ: All in all, it looks as though things are looking up. Especially for the Intrepid Trio. Formerly known as the Loveless Trio.

GABI: They really did seem to be pretty unlucky in love.

LIZ: Not anymore!

GABI: Emma and Charlie have had some real trials and tribulations, but both seem to have found their happily ever afters.

LIZ: Gosh, I hope so. But let's not forget, there's still Harrison.

GABI: Pfft.

LIZ: What? What was that sound of abject disbelief for?

GABI: Harrison is a good-time guy. He's the epitome of the bachelor. He never takes things seriously, and I bet you a venti mocha that he will never settle down.

LIZ: Oh, you are so on.

[excerpt ends]

35

Wesley

A little down the road

We'd only been in Devon a few days when Charlie threatened me with his angry cock.

"Come on, don't be a chicken," Charlie said enthusiastically and with an impressively straight face.

"He never tires of those jokes," Kate said with a patient sigh.

"And you never tire of my angry—"

"Okay, sir, that's quite enough of that." She swatted his bottom. "And he's the sober one here." She kissed his cheek before going over to where Emma and Agata stood chatting.

Charlie chatted happily about his new family of chicks as he led me to the coup. I smiled at Emma as we passed and luxuriated in her easy, returned smile.

"I'm telling you. Could not walk straight for days," Agata said as I passed.

Nope. I would not be slowing down to take part in that conversation.

"It's really easy to get started," Charlie explained.

"This is really great, Charlie. But Emma and I are thinking of starting a clothing line, not a farm."

"I still think you should consider an all profits to charity line of organic food. You could use The Vicarage eggs."

"We'll think about it. We have time to decide."

Neither of us was in a rush to get back to work. We were more interested in making up for lost time and learning about each other's bodies. I looked back at Emma, who smiled at me from across the yard.

I was at ease and happy the smile never left my face.

Harrison cornered me several beers in. I narrowed my eyes to focus on him. He narrowed his eyes to focus on me. We both swayed.

"Listen here, mate," he said and then burped. "'Scuse me." He gripped my shoulder. Maybe he was trying to threaten me. Maybe he was trying to balance. Either way, I did the same so that we both had a hand on the other's shoulder, our heads down, and glaring at each other. Or maybe not glaring? Maybe just unable to hold our eyes all the way open.

Harrison spoke, and my mind processed it on a delay. "You're'ight."

"What?" I asked.

"You are all right."

"Oh. Thanks. I know."

He chuckled deeply. "Imserious."

"M'too."

He shook my shoulder. "You loved her in a way Charlie and I never could. You saw her in the way she needed to be seen, you know?"

I didn't know. What was he talking about? I nodded.

"Charlie and I were teenagers. We discovered breasts and fame and breasts, you know? We dinnit know. We dinnit. And the media was so bloody tough on her. And she was always so special. All bark and smooshy, you know?"

No. I still didn't follow. I did like boobs. I nodded.

"Thank you for loving her as she needed to be loved. Thanks for being there for Emma when we weren't," he said.

Oh. Yes. I followed. Emma. Oh, Emma. Emma's boobs. My Emma. She was mine. I got to love her. What a wonderful, beautiful world we lived in where love existed. And I got to play with Emma's boobs whenever I wanted.

"Never hada choice," I said, my throat suddenly tight. "It was like breathing, loving her."

Harrison nodded, emotion welling in his eyes. I nodded, emotion welling in my eyes.

"I tried not to. I tried to keep her away," I said with a disappointed shake of my head.

"Yeah. Keep her away," he said seriously.

"No. Don't keep her away."

"No." He reared back. "No, don't push her away. She needs your love," he said just as seriously.

"Exactly. I need to love her. Nobody else will ever love her like I can."

"Yeah, keep her close." Harrison swayed. "She's just so good, you know?" he said, starting to cry.

"I know. She's the best," I said, also crying.

"She's perfect," Harrison said.

I nodded but then shook my head. "No. Not perfect. Better than perfect." I sniffled and wiped my nose on my sleeve.

"Yeah. Not perfect. She's Emma," he said.

"We're lucky to even know her," Charlie said, emotion in his eyes.

Charlie? When did Charlie get here?

"So lucky," I agreed, clapping his shoulder and bringing him closer into the circle. The three of us stood, swaying in our huddle, holding each other's shoulders, crying over the most wonderful woman in the world. Or at least Harrison and I were swaying. Charlie seemed to be trying to hold us upright but happy to be there.

"And your love is so beautiful," Harrison said. And then, also just noticing Charlie, he pointed at him. "And you and Kate. It's so fucking beautiful."

"It's the most beautiful thing in the world," Charlie said with a smile.

"It is." Harrison sobered a little and stood still. "I want that. I want that so bad," he admitted. "I thought maybe but no. Not for me, I guess."

"You'll get there, mate," Charlie said. "It'll happen."

"Nobody takes me seriously. I—"

"Oh, for the love of God. You boys are pissed to high heaven." Emma came up to us and crossed her arms.

Kate was at her side, smiling with large doe eyes sparkling at the scene she found. "Oh, this is so precious," she said.

"They can hardly stand," Emma said, but she was smiling. She was so beautiful there with her hair down and her summer dress. Happy and at ease. My beautiful Emma.

I fell off the guys, and they stumbled. "There she is!" I went to her, arms in the air, exalting to the sky. "The most wonderful woman in the world!"

"Aw. Let's get you some water. Are you crying?"

I nodded. "I am a man who feels deeply and shows his emotions."

"That you are. Come on."

Later, after much water and food, I was sobered up but still bubbled with emotion as though I were drunk.

Kate and Charlie, Harrison and Agata, Emma and I sat at the large outdoor table as we passed around dishes of delicious food. I sat with my arm around Emma. I looked around at the people I now called family and felt true happiness.

Nothing else existed but these moments. The fame and money could never compare to the warm summer air filled with the scent of flowers and the woman I loved. Power to control would never be better than laughing at inappropriate cock jokes until it hurt with good people.

Anytime the doubt would creep in, when fear would cause me to default into my icy mask of protection, Emma was here by my side to thaw me out and squeeze my hand.

I loved and was loved in return.

And there wasn't any more to it than that.

* *

Curious about what's going on with Harrison?

Read on for a sneak peek of Down For The Word Count, a found family, single guardian romance from Piper Sheldon.

Order here or visit pipersheldon.com.

DOWN FOR THE WORD COUNT

Harrison

Several weeks ago

Practiced smile locked into place and eyes meeting hers for the appropriate amount of time, I nodded to show I was listening and interested.

Truthfully, I had no idea what the shop clerk just said.

"The love they're shown is just as important as the quality of the air or the pH of the soil. Everything has to be just right," she went on.

My head continued to nod in her direction, but my eyes roamed around the tourist shop named Brooks' Baubles and Books. Honestly, I'd checked out two sentences in. If I came across as not listening, it wasn't because I was rude, only that if a topic didn't interest me, trying to hold the thread of conversation felt like trying to track a single cloud as it morphed and shifted with others. And that was on a good day. Today, my focus was more difficult than ever. The woman speaking was charming enough, but I couldn't stay centered when the background music played so loudly, and the couple over by the artesian hand towels argued about the bottles of wine they splurged on. The bell above the door rang at sporadic intervals, a brunette woman with her back to me fidgeted with the postcard rack, and trinkets down the row sparkled for my perusal.

And louder than anything was my concern for my longtime friend and father-like figure, George Sedar. My worry was a man yelling into a bullhorn, demanding the lion's share of my attention.

Once this movie wrapped, I *would* visit more often.

"Hello?" she asked, following my wandering gaze before coming back to my face to scrutinize it closely. "Are you local?"

"Nah. Just passing through." I turned away, not wanting to be studied too closely, lest my features become recognizable.

My inability to focus was one of the many reasons people thought I was a bit thick. But didn't everybody struggle to maintain a conversation? Didn't everybody receive the input around them at full blast all the time? It was impossible to stay focused on the growing conditions of a particular grape when I wasn't a big wine drinker to begin with.

In her defense, being in Sandia, the "hidden gem" wine town in Northern California, typically meant that one *was* interested in the fancy grape knowledge she'd just been sharing. This was probably a spiel she gave to a hundred tourists a week.

"I swear we've met," she said. Her head tilted, examining me closer as I tucked my chin. She couldn't have been thirty, which meant chances were she'd easily know who I was. Not vanity, just statistics.

"Not likely," I said, using *Hank*, my Southern American persona. A slow-talking Southern drawl was like slipping into a familiar character, another layer of defense against notoriety. I tried my best to speak as little as possible as she continued. Not just because I had no idea what to say, but with every second that ticked by, she would likely realize that I was *the* Harrison Evans, uber celebrity.

I picked up another item as she spoke. It was a simple bottle opener with the town name etched on the side. I made it dance by pulling on the square head of its spiral body. Arms up. Arms down.

"Wheee." I brought it higher so she could see it looked like an excited person doing jumping jacks, but she didn't seem entertained. Her brow arched as her spiel trailed off.

"Excuse me. I'm needed over there," she said, scooting away hurriedly.

I set the trinket back down with a sigh. I only came down to town from George's place to get some space to think. His house was thirty minutes away, higher into the surrounding Mayacamas Mountains. I'd been filming so much these past few years that visiting happened less often. Ever since George's other half, William, died, I found it harder to return.

My best friend Emma Flynn would say I was uncomfortable dealing with my own impending mortality, and the loss of someone that close shoved that unavoidable fact in my face.

My other best friend Charlie Downing would just slap me on the back and tell me that time was a gift not to be wasted.

But Charlie had found Kate, and Emma had reunited with Wesley and were happily in love—or pretending not to be, as was the case with Emma—so their optimistic views on life couldn't be taken as gospel.

My truth lay somewhere between. I was wracked with guilt and an overarching sense that something was wrong not only with him but in my own life. I felt stuck between two worlds yet fully in neither. The world of celebrity and fame, and the world of George and my past.

But I was here now. That mattered.

I discreetly shuffled away, feigning interest in goat milk soap as the woman chatted with another tourist. I couldn't shake the feeling of being watched, even with my "normal American" disguise. That was to be expected. I was grateful for my fame, but it came at a cost I'd been paying since I was eleven and made the life-changing decision to join the cast of what would be the international phenomenon *Terraformative*.

George's health couldn't be that bad if he were still writing. I'd been repeating that sentence like a mantra. His last two books were well received not only by the frothing fanbase but also by notoriously hard to please reviewers. So things couldn't be *that* bad. Sure. He forgot my name from time to time, calling me Adam, but that was bound to happen to anybody close to ... How old was George these days? I couldn't recall, but he'd met hundreds of thousands of people in his lifetime, so he mixed my name up with my character from his novels. No. Big. Deal.

I moved to a bin of what appeared to be various miniature farm animals.

Who were these shops for? Who bought these incredibly overpriced knickknacks? In my hand, I turned around a tiny fluffy chick with literal twigs for legs.

"It's alpaca fur."

I jumped slightly. The woman was back.

"There's a farm up the road, and it's locally sourced," she explained, misinterpreting my examination of the petite poultry as interest.

"Very cute." I gestured with it as I checked the price on the bottom of the fluff ball on sticks, *yeesh*—very overpriced rubbish. "But not cheap, cheap."

She gave a polite smile with a glimmer of worry behind her eyes. "Let me know if you have any questions." She smiled as she backed up.

"Cheep." The chick in my hand answered as I waved it at her.

She opened her mouth and closed it again, deciding to make a polite sound of "hmm" before backing away slowly and busying herself with another shelf. On the other side of the store. Away from me.

It was a familiar feeling. Despite being one of the most well-known people on the planet, very few people *knew* me, which was terribly isolating.

Maybe it was that my hair was longer than it'd been since the seventh season of *Terraformative,* and my beard was more unkempt than Harrison Evans's usually beard-free style, thanks to the latest movie I was shooting. I didn't have time to clean up before this surprise visit to George. Between the beast-mode hair, hat, and sunglasses, I must have looked a little less like her usual clientele: the elite on holiday.

After another few minutes of wandering and worrying, *not worrying*, about George, I slipped out discreetly. The shop owner was distracted, and I didn't need to give that awkward wave of "thanks for having me, sorry I didn't buy anything" and risk seeing the judgment in her eyes. Maybe I should have bought that damn little chick to send to Charlie and Kate. Hell, I could probably buy the whole store, but gifts should mean something more than a way to show that you had the means to purchase them.

I left the small shop filled with expensive wooden cheese boards and silver inlaid cutlery and slowly made my way down Main Street. The twists of evergreen around the lampposts and twinkling fairy lights decorating the perfectly manicured tree-lined street hinted that Christmas was just around the corner. The picturesque small town of Sandia thrived with tourists but was still fully in the hidden gem territory. The surrounding mountains protected it, and its famous watermelon wine kept it flourishing.

I wasn't quite ready to go up the mountain and return to

George's just yet. When it was just George and me, it could be painful. I sometimes struggled to meet his gaze because of my guilt at my absence in these years since *Terraformative* wrapped. And that made me feel lower than a rubbish bin. At least his tiny ward, Collette, was a welcome distraction. I saw so much of myself in her as a child, a constant reminder of the family I'd thought I'd have by now. My stomach twisted uncomfortably, and I shoved the thoughts away and the overstimulating distractions around me by reaching for my earbuds.

I hit play on my watch, and the voice in my earbuds started the next scene. A female voice with the careful optimism that only AI had read the action beat of my current manuscript.

Fade in. Ext. A small cabin set back in a densely wooded area. A soft glow comes from the windows, but the man on the front step hesitates before reaching for the handle.

Ever since I discovered the magic of listening to my screenplays, memorizing my lines came a lot easier than when I tried to read the words on the page that tended to blur and lose my attention. It also blocked out the outside world so I could fully sink in and focus.

Just one of the many reasons I had been identified as a dumb kid, reliant on my looks and knack for acting. Practicing my lines helped distract me as I wandered the small town, known for its slanting slopes and dry, mild climate.

"This is the end for you," my prerecorded voice said as I spoke quietly along out loud. I tucked my head as a passing retired couple glanced at me.

My mind kept going back to George and the worry that settled deep in the marrow of my bones.

He was the most important person in my life along with my two best friends. I couldn't lose ...

No. I wouldn't go down that path.

"It's too late," the robot voice said.

"Excuse me!" a woman called out.

That was odd. I didn't remember that line. This was a high-budget action flick in the newest mystery detective Simon Harris series remake. I didn't recall a woman in this scene. I frowned and continued to walk.

"You've run out of chances," I said.

"Excuse me!"

That time I was sure that hadn't been in my earbuds. I stopped and turned just as a woman was halting her jog up to me.

So much for incognito Harrison Evans. I didn't mind a selfie with a fan but was surprised to have been discovered. I straightened my shoulders and slipped on my Hollywood smile. I wouldn't need *Hank* since I'd already been identified.

The woman in question stopped in front of me, halting with her hands on her knees, taking a few breaths. "You ... walk ... really fast," she said through her pants.

I smiled, disarmed by her cheek. I didn't often receive an accusation from a fan right out of the gate. As she straightened, her features focused into view. Full pink lips on a wide smile slightly parted in exertion. High color in her sharp cheekbones, dark, curious, almost sleepy-looking eyes, and soft brown waves of hair flowed down her shoulders. I imagined a camera cutting sharply to a zoomed-in shot of my pulse rapidly picking up its tempo, my pupils dilating, and my intake of breath. Tiny details to show that my very human body was having a very human response to her.

She was astoundingly beautiful and as familiar as a friend in a dream.

"Hi," she said with a wave of a hand.

"Hi," I said in return, still feeling caught off guard and awestruck.

Awestruck.

It hit me then why I felt like I knew her. She had the same coloring and wide smile about her of this early nineties soap star that my mum watched when I was a child. Something about how her lids sat low on her eyes gave her a sleepy look and, combined with her low, raspy voice, was alluring. She was impossible to look away from, not that I wanted to. My gaze was eager to capture every detail of her that wasn't covered by her heavy winter coat.

"This is a little awkward," she said in her American accent.

"Don't worry. This happens all the time," I said.

She tilted her head. "You're British?"

That didn't usually come as a surprise. I have played Americans, even a Russian once, but Adam Abbots was undoubtedly my most famous role. People often yelled, "To be human is to endure!" as I walked down the street, and I'd salute back as I had in *Terraformative*.

"I am. Londoner, I'm afraid."

"Huh." She cocked a hand on her hip. "You know I have a friend ..." Then she waved her hand through the air as though erasing what she said. "Never mind. You don't know him."

"No. I might. All ex-pats here in the US know each other," I said. "We have a group chat where we are remiss over the lack of beans on toast and the strict dental regime." Her glorious mouth split open into a huge smile, revealing a perfect set of pearly whites. I gestured to her mouth. "Case in point."

She self-consciously brought a hand over her dimming smile. I cursed myself.

"Well, now this makes things even more awkward," she said.

"Excuse me." A group of at least a dozen geriatric tourists was headed right where we blocked the walking path.

I stepped out of the way under an awning of another tourist shop, gently guiding her by the elbow. My hand hummed with warm energy when I made contact, even through her jacket, and she glanced where my hand briefly touched.

A passing senior dropped her map, and I quickly grabbed it and returned it to her.

"Thanks, doll," she said, patting my arm and then catching up with her group.

I returned to the cove with the mysterious, beautiful woman. Sparkling white lights hung around us, closing us off.

"Yep. Super awkward." The stranger looked at me with gleaming light reflected in her eyes.

"Why is it awkward?" I asked, my voice lower, as somehow this setting made our conversation deeply intimate.

"It appears that you're both funny and polite." She gestured to the passing group, avoiding my eyes as she said it.

"I'd think that be a good thing. I'm a professional after all." I gave what I hoped was my most Harrison Evans, good-natured smile.

Her mouth hardened, and her eyebrows slashed down. "Are you admitting to being a professional shoplifter?"

My smile dropped. "Excuse me?" I glanced around, worry growing. "You didn't stop me for a—"

I couldn't even finish the question. It felt absurd now.

"Empty your pockets, buddy. And I won't alert the authorities." Her eyebrow raised with a teasing reprimand, but my pulse thumped in my throat.

"I am *not* a shoplifter, I assure you," I said, holding her gaze with all seriousness. This would not be tomorrow's headline.

"You know, I believe you. But still. Humor me," she said gently.

I checked the first pocket of my Mac; a crumpled receipt, a rock Collette found for me and told me was lucky. I proffered my loot.

"See?"

"Nice rock. Other one." She crossed her arms and tapped her foot.

Earbuds case, phone, keys to George's and ...

"Oh bloody hell," I said in horror.

A little fluffy chick with stick legs and an exorbitant price tag.

"I didn't—I would never," I sputtered.

I looked up and around, trying to collect my thoughts. Was this a prank? Was there a hidden cameraman? The clickbait headline unfurled in my mind, "Intrepid Trio heartthrob Harrison Evans secret kleptomaniac?"

"It's okay. It's okay," the woman who was most certainly *not* a fan said.

She went to pluck the little chick from where it sat in my hand, trembling slightly. Before she could take it, I closed my fingers around it. Our hands brushed, and she pulled back like she'd been zapped. I tucked it away as I reached for my wallet instead.

"I'm mortified," I admitted. "But I'd like to keep it."

I thrust twice the price tag in cash at her, but she didn't check. Her mouth pulled in an indulgent, albeit pitiful smile as she pocketed the cash.

"I know you didn't mean to. I was watching you in the shop. You seemed distracted," she said. "I was kidding about calling the authorities. I'll let you off with a warning. This time."

I ran a hand over my face. "I should go apologize..."

"It's okay. Really." She reached for my arm before dropping it awkwardly. I wish she'd have completed the gesture. It might have helped keep me from melting from embarrassment. "It's my friend's shop. She's the one who sent me after you. You were talking to her. Well, she was talking at you. She's not concerned about it. Actually, she thought it was funny. Do you know her? She seemed to know you."

"I didn't … no. I was distracted."

She lowered her head until my gaze found her's again. "Really. It's not a big deal. We won't put your picture by the register."

"Ha." Only a moment ago, I had been expecting a picture. Just not that kind. "Right." I nodded as I ran my hand over my stupid beard. I was suddenly keenly aware of how much I wished she recognized me or at least saw me at my best and not like this. A hairy, self-absorbed, shoplifter.

"Are you okay?" she asked carefully.

I scoffed. "You shouldn't be worried about the criminal. You would make a terrible copper."

She laughed softly. "For many reasons. But are you?"

I didn't feel okay. Hearing her gentle question seemed to unlock this intense pressure in my chest.

I felt absurd and somehow like a child who had no idea what they were doing trapped in an aging man's body. Time passed too fast. People I cared about got older. My youth felt like a lifetime away. My two best friends were creating their own families away from me. It was like I was dunked in the undertow of life, and nothing I could do would get my head above water.

I couldn't say any of that. Basking in the focus of those compassionate green-brown eyes—I hadn't noticed the little flecks of green before—all the thousand swirling thoughts calmed down to one distinct longing.

I swallowed. "Have we met?" I asked without meaning to, avoiding the complicated answer to her simple question. There was something about her. A rising need that almost felt like panic to figure out what this connection was flowing between us. Like a magnetic pulse that couldn't be seen but only felt. "I feel like I've known you," I added, breathless with my throat too tight.

She hesitated, probably because of my awkward phrasing.

"You know, I thought you looked familiar too," she said after a moment. "Are you a local? Sometimes I help out at my friend's shop, Brooks' Baubles and Books." She gestured back toward the shop I'd visited.

"No. That's not it." I couldn't stop memorizing the details of her face. The swoop of her lashes. The curve of her neck. Time raced by. This odd interaction would end too fast.

She shrugged. "Maybe just one of those faces." She glanced back in the direction of the shop. "I better get back. Just in case she really does call the police."

My eyes widened.

"I'm teasing," she said with a laugh. She reached for me again, looking at her own hand like it was a stranger. When she dropped her arm, still not making contact, I reached out without thinking to hold her sleeve.

"Wait," I said.

Her full lips parted in surprise but not fear. Hopefully.

I couldn't let her go. This couldn't be the end. I felt a frantic desire to get more information and learn something about her. This brief, terrible interaction could not be her only impression of me.

"What's your name?" I asked. Hopefully, the edge of desperation wasn't as noticeable to her.

She chewed her lip, her brow furrowing. "I'm sorry. I really have to go."

I swallowed as my heart dropped to my trainers. "Right. Of course." I let her go and tucked my hands back in my Mac.

She wasn't interested. A distracted, petty criminal didn't attract her. There were a thousand reasons this witty woman would tell herself to get away.

"Good luck with the kleptomania," she said, keeping her voice friendly as before but already walking backward and away from me.

Forever.

I chuckled once, balling my hands in my pockets, stopping myself from reaching for her and making even more of a fool of myself. I respected a woman's wish the first time she spoke them.

She backed into a street chalk sign advertising lavender lattes and almost fell over. By the time I took two steps forward, my body reacting on instinct to get to her, she had righted herself and the sign, chuckling nervously and dusting chalk off the sleeve of her jacket.

"Oops. How'd that get there?"

I smiled but couldn't get the other half of my mouth to lift.

She turned and took three steps away. Her brown waves flowed down her back. Her long legs shapely in tight jeans. I watched her longer than I should for someone who wanted to come off as *less* weird. She stopped suddenly, fists balling once before turning back around.

I stepped closer, feeling my eyes widened hopefully.

"But I'm around, at the shop sometimes," she called a couple of yards away. A passing family crossed in front of her and she tucked her hair as they shuffled on. "So you know. If you feel like trying your luck again."

"Right. Brilliant," I called back.

She ducked her head, smiling. "Okay then. I'll see you around. Maybe."

I waved like a big, goofy goober. She disappeared around the corner, glancing back once more with a shy smile. I'm not sure how long I stood there blinking happily in the thin winter air. I didn't even reach for a cigarette. I'd been meaning to quit anyway. Collette had caught me yesterday when I'd thought I'd been sneaky and made me feel terrible when she started asking all sorts of questions about it. The sun shone a golden hue. The birds chirped giddily. Passing pedestrians chatted happily.

Everything felt brighter and more alive.

Today was a new day. A fresh start. I'd be up here visiting George more. He was absolutely fine. I didn't need to worry about a thing. The world was a beautiful place. And maybe I'd swing back into town and get that little chick for Charlie and Kate after all.

Visit pipersheldon.com for more information!

ACKNOWLEDGMENTS

Oh boy, I always worry as I write these that I'm going to forget someone because I am overwhelmed by amazing support but extremely distractible at the end of the day. Here are all my thanks in no particular order.

First and foremost, thanks to you reading this. I am a person who loves to read the little love notes authors leave so it makes me happy that you are too. Thank you for reading this book. I hope you loved Emma and Wesley as much as I do.

To Brooke for being an early reader and a constant champion. For not even commenting when I lay on the ground in the middle of a conversation or conjure magical gusts during an epic horror movie retelling that cause us to have heart attacks.

To Nora for letting me fret and talk ad nauseam, and reminding me that I ALWAYS DO THIS and to just keep moving forward. Thanks for all your brilliant ideas and for overall just being the best. Look at us!

To my Dramione dream team; Karla, Penny, Chelle, and Brooke. Tell Crookshanks I said pspspsps.

To Lynsey for always listening to my lamenting voice memos and also reminding me that I ALWAYS DO THIS ... I'm sensing a theme here.

To Tracy, for reading the roughest, earliest version of this book and still giving me hope.

To my husband, who quite frankly, is so good at being a partner that I struggle to write a hero that lives up to you. Tone it down a little, man, wouldja?

To Pipe's Peeps, who are a constant source of joy and pride. I love all my #VIPeeps.

And to all my friends and family who support me without fully understanding this wild, wonderful world of Romance and most likely won't see this, but cheer me on nonetheless. I am eternally grateful.

ABOUT THE AUTHOR

Piper Sheldon writes Contemporary Romance and Paranormal Romance. Her books are a little funny, a lotta romantic, and with just a little twist of something more. She lives with her husband, daughter, and elderly dog at home in the desert Southwest. She finds writing about herself in the third person an extreme sport in awkwardness.

Sign up for her newsletter here!
   http://pipersheldon.com/newsletter

If you are a Piper Sheldon fan, join her Facebook reader group to get all this insider info!
   Pipe's Peeps (Piper Sheldon Reader Group)

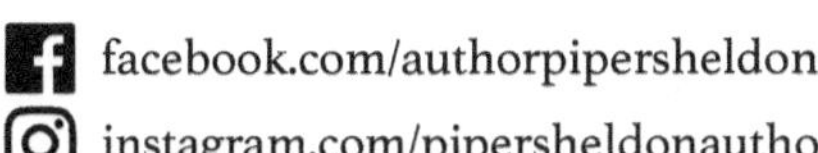

facebook.com/authorpipersheldon
instagram.com/pipersheldonauthor

ALSO BY PIPER SHELDON

Unlucky in Love Series - Contemporary Celebrity Romance

Stranger Than Fan Fiction

Better Date Than Never

Down For the Word Count

Slippery Slopes Series - Small town, Romantic Comedy

All Downhill From Here

All Joking Aside

The Unseen Series - Paranormal Romance

The Unseen

The Untouched

Cozy Creek Collection - Small Town Romance, collaborative series

Fall Shook Up

Smartypants Romance

The Scorned Women's Society - Small Town Romance

My Bare Lady

The Treble With Men

The One That I Want

Hopelessly Devoted

It Takes a Woman

The Teacher's Lounge - Small Town Romance, collaborative series

Band Together

You can find all of Piper's books at pipersheldon.com or on her author page on Amazon.